DEX HAVEN

KINGDOMS OF ELDORIA BOOK 3

STARLIGHT & FIRE

II

Mean Man,

You are the fire that keeps me
warm at night, and were the
only light in my otherwise dark and
lonely existence all those years ago.
What an amazing road it's
been. Let's keep riding.

CONTENTS

AUTHOR'S NOTE

This book contains mature elements and is suitable for mature readers 18 years and older. I didn't include any triggers, everyone consents in a most lovely way. The steam is steamy and the heat it hot. You have been warned.

"She has fought many
wars, most internal.
The ones that you battle alone,
for this, she is remarkable.
She is a survivor."
— Nikki Rowe

CHAPTER 1

Rising from the Ashes

Callie

Blended scents of sage and lavender tickled my nose. It was so much sweeter than the smells of sulfur and rot that I'd smelled for the past several weeks in the Underworld. My eyes finally opened and the canvas of the healer's tent came into focus. It stretched above me. Sunlight made it through the seams. It was almost pretty. Gah, I missed the sunshine. My senses were rougher, sharper: the creak of the cot beneath me, the dull, grinding ache that pulsed through every inch of my body. The kind of pain that went deeper than cuts and bruises.

A quiet, soothing voice broke through my haze. "Easy now." An older woman with kind eyes leaned over me. She dabbed at my forehead with a cool cloth. I hadn't had a kind touch in so long it almost made me cry. "You've been through quite a trial, child."

I tried to smile. I'm sure it looked forced. My lips were so dry, they must be cracked. When I spoke, my throat burned something awful. My words came out in a raspy whisper. "Thank you."

It wasn't much—barely louder than a breath—but it was the polite thing to do, to say "thank you" at least in Texas it was. Ah... Texas. The place I'd never see again. And then, like a door slamming open in my head, the memories rushed back in, washing over me and dragging me under.

Ignis.

His face rose in my mind. How could someone I met just one time have left a hole in my heart and an empty spot in the middle of my gut? I can see his beautiful face—sharp and vivid, every detail like it had been burned there right into my brain. The strong, angular line of his jaw. The fire in his amber eyes— eyes that had softened, just for a second. Just long enough for my dumb chest to fill itself up with what? Hope? What kind of idiot am I? You don't fall in love with a man after one look. One touch. That's crazy train stuff. But I saw his face. He felt one hundred percent of what I felt. At least he didn't deny it.

"We are Fated Mates," he'd said. I wasn't sure what that meant, but it had to be good, right?

For a fleeting moment, I thought that had to mean something. But as fast as that thought came, he shot it down. His face turned ice cold. The stone cold look he gave left no argument.

'You're not from Aurelion,' he'd said. Then the next words sealed the deal. 'This is impossible.' He may as well have stabbed me with a knife. That's how it felt in my gut.

Of course, I'd never heard of such a thing, but boy, I sure as hell felt it. And I still feel it. This awful emptiness in the very middle of my being. I squeezed my eyes shut, trying to block out the memory, but it clung to me like a sticker burr sticks to your socks when you walk through the pasture without boots on.

When I opened my eyes again, the healer had moved on, bustling quietly around the tent. My eyes drifted with her, landing on bundles of dried herbs strung up from the ceiling —fennel, rosemary, sage. Their earthy scent filled the space, mingling with that ever-present Aurelion sweet smell of grapes. Of course, it's blending with the smoke of the remains of the rift. That is not a pleasant mix. But I don't mind when I catch the whiff of spices. It's all very confusing to my nose.

Outside, the camp buzzed with life—or maybe chaos was a

better word. The rustle of the tent walls didn't do much to muffle the clang of weapons or the clipped shouts of training soldiers. Occasionally, there was the distant *whoosh* of some kind of arrows or something, followed by a sizzle of water being added to something like they're mixing fire and water. Other things rattled the ground just enough to remind me where I was.

Where *he* was.

Everything here felt so alien, so far removed from the life I used to know. I closed my eyes and let my mind wander back to wide-open fields under an endless sky and the gleaming steel of the farm equipment I used to sell. I could almost hear the steady vroom of machinery, smell the hay being baled in the fall, or rich soil being tilled. God, what I wouldn't give to be back there right now—buried in spreadsheets and sales calls, where the biggest crisis was a botched quarterly report, not war, monsters, or the rejection of a fire king with enough ego to fill Texas panhandle to coast.

The ache of homesickness was overwhelming. But there was no going back. And since I had to stay here, that meant I had to fight. I felt that spark that always drove me. They called it stubborn. I called it tenacity. Doubt me at your own peril. Things look bad at the moment. I'm down, but I'm damn sure not out.

I might be bruised, beaten down, and literally missing chunks of hair thanks to this mess, but I was still *me*. Callie Langston. And Callie Langston didn't let anyone—not even an infuriatingly gorgeous fire king with all the emotional range of a brick wall—define her worth.

I let out a slow breath; the thought settling in my chest like a layer of armor. Leaving Aurelion wasn't just something I *wanted* to do; it was something I *had* to do. I'd already lost the life I'd built once. I couldn't lose more—not my pride, not what little was left of my heart. Ignis had made his position painfully clear, and I'd be damned if I hung around hoping for scraps of his acceptance.

"Alright, Callie," I muttered, trying to inject a little steel into my voice. "Time to get your ass in gear."

Carefully, I shifted and pushed myself upright. The dull ache that had been my constant shadow since the Underworld flared in my lower back for a moment, sharp enough to make me suck in a breath, but it faded quickly. Then I tested my fingers, I flexed them slowly. I thought they'd be too stiff to bend. But they weren't. My hands moved with ease, no pain. I couldn't believe they felt fine.

"Well, I'll be damned," I murmured. "Guess being a revenant comes with a few perks."

I swung my legs over the side of the cot, my bare feet warmed by the Aurelion earth. It sent warmth up my spine, snapping me into focus. Outside, the steady rhythm of soldiers' boots blended with the sharp clang of weapons reminded me once again of the dangers outside. Even here, in this moment of near quiet, Aurelion still lived in the shadow of war. I thought I smelled something cooking nearby. My stomach gave a soft, traitorous growl, but I ignored it.

"Focus, Callie," I muttered, shaking my head. "Bigger things to handle right now."

I planted my hands on the cot and pushed myself upright to standing, slow and cautious, testing my strength. My legs wobbled under me but held steady. One step, then another, each one small but enough to remind me I was still here. Still standing. Somewhere deep in the hollowed-out space where exhaustion had taken root, I could feel it—a tiny ember trying to spark back to life.

"Hey," a harsh male voice called from outside the tent. Made me about jump out of my skin. "Everything good in there?"

I froze. "Just fine," I called back, trying to sound like I was simply laying on my cot like a good patient. Not like I was standing on legs that could give out at any second. "Don't need a thing."

I exhaled, relieved at the sound of his boots shuffling away. My grip tightened on the cot's edge for a moment before I straightened up again. "Alright, Callie," I murmured under my breath, standing up straight. "You've handled worse than this. Just another day at the office, right?"

Ahead of me, the tent flap swayed in the breeze. Just a few steps and I'd go through it and on to whatever lay ahead.

"Let's do this," I said, my voice firm with the all grit that my adoptive parents had raised me with.

I slipped outside, moving carefully, trying my best to blend in. The temperature was uncomfortably hot and humid. It rivaled Texas on a September day. Everything about this place felt alive in the worst way—charged and crackling. In the distance, low, guttural roars rolled through the camp, faint but unmistakable. Even with the rift closed, its dark magic still lingered, faint and evil, rippling beneath my feet.

One thing at a time. First, I needed to find Olivia.

Eldric

"Well, Eldric," I muttered, my voice low as I scanned the craggy expanse of the barren landscape. "You've done a great job there."

The air smelled rancid. Smoke and brimstone was a reminder that Underworld creatures had been here recently. I caught a flicker of movement. Something was there, in the shadows, watching.

"Come on, then, if you're coming." I teased. "Let's see what you're made of."

The silence went on and on. Finally, the thing finally stepped out of the shadows. It moved with a jerky gait. Its form was unnatural and twisted. Limbs jutted out at odd angles, and its flesh gleamed with a sickly toxic sheen. In other words, this thing was gross. The weirdest part of it was the fact that it had too many eyes and they all blinked out of sync. It seemed like it didn't know where it was looking.

A wave of revulsion hit me, and unease settled in my chest. "Well, aren't you're a charming abomination?" I said, trying to make ready for its first move.

It opened its giant mouth and lunged for me. Glass like teeth gnashed trying to take my head off. Dark magic pulsed through me, sharpening my senses. It pushed my nerves right to the edge.

"Really?" I said, sidestepping another snap of its jaws. "That all you've got?"

I was clearly irritating it because the angry howl it released was full of rage. Its many eyes were darting this way and that. I tried to guess where it would strike next.

"You know," I told it, "this is more of a workout than I've had in some time."

It got close enough for me to release a way of dark energy, tendrils of my shadows biting like whips. Finally, I released a vortex of energy shadows, causing the creature to explode outward. My body felt the strain immediately—my breaths came hard and shallow, sweat dampening my skin.

It wouldn't hold. Not for long. I could feel the edges of the spell fraying already.

"Come on, Olivia," I muttered under my breath. "Where are you hiding?"

Movement flickered at the edge of the haze, pulling my attention. But the figure stepping out of the gloom wasn't Olivia.

It was him.

Farin Thalassa.

Of all the people I could run into in this gods-forsaken wasteland, it had to be him—the King of Thalassa.

Behind me, the vortex sputtered out, leaving the creature nothing more than a smoldering pile of toxic goo.

"Oh, my," I said, my voice showing just how surprised I was. "Farin Thalassa. Now *this* is a surprise? I've got to say, royalty wasn't exactly on my to-do list for today."

His deep brown eyes narrowed.

"Eldric Alinar," he said finally, his voice smooth but accusing. "Tell me why I shouldn't end you right here, right now."

I didn't need to guess if he meant it. Farin Thalassa wasn't the type to bluff, and after everything I'd done—the chaos, the blood, the wreckage I'd left in my wake—he had every reason to want me gone. Hell, if I were in his place, I might've gone ahead and ended me. The distant roar of rift-born creatures echoed across the wasteland, adding weight to an already unbearable silence.

"Uh, Farin," I said, keeping my tone light, steady, as if he wasn't contemplating my demise at this moment. "This meeting is definitely not a coincidence, I promise you. I'm looking for Olivia—not for any nefarious reason, I swear." In a gesture of peace, I raised a hand, hoping to slow him down. "I've got news about her friend Callie. That's why I'm here."

When I said her name, his brow furrowed. Just a flicker, but it was enough to crack that perfect, stone-cold mask of his. For a second, I knew I had his attention.

"You see," I said, leaning into the moment as his sharp eyes pinned me. "I was the one who got her out. She's alive because I helped her escape from the Underworld myself."

For a moment, he just looked at me as though he was deciding if I was telling him the truth. I tried to make my face look as honest as possible. Which is a look I'd never gone for in my life. I wasn't even sure *how* to look honest. Farin's face didn't give much away—he was frustratingly good at that—but his silence said plenty. A flash of disbelief flickered across his features, gone almost as fast as it came, replaced with pure, calculating suspicion.

"Explain," he said, voice low, sharp, and absolutely deadly. "And don't waste my time with riddles, sorcerer. I'm not in the mood."

Nearby, one of his soldiers made a move to step in, like they thought I was some kind of threat, but Farin waved them off without even looking their way. He didn't need backup. He didn't need anyone to do his dirty work. Not when his eyes were locked on me like I was the predator he was going to under his blade in a matter of minutes.

For once, I wasn't interested in playing games either. Not now. Not with what was at stake. I looked him straight in the eyes, trying to channel someone he could believe.

"Your Highness," I said, voice even though the weight of his stare made me want to squirm. "Callie is going to be very important in the battle Eldoria is going to wage against Magda."

His jaw tightened, tension rippling through his shoulders, and I could practically hear the gears turning in his head. I knew he didn't trust me. I wouldn't either, if I were him. The things I'd done... well, they didn't exactly scream reliable ally.

"You talk of serious matters," Farin said, his words slow and deliberate, like he was piecing something together in real-time. "And let's not forget, Eldric, you've always had... questionable loyalties."

I nodded my head slightly, letting him know I understood and acknowledged the truth in his words. "You have every reason to doubt me," I said. "But there's one thing you *don't* know—something I only recently discovered myself. Callie is my cousin. Blood ties us together, Your Highness. I wouldn't hurt her. My only goal was to save her. To get her out of that hellish place."

Farin's expression shuddered, just enough for me to catch a hint of surprise, before he went back into his guarded stance.

"Family, hmm?" he repeated. His voice had a trace of doubt.

A warm breeze blew through the trees, carrying with it the faint scent of smoke. Farin looked briefly toward the towering walls of Aurelion. His expression was unreadable, but I didn't have to guess too hard to know who thought about. He wondered if Callie was, in fact, in there..

"Very well," he said at last, his tone as cool as ever. "I'm willing to give you the benefit of the doubt. But tread carefully, Eldric."

I gave him another nod, the feeling of relief flooded through me. At least he was willing to listen to me. "Thank you, Your Highness. Even if you don't fully trust me, giving me a chance to prove that I can be a man of my word is appreciated. My priority now is to find Olivia and let her know Callie is safe inside Aurelion's walls. She was seriously injured in the Underworld and wasn't strong enough to travel with me."

Farin's hand moved almost reflexively to the hilt of his sword. "If you're lying to me…"

"I'm not," I said quickly, lifting my hands again in a gesture of peace. "I understand your mistrust—I've earned it, I know. But in this, we are on the same page, I swear it. Callie's safety is what is most important to me."

For a moment, the tension between us felt as tight as a bowstring. Farin's eyes bored into mine, dark and unrelenting, like he was searching for even the smallest crack in my story. Finally, he gave a curt nod, though his grip on his sword didn't loosen.

"Alright," he said. "I will take you to Olivia. But mark my words, Eldric—if this turns out to be some ploy, you will not leave this realm alive."

I lowered my head and acknowledged the warning. "Understood, Your Highness. Lead the way."

The rugged terrain stretched before us as Farin set a brisk pace. Every step he took was deliberate, his movements efficient and decisive. He constantly looked back and forth across our surroundings, scanning for potential threats. He carried himself like a man who'd spent a lifetime on battlefields. Even though Eldoria had not seen a war in over 50 years. Perhaps his current state of vigilance was due to the reality that he missed the fact that his wife was plotting horrible things right under his nose for years.

9

But no one could question Farin's goodness, loyalty, and honor. It was no wonder he was chosen to take the throne after Nerissa's treachery was exposed. He was a natural leader—disciplined, formidable, and unshakably faithful to his people.

As the silence stretched between us, punctuated only by the crunch of our boots on rocky ground and the distant, guttural roars of rift creatures, Farin finally spoke.

"Tell me," he began, his voice steady but laced with suspicion, "how exactly did you come to rescue Callie from the Underworld? You were Magda's most trusted lieutenant, her right hand. Surely you can see how this entire story reeks of deception."

I shook my head, the weight of my guilt pressed heavily on my shoulders. "Your skepticism is warranted, Highness. I fully deserve every ounce of distrust you have for me. I'm not proud of the things I've done, nor the monstrous deeds I am unquestionably guilty of." My voice wavered for a moment, but I forced myself to continue. "There's no excuse that can absolve me. But I can tell you this: something changed within me during the weeks I spent in Callie's presence."

I met Farin's unflinching gaze, willing him to see the truth in my eyes. "It's the first time in longer than I can remember that I've felt even the faintest hint of what it means to have a family. Every time Magda forced me to harm her, it was like striking at myself. The pain... it was unbearable. Something within me —something I cannot fully explain—convinced me that the only chance I had at redemption; at peace, was to get Callie to safety." I paused, my voice thick with emotion. "And somehow, Eldoria felt like the key to that peace. To what little redemption I might still hope for."

He held my gaze, his dark eyes sharp and calculating. His inquiring look told me he was listening intently to my explanation. Farin Thalassa was a man of extraordinary discipline, as relentless in seeking truth as he was in map making. He was patient enough to root out lies from the best storyteller. I did my best to share what was in my heart. That I truly sought redemption made my story easy to tell.

"Very well, Eldric," Farin said at last, his deep voice measured but not unkind. "I am a man who has also stood at a crossroads more than once in my life. Never to the degree to which you find yourself, of course," he added with a pointed glance. "I've been adjacent to evil, never the one to deliver it. But my inaction, my failure to confront it, has allowed much of the destruction that plagues our realm. For that, I bear responsibility."

He straightened, his tone hardening. "So I cannot, in good conscience, hold you solely in judgment for your actions. But neither can I offer you trust without worthiness. That, my boy, you will have to earn."

A lump rose in my throat, but I swallowed it down. "That is all I ask, Your Highness."

Farin's lips pressed into a thin line, but he nodded curtly. "Let us head to Vesparra. That is where we'll find the king and queen you're looking for—for you won't get near Queen Olivia without also being in the presence of His Highness, the king as well."

The mention of Cadence Vesparra sent a shiver of apprehension racing down my spine. My hands clenched at my sides as I envisioned the coming confrontation. There was no doubt in my mind that I would pay a steep, physical price for my past deeds when I faced Cade.

Still, I forced myself to lift my head, determination hardening my resolve. I deserved what was coming—and I would face it, if it meant I had even a slim chance of making things right. And that chance was likely very thin.

CHAPTER 2

Battles of Heart & Kingdom

Ignis

Tension filled the late evening air. Even so, a brilliant sunset cast the horizon in beautiful shades of orange and gold. I stood on a low hill at the edge of Aurelion's northern border, scanning the quiet expanse of desert that stretched endlessly before me. Jorvahn Pyreth, the general of my armies and oldest friend, stood at my side, his face as inexpressive as ever. Although his sharp hazel eyes missed nothing. He'd been my right hand for years, a trusted friend and voice of reason even when I didn't want to hear one.

The crown is never heavier than in times of strife. Thank the Goddess that for now, my kingdom, and my people, were safe.

In the distance, I could make out the silhouettes of grapevines swaying gently in the breeze, a promise of the sweet wines that would flow once more when these battles ended and we once again enjoyed peace.

"Aye, so we made it through yet another rift openin', Yer Majesty." Jorvahn's deep voice reverberated with his Aurelion brogue, pulling me from my thoughts. "How many more do ye think there will be?"

I turned to face my general. His handsome face carried a deep weariness we were all beginning to feel.

"There is no way of knowing, my friend. Today's rift was odd. It was opened for such a shot while. I don't know what that meant. Magda is up to something. I have a feeling it's all coming to a head sooner than we think. I just hope that we'll be able to handle it when it does."

Jorvahn nodded as his eyes swept over the battlefield. "The eastern defenses held weell," he mentioned. "But the southern wall…"

A feeling of concern washed over me. "We'll need to reinforce it," I said, already calculating the resources we'd need. "Perhaps with those new stone formations we discussed?"

"Agreed," Jorvahn said. A bit of a grin crossed his face. "Yer skill in fortifyin' never ceases to amaze me, Ignis."

I let out a small laugh, letting go of the tension from my shoulders. How long had we been standing here, planning, strategizing? "How many battles had we fought side by side?"

"Too many," Jorvahn said. I hadn't even realized I'd asked that last question out loud. "But there's no one I'd rather stand beside."

I gave him one of my rare, genuine smiles. "The feeling's mutual, my friend."

As the last rays of sunlight slipped below the horizon, the familiar ache I felt more and more settled in my chest. This land, these people—they meant everything to me. I would give my life for them without hesitation.

"Let's head back to the city," I said, finally stopping my contemplation and looking away from the darkening landscape. "There's still so much to do."

Jorvahn nodded and fell into step beside me as we made our way back toward the glowing lights of Aurelion. The evening breeze carried the sounds of the city—guards on their rounds, the crackle of distant fires, the hum of life continuing, only now there was an undeniable feeling of fear underlying every action.

As king, it was my duty to keep this city, these people, safe from our enemies. The latest battle was more of a skirmish, but it was a wake-up call because it happened at our borders. I couldn't help but think it was just the beginning of something much bigger. A storm was coming; I could feel it deep in my gut.

Whatever came next, I knew one thing for certain: Aurelion would stand. I would make sure of it, even if it cost me everything.

Then, movement caught my eye. I saw a woman walking along the expanse beyond the city's borders, where the light was quickly fading.

Callie.

She was walking toward us; her steps were slow and unsteady, like every movement was a struggle. She shouldn't be out here like that; barefoot, her clothes in tatters, her blonde hair a matted, uneven mess. But even like this, she was the most beautiful woman I'd ever laid eyes on. Her green eyes, even though dulled with exhaustion, still held a spark of fire as she trudged along.

My heart literally hurt at seeing her like this. What was she doing out here? How had she even made it this far?

"Callie!" I called, my voice sharp with concern. "What in Vesperia's name are you doing outside the city walls?"

She stumbled as she looked up, just noticing me. Her eyes locking onto mine. For a brief second, her expression held a glimmer of—relief, maybe even hope? But just as quickly, it hardened into indifference.

I took a cautious step toward her. Every muscle had to fight for my restraint. She still smelled like smoke and earth, wearing that damned filthy tattered rag of a dress. I wanted to grab her up and take her to my chambers and see that she was given a hot bath filled with lavender and chamomile, pampered like a queen should be pampered. But I had to shake that thought away. She was not my queen.

"It's not safe out here," I growled, even as my eyes moved over her, cataloging every detail, searching for injuries.

Every instinct screamed at me to close the distance, to shield her from whatever had brought her to this state. But there was no way that I could. I couldn't have her, so what would be the point? It would only make it more difficult to let her go again. Callie was an outsider, and while my people may accept her one day, my council of nobles never would.

"I had to leave," she said. Her voice sounded rough. I wondered if she'd even eaten or had anything to drink. But even in this state, she seemed determined. "I need... I need to get to Olivia."

I still could not believe she'd walked all this way in the shape she was in. By the Goddess, I stood there, my fists clenched at my sides. I fought an internal war before I spoke. "You shouldn't be here," I managed. Truth is, what I wanted to say was, *'I'm glad you're here.'*

She lifted her chin, face full of defiance, and flashed her beautiful eyes at me. Even in her weakened condition, with dirt and blood staining her dress and exhaustion lining her face, she was magnificent.

"I shouldn't be a lot of things," she shot back, her voice unsteady but laced with steel. "But here I am. Olivia needs me."

The mention of Olivia's name hit me, dragging my focus back to the urgency behind her words. I saw it then—the way her fingers twisted in the torn fabric of her dress, her effort to hold herself together despite the cracks threatening to break through.

"It's dangerous for you to be out here alone," I said, my voice softening despite myself. "Especially for someone in your... condition." My gaze looked down at her filthy dress and, catching on her bare, dust-streaked feet.

She laughed at that. "Danger? You don't know the half of it, *Your Majesty.*" The title landed like a slap. "But I've made it this far, and I'm not stopping now. So either help me, or get out of my way."

She clearly had had enough of this conversation—enough of

me and my shit.

"There's a portal," I said. "I can… I'll take you there."

Callie seemed just as surprised to hear those words as I was to say them. Her eyes widened just a bit, her guarded expression lessened enough to reveal a look of gratitude. "Thank you," she murmured, her voice quiet.

I gave her a nod and turned before I thought too long about how the fact that she seemed surprised that I would help her bothered me. I'm her mate. Of course I would help her. But I guess I'm not really her mate. Why would she expect help from me? Fuck.

As we walked, the distance between us grew. I don't mean the physical distance. The silence was deafening. I was painfully aware of every step she took behind me. She breathed in and out with steady breaths.

The path to the portal was uneven and rocky. Callie stumbled once, catching herself with a soft curse. Instinctively, I reached back, my hand brushing hers before I realized what I was doing. It was barely a touch, but the connection caused a reaction. My body recognized who it belonged to.

"Careful," I said gruffly.

"I'm fine," she replied, her tone clipped. But when I glanced back, she was rubbing her hand where mine had been. Her expression said she was anything *but* fine. She had clearly felt the same thing I had at our touch. I needed to be more careful about touching her. It wasn't fair of me to do that to her.

I swallowed hard when I saw the distant glow of the portal. The swirling energy shimmered like starlight, a beacon of escape in the twilight.

When we reached it, I stepped aside and gestured toward the portal with a stiff motion. "It'll take you to Vesparra," I said, my voice low. "You'll be safe there."

Callie hesitated, her eyes locking onto mine. For a moment, the world came down to just the two of us. The sounds of the desert faded into the background. She hesitated just for a moment and looked at me. Goddess, she was the most beautiful thing I'd ever seen. It literally pained me to let her go.

"Thank you, Ignis," she said, her voice barely above a whisper.

I nodded, unable to say anything. She turned and stepped into the swirling light. I watched as the portal closed around her.

And then she was gone. I'd ruled Aurelion for 46 years. I'd never experienced a sacrifice like this.

Duty had come first.

"Yer a fool, Ignis," Jorvahn's gravelly voice cut through my musing.

I turned to face him, not appreciating the disrespect. "Mind your tongue," I snapped, but the words lacked their usual bite.

"Yer Highness," he said, his tone steady, "Surely I've earned the right to speak plainly. And what I see is a man lettin' outdated prejudices rob him of somethin' precious."

Maybe I was just angry at the situation, or angry at myself. "You overstep, Jorvahn," I barked. "The laws of our kingdom—"

"You are the law," he said. "But love? True connection? That's rarer than Runestones o' Resonance. And far more valuable."

I opened my mouth to argue, but he pressed on, his voice softening. "I lost my mate, Ignis. Thirty years ago. And not a day goes by that I don't feel that absence."

The raw pain in his voice silenced me. For the first time, I saw the depth of sorrow etched into the lines of my oldest friend's faced.

"In yer case, it's somethin' even deeper," he continued. "Somethin' divine. The Goddess chose her for you, Ignis. That has to mean somethin'. You have a chance at somethin' real, somethin' that most of us could only dream of."

He gestured towards the dormant portal, the shimmering light now dimmed. "Don't throw it away because of some arbitrary rules set down by men who died long ago."

His words hit deep. I'd forever lived my life dedicated to tradition, duty, and pride. I turned away, unable to meet his eye. I looked at the last light of evening over my kingdom, a kingdom I'd dedicated my life to. A kingdom that I loved. The evening light painting the horizon in fiery colors of crimson, yellow, and amber, its beauty a reminder of all I had to lose.

"It's not that simple," I murmured, more to myself than to Jorvahn.

But even as I said it, I felt my resolve started to crack. The warmth of the fading sunlight whispered the possibilities I never dared to consider.

CHAPTER 3

Trust but Verify

Olivia

A shiver ran down my spine, stopping me mid-step. The air crackled, heavy with an energy I couldn't see but felt everywhere, setting every nerve I had on edge. I spun toward Cade, my breath caught when I saw his blue eyes already locked on mine. My heart about beat out of my chest when I saw he was also worried.

"Tell me you felt that?" I whispered, my hand held over my fast-beating heart.

Cade gave me a nod. "Yes, my love, I heard it. Something's happening in the courtyard."

We didn't need to say anything else. We broke into a run, the stone corridors of Vesparra Castle blurring past in streaks of shadow and flickering light. My bare feet slapped against the cold floor, but the sting barely registered. The hum of magic could be felt all around.

We ran out into the courtyard and I could not believe what I was seeing. This was something we certainly did *not* see every day. A shimmering portal was standing square in the center of the courtyard, its lights cast an eerie glow all around. But it wasn't the portal appearing that was the most surprising thing that happened. It's what the portal brought.

Right before it dimmed, two figures stepped through its swirling depths, their outlines stark against the glow. My eyes locked on the first, and I let out a sharp breath. Grandpapa. I'd know his broad shoulders and steady presence anywhere. I always loved seeing him, although his visits were usually less of a production.

But the dude next to him was not just unwelcome, he was wanted dead or alive. Mostly dead. Eldric Alinar. The man who had not only tried to claim Eldoria as his own, but he also tried to claim *me* as his own! He stood bound, shimmering magical restraints coiled tightly around him, holding his power in check.

"Goddess above," I breathed, my fingers instinctively reaching for Cade's hand. His warmth steadied me, but my heart was still hammering against my ribs. "What in tarnation is goin' on here?"

Cade's grip tightened around my hand as his voice dropped to a deep rumble that sent a shiver through me. "Stay behind me, Olivia."

Now, as much as I love my sexy alpha male wanting to go into protection mode, I pulled my hand free, planting my feet. "Now hold your horses, darlin'. I'm not a scaredy cat who needs savin,' that girl is gone."

I kept my eyes on Eldric, watching him closely as I spoke. Something about him wasn't right. Even with the magical bonds holding him, the arrogance he always carried was gone. For once, he didn't look smug or full of himself. When I caught his eyes, I saw something I never thought I'd see: humility.

"Grandpapa," I said, as I kissed his cheek. "You wanna tell me why you gotta a tied-up polecat in my front yard?"

His demeanor was as calm as always, but I could tell he was tired as well. "My sweet granddaughter," he said with unyielding confidence, "I promise, there's a good reason for this."

I trusted my grandfather implicitly. If he said there was a good reason, then there was a good reason. "Alrighty then. I trust you as much as I trust this man standin' here next to me."

I looked up at Cade. "And I know you'd never bring anyone into my home who would hurt me." I looked back at Eldric and I did not get any bad vibes from him at all. Which was freaking me out a little.

Grandpapa started to reply, but before he could, I raised my hand to tell him to give me just a minute as I turned my back on him. I put my hand over my heart. I felt the magic of the Goddess Star flaring. It started at the point of the star mark and curled around inside until I felt it radiate through my mate mark and beyond. I looked at Cade. His eyes were locked on mine. I knew he felt it, too. Eldric, being here, was a part of this war. It seemed he was meant to be here. A feeling of peace washed over me. Cade gave me a look of reassurance.

Out of the corner of my eye, I caught movement. Red Claw, my Twixit friend, was sitting on a raised stone nearby. His wings shimmered in the fading sunlight and the iridescent colors made me smile. His glowing eyes were steady, looking at me.

"*My lady,*" Red Claw's familiar voice rang through my mind. "*The bound one... his aura holds no ill intent. The darkness that I expected to see in him must have somehow receded, like shadows in the sunlight.*"

I nodded and acknowledged Red Claw's insight. "*Thank you, friend,*" I thought back. The telepathic connection between us was as natural as breathing. "*Keep watch and let me know if you sense even a hint of danger.*"

Red Claw's ears flicked toward a distant noise, but his eyes never left mine. I loved the connection we shared. The Wyldcaster magic I was blessed with was the favorite of all my gifts. The ability to communicate with the creatures of Eldoria and the Dragonia was the thing fairytales were made of.

I turned to Cade. I knew he would not like what I was going to say. The Goddess Star hummed faintly against my skin, almost as if urging me forward. "Cade," I said carefully. I tried to use my sweetest but most serious voice. "We should release

Eldric."

Cade didn't just stiffen—he turned to stone. The heat of his frustration rolled off him in waves, scorching the air between us. His jaw locked so tightly I thought it might crack, and when he finally spoke, his voice was sharp enough to cut. "You can't possibly mean that, Olivia. That man has done nothing but destroy everything he's touched. He hurt you, stole from you, tried to tear down everything we've built. You want me to just... let him go?"

"I know exactly what he's done," I said, cutting in before his anger could build further. My hand found his arm, my fingers pressing gently against the hard line of his muscles. He was so tense, I could feel the fight simmering beneath his skin. "But listen to me. He's not the same man we faced before. I know it sounds crazy. I can't explain it—just feel it. There is something different about him now, and letting him out of those bonds is just the right thing to do."

Cade's eyes narrowed. He looked at me like he was searching for the screw that had come loose. I know he wanted answers as to why I felt this way. But there's no way to show someone a gut feeling. For a moment, he was completely still, as though he had to come to terms with this wild change of circumstances. Then, almost reluctantly, his shoulders eased —though only slightly. His sigh was low, the sound brushing past me like the whisper of a reluctant wind.

"If he so much as breathes wrong..." The words hung in the air, unfinished but heavy with meaning. They were more than a warning; they were a promise. Cade wasn't giving in—he was bending. For me.

"He won't," I said, though my heart hammered harder with every passing second. "We'll handle this. Together. No matter what happens."

His hand came to rest lightly on mine, but the tension in him remained. "Your compassion will always amaze me," he said, with a frustrated sigh. "But Olivia, compassion can be as dangerous as it is noble. If this backfires…" He trailed off as he gritted his jaw, struggling for words. "I won't risk you. Not you. Not our people."

You've heard of tension being so thick you could cut it with a knife? Well, you'd need a chainsaw here. Cade wanted to protect me, and I loved him for it. I wanted him to trust my judgement. If anyone should hate Eldric, it should be me. And I know Cade went through his own hell when I was in the Underworld. But this felt right. Sometimes, risks had to be taken.

"Cade," I said softly as I took a small step closer. I grabbed his hands in mine. "I hear you. I really do. But we can't afford to let fear keep us from doing what needs to be done. If we're going to face what's ahead, we need every bit of help we can get. Even if it's… unconventional."

His jaw clenched so tightly it looked like it might crack. He stared at me like he was searching for some kind of loophole in my words. The courtyard felt impossibly still, the wind barely rustling the castle banners. I knew what I was asking —it wasn't just trust in Eldric. It was trust in me. In my gut instincts.

After what felt like an eternity, Cade exhaled a long, slow breath. His shoulders dropped slightly, though not enough to feel like a real victory. "Fine," he said at last, his voice flat but simmering with warning. "But so help me, if he tries anything, anything at all, he'll regret it."

"I support that," I said quickly. "If he tries anything, we'll be all over him, life a chicken on a June bug."

Cade gave me a typical, 'Starlight, I have no idea what you're talking about' look, but at least I'd gotten a smile out of him. He finally turned toward Eldric. He methodically moved to him and with a single, sharp gesture, the glowing magical bonds dissolved into the air. Eldric straightened, rubbing his wrists as if the bindings had actually hurt him. His green eyes flicked from Cade to me and back again, his expression as guarded as ever. But I saw something more. Could it be shame? Gratitude? I couldn't quite put my finger on it, but I can tell you what it wasn't. Contempt. Arrogance. Pride. None of those things were there at all.

The tension rose a few degrees as we stood there. Things were more than a tad bit awkward. Thank goodness for Grandpapa.

He'd been standing off to the side in the same unassuming manner he always displayed. I guess he realized we had come to the point where we needed a small intervention. In his easy going manner he stepped in and calmed the situation. His voice held a slight trace of humor when he spoke. "Well," he said, as he broke some of the tension with a clap of his hands, "This should be fun."

I busted out laughing despite myself.

"If I may," he began again, with a slight bow of his head respectfully to Cade and me. "Our esteemed guest has a tale worth hearing. One that might illuminate why I brought him here, despite... past transgressions."

I forced myself to keep my gaze steady, though my pulse quickened. "Go on," I said, wondering what we'd hear next.

Grandpapa nodded. "Eldric has told me he is no longer our enemy. He is apparently a man seeking redemption. And perhaps a bit of a hero as well."

I was more than a little confused. The redemption part I understood, but a hero? I turned to Eldric and looked him square in the eyes. "Is that true?" I asked, expecting him to be honest with me.

Eldric nodded. I couldn't really read his expression except for the undeniable sincerity I saw in his eyes. "Yes," he said simply, his voice devoid of its usual arrogance. "It's true."

Grandpapa looked at us. I could tell he was examining the words Eldric spoke as well. "As you know, Eldric was in the Underworld with Callie," he began, his tone neutral, though the corners of his mouth curved faintly upward. "Things apparently devolved into a rather precarious situation." Grandpapa's voice took on a sarcastic tone. I swear he was channeling Denzel Washington. "Being the gallant soul he is"—here, he allowed himself a small, ironic smile—"he facilitated her escape."

My eyes snapped to Eldric's as my breath caught in my throat. "WHAT?"

Grandpapa put his hand up to stop me. "I understand they made their way out of a rift," he continued, recounting the story from his memory, "and found themselves on the outskirts of Aurelion. A most fortuitous location, given its proximity to the kingdom."

I was about to jump out of my skin as Grandpapa continued his methodical telling of this revelation regarding Callie. I could tell he was watching Eldric for his reactions, not just relaying facts. His dark eyes flicked between Cade, Eldric, and me, noting every emotion, every shift in stance.

"Callie's here? In Eldoria?" I was beyond ecstatic at the thought. "You got her out? She's really out of the Underworld?"

Eldric gave me a decisive nod of his head. "Yeah. I got her out. She was weak, so I left her in Aurelion so I could find you as quickly as possible."

I noticed Cade had relaxed just a bit, as his eyes caught mine. Grandpapa's bombshell about Eldric's rescue of Callie changed, at least for now, his opinion of his enemy. We needed more information, though.

"We need to find her," I said, pacing around the courtyard. "We need to find her and we need to get her to Vesparra, where she'll be safe."

I could not believe she was in Eldoria and as close as a portal away. My mind was racing. I was thinking of getting that portal going again and heading right back into Aurelion. But geez, those Aurelions are such dicks. They hate everybody that's not Aurelion. But I'm the Chosen One. I dare then to not allow me entry. The circle I was pacing had gotten wider and wider. The thought of Ignis made me furious. I needed some anger management when it came to that guy.

I looked up, and I was a pretty good distance away. The men were huddled up talking. I wandered back to them, thinking about Callie and Aurelion. My pace increased, and I was almost stomping, forgetting I still had bare feet by the time I got to them. Cade looked at me with a raised brow. I caught his voice through our bond.

"Starlight, I feel your agitation. You're seething. And you're going to cut your feet. Let's go inside so you can at least get some boots on."

I'd made it to their little pow wow.

"Alright," I said, my voice shook a little with the anger I felt. I met the eyes of every person in the courtyard—Cade, Grandpapa, Eldric. "Let's make a plan. And Grandpapa, how was there a rift open we weren't told about?"

Grandpapa looked as sheepish as I'd ever seen him. He straightened his shoulders, but there was no mistaking the contrition in his voice.

"Olivia, it was only open for a few minutes, and only a handful of creatures escaped before it sealed itself up tight. We had command centers and sub-hubs fully staffed and operational. Everything worked exactly as we drew it up. There was no need to bring you or the Dragonia into the fight this time. We would have debriefed you in due time, but we had this situation,"—he gestured toward Eldric—"that expedited the information dispersal."

I locked eyes with Cade, a silent understanding passing between us. His jaw was set, determination etched into every line of his regal face. The surrounding air seemed to hum with unspoken strain, a mixture of anticipation and resolve.

"Well," I said, my voice clipped but calm, "I'm glad the systems held. That's great news. But now, we'll need to hurry with our next steps."

Cade's deep voice cut through the courtyard like a blade.

"Magda will be raging when she learns she's lost both Eldric and Callie. We've bought ourselves some time, but not much."

I nodded, adrenaline sparking to life. "Eldric might be our best chance at understanding what we're up against," I said, casting a glance at the man standing as still as he had been when he was restrained. His eyes met mine, and I saw the same look of contrition I'd seen earlier.

"You really think we can trust him?" Cade asked, he still was wary, and rightfully so.

I took a step closer to Eldric, looking into his eyes once again, then looked away. "I think we need to trust our instincts, and mine say we can trust him. But," I added, trying to sound as harsh as I could, "at the first sign he's up to something no good… we fry his ass."

I think I saw the corners of Eldric's mouth turn up ever so slightly, but he wisely kept it shut. Meanwhile, Cade begrudgingly gave me a nod of approval.

I hit the castle doors and tossed over my shoulder, "Let's head inside and get this little party started," The tension still lingered, but I could feel things loosening up.

I waited at the entry as Cade led Grandpapa and Eldric inside. Before we'd taken five steps into the foyer, I heard a tiny knock at the door that barely registered in the grand hall. For the first time in a long time, I dared to hope.

"Callie?" I whisper-shouted.

My bare feet slapped against the cool tile as I bolted for the door. The scent of night air rushed in as I flung it open. And there she was. Filthy, bloody, and dressed in rags. And she was the most magnificent thing I'd ever seen.

A yelp of pure happiness flew from my mouth as I threw my arms around her. "Callie! Oh my God, it's you! It's really you!"

She stiffened for a moment in my embrace, but then she melted into me, her arms wrapping tightly around me. "Ollie," she murmured, her voice thick with emotion. "I didn't think I'd ever see you again."

I held her close and felt her warmth—her realness, sink into me. I had no idea what lay ahead, but by the Goddess, this was a miracle. And right now I was just going to soak it in and let myself be happy, just for this moment.

CHAPTER 4

Bonds that Cannot be Broken

Callie

I stood frozen in front of Olivia's door, my whole body trembling as my heart thudded painfully in my chest. Every ounce of strength I had left felt like it was slipping through my fingers, the weight of what I'd endured pressing down until I could barely breathe. My hand shook as I raised it, hesitating for just a second before I managed to knock—barely. My knuckles hadn't even made full contact with the wood before the door was pulled open.

And there she was. Olivia. My best friend. My family.

"Callie?" That voice. That sweet Texas drawl that I didn't think I'd ever hear again. It washed over me like the softest wave. Relief flooded my soul, and when I looked into those deep purple eyes, the dam broke. My knees gave out, and before I could stop myself, I was falling forward, collapsing into her arms. "Ollie," I choked out, my voice barely above a whisper, raw from everything; emotion, lack of water, disuse. I buried my face against her shoulder, and oh god and her scent hit me —stargazer lilies. It was like a lifeline. I'd been lost for so damn long.

Her arms were already wrapped around me, holding me up. It was like she was trying to absorb all of me. "Callie. It's you. It's really you. Shhh. I've got you, sugar," she said softly. Her words were everything.

Sobs tore from my throat. I couldn't stop them if I wanted to. I clung to her like a child holds their favorite teddy bear. I knew I was getting snot and tears all over her pretty dress. But I couldn't stop myself. And my beautiful best friend just continued to rub my back and whisper sweet words of comfort to me. It had been so long since I'd had a kind word or a comforting touch. And for a brief moment, I believed everything was going to be ok.

"Shh, darlin'," Olivia said, as her hand ran through the filthy stands of what was left of my once beautiful hair. Her touch was gentle, but she didn't hesitate to touch me. "You're home now. There's nothin' gonna hurt you here, Callie Girl. Nothin' or no one."

I really wanted to believe that was true. I wished she could stop the memories that popped up when I least expected them —that dripped off of me like oil, dark and impossible to wash away.

"I was afraid I'd never get out of there." I told her.

Olivia leaned back and took my face in her hands. "Listen here, Callie Langston," she said. "I would've moved heaven and earth to find you. You hear me? There's no force in this realm or any other that could've kept me from bringin' you home."

I believed every word she said.

"That's my girl," she whispered. "Now, let's get you inside and settled. You look like you could use a hot meal and about a week's worth of sleep."

As she guided me into the warmth of her home, for the first time in forever, I wasn't afraid. I know I had a ways to go, but I was now in a place with people who cared about me and hopefully I could fight my way back to being me.

"Cade, come say hello to Callie," Olivia called over her shoulder.

The most handsome man I'd ever seen—well, next to Ignis— stepped out of the shadows.

"Starlight has told me so much about you." He said, "It feels like I know you."

"I can see by the look on her face that you're the man of her dreams, Majesty. You treat her really well, I can tell. It's a good thing too, or I'd have to hurt you," I told him with a small wink.

Olivia busted out laughing. God, how I've missed that sound.

"Even hanging on by a thread, you still manage to throw out zingers, Callie Girl. That's how I know you're gonna be okay." She gave me another quick hug.

"I'm taking her up to her room. Can you ask Francois to bring up some kind of stew? She's gonna need something hearty to eat tonight."

Cade smiled and pressed a kiss to Olivia's forehead. "It's my pleasure, sweetheart."

I let Olivia lead me through the winding corridors of her home. The plush carpet felt soft beneath my bare feet.

After heading up a flight of stairs, Oliva opened a door off of one of the many hallways. "Here we are. Your own little sanctuary."

The room that greeted us was lovely, and it seemed to ease my weariness.

"It's beautiful," I murmured, my voice barely above a whisper as I drank in the peaceful atmosphere.

Olivia's smile was bright, brimming with pride. "I think it's beautiful, too. And best of all, it's safe. And right now, that's what matters most."

I sank onto the plush bed. It felt like a lifetime ago that I'd been selling tractors, worrying about quotas and commissions. Now, I was adrift in a world of magic and monsters, unsure if I belonged anywhere at all.

"What am I now, Ollie?" I whispered, the words catching in my throat. "I died. And now... I'm not human anymore, am I?"

Olivia knelt in front of me, taking my hands in hers. "You're still you, sugar. You're still my Callie."

I swallowed hard, steeling myself for what I needed to say. "I need to tell you something."

Her expression shifted. "You can tell me anything, Callie."

"You know I was born in the Underworld. Both of my parents were born there too. That makes me... a creature of the Underworld, Ollie." The words tasted bitter as they left my mouth. "When I said I died, I wasn't speaking metaphorically. I literally *died*. But here I am."

Olivia's face softened. "What does that mean, Callie?" She pulled a chair closer. "What does that make you?"

"Apparently, I'm a revenant." I told her. "That means, if I knew how to use my powers, I could... reanimate the dead or something. I can heal myself too. Which lately has come in handy, even if I'm not doing it on purpose. Oh, and I could tear worlds apart, according to Magda. I don't *know*, Ollie! I don't fully understand *what* it means. But it sounds like I'm the worst kind of monster there is!"

She grabbed my hands again.

"Now you listen to me, Callie Marie Langston," Olivia said, her voice firm. "You are not a monster. You're the most precious friend a person could ever have. You *saved* me, Callie! When I was a lost and lonely girl, you saw me. No one ever *saw* me before you!"

"Monsters don't drag lonely people up out of a pit. They don't. So I better *never* hear you refer to yourself as a monster again, you hear me? You may have some kind of big, evil power that you didn't ask for—mind you—but we will find some way to use that power for good. That's what we do. And mark my words, we're gonna figure out how to use that power to bury Magda so deep in hell she'll never even *think* of trying this nonsense again."

Her words comforted me. "Well, that's not all," I said. "I have a cherry to go on top of the crap sundae that is my life."

"Ah, geez, what else, sugar pie?" Her exasperated affection brought the smallest flicker of a smile to my lips.

"I also discovered I have a True Mate," I confessed.

Her face lit up with a radiant smile. "But that's wonderful news! Speaking from experience, a True Mate is as good as it gets, baby doll!"

I winced, the memory still raw. "It might be... if your mate doesn't reject you. He couldn't even look at me," I choked out. "Like I was... wrong. Tainted."

Her smile faltered. "Wait. How could you have found your True Mate? You've only been here and... oh no... don't tell me... please." She leaned closer, searching my face for confirmation. "The only other place you've been is Aurelion, correct?"

I nodded, biting my lip to keep the tears from falling.

"Your True Mate couldn't possibly be King Ignis Aurelion, could it?"

I let out a mirthless laugh and sang, "And BINGO was his name-O."

Her face twisted into a storm of fury, indignation, and determination. "I will kill him myself."

"It's okay, Ollie," I said quickly, the words tumbling out in a desperate attempt to soothe her. "I wouldn't force myself on someone. I'll... I'll learn to get over it. And I'd really rather not talk about it now, if you don't mind."

Olivia shook her head. But I could see the wheels turning behind her eyes, plotting something she hadn't yet shared.

"What happens now?" I asked softly.

Olivia sat down beside me, wrapping an arm around my shoulders. "Now, we rest. We heal. And when you're ready, we figure out our next move. Together."

I leaned into her. "I'm scared, Ollie," I admitted. "Everything's changed, and I don't know who I am anymore."

"You're still the strongest, most stubborn woman I know," Olivia said firmly, her hand tightening on my shoulder. "And I'll be right here, remindin' you of that fact every single day if I have to."

The road ahead was uncertain. My future was a mystery, but in this moment—wrapped in Olivia's care—I allowed myself to hope.

Olivia

The corridors of Vesparra Castle were a labyrinth of stone and tapestries. Cade and I escorted Eldric toward his quarters for the night. I was still thinking of Callie. I was happy she'd had a nice bath and a hearty meal. The color had started returning to her cheeks before I'd left to meet Cade when Grandpapa had departed. Eldric walked a few paces ahead of us. His movements seemed calm and unassuming, even though Cade's shoulders held a good amount of tension. There was an awkward silence as we walked..

Out of the gloom, a silver-haired figure emerged, her arrival a surprise to all of us, her included.

Seraphine yelped. "Oh Goddess! I didn't hear you coming down the hall. I'm sorry." Her eyes immediately landed on Eldric. A flash of recognition crossed her face, but there was no recoil at the recognition. Interesting.

The moment Eldric caught a glimpse of her, his steps faltered slightly.

"You must be Seraphine," Eldric intoned quietly, almost reverently. "Word of your beauty precedes you. I don't believe we've been properly introduced."

Seraphine looked at him closely. Her navy eyes seemed most interested. She gave him a small smile. "We haven't," she said, her tone light. "But, of course, I know who *you* are." That was almost said as a threat.

Well, so much for the tension having disappeared. I felt Cade's anger rising through our bond. I needed to move things along. He stiffened beside me like he was about to go into attack mode.

"Alright, what's happening here?" he demanded. His eyes locked on Eldric. "Seraphine, you shouldn't be anywhere near him. He's not to be trusted."

I put a hand on Cade's arm. I felt he was about to lose it.

"Cade," I murmured, trying to keep my voice soothing despite the unease that knotted my stomach. "Let's try to keep a cool head. We're all adults here—"

"No, Olivia. You don't get it." Cade's words echoed in the hall. His focus never wavered from the two in front of us. "There's something that isn't right here. Eldric, if you're using compulsion on my sister—so help me—I'll make you regret it."

Seraphine turned to Cade, her eyes narrowing with unmistakable anger. Her voice was calm, but the steel beneath it was impossible to miss. "Brother," she said, her tone biting, "have more respect for me than to think I could be manipulated so easily."

Cade had shown amazing restraint. He could have had Eldric against the wall by his neck.

I took a deep breath and centered myself. "Highness, I understand why you're feeling suspicious. But, if anyone has reason to hate this man, it's me. His abuse left me terrified."

Eldric looked at me. I held his eyes for a moment and saw the torment inside him. His expression was filled with regret. It was like he was silently asking for forgiveness, a forgiveness I wasn't sure I could give. But as difficult as it seemed, I knew I had to try. This man could very well be the key to Eldoria's victory over Magda.

"But sometimes," I continued, "the most unexpected associations can lead to the greatest allies. How 'bout we just observe for now, okay?"

Cade's stance relaxed slightly, though I could still see the stress in his jaw. Thankfully, he said nothing more, his silence a sign of the internal battle he had going on.

As we stood there, I felt like something was happening that was likely going to change things. Cade was probably going to have to deal with something that was going to be unpleasant for him.

"Seraphine," I said. I hated to get in the middle of anything between the two of them. "You know your brother's only concerned about your safety. And you know why he's suspicious of Eldric."

She looked at me with love, letting me know she wasn't upset that I spoke to her about this. "Of course, Olivia. And I'm certainly no fan of his, not after everything I know he did to you. I would never do anything to cause you pain. I agree it's wise to observe for now. But..." She straightened her shoulders, her voice gaining confidence. "I reserve the right to have my own feelings on the matter."

I grabbed her hand, squeezing it gently as I leaned in. "Of course, sister. I have no reason to doubt your judgment—especially in matters of the heart." Lowering my voice to a whisper, I added, "But please, be careful. He's shrewd. Protect yourself until you're sure of him."

She gave me one of her beautiful smiles, then kissed my cheek, her touch warm and reassuring. "I promise, Olivia. I'll be very careful whenever I'm near him."

CHAPTER 5

Sparks of Passion Flickers of Doubt

Olivia

We'd deposited Eldric in his room and stationed Twixits at both the balcony doors and the main entrance. Guards patrolled the hallway and the grounds near his chamber. Every precaution had been taken—we weren't about to risk this being a trap.

I breathed slowly, trying to relax and calm the thoughts that were racing through my mind. The stress of the last few hours pressed in on me like a weight on my chest. Then the charged encounter with Seraphine and Eldric kept replaying in vivid detail over and over. I swear I was going nuts. I know they are adults and they're gonna do whatever they're gonna do no matter what Cade and I think. It's silly to worry about it.

"Cade," I said softly, interrupting the quiet. "I need to contact Amaya. I'd like to tell her about Callie."

He gave me a light kiss on my forehead. "Of course, my love. I think I saw your crystal in our chambers. Go ahead and use it in there. She'll be excited to hear from you."

Good Goddess, I love this man so much. Making my way to our sanctuary, I pushed open the heavy wooden door, and I was immediately surrounded with the scents of leather and lilies. It's amazing how those scents are now what I most closely associate with *home*. That word means so much to me now.

I crossed to the night table on my side of the bed. I picked up the small, faceted crystal that normally rests in my pocket. Its surface glimmered faintly in the low light of the candles in our room. I closed my eyes, sent a small portion of my energy into the crystal, and recited the brief spell that would activate the connection to my sister.

"Amaya," I called, my voice echoing faintly through the crystal's facets. "Can you hear me, sis?"

A heartbeat later, her voice rang through, clear and light. "Olivia? What's wrong?"

"She made it out, Amaya," I said, my voice breaking as tears of relief dripped down my cheek. "Callie. She's safe."

Amaya's gasp reverberated through the connection. I could feel her joy all the way to Vesparra. "Oh, thank the Goddess! How? When? Is she... how is she?"

"Shaken," I admitted, my heart twisting as I spoke. "There's so much to explain, but it's too tangled for crystal-speak. Cade's calling a meeting at the Crystal Citadel tomorrow. Can you come here beforehand? We need to talk face-to-face."

"Wild hellhounds couldn't keep me away," she said. "I'll be there at first light. Love you."

The crystal dimmed as the connection closed, and I let out a shaky breath. I felt Cade's presence behind me, always my pillar when I need him. His muscular arms encircled my waist, pulling me against his chest.

"You did well, my queen," he murmured, his breath warm against my ear. "But our work is far from over."

"We'll know more after tomorrow," I said, leaning into him. "We need Eldric to lay out what he knows for everyone at the Crystal Citadel."

The weight of responsibility hung heavy between us, there's almost never a moment's peace. I longed for the day when we can just be normal people, well, normal vampires, and magic wielders, whatever. I just wanted to be able to live without the threat of death constantly at our backs.

I slipped from Cade's embrace, the plush rugs soothing under my bare feet as I made my way to Callie's room. Torchlight flickered along the corridor, casting soft, wavering shadows, and the calming scents of home wrapped around me calming frayed nerves.

I eased her door open and stepped inside. Callie laid curled on her side, her chest rising and falling in the steady rhythm of deep sleep. Moonlight spilled through the window, painting her face in a silvery glow, softening the lines of worry etched in her features.

Relief flooded me, so overwhelming it brought a lump to my throat. "Oh, Callie," I whispered, my voice barely audible. "You're safe now, sugar. I promise."

I lingered for a moment, memories of our past rising like a tide—sun-drenched laughter, whispered secrets under a canopy of stars, her stubborn presence when I'd needed her most.

Reluctantly, I stepped back, easing the door closed behind me. The lavender-scented air followed me as I returned to Cade, resolved to keep safe the people I loved.

Cade

Olivia entered our bedchamber, her steps weary, but her expression one of peace at knowing her best friend slept under our roof tonight. She still carried too many worries on her shoulders—those of our kingdom, her sister, the looming threat of war. I longed to ease her burdens, even if only for a night.

"She looked so peaceful," Olivia said as she undressed for bed.

"So do you, when you allow yourself to rest," I told her, moving to her side. My fingers traced the curve of her cheek, feeling the tension beneath. "Come here. Let me take care of you tonight."

Olivia leaned into my touch, her eyes slowly closed, a silent acknowledgment of her exhaustion. "Cade, I don't know if I can relax. There's so much—"

"Hush," I said, tenderly lifting her chin. "For now, there is only you and me."

I led her to the adjoining bathing chamber, where the flicker of candlelight cast shadows on the stone walls. Steam rose from the copper tub, scented with lavender and chamomile, filling the air with soothing fragrances. I had prepared the bath for her while she tended to Callie. I was determined to create a relaxing oasis for her to come back to.

"You did all this?" Olivia's voice held a note of surprise as she took in the scene.

I smiled as my hands worked to unfasten the clasps of her gown. "I'd do anything in my power to give you a moment's rest, Starlight."

The fabric pooled at her feet. And even now, her beauty amazed me. The scars on her back told stories of her strength. They were a roadmap of her suffering. I pressed a kiss to my mating mark, and she moaned against my lips.

"Into the bath with you," I urged and held her hand as she stepped into the warm water.

I knelt beside her and gathered her long, dark hair, carefully pinning it atop her head. My fingers worked methodically as I massaged the tension from her neck and shoulders. I felt each knot unwind under my touch.

"Let it all go," I murmured close to her ear. "The kingdom, the war, every worry. For now, there is only this moment."

I looked at Olivia, and a spark of mischief found her eyes amid her tiredness. "You're soundin' awfully poetic tonight, Highness. I reckon you've been readin' a book or two from that fancy library of yours, huh?"

Oh, how this woman made me happy. "Perhaps your country charm is rubbing off on me, darlin'."

Her laughter echoed off the stone walls, filling the room with her warmth. It was the sweetest sound I'd heard all day.

The scent of lavender and chamomile filled the air around us as I worked the soap into a lather in my hands. Running: Carefully, I ran my palms along Olivia's arms until I felt her muscles begin to relax beneath my touch.

"I worry about you, you know?" As my fingertips traced her collarbone, I told her. "You carry too much, baby. You don't have to carry everything alone. Let me help you."

She closed her eyes and laid her head back against the edge of the tub, fully relaxed. "You already carry more than your share, Cade."

I dipped my fingers lower, skimming the swell of her breasts. A soft gasp escaped her lips, sending a thrill through me. I loved the way she responded to my touch, always ready.

"You're so beautiful, Starlight," I told her, my voice filled with desire.

"And your touch is everything," she breathed as she arched into my hand, her body telling me of her need for this moment of peace.

I explored her body with reverent touches as I mapped every curve and valley like it was my last touch. As my fingers found their way between her thighs, Olivia's breath hitched.

"And the way your body understands who holds the keys to your pleasure makes your king truly happy, Starlight."

"Highness," she whimpered, her hips rocking against my hand in an unspoken plea.

"I've got you," I assured her, my fingers entering her tight opening while my thumb found that sweet bundle of nerves that would send her spiraling. I rubbed a bit harder and faster, moving my fingers back and forth. "Let go, Olivia. I'll always catch you."

Her climax built slowly, and I watched as she finally went over the edge. Her face told the story as her body writhed under my touch. The sounds she made when she came were the sweetest music.

As she shuddered against me. I felt in our bond the pulsing

the rhythm of her ecstasy and there was no better feeling of satisfaction than to know that I'm the one who took her there.

In that moment, as Olivia trembled in my arms, I knew what true contentment felt like. And I knew that I'd do whatever it took to give her these moments of serenity as often as I could.

As Olivia's breathing steadied, I pressed a gentle kiss to her temple. "Let's get you dried off, sweetheart," I told her, reaching for the soft towel I'd set aside earlier.

I helped her stand as the water cascaded down her curves. Then I wrapped a towel around her and took my time patting her skin dry. Olivia's eyes locked onto mine. The trust and affection I saw there made my heart swell.

"You're somethin' else, Cade Vesparra," she drawled, her Texan accent more pronounced in her relaxed state.

I smiled at her, tucking a damp strand of her dark hair behind her ear. "I could say the same about you, Olivia Ilyndor Vesparra."

She yelped as I scooped her in my arms, laughing as I carried her to our bed.

"I'm capable of walking, you know," she teased, but didn't make any effort to leave the comfort of my embrace.

"I know you are, but there's nothing I love more than caring for you," I told her as I laid her on our bed.

"No one cares for me like you do," she replied.

I trailed my fingers along her neck as I laid down next to her. "You deserve every ounce of care I can give you, Starlight. And so much more."

She cradled my cheek in her hand, her thumb tracing my lower lip. "Show me, Highness."

I lowered my head and trailed her lips with my tongue. She opened her mouth for me and I kissed her with all the love and passion I felt for her. Her arms wrapped around my neck, pulling me closer to her. She ravaged my mouth as much as I did hers. Kissing, tasting, exploring.

I pulled back so I could continue down her neck. I sucked

and kissed the sensitive area toward her shoulder where my mate mark was. The magic there always gave a rush when the sensation of my tongue and lips played there.

"Cade," she gasped as my tongue found its mark. "Oh, sweet Goddess…"

"Yes, the Goddess gave us each other, Olivia. Our love, our mark. Our bond. I can never thank her enough."

I kissed my way down to her beautiful breasts. Poets wrote odes to beauty such as these. I took one hardened nipple into my mouth, my tongue dancing around it, then sucking until I released it with a subtle pop. The other side begged for the same treatment, so I happily made my way to it, sucking and gently nibbling all around. I longed to sink my fangs into it, and one day I surely would.

I licked my way down to her cute navel and circled it with my tongue, continuing my journey down her beautiful, firm belly ever closer to the object of my desire. Her scent drove me wild as I edged closer. Her gorgeous bare mound seemed to beckon anytime I was near her naked form.

"Olivia, my love, your beautiful pussy calls me, and I must answer," I told her as I gently licked within her folds.

"Oh gods, Cade!"

Her body jerked.

"Now, my darling, I'm going to need for you to spread those fucking thighs for me. I should not have to ask."

I took my hands and spread her wide open for me, positioning them to where I had the best access.

"Look at how you drip for me, angel. So fucking wet. So fucking mine."

I buried two fingers deep inside her, thrusting them in and out, curving them slightly until I hit that soft area that made her lift her hips in the same rhythm.

"Cade, please. I need to come!"

"You beg so prettily, Starlight. You are so godsdamn beautiful when you beg."

"Now! Highness!"

"Alright, good girl."

I leaned down and added my tongue to her swollen clit as my fingers continued their sweet assault. Moving my head from side to side, the flat of my tongue pressed in, and it didn't take long until she cried out, her body twitching and pulsing as she came and came.

I lost myself in pleasuring her, savoring every moan and whimper. The taste of her on my tongue, the scent of her arousal, the way her thighs trembled—it was intoxicating.

I then licked my way back up her body until I took her face in my hands. I kissed her deeply, like I was a dying man and she was my oxygen. And then I entered her in one deep thrust. Her legs wrapped around me, her heels digging into my ass, urging me in deeper.

"Gods, you feel so good, Cade."

"You are a miracle, Starlight."

I pounded into her, lost in her essence.

As Olivia's body tensed beneath me, she gasped under my touch; I knew she was close. I could feel her pleasure building, a crescendo of sensation that mirrored the pounding of my heart. Her fingers tightened in my hair, urging me on.

"Cade, please," she whimpered, her voice raw. "I need... I need..."

In that moment of vulnerability, I struck. My fangs sank into the soft flesh where her neck and shoulder met, and her blood —rich, sweet, intoxicating—flooded my mouth. Olivia cried out, but it wasn't in pain. The bite heightened her pleasure, prolonging her release.

"Yes," she moaned, her body arching off the bed. "Take me, Cade. All of me."

I drank deeply, feeling our bond strengthen with each swallow. Olivia's surrender was complete, her trust in me absolute. As I fed, I could sense her emotions flowing into me— love, desire, contentment, and a bone-deep sense of belonging.

My climax followed hers, indescribable each and every time. It was a feeling that started in my heart and radiated completely throughout my being, filling every one of my senses with her. It was remarkable.

When I finally withdrew, licking the puncture marks to seal them, Olivia lay boneless against the sheets. Her eyes were heavy-lidded, a dreamy smile played on her lips.

"That was..." she murmured, unable to find the words.

"I know," I replied, pressing a tender kiss to her forehead. "Rest now, my love."

I reached for the soft cloth I'd set aside earlier, gently cleaning her sweat-dampened skin. Olivia's eyes fluttered closed, a contented sigh escaping her.

"Do you love me?" she asked, her voice already thick with approaching sleep.

"How can you ask?" I queried, settling beside her and drawing her into my arms.

"Just checking." She whispered as she drifted off, safe and cherished in my embrace. I wondered at the depth of our connection. In her, I'd found not just a mate, but a partner in every sense. Together, we were a force to be reckoned with.

Eldric

I stood looking out the window of my chambers to the moonlit gardens below. My mind was a whirlwind of thoughts that I could not seem to shake. My encounter with Seraphine earlier had stirred something within me that was dangerous, seeing that I was under her brother's roof.

Her eyes had seemed to see right through me. What *was* that? And the unexpected connection of energy was potent. It left a humming in my veins that had yet to quiet.

I ran a hand through my hair, trying to calm the chaos inside. I hadn't tried to be a man of introspection in ages. I'd been too busy with my evil plans. I never wanted to examine myself, afraid of what I'd find. But now, it's all I do. And yet, Seraphine had looked at me like she didn't care about my past —the man I used to be. She seemed more interested in the man I had become.

I turned away from the window. What could she possibly have seen in me? Whatever it was, I didn't deserve it. Not after the blood on my hands, the betrayal etched into my soul. Still, the thought of redemption—is this available for someone as wicked as I had been? Could the Goddess give grace to someone like me?

I truly believed that returning to Eldoria would be the place that I'd find peace. Honor was a thing that I was chasing. Was it attainable? Would I be allowed to prove myself? Tomorrow was the first of many steps toward that goal. Tomorrow's meeting at the Crystal Citadel would be my first step on that path. I had information about Magda—secrets I'd hoarded even as I carried out her will. Sharing it freely would be the first stone laid on the road to redemption. There was no easy road to victory, not without the inside knowledge I possessed.

But it wasn't just Magda that weighed on me. Cadence Vesparra had to be told the truth about Callie's powers. He needed to understand what she was and the implications of her existence. It wouldn't be a simple conversation, but it was imperative. Callie deserved better than secrecy. She deserved a chance to control the power she hadn't asked for.

I let out a breath I hadn't realized I'd been holding, the faint scent of sandalwood from the room's hearth grounding me. Tonight, for the first time in what felt like an eternity, I would allow myself to rest. A hot shower to cleanse the filth of the Underworld, a soft bed to cradle my weary body—these were welcome luxuries I'd not had in ages. Tomorrow, the fight for redemption would begin in earnest.

CHAPTER 6

Scissors, Secrets, & Sisterhood

Olivia

The soft glow of morning crept through the sheer curtains, nudging me awake. A spark of excitement fluttered in my chest as my mind caught up. *Amaya's coming.*

I'd barely swung my legs over the side of the bed when a familiar voice rang out from the hallway.

"Olivia! Where's my favorite sister hiding?"

My heart skipped. "In here, you menace!" I called back, already grinning.

The door slammed open and my little sister came crashing in.

"There you are!" she cried.

Laughter spilled from my mouth. "Gods, I've missed you," she breathed.

I squeezed her tighter. "Missed you too, sis. More than you know."

Her expression darkened.

"What's wrong?" I asked, my smile faltering.

She hesitated, biting her lip. "I saw Callie on my way in." Her voice dropped, "Oh, Ollie... what that witch did to her..."

"I know," I said quietly. "It's awful. But she's strong. She'll make it through this. She has to."

"Well, at the very least, we can do something about that hair. Where are your scissors?"

I raised an eyebrow. "Oh? And when did you become a hairdresser?"

Amaya was already digging through my drawers, tossing things aside in search of her prize. "I didn't. But I *am* someone who refuses to let my friend walk around looking like she lost a fight with a lawnmower." She held up a pair of scissors in triumph. "Now, are you gonna help or just sit there looking skeptical?"

I snorted as I led Amaya down the hall. The second we stepped into Callie's room, her eyes lit up—not all the way, but enough. The weight she carried was still there, lurking just beneath the surface, but for a moment, she looked like *her* again.

"Alright, missy," Amaya announced, flipping the scissors in her hand like some kind of battle-ready warrior. "Time for a little follicular justice. Trust me, you're gonna *own* this pixie cut."

Callie didn't hesitate. She just nodded, already rolling up her sleeves like she was about to fight for it.

Amaya yanked a stool into place, patting it like she calling a small child to sit. "Up you go."

Callie sat without a word, letting Amaya drape a sheet around.

As Amaya got to work, I dropped onto the bed, watching. My fingers toyed absently with my own strands before a memory surfaced, one that made me smile despite everything.

"You know," I said, "Callie did this for me the first day we met."

Callie's eyes met mine in the mirror. "Gods, I forgot about that disaster," she rasped, voice rough but warm. "That nightmare of a foster mom really went for the *artistic* approach, didn't she?"

I huffed out a laugh. "Yeah, if by artistic you mean *butchered beyond repair*. You saved me from walking around looking like a deranged poodle."

"And now it's my turn to return the favor," Amaya cut in. "Consider it balance restored. But let's be real—the hag who did this to you? *Way* worse than the one we got stuck with."

The air in the room shifted, something lighter settling in. It wasn't much, but it was something. Snip by snip, strand by strand, I could see it happening—Callie, taking back a little piece of herself. A tiny victory, but a victory nonetheless.

With one final flourish, Amaya stepped back and flicked a stray hair from Callie's shoulder. "There," she declared, setting the scissors down. "So? What's the verdict?"

Callie tilted her head, studying her reflection.

"I... I love it," she whispered. "Thank you. For this. For... everything."

I yanked her into a hug, dragging Amaya in too, squeezing them both tight. "That's what family does," I said.

Eventually, I pulled back, sniffing once before schooling my face into something less sentimental. "Alright, alright. Enough feelings. We're just getting started with this transformation."

Callie arched an eyebrow. "Oh?"

I grinned, crossing the room to grab the bundle I'd hidden earlier. "Go on," I said,. "Open it."

She unwrapped it carefully. As the dark leather came into view, the air seemed to shift. The intricate patterns etched into the material shimmered under the morning light, faintly catching on some unseen magic woven into the design.

Callie sucked in a breath. "Ollie..." She ran her fingers over the supple leather. "These are... *beautiful.*"

"Try them on."

She stepped behind the dressing screen in the corner. When she emerged, the difference was immediate. The leathers perfectly.

She didn't just *wear* them.

She *owned* them.

"Well?" Callie asked, "How do I look?"

"Like a damn warrior," Amaya said.

My smile widened as I nodded. "And not just any warrior. Those leathers aren't just for show—they're laced with protective magic. You're in this now, Callie. No backing out."

Callie met my gaze. "Oh, I'm not backing out," she said. "I *like* it. And I'm ready—thanks to you."

Just then, Amaya's stomach let out a wolf-sized growl.

"Alright, alright," I said. "Let's feed you before you start chewing the furniture."

We ventured down the hall back to my room where my lady's maid, Margaret, had set the table with a beautiful breakfast.

"Okay," Callie said, pointing her fork at me with a sly grin. "Remember that time in college when we tried to sneak into that *very* exclusive club?"

A groan ripped out of me as I buried my face in my hands. "Oh gods, don't remind me. *What* made you think we could pass as elite country club members?"

Amaya perked up. "Hold on. I haven't heard this one. Spill. Now."

Callie, ever the storyteller, launched into the tale. I let myself get lost in it.

For a moment, just a small, perfect moment, I let go of the worry. The fear. The weight of everything waiting for us outside this room.

Right now, we were just three women, sharing old stories over breakfast.

Callie set her coffee down and turned to Amaya, a teasing gleam in her eyes. "So," she said, "how's mated life treating you? Is being a Luna as overwhelming as it sounds?"

Amaya smiled. "Kaelen is... amazing. Truly. He's the best man I've ever known. Patient, kind, and fiercely protective. I couldn't have asked for a better mate if I'd picked him myself. Honestly, the Goddess knew exactly what she was doing when she paired us." She said, shaking her head. "Though, I'll admit,

I was skeptical in the beginning. Kaelen had to put up with *a lot* of my nonsense before I came around."

Callie's expression shifted. "That sounds... incredible. Like a dream." Her voice was quieter now, almost hesitant. "And, against all odds, I found out I have a Fated Mate, too."

Amaya froze, her coffee halfway to her lips. Her eyes shot wide, and the cup nearly tipped. "Wait, *what?*"

"Callie, that's amazing!" She burst out, leaning forward. "But... how? When? Tell me everything!"

Callie let out a hollow laugh. "It's not exactly the fairytale you two seem to have," she said, shaking her head. "Mine was more like fate smacking me upside the head with a reality check." She paused. "He found me by accident—or fate, I guess. I was lying by the city walls, barely conscious. He must've come to see if I was alive. He touched my face, looked into my eyes, and asked my name. That's when I felt it. This... pull. Like something inside me had just clicked into place. Like I'd been anchored to something I didn't even know I needed."

Her voice wavered as she continued. "I didn't even know what a Fated Mate *was*. But he did. And he told me."

She turned her head. "He carried me to the healer's tent, sat me down on a cot. And then..." Her voice broke, and she shook her head. "He said he didn't want me. He rejected me. And he walked away."

Amaya's jaw dropped. "NO. HE. DIDN'T!" she exclaimed. "Who is this jackass? And what in the *blue blazes* is wrong with him?"

I cleared my throat. "So... her mate is, uh, Ignis."

Amaya froze mid-motion, her coffee cup hanging precariously in her hand. "Oh, for crying out loud. Ignis? Really?" She set the cup down with a thud. "Well, good luck, Callie. You've officially signed up for the toughest mate on the planet."

We groaned in unison, because, well... she wasn't wrong.

Ignis had a reputation, and not just because of his fire magic.

The man was stubborn. To an unreal degree. "Do you think the war's changed him at all?" I asked, though I couldn't keep the bite of irritation out of my voice.

Amaya tilted her head, considering. "Honestly? Hard to say. He came to Kaelen's and my mating ceremony, but the whole time, he looked like he'd rather be anywhere else. I think he's so tied up in the rules of his kingdom that he's afraid to do anything that might upset the balance."

Callie crossed her arms and leaned back, her tone sharpening. "Sounds like a man who's trapped by his own traditions. He's so stuck, I doubt he even knows how to break free—assuming he wants to."

"That's not an excuse," I snapped, heat flaring in my voice. "He still has a duty to Eldoria. And don't get me started on how long it took him to send troops to fight Magda. If I could've throttled him back then, I would've."

Amaya snorted, her eyes narrowing as she leaned back. "Throttle him? That's too nice. I'd punch him. Right in his stupid, smug face. And if I see him at the Citadel today?" She smirked. "Someone's going to need to hold me back."

Callie flinched, her arms tightening around herself. "Wait—the Citadel? Do I have to go?"

My voice softened as I reached out to touch her arm. "It's up to you, Cal. No one's gonna make you do anything you're not ready for. But if you're there, it might help. Just... think about it, okay?"

Amaya put her hand up to stop the conversation. "But wait. How did you wind up injured in Aurelion in the first place?"

"Oh, my stars!" I shouted. "I'm sorry, Itty Bitty! I told you Callie got out of the Underworld, but didn't tell you how!"

I gave her a quick run-down on Callie's rescue, including her relationship with Eldric and how he ended up here, in Vesparra.

Amaya sat shaking her head, a little stunned for a minute before she spoke. "It's kinda weird." She said. "I really don't have any bad feeling about him being here even though I know I should after what he's done. Maybe the Goddess has given me an extra dose of grace or something. Kaelen's gonna want to rip his head off, though."

I laughed at that. "Oh, trust me. I've had to talk Cade off the ledge, too. But I somehow believe this is all a part of the bigger picture."

The disbelief lingered in the room for a beat before I decided it was time for a distraction. Sitting back, I let a sly grin take over my face. "Speaking of Eldric, wait till you hear what happened with him and Seraphine last night."

Amaya leaned forward, her eyes gleaming with curiosity. "Please tell me you're kidding. No way something happened between the two of them."

"Oh, it happened," I said, the memory pulling a laugh out of me. "I don't know if it was flirting or fighting or something in between, but the tension? You could feel it from a mile away."

"I still can't believe it," I admitted, shaking my head. "The man who tried to steal my magic, the same man who terrorized so many, now standing there, all mesmerized in front of Seraphine. If I weren't living it, I'd swear it was a fairytale gone wrong."

Amaya snorted, a laugh escaping her lips. "Evil Eldric wouldn't know what hit him. Maybe he really is trying to change. Hopefully, he can help us against Magda."

I nodded, her words echoing the thoughts that had been swirling in my own mind. "I sit here in disbelief at my own ability to forgive that man for all the evil and heartache he caused me just months ago. I can't explain it. It must be a combination of Cade's love and the influence of the Goddess. You'd think I'd wanna yank him up by those curls of his and kick him square in the nads."

Callie barked out a laugh, nearly spilling her coffee.

"But somehow," I continued, "I find myself hopin' he's acting in truth. That he'll help us end this nightmare once and for all."

We both turned to Callie then, the weight of the conversation settling between us. She was the one who had truly suffered the most at Eldric's hands. The horrors he'd put her through... I couldn't blame her if she still hated him with every fiber of her being.

"Oh, Callie Girl." My voice softened as I reached across the table to take her hands in mine. Her fingers trembled slightly, but she didn't pull away. "I'm so sorry. We must sound like total jack wagons, sittin' here talkin' like this with you right here. You suffered horribly at his hands, and we're actin' like he should just get a free pass. I hate everything he did to you. Please know that."

"Ollie, stop." Callie's voice was steady, her green eyes locking onto mine. "I understand your feelings. Believe me, I'm struggling to reconcile my own. Eldric is the only genuine family I have—or at least that I'm willing to claim—in this realm. He risked his life to get me out of the Underworld. That has to count for something."

Her fingers tightened around mine, her gaze unflinching. "Every time Magda forced him to hurt me, I could see it in his eyes—he didn't want to do it. But if he hadn't, she'd have gotten someone else to do it. And it would've been so much worse."

Her voice wavered, but she pressed on. "He made the choices that got him there. I won't sugarcoat that. He walked into that darkness of his own free will. But... he's trying to claw his way out. None of us are perfect. None of us have done the evil he has, either. But damn, doesn't everyone deserve at least a chance to redeem themselves?"

Tears welled in my eyes before I could stop them. I swiped at my face in frustration, laughing weakly through the emotion. "Dadgummit, why am I cryin'? OK, come on, y'all. We all agree. We're just freakin' good people. That's it."

I sniffled, the hint of a smile tugging at my lips. "Alright, these are the things we know; Ignis is a gigantic butthead for hurtin' Callie. And trust me, he'll regret it. Eldric is also a gigantic butthead for hurtin' all of us. And he already regrets it. And Cade and Kaelen are perfect."

At that, we all burst out laughing, the sound ringing through the room like the first rays of sunshine breaking through storm clouds.

CHAPTER 7

Shadows of Redemption

Eldric

I paced the length of my chambers, each step a drumbeat against the stone floor, echoing the turmoil within me. With every turn, it seemed the walls moved closer, pressing upon me the weight of my sins. How could I face Cade after all I'd done? The memory of the pain I'd inflicted grated across my raw nerves.

"You have to try," I muttered, raking a shaking hand through my tangled curls. "This may be your one chance at redemption."

My eyes flickered to the mirror opposite the room, and I caught a glimpse of myself: piercing green eyes on a face that at one time might have been called handsome now seemed repulsive based on the life I'd lead. My jaw clenched, and I turned away, not able even to look at my own eyes.

A soft knock buckled my knees from my spiral of self-loathing. My heart went still. This was it—the moment of reckoning.

"Enter," I called, surprised by the steadiness of my voice, though my hands clenched into fists at my sides.

The door creaked open to admit a figure that seemed fragile and unyielding all at once. A woman stepped inside, her presence a curious mixture of fragility and command. Her dark eyes, sharp and steady, met mine without flinching.

"Eldric," she said, her voice low but full of command. "I am Ilyria, the Vesparra Court Mage. His Majesty has requested that I escort you to his study. I understand you have information of importance to impart."

I nodded, drinking in the vision of her. Threads of gray wove through what was once ebony hair, a sobering reminder of how many years she had given to this kingdom—the very kingdom I had tried to all but destroy.

"Yes, ma'am," I said, my voice no louder than a whisper, the words heavy in my throat.

She cocked her head sideways, an unreadable mask of expression. "I must say, I was quite astounded to have word of your arrival at the castle," she said, her voice cold as cut glass. "You caused us a great deal of pain, Eldric. Her Highness was not the only one who suffered torture at your hands."

Her words were a blow, thick with accusation and veracity. It weighed in between us alive, relentless. My throat started to shut, but I forced myself to meet her gaze, hard as it was.

"I know," I said, hoarse with my guilt. "And I'll carry that every day."

Her expression softened, though only slightly. "Then let us expect your actions now will outweigh the pain you've caused," she said.

"I realize my actions are unforgivable." The words tasted bitter on my tongue, each syllable heavy with regret. "But on what little honor I have left, I swear to the Goddess—I will do my best to make this right. I had been complicit in Magda's destruction, in her betrayals. I can't undo it. But maybe I can atone for it." My voice trembled, revealing the weakness I hated in myself. "I just … I just hope I can find redemption."

Ilyria smiled a small, sad smile, the kind that came from a lifetime of experience and lessons learned the hard way. "Hope, Eldric, is a dangerous thing," she whispered. "But sometimes that's the only thing we have."

Then, out of nowhere, she reached out her hand. An

invitation? A challenge?

I hesitated. The weight of my shame kept me there glued. But after a moment, I pushed myself to go, to accept. My fingers wound around hers, the warmth of her skin jarring against the cold knot of self-hate in my chest. A soft vibrato of magic thrummed under her fingertips, a gentle echo of her power.

Together, we emerged from the isolation of my chambers. Anxiety coiled around me, thick and damning. Every step forward seemed like walking a razor's edge, taking me either to salvation or to my demise. I wasn't sure which one I deserved more.

Torchlight flickered as it danced across the polished stone walls, casting images of dancers, and gaunt faces of times long lost in a roaming tableau in search of a stage, within the ever reacquainting shadows. Tapestries hung here and there depicting scenes of long-past battles, relics attesting to the great burden of strength the Vesparran line still bore.

"I had never really thought about the inside of this castle before," I said softly, feeling as if speaking too loudly might call forth the spirits that once stalked these halls. "The power it wields doesn't shock me... but the legacy does."

Ilyria's clasp tightened for a moment, anchoring me. "And now?"

I felt the question's weight sitting atop my shoulders, and I swallowed it hard. "Now I realize what I was about to destroy."

We rounded a corner, and the sight of the elaborately carved double doors to Cade's study came into view. My steps slacked, dread coiling stony fingers on my spine. The elaborate wood loomed larger with every breath I inhaled, the intricate carvings an unspoken accusation.

With every heartbeat growing louder in my ears, I moved on, the icy dread of what would await continuing to seep into my very bones.

"Ilyria," I whispered as loud as I could over my pounding heart, "do you think he'll listen? That he'll take me at my word that I'm really trying to help save the realm?"

She halted mid-stride and turned toward me. She looked old —old in the way people in history books looked, with all the light sucked out of her. "You cannot take back what you did, Eldric," she replied, the tone of her voice tempered but sure. "But every moment is an opportunity to create a new path. Remember why you're here."

I closed my eyes and allowed her words to settle over me. Callie's face flashed in my head—her strength, her pain, the forgiveness I saw in her, even when I didn't deserve an ounce of it. My chest was heavy with the knowledge, but it was also my anchor; it gave me purpose.

As I dared to open my eyes, terror turned to resolve. "For Callie," I said softly. "For the realm. For an opportunity to correct my mistakes."

Illyria dipped her head in what could be a sign of favor; some warmth crept into her expression. "So then let that be your north star."

The study doors loomed, a heavy oaken presence before us, forged into arcane patterns that glinted in the torchlight. Their tremendous weight matched the gravity of the events to follow.

I stood up straighter, readying whatever resolve remained in me. The "me" of just months ago would have gone is with an arrogance and smirk. But I wasn't that man anymore — or at least, I was trying not to be. I'd face whatever judgment that was to come, with as much humility and honesty as I could muster.

"Are you ready?" Ilyria inquired, her hand hovering just above the door.

I took a deep breath and allowed the air to fill my lungs and steadied myself. "As I'll ever be."

My soul shook at the echo of her knock in the corridor. It was a point of no return, the moment where everything would either disintegrate or remake itself.

I entered Cade's study when the doors opened and the air grew thick around me with an intoxicating mix of power and memory. As the smell of old paper, varnished wood and leather wafted through my nostrils, I felt as if I was at the foot of a mountain of knowledge steeped over centuries.

I felt my eyes being drawn to the figure who looked out the window. Highlighted by the golden morning sunlight, Cade Vesparra, the Vampire King, stood before me, his broad frame cast an intimidating shadow. He was all muscle, even at rest, and his silent energy filled the room.

Around us were rich, dark furnishings—ornately carved bookshelves piled high with ancient tomes, a massive desk of polished ebony, plush velvet chairs that seemed to have whispers of hushed conversations and weighty decisions. The golden rays of the flickering light from the ornate candelabras danced shadows on the walls, turning all corners of the room mysterious.

I swallowed hard, easing the anxious knot in my throat. "Your Majesty," I said, bowing my head respectfully. I maintained a calm inflection, hiding the tremors of guilt that throbbed just under my skin. "Thank you for giving me this audience."

Cade looked away from the window, his piercing eyes locking on mine. His scrutiny felt almost heavy, and I battled a desire to squirm beneath his gaze. His smooth, jet-black hair framed features that resembled porcelain—beautiful, but unforgiving.

"Eldric," he said, with tone cool and measured. The single word packed multiple meanings—acknowledgment, caution and even a glimmer of curiosity. "You've come with information, I hear. Speak freely."

I breathed in deep; the air laced with a faint trace of magic that hummed around us, crackling away at the edge of my awareness. This was it. My opportunity to show them I was not the man they recalled. That I might be more than my past sins.

The words I said next could change the fates of the realm. No pressure, right?

"Your Majesty," I started, my mind scrambling for the right words, "I have much to tell you about Callie—and the power held within her. It could help change everything we believed we knew about the balance of magic in Eldoria."

I stopped, feeling the gravity of the discovery settle heavily upon me. The atmosphere felt thick now, the silence in the air magnifying my revelation. "I don't know if you knew this, but Callie and I are cousins. My father was her late father's brother."

Cade gave a slight nod, his face inscrutable. "I have been informed of this fact."

The knot in my chest loosened just enough that I was able to exhale. I continued, my voice low but urgent. "Callie... she was born to parents born of the Underworld, their bloodlines imbued with enormous magic. That legacy granted her powers that challenge our understanding of life and even death."

The whole time I spoke, Ilyria's stare searing through me. Out of the corner of my eye, I saw her eyes widen, an infinitesimal flash of fear that rippled across her otherwise placid features. It was the kind of fear that comes from knowing the seismic weight of my words.

"These powers," I continued, my throat constricting as the weight of what I was about to say settled over me, "they're complicated... and dangerous. Callie was born a revenant. This means her abilities will enable her to connect with the dead in ways that make little sense." A chill ran through me. Cade's eyes never wavered. "It's as if that veil between death and life is little more than a gossamer curtain to her."

While Cade's face didn't change, I didn't miss the minute clenching of his jaw or the way his hands curled just slightly at on his desk. He definitely understood the weight of this news.

He said in a low and commanding voice, without leaving room for hesitation, "Go on."

I swallowed, struggling with the dryness in my throat. "Remember," I said hesitantly, "she doesn't know how to use these powers. She's also just also learned about them herself —a few weeks ago. Magda had attempted to break her, tried to pound the strength out of her, but Callie's resolve had been powerful. She resisted at every turn."

Those words hung in the air like smoke, and I watched as Cade gripped the sides of this desk, knuckles white as he fought to digest the cruelty Callie had suffered.

I took a deep breath. The smell of faded pages and stale candles lingered in the air. "At this stage," I said, "the only part of her magic she's accessed is her body's ability to speed up its healing. And even that is done involuntarily."

Cade's eyes flared to life, anger simmering just beneath the skin. I sensed the storm brewing inside him as he struggled to process the meaning of what I was saying.

I paused, the gravity of what came next almost unbearable. But there was no going back now. "If Callie were to embrace her powers completely, she would carry deadly abilities that the vast majority of us could hardly even imagine."

Cade's eyes drilled into me like he was looking for some sign of deceit, but I stared him down, letting him read the fear that coincided with my earnestness.

I spoke again, but my voice hardly carried above a whisper. "Callie can bring the dead back to life. And yes, it's as terrifying as it sounds."

That dialed up the tension in the room tenfold. The heavy silence was broken only by Ilyria's sharp intake of air.

Cade's eyes narrowed, the flare of fury in their depths dulled by frigid calculation. When he spoke, his voice was as smooth and dark as the shadows pooling in the corners of the room. "Explain, Eldric," he ordered.

I walked a few steps and never made a sound on the elaborate carpet beneath my feet. "Imagine, Your Majesty," I started, the burden of my words weighing heavily on my tongue, "an army that never really dies. Soldiers who come back the hundredth time, the thousandth time, immune to fear, to pain, to... mortality." The idea left a bitter taste in my mouth, unwanted memories of Magda's depravity rising unbidden to the surface.

The room was silent, except for the faint crackle of the fireplace. The oppressive stillness bore down on my skin as Cade's eyes darkened, his brain clearly whirling. I almost imagined the cogs spinning, this brilliant mind weighing the strategic utility of such power against the enormity of horror that lay in its simple existence.

"There's more," I went on, but my throat felt constricted, as though the air were pushing back against my next admission. "Callie has a different gift—she knows that death is coming before it happens. On a battlefield, this could be priceless: predicting outcomes, saving lives."

Cade leaned forward a little, and his keen gaze speared me. "And how might this power impact Callie?"

I paused, closing my eyes briefly as I wrestled with the answer. "I believe it would be devastating," I admitted. "To constantly feel the approach of death, to hear its whispers creeping closer with every breath. I fear it would break her without a way to shield herself from it."

My words fell over the room like stone, a blanket so heavy that it put all but the firelight out. The air hung heavy with unsaid possibilities, with the lines between salvation and demise growing perilously thin.

I breathed deeply; the air had a slight tang of wood smoke. "There's something else we need to talk about," I said. "There is another detail of Callie's power."

Cade's brow furrowed. "Continue," he said.

"Callie," I said, "can channel spirits."

Cade's eyes narrowed. "Channel spirits?" he asked. "Explain."

I nodded. "She has the ability to mediate between the living and the dead, and the dead speak through her. It's like she's in between our world and the next world. She's both there and here at the same time." I paused, then continued, "The insights we could get, the knowledge."

Cade leaned back in his chair, his face inscrutable, though the brief glimpse of doubt in his eyes did not go unnoticed by me.

"But the dangers," I said, "are just as great. Continued channeling may compromise Callie's identity. She could get lost in the all the voices without being able to discern her thoughts from that of the spirits she channels."

Ilyria's dark eyes softened then, and she shook her head. "To lose oneself." She said, "It's worse than death."

"And then," I said, "there's the question of her immortality."

"Immortality?" Cade asked.

"Yes," I said, turning back to meet his intense gaze. "A blessing and a curse that will never not be intertwined. Callie cannot truly die. Her body heals... but not without cost."

"Each time she 'dies,' she feels the full, excruciating pain of her demise. And with every regeneration, a piece of her soul— her essence—fades. It's as though death chips away at who she is, little by little."

The dawning horror in Cade's eyes mirrored my own when I first learned this terrible truth.

"Magda would use this against her," I went on. "Think unending torture, aware that she can't escape through death. She would revel in tormenting her, taunting her. It would be an everlasting punishment."

The silence that followed was only broken by a rumble of distant thunder. I could feel the charged air pressing down on all of us, the reality of Callie's "gift" weighing heavier than I could stand.

Ilyria put a steadying hand on the edge of the desk, her face white but firm. "The price of this kind of power... It's almost unimaginable."

Cade's protective rage radiated from every line of his body.

"There's... one more thing," I said. "It's likely that Callie is able to open portals to the Underworld."

Everything felt static charged with heaviness. In the quiet, I could hear Ilyria inhale sharply, yet again.

"Portals?" Cade's voice dipped dangerously low, the edge slicing through the taut air. "To Magda's realm?"

I nodded, locked eyes with him, and willed him to see the seriousness of what I was saying. "The strategic possibilities are... considerable. We could conduct a surprise attack, gather intelligence."

"But the risks..." Ilyria said.

"Are immense," I said. "One false step, and we risk unleashing unspeakable horrors on Eldoria. And what if Magda gets control of Callie's power?"

I stepped to where I could see both of them, fists balled at my sides. "No power comes without a heavy physical price, and Callie pays dearly for each one of these powers. The effects are the same as when any of us use our own magic—it drains you. Callie's strength might make her able to work her magic longer before falling apart, but fall apart, she will. And the bigger threat is if Magda were to harness this power." My voice became increasingly frantic as I explained. "That's why she fought as hard as she did to keep Callie inside the cage. That's why I now imagine she is raging."

Cade turned away, and his wide shoulders stiffened as he gazed out the window. The storm that had been churning towards them on the horizon mirrored the chaos in the room, the very atmosphere heavy with static and tension. A distant roll of thunder was like the theme of choices to come.

I could see the heaviness covering him, the weight of a kingdom's fate pressing down like a shroud. His hand gripped the top of the windowsill; the tendons of his forearm stood out in stark relief.

The silence stretched, full of possibility, until Cade finally spoke. His voice rang low but confident, piercing the stillness like a knife. "We'll see that Callie's power is never seized by Magda. Whatever it takes."

Then he asked the question I feared, the one that would force me to face my deepest shame. "How can Callie not know what her powers do and how to use them?" His tone was soft, but his eyes burned with a fierceness that allowed for no deflection. It was a fair question—one I wished I wouldn't have to answer.

I took in a deep, steadying breath. "When Callie came to the Underworld, she was a lot like Olivia," I started carefully. "She didn't know magic was real. But, unlike Olivia, she had no one to guide her. She drifted alone for weeks, and Magda... more or less ignored her."

The blood in my veins ran cold. To say it aloud would make it even more real. "For the simple reason," I added, my voice breaking, "that she had Olivia. And she didn't believe she needed Callie."

Cade's face fell and his fists tightened at his sides. The murderous glare in his eyes churned my stomach, but he held himself together, his voice cold and concise. "Continue, Eldric."

I nodded, swallowing hard. "The next target was Callie after Olivia and Amaya were freed." Magda was furious. And she... My voice fell, bitter over what I'd seen. "She finally just came out and told Callie what sort of Underworld creature she was. Callie, of course, didn't know what a revenant was. But Magda played that ignorance against her. She tormented her with the knowledge, told her she was the worst kind of monster ever born."

My voice broke, but I made myself go on. "And Callie... she took it. All of it. Every impulse to let loose with her magic. I don't know if it was because she didn't know how—or because her goodness wouldn't let her."

The silence in the room was palpable, the tension like a vice squeezing us tighter around the core. Cade's jaw worked as he fought against his rage, that sharp look, drilling into me.

When he spoke, his voice was low and firm, every word a promise. "We have to be very careful here. Callie's powers might be the thing that helps turn the tide of this war—but at what cost?"

He adjusted his body so that he was facing us completely, the force of his presence owning the room. His eyes were full of feral heat, and they set my skin alight. "We are going to protect her. We are going to guide her. But we also have to be ready for the worst."

The weight of his words washed over me, suffocating with their sincerity. Ilyria nodded, her lips drawn into a grim line. Firelight flickered across her face below, putting her own thoughts in stark relief.

By the end of the meeting, hope and dread coiled in my stomach, a highly flammable mixture that felt on the verge of combusting. Our choices today would determine Callie's fate —and possibly of all of Eldoria's. And as I gazed into Cade's focused face, I knew that whatever happened next, it would try us all in ways we couldn't yet fathom.

CHAPTER 8

Callie's Burden

Cade

The atmosphere was heavy in my study with the gravity of Eldric's words. Everything he had said about Callie's powers settled heavily over my mind. I stilled in front of the massive bookshelves filled with ancient tomes. None of them echoed the tempests writhing through me. I felt a tightness twisting in my gut as I tried to process everything I'd just learned about the power that Callie held.

My fingertips grazed the spine of a leather-bound volume. I needed to touch something familiar as I thought about Callie, Olivia's sweet friend, who hadn't asked for any of this. Now that I knew the powers she carried, and how they could affect the outcome of the coming war, I worried for her. The instinct to keep her safe from the claws that break through the rifts battled with the sobering truth: her necromancer power might hold the key to protecting us all.

"Dammit," I muttered, my voice barely above the hiss of the candles. The burden of keeping not only my kingdom, but now this vulnerable woman, safe pressed on my chest like the physical weight of iron.

I shut my eyes, extending through the ghostly strings of my connection with Olivia. Her presence greeted me right away —warm, soothing, as necessary as the air in my lungs. The connection grounded me, like a vessel dropping an anchor during a tempest.

"Starlight," I called out to her mind; the thought colored

with both urgency and tenderness. *"I need you, my love. Bring Callie to my study."*

Even across the sprawling expanse of the castle, I could feel Olivia's pulse quickening, her breath catching softly as my words connected with her. Her worry brushed against me like a breeze, coaxing the scent of stargazer lilies, anchoring me deeper.

"What's wrong, Cade?" Her tender voice filled my mind, caressing my frayed nerves.

"Eldric's information regarding Callie," I let her know. This was something that all three of us needed to talk about.

Olivia's iron will coursed through the bond between us. She had become an incredible queen for Vesparra and leader for our forces. Just to be with her soothed the rough places in my mind. *"We're on our way,"* she told me, love and strength pouring into me like a river, fluid and persistent.

While waiting for them, I walked the length of my study, the plush rugs soft against my boots. The elaborately decorated fireplace whispered with the crackle of dying embers that bathed the walls with flickering shadows that only bitterly failed to reach through the cold weight sitting on my breast.

"We're going to help her through this," I promised the empty room, my voice low and fierce. "Whatever it takes."

The words hung in the air, a solemn promise, also a challenge that must be met. With the first tap of oncoming footsteps in the hall, I stiffened and squared my shoulders. I would be damned if I let my world fall or let my any harm come to my family.

I sensed Olivia before she entered the room, her warmth skimming through my consciousness like the first light of day. The study door creaked open, and I turned, expecting to see both my mate and Callie. Olivia came through alone, her purple eyes twinkling with an emotion I couldn't pinpoint right away—concern mixed with something weightier.

"Where's Callie?" I said, my brow knitting as anxiety washed over me.

Olivia exhaled softly and closed the door with careful deliberation. "She's still with Amaya. They said they were going to have another cup of coffee."

Frustration bubbled just below my skin, ready to erupt. My jaw clenched and my voice wavered as I tried to keep my tone steady. "I asked you to bring her here."

"I know, sugar," Olivia said with a drawl thick with her own telltale signs of stress. "But Amaya thought it would be best if we spoke first. She's concerned about overwhelming Callie."

I ran a hand through my hair. My voice was tight with frustration. "Coddling time is over, Olivia." The impatience in my voice betrayed my internal concern. "This is too important to wait."

Olivia flinched at my shortness with her. Her raised eyebrow told me she wanted to let loose on me. Surprisingly, she crossed the room and gently rested her hand on my arm. The touch sent a spark through me. She had a way of calming the storms that raged with those simple touches.

"Darlin' I understand that. But remember, Callie's literally been through hell. We need to be careful."

I closed my eyes and drew in a deep breath. Olivia's unique fragrance of stargazer lilies and sunshine grounded me. When I opened my eyes, her gaze was steady. It was like she was determined to fill me with her peace.

"You're right," I reluctantly admitted. "It's just... I don't know how much time we have until Magda strikes again. We're in uncharted territory here, Starlight. What am I supposed to do?"

She gave me a small smile. "Probably burn the entire realm to the ground trying to protect everyone."

I laughed, despite the weight that seemed to crush my chest. "I'm trying to prevent that, not make it worse."

The gravity of our situation could not be denied. We felt it everywhere. The flickering firelight couldn't warm the room enough to cancel the chilly feelings that seem to surround us.

"So," Olivia said, her fingers threading through mine. "It's always somethin', huh?"

The creak of the heavy oak door pulled my attention away from her. Callie stepped into the study. She looked ready to take on whatever I had to tell her. She looked totally different, dressed in the leathers Olivia had made for her. They caused her to stand tall and exude a confidence that I had yet to see. Cleaned up with her hair no longer a choppy mess, it also seemed to give her the will to face what was coming her way.

The sight of her still-healing injuries caused a surge of anger to flare in my chest. Though her healing abilities were evidently at work, the faint marks left on her pale skin stood as glaring reminders of the horrors she had endured. The thought of what Magda had done to her made me want to find that bitch and rip her head off.

"Callie," I said, trying to keep my temper in check.. "Come in."

Olivia got up and pulled Callie into the room. The bond between the two of them is obvious in every gesture.

"There's that girl," Olivia sang as she sat her in one of the large velvet chairs in front of my desk. "Alright now, Cade's gonna give us the lowdown on everything revenant, I assume, hmm?"

I couldn't help but smile as she looked my way. I could only assume "lowdown" meant information.

"Ah, yes, Starlight. The lowdown." I said. I was hopeful my tone could switch to sounding a bit more serious. "We have much to discuss."

Callie hesitated a moment before sinking into the chair. She looked less than comfortable as her fingers twisting nervously in her lap. I hated she felt uneasy, but hopefully I could present things in a way that wouldn't be too overwhelming.

I crossed my arms and leaned against my desk. "Callie," I began. "I know that you, like Olivia, have been tossed into this world of magic and magical beings not knowing its origins or history. Learning that you are a part of that world must be terrifying."

She gave a little nod.

"And for you, it's been more terrifying because your introduction was in the Underworld at the hands of the cruelest creature of them all. I hate that for you. We all do. But thank the Goddess, you're here now."

Olivia reached out and gave her hand a squeeze and continued to hold on to it.

"Now, we need to discuss you specifically and your magic, your revenant abilities, which are many and incredibly powerful, as you may or may not have discovered."

She spoke up then.

"I only know what Magda told me, and that was only bits and pieces."

"Ok. Well, I think it's best we throw out what she told you and start with what Eldric shared with me this morning. My goal here is to help you understand the nature of your powers and unravel some of the mystery surrounding them. You power it's not something to be feared."

I saw her shoulders tense at my words as she looked down at her hands.

"Callie, look at me. Your powers are not a curse. They are a gift—a rare and extraordinary ability that sets you apart."

Her brow furrowed, frustration flickering across her face. "I get it. I do, in as much as I get that I was born in this freakin' horrible, hellish world I hadn't even heard of until a few months ago. And that my birth parents were some kind of royal creatures. But other than that? The rest of my life, I was just a normal girl from Texas. It's hard to wrap my head around the fact that I could have *any* magical powers at all. The only power I ever had before was getting a farmer to sign on the dotted line."

"I promise you, Callie, you've always been far from normal.

Your revenant powers grant you extraordinary abilities. Let's just start with one you're probably already aware of. You have accelerated healing—which just means your wounds heal faster than humans and even other magical beings."

Callie shifted uncomfortably in her chair, but gave a small shrug of her shoulders in acknowledgment.

"Most of your other powers surround a spooky subject that most people find off-putting simply because of the unknown. You have necromancer powers. Which just means your powers surround the dead. That seems macabre, but death is not something to fear," I continued. "The spirit world surrounds us all. Your magic makes you more attuned to it. With time and mastery, you'll be able to communicate with the dead. I know that sounds frightening, but it could prove invaluable in our fight against Magda."

Her gaze darted to Olivia, panic flashing in her eyes. "I don't know that I *want* to talk to dead people—like that creepy kid in that *Sixth Sense* movie. 'I see dead people'—ugh, it gives me the willies."

Olivia busted out laughing, the sound lightening the tension in the room.

"Callie Girl, you don't have to be creepy. You can be like the cool medium in that movie *Ghost,* you know—'You in danger, girl.' That's more your speed."

Callie's lips twitched despite herself, and soon they were both giggling. The laughter softened the moment, giving me the chance to broach the next, more difficult subject.

"Now, Callie," I began, my tone serious, "this next ability is the most impactful and likely the most uncomfortable to discuss. Your power also gives you the ability to... reanimate the dead."

At that, Callie shot out of her chair like a spring, her hands wringing together. "OH, FUCK THAT!" she exclaimed, pacing the room. "Uh uh, no way. I'm not creating a zombie army! I know exactly how *that* turns out. *Walking Dead,* anyone?"

I frowned, not understanding the reference. It seemed to be from the mortal world. I glanced at Olivia, who was suppressing another laugh, her shoulders shaking.

"Callie, I know it sounds terrifying," I said, keeping my tone steady and calm. "I get that. This is a tremendous responsibility, but I believe you can handle it. If there's even the slimmest chance that your powers can help us defeat Magda—permanently send her back to the Underworld if she escapes—we need to consider every option. But let me be clear: no one will force you to use your magic. You won't be asked to do anything until you've been trained, until you fully understand how your power works, and how it affects you mentally and physically."

Her green eyes widened, a storm of awe and fear swirling within them as she slowly sank back into the chair. "But how?" she asked, her voice trembling. "I don't know the first thing about... any of this."

Pushing off the desk, I knelt before her, ensuring my gaze was level with hers. "That's where I come in," I said, my voice soft but resolute. "I promise you, Callie, that I, along with Olivia and the others, will help you. We will train you, guide you, and teach you to harness your powers—to control them instead of letting them control you."

I reached out and placed a hand over hers. Her fingers trembled beneath mine, a slight but telling sign of the battle waging within her. "You are safe here, Callie," I continued, my words deliberate and measured. "You are under my protection. And I swear on my life, no harm will come to you while you're learning to master your abilities."

As I spoke, I felt Olivia's hand settle on my shoulder. Her touch was firm, and our bond hummed in the background of my mind—a source of silent strength, unyielding and true.

Callie's gaze flickered between the two of us. Slowly, her rigid shoulders began to loosen, the tension easing just enough to let her voice break free. "Okay," she whispered, barely louder than the crackling of the fire. "I trust you. Both of you."

I straightened, turning to meet Olivia's eyes. The warmth that had passed between us earlier had dissipated, replaced by something far more intense. Her gaze held a storm of emotions—concern, resolve, and something unspoken that sparked between us, sharp as lightning and just as electric.

"Now, Cade, there's something we haven't told you," Olivia said, her voice barely above a whisper. The scent of her distress —a sharp, bitter tang cutting through her usual honeyed fragrance—made my fangs ache beneath my gums. Whatever she was about to say, I knew I wouldn't like it.

"Look, I'm just gonna give you the highlights, or lowlights, of what's happened. When Callie first arrived in Eldoria, she came up just outside Aurelion's gates. Eldric was in a rush to find us, so he carried her into the city and left her by the walls at her insistence. Well," Olivia hesitated, her hands fluttering in that telltale way of hers, "wouldn't you just know it? Fate decided to meddle. And who should find her but our ol' buddy Ignis?"

My jaw tightened. Whatever was coming next, I was sure it would be worse than I imagined.

"And," Olivia continued, her tone dropping conspiratorially, "he sees this battered, bruised, and beautiful woman, semi-conscious on the ground. Of course, he runs to help her. And…when he touched her face? Badda boom, badda bing! He discovered she's his one True Fated Mate."

"Starlight," I said, my voice low and filled with disbelief, "you have got to be shitting me."

"Nope," she replied, popping the 'p' with a sharp nod. "And whatever you're thinking, Highness, it's exactly what that weasel-faced, good-for-nothin', piece of horse poop did. He rejected my Callie Girl, and I'm gonna kick his royal hiney when I see him later today!"

Callie shrank into the chair, curling her legs up to her chest. Her pain radiated through the room like a palpable force tightening my chest. I dropped to one knee in front of her, my voice softening.

"Callie, Ignis is an ass. We all know this. But he's also a good man. Don't give up on him just yet. I'm so sorry he hurt you, truly. He's fighting a legacy of pride and backward traditions, trying to break free of the ones that came before him. But that doesn't make what he did right."

Her green eyes, filled with unshed tears, searched mine.

I continued, my tone firm but gentle. "It's going to be important, more than ever, that you control your powers in the midst of your pain. You don't want to do actual harm to him, Callie. That would hurt you just as much as his rejection. That's the curse of the mate bond—it cuts both ways."

Tears spilled down her cheeks as the hurt overwhelmed her. Olivia was instantly by her side, her hand stroking Callie's arm in soothing circles.

Callie gave a laugh and spoke through her tears, "Well, ain't that just the way it goes? I finally have the ability to give as good as I get, and I'm not allowed to give it."

Together, we stood as Callie wiped her tears away, her spirit flickering back to life despite the weight of her heartbreak.

Olivia wrapped Callie in a tight hug. It was like she could impart literal magic through her touch. Callie straightened, and her face lit up with a bright smile. "I've never let a man keep me down," she said, her voice firm. "And I'm not about to start now."

I admired Callie for her bravery in the face of what had to be an incredibly painful situation. She Olivia and I made our way toward the dining room, Olivia's hand nestled firmly in mine. I couldn't help but want to kick Ignis' ass for not only hurting Callie, but himself as well. He was trading this incredible feeling for the outdated traditions of his kingdom.

The atmosphere shifted the moment we entered the dining room. I'd already given my Circle the information regarding Eldric's apparent change of heart and Olivia's insistence that she had a gut feeling that he's sincere and she'd forgiven him. Everyone seemed to be getting along so far. My irritation still lingered, however.

"Well, don't we all look cozy," I muttered under my breath, noting the way Seraphine leaned towards Eldric, her silvery hair cascading over her shoulder as she laughed at something he'd said.

Olivia squeezed my hand, her grip a gentle reminder. "Play nice," she whispered, her tone laced with amusement.

My jaw tightened as I watched them. How could Seraphine, my sister—the strategist, the one who always saw through veils of deceit—be so at ease with him after everything he'd done?

"Highness," Olivia's voice pulled me from my brooding thoughts. "I want to introduce Callie to Miranda."

I nodded, forcing a smile as Olivia guided Callie toward her cousin. Despite my irritation at Eldric's presence, a swell of pride rose in my chest. Olivia carried herself with grace and quiet authority, every inch the leader I knew her to be.

"Miranda," Olivia said, her excitement unmistakable, "I'd like you to meet my best friend, Callie. Callie, this is my cousin, Miranda, the Queen of Ilyndor."

Miranda rose swiftly, her black curls catching the light as she practically flew across the room to envelop Callie in a warm hug.

"I've heard so many stories about you!" Miranda exclaimed, her tone effervescent. "I feel like I know you already."

Callie blinked in surprise, but her lips curved into a smile as she returned the embrace. Miranda's genuine warmth and enthusiasm were infectious, breaking through any lingering unease.

I felt a knot of tension I hadn't realized I'd been carrying start to loosen. Callie's shoulders relaxed, and a genuine smile spread across her face. "All good things, I hope?"

"Of course," Miranda replied with a conspiratorial wink.

"Though she may have mentioned something about a certain incident involving a stolen boat and a furious fisherman..."

Callie groaned, her eyes sparkling with mischief. "Oh god, she didn't. Ollie, you promised never to tell that story!"

Olivia couldn't help her laughter. "I'm sorry, Cal, but it was just too good not to share."

As the introductions continued, I wondered at the strange twists of fate that had brought us all together. The dining room, that usually ended up being a place for strategy and negotiations, now buzzed with an energy that was almost... hopeful.

Even so, the underlying feeling of dread was always there. From one minute to the next, we could be called to battle. We all knew that any meal could be our last. My gaze drifted across the table until I met Eldric's eyes. For a fleeting moment, something flickered in his eyes—regret? remorse? In that brief second, I felt he was searching for something intangible.

As the women fell into easy conversation, I was unexpectedly swept up in the lightness of the moment. Even Eldric and Seraphine seemed to relax, their earlier tension melting away as they joined in the banter.

"So, Callie," Seraphine asked, leaning forward with genuine curiosity, "what was it like growing up in Texas?"

Callie's face lit up, her enthusiasm cutting through the lingering shadows of her pain.

"Oh, there's no place like Texas! Especially in the spring when the bluebonnets are in bloom. There are these fields that look like oceans of blue and white flowers. Families stop on the side of the road to take pictures with their kids—it's practically a rite of passage. Every spring, my parents would schedule a day just for that. We'd head to the Bluebonnet Festival for photos and lemonade. We never missed..." Her voice faltered, trailing off as memories overwhelmed her.

Olivia immediately reached out, taking Callie's hand and giving it a reassuring squeeze. "Oh, Cal, you know we have some lovely flowers here, too. And beautiful coastlines and forests. There's so much to see, honey. This place will feel like home sooner than you think."

Callie looked up and gave a grateful smile.

Olivia's face seemed to hold a mix of emotions. I knew she was so glad that Callie had opened up and was feeling more at home here. But at the same time, there was no way not to feel so sad for her because of the rejection she felt from the mate bond.

Olivia's voice rang in my mind through our bond. *"Cade, my heart is breaking for her."*

I nodded slightly, sending my love through the bond. Aloud, I said, "Maybe we could arrange a visit to the coast soon. I'm sure King Farin would love to see his granddaughters for an extended stay. Once this war is behind us, we'll all need a long holiday."

The table erupted in agreement. We, of course, all knew that this suggestion could possibly just be a fanciful fantasy at this point. I'm just hoping Farin will have a kingdom for us to visit. But for a small moment in time, we weren't royals, warriors, or strategists bracing for war. We were just friends sharing a meal and laughter.

CHAPTER 9

Dragonia Encounter

Olivia

I stepped out into the warm afternoon sun of the courtyard, anticipation coursing through me. I had called the Dragonia to meet Callie. The air hummed with an otherworldly energy, making my skin tingle. Cade's hand found mine, his touch grounding me as we led our small group past the castle walls to the training fields. He was broody and irritated because Seraphine had insisted that she and Eldric would follow shortly. I mean, it was her business. His sister was a grown woman, and all he could do was to trust her judgment. I had a feeling that soon his irritation would reach new heights regarding those two.

"Ok Callie Girl! Are you ready to have your mind blown?" I could hardly contain my excitement. "The Dragonia are... well, there's nothing quite like them."

As we cleared the gates and stepped into the open field, a grin split my face, as it always did at the sight of the magnificent creatures that made up the Dragonia. Emerald scales shimmered in the sunlight as Eryndor soared high above us. Not to be outdone, Scorn swooped down, his obsidian scales glinting faintly as his long wyvern tail passed close enough to fan our hair back.

"You just have to make trouble, don't you, Scorn?" I yelled. Laughing as I ducked.

Callie was as still as a stature, staring at me like I'd lost my mind.

I was so happy when my beautiful friend, Thyra, the gorgeous silver-gray Pegasus walked up, her lavender main flowing around her. She gave Callie a gentle nudge. This startled her and she spun around, speechless.

Then Thyra spoke to me, telling me the words she'd like to convey to Callie, her voice melodic and kind. "*This child has a troubled mind. Tell her to trust things will be okay.*"

Callie's trembling hand reached out to Thyra's muzzle, talking softly to her.

I stepped closer, tapping her arm lightly. "Thyra wants me to tell you to rest your troubled mind. You need to believe that things will be okay."

Callie turned her wide-eyed gaze to me, then back to Thyra. "Thank you," she whispered, her voice trembling with emotion.

Thyra gave a gentle jerk of her head, telling her, "*You're welcome.*"

And then, the ground shook as heavy footsteps neared, each step rumbled through the earth. Vaelith moved toward us, his massive form casting a shadow that seemed to stretch for miles. I turned to Callie, wanting to jump up and down.

"And now, Callie. This is the one I've been wanting to introduce you to."

For a minute, I thought she might pass out. "Oh my God," she breathed. "Now that... he's... *definitely* a dragon."

I was laughing as I walked over to my gigantic friend. Vaelith's scales shimmered in hues of iridescent silver, a prism of colors. "Callie, let me introduce you to The Big Guy. This is Vaelith, otherwise known as The Ancient One."

For a moment, Callie just stood there. Her expression could be best described as a combination of awe and disbelief. Then she shook her head as if she was trying to wake herself up and stammered, "I'm sorry. I'm Callie Langston—or, well, I don't even know what my actual name is anymore. I'm just Callie now, I guess, and I'm thrilled to meet you, sir."

Vaelith lowered his massive head, his turquois eyes glowed with wisdom. *"Tell her I am happy to make her acquaintance."* His deep voice echoed in my mind.

I grinned at Callie. "He says he's happy to make your acquaintance."

"This," Callie muttered under her breath, her gaze fixed on Vaelith, "is the craziest thing I've ever seen."

Vaelith's voice filled my mind once more, his tone solemn. *"This little one has been through much. She has yet to face all that lies ahead for her. There is still heartache on the horizon, but she must stand strong and resist the temptation to use her power selfishly, though the appeal will be great. Tell her to be wise. She must listen to her heart, even when it is hurting. Heartbreaks have a way of mending. Things that seem gone forever often return. Tell her not to lose faith. Not to lose hope. To believe in the power of love—and in each other."*

I stepped closer to Callie and took her hands gently in mine. "He has a serious message for you, honey," I said, my voice soft. Then, word for word, I relayed Vaelith's message.

When I finished, Callie hesitated, her chest rising and falling as though she were struggling to catch her breath. Then she stepped forward, and Vaelith lowered his massive head toward her, his eyes watching her intently. Tentatively, she reached out; her trembling hand brushing against the warm, scaled surface of his face.

"I promise," she whispered, her voice breaking. "I'll remember your words. I'll do my very best to heed them... even though I'm terrified of what the future holds." Tears traced silent paths down her cheeks, falling to the ground below.

Vaelith's voice resonated once more, calm and steady. *"Tell her we believe in her."*

I placed a hand on Callie's shoulder, anchoring her as the weight of the moment settled over us. "Callie," I said gently, "he wanted me to let you know—they believe in you."

She nodded, her tears glistening in the sunlight as she quickly wiped them away. "Thank you," she murmured, her voice trembling but steady.

Eldric

I headed out toward the courtyard with the others when Seraphine's hand grabbed mine and pulled me back. Her grip was firm but wonderfully delicate as she let me know she intended for me to stop.

"I told my brother we'd follow along in a little while," she said with a smile in her voice.

This was worrisome to me. "And he was ok with this?"

She crossed her arms across her chest with an edge of defiance. "Well, what could he say? I'm a grown woman with a mind of my own."

I could see how this beautiful woman had a way of getting what she wanted. I couldn't help but smile. But then the reality of the situation sank in.

"And I've been an enemy of your family—hunted and hated," I said, the weight of the words sitting heavily between us.

Her expression softened, her posture losing some of its steel as she slowly stepped toward me. "Eldric," she said, her tone now softer, "clearly, things have changed. You've changed. I can feel it."

Her tone instilled me with a jolt of conviction. She leaned in, close enough for me to make out the flecks of silver in her deep navy eyes, close enough that I felt exposed in a way I was not accustomed to.

"Sera," I whispered, the name tumbling off my tongue like a secret. "What are we doing here?"

She exhaled strongly. The exasperation of it pulled at the sides of my mouth even in the gravity of the moment. She was like a storm, smothering me with my blood hammering in my ears as I felt her nearness.

"Don't sit there and tell me you didn't feel the chemistry between us," she said, locking eyes with me. "I am one hundred and twenty-five years old, Eldric. I'm too old for games. There's something between us. You know it, and I know it."

Her brashness wasn't surprising — it was part of what attracted me to her. But to hear those words spoken so plainly tightened my chest.

"I felt it too," I said, the words tumbling from my mouth before I could catch them. My hand moved, brushing the silken strands of her silver hair out of the way. My fingers hovered at her neck, her skin warm under my touch. The feeling shot through me unbidden, a shiver. My thumb grazed over her cheek, and she closed her eyes for a moment.

"I just don't know what we're supposed to do with these feelings," I admitted, the inner struggle in my voice audible. "I've never been so conflicted before in my life."

Her little hand lifted to grab my wrist, holding my hand where it lay on her neck. Even as it electrified the space between us, her touch steadied me.

"What I want you to do, Eldric," she said, her voice barely a whisper, "is what you feel is right." And when she stepped closer and the distance vanished between us and she didn't look away. "And what I think feels right in this moment is for me to taste your lips on mine."

Her head tilted back into my hand, her face tilted up to mine, so delicate, so small in my hold. All that closeness, the audacity of it—it was too much.

I lifted my other hand, cupping her face in my palms, the rest of the world fell away. Our breath mingled, and with that breath, I gave in to the force between us.

"How can I not accept what my lips crave so desperately, too?" I dropped my voice low and raw, leaning in.

I bent down and kissed her lips. It was gentle at first, a timid exploration of uncharted territory. But when Seraphine's lips moved against mine, something sparked between us, flared into a blaze. Her hands ran up my chest, grasping the material of my shirt, holding me in closer. I kissed her deeper, my tongue wanting in, and she opened up right away.

Time stood still as we reveled in our passion. And suddenly the rest of the world disappeared until all that was left was the softness of her lips pressed against mine, the heat of her body against my chest—and the thundering of my heart.

When we finally pulled away, both breathless, I pressed my forehead to hers. Her eyes were shut, a tiny smile on her face.

"That was," she whispered.

"Incredible," I completed for her.

She opened her eyes, silvery depths awash in emotion. "Eldric," she said, fingers moving over the line of my jaw. "I've never felt anything like this."

I took her hand in mine and kissed her palm. "Neither have I, Sera. But we need to be careful. There is a lot there at stake here."

Her expression turned serious, and she nodded. "I know. But there's no denying this thing between us. It feels... important, in a way. This is part of something bigger."

I sighed and ran a hand through my hair. "I feel it too. But your brother"

"Cade will come around," she said decisively. "When he's seen how you've changed. And he trusts my judgment."

I wasn't so sure, but I didn't express my doubts. Instead, I wrapped her tight in my arms again, relishing the sensation of her in my embrace. "I guess we should rejoin the others," I said into her hair.

Seraphine hesitated, then stepped back and nodded. "You're right. But this discussion is not finished, Eldric."

I smiled, my chest warming at her words. "I could never dream that it was over, my lady."

We walked hand in hand to the training fields. As we got closer, I saw the wonderment on Callie's face as she interacted with the Dragonia. Their grandeur took my breath away, but experiencing their majesty through her eyes made it even more unforgettable.

Cade's sharp gaze shifted to our clasped hands, his jaw tightening slightly, but he remained silent. Olivia, though, met us with a knowing smile.

"So nice of you to join us," she teased, her smile warm and playful.

I still hadn't gotten over the magnitude of Olivia's forgiveness. The atrocities I'd committed against her had earned me no mercy, and yet there she was, trusting me with her life. As if she'd read my mind, Seraphine squeezed my hand reassuringly.

"Olivia is not like any woman I've ever known, Eldric," she said in a soft voice, her silver eyes holding mine. "Like I swear, her heart is bigger than the Goddess's herself. If she says she's forgiven you—it's finished. Stop beating yourself up about it. I don't get how she has so much grace either, but we're lucky we have her. She is goodness and light, and we simply have to accept that and be thankful she's one of us."

At that, Callie walked toward us, a sheen on her face the likes of which I'd never seen.

"Hello, cousin," she said cheerfully. "You're looking good this morning."

"Morning, Callie. You look well-rested. How are you feeling?" I hoped she could hear that concern in my voice.

Her smile softening, and for the first time, I noticed a glimmer of relaxation in her expression.

"I actually feel so much better," she said. "Clean, fed and my hair combed? More than I'd dare to dream a few weeks ago. Oh, and I never had a chance to thank you for getting me out of that nightmare, Eldric. So—thank you."

Before I could answer, she took a step forward and enveloped me in a hug. I was caught off guard by the gesture, so I froze momentarily and then awkwardly hugged her back. I realized no one had hugged me just because they wanted to in so long. The feeling humbled me, and deeply moved me.

I cleared my throat, swallowing the lump that had formed.

"I figured it was the least I could do, after… everything." The words broke, too heavy to complete. I could not bring myself to say it out loud, after the way I tormented you.

She pulled back, a hand on my arm, green eyes meeting mine.

"Eldric," she said forcefully but kindly, "it's all right. Thanks for getting me out of that place. You don't have to worry about anything else, OK? All that matters is beating Magda and throwing her back into the Underworld for good. That's the priority now. We're not looking back. And I mean that."

Her forgiveness hit me like a physical blow; it knocked the air out of me. All I could do was shake my head for a moment. "Thanks for this, cousin," I said, the words coming out as a whisper.

She gave me a light pat on the arm, then turned and walked off toward Olivia, who waited with the Dragonia. As I watched her walk away, I felt a deep sense of gratitude.

"There are spectacular women in this place," Seraphine said quietly, puncturing the silence.

I couldn't have agreed more.

Cade

I could hardly believe my eyes when Eldric and Seraphine strolled onto the training field hand in hand. Olivia, of course, just gave them a wink, like she'd known this was coming all along. That mate of mine…she never ceases to make me scratch my head.

It wasn't long before Kaelen made his way over, his expression a mix of disbelief and irritation.

"What in the Goddess's name is going on with your sister and *that beast*?" he demanded.

I gestured for him to walk with me toward Zarvyn, the sleek dark-scaled dragon with the molten golden underbelly I'd prepared for him to ride to the Citadel today.

"Fuck if I know," I muttered. "Something happened between them last night when I was taking him to his chambers. I guess the Goddess has another twist to add to this tangled web."

Kaelen shot me a look of pure incredulity. "And Olivia's just...fine with this?"

I couldn't help but laugh. "Oh, she thinks it's *grand*. Sometimes I wonder if she's cracked as a used shadow shard." I grinned, holding up a hand to cut him off. "And before you go judging my mate, let me remind you—your little Luna is riding right along to this 'forgiveness fair.'"

Kaelen stopped dead in his tracks, his expression darkening. "No. My Luna is too fierce for that nonsense. Her wolf would want to shred his throat."

I let out a bark of laughter, clapping him on the shoulder. "No, brother. Her wolf would probably play fetch with him now."

That was enough to set Kaelen off. He stormed toward Amaya, who was in the middle of a lively chat circle with the other ladies. The sight of him cutting a path through the field like a thundercloud almost made me pity her—almost. I followed at a casual pace, curious to see how this would unfold.

By the time I caught up, Kaelen had pulled Amaya to the side, his voice low but far from subtle.

"Amaya," he said, his tone laced with disbelief, "you're telling me you're just fine with this? With Eldric? After everything he's done?"

The ladies nearby exchanged glances, clearly trying not to eavesdrop too obviously. Olivia, bless her meddling soul, had an amused sparkle in her eye as she whispered something to Callie. I resisted the urge to shake my head.

This was shaping up to be a very *interesting* morning.

Her expression was a mix of surprise and amusement.

"Well, husband, I trust the King of Vesparra and the mate of the Chosen One."

Oh, she went straight for the gut with that one. And she wasn't done.

"And furthermore, I believe people can change. If they sincerely ask for forgiveness, who am I to withhold it? Also, Alpha, let's remember—we're fighting an *almost* unwinnable war against a GODDESS. Last I checked, none of us are gods or goddesses. Eldric's been on the inside. He has knowledge that might give us the edge we need to defeat her. If he's sincere—and I believe with all my heart that he is—then we'd be damn fools not to let him help us. Geez Louise!"

I did not know who Louise was, but she sure seemed to drive Amaya's point home. Fuck. I wouldn't want to be on the wrong side of *that* Luna.

Kaelen cleared his throat, clearly trying to recover what little dignity he had left.

"As long as you feel secure in the situation, then I'm okay with it," he said, his voice gruff.

Amaya smiled, softening instantly. She stepped closer and placed a kiss on his lips. "I can assure you, my Alpha. Somehow, the Goddess has given me peace over this. I feel perfectly secure in the situation. Thank you for your love and for always being so relentless in protecting me."

The women around them looked ready to burst into applause as Amaya returned to their circle. Kaelen, however, stomped back toward me, his jaw tight.

I couldn't stop the grin tugging at my lips. "Everything secure?"

"Shut the fuck up, Cade," he growled.

CHAPTER 10

Crystal Clear Strategies

Cade

The ground shook beneath our feet as the roar of dragon wings filled my chest, culminating in a crescendo as we swept over the Crystal Citadel. Eryndor's emerald scales shone in the sunlight like glittering jewels, with patterns of radiance and rainbow colors that rippled across the courtyard below. I took a deep breath of the crisp mountain air, tinged with the scent of ancient magic.

As gargantuan claws descended, I cast a wary eye toward the glinting spires of the Citadel. It was a building saturated by the ages, but it concealed depths as deep as its roots. Kaelen and Amaya readied to descend, Zarvyn's obsidian shape looming in our periphery as a dark portent.

"Stay sharp," I whispered to Eryndor while patting his rippling neck. He rumbled his agreement, eyes darting lazily around the forest with concentration.

After landing, I disengaged from the saddle, my boots making a gratifying thud on the forest floor. Power thrummed through me, Vesparra blood magic singing in concert with the ethereal energy of this place.

Kaelen dropped beside me, his wolf's senses scanning our surroundings, his gold-hued mane glittering in the light above him like a halo. Amaya slid from Zarvyn's back into the embrace of her waiting mate, the motion of her blonde curls bouncing, her own senses heightened, fully immersed in her wolf mode.

"Well, this is a lovely welcoming party," Kaelen quipped, gesturing to the throngs of mages and guards that lined the courtyard. Their posture seemed to be chiseled from tension, their faces statuesque.

I grunted in agreement, aware of the palpable uneasiness. "This is not the time to lower our guard."

Amaya's blue-green eyes widened with wonder as she took in the towering crystal structure. "Every time I see this place, I'm awed. When the Goddess creates a thing, she doesn't half-step," she said, her tone slightly reverential.

Watching her, still so young, so innocent despite everything she had been through, a rush of protectiveness shot through me. I locked eyes with Kaelen, recognizing my own concern reflected there.

"We've done a good job of keeping this place protected," I said, a bit of pride and relief in my tone. "Thank the Goddess for Farin and all his thoughts on security."

Olivia slid from the back of Vaelith, her dark hair swept behind her like a silk banner. Her eyes met mine for an instant, and I saw the fire of her temper flickering in them, barely contained. My heart tightened at the image. I recognized that look. I hoped she wasn't looking for a fight with Ignis.

"You alright there, honey?" she called to Callie, her drawl a sharp contrast to the otherworldly settings.

Callie climbed down the saddle ropes from the silver dragon's back, her cropped blonde hair only slightly windswept and her wide green eyes filled with wonder. "That was... amazing," she breathed, her voice quivering with excitement. "I've never experienced anything like it. It was like... like flying through sunshine."

Despite the apprehension everyone felt, Callie's enthusiasm made the air feel a little lighter. The Crystal Citadel towered high above, its prism spires reflecting light and casting colored rainbows across the ground. The sight was nothing less than breathtaking.

"Good to hear you liked the ride," I said, attempting a lighthearted tone. "But stay sharp. We have our best warriors here, but we still need to remain vigilant."

A sudden crackle of energy tore through the air, raising every hair on the back of my neck. I spun, my hand instinctively going to the sword that at my hip.

A brilliant portal appeared in front of us, shimmering with golden light. Four figures appeared.

Miranda was the first one through. Her dusky caramel skin was aglow with otherworldly light, her black curls glossy with the sheen from the golden light, her posture regal and relaxed. Thorne was right behind her, his hulking form fully clad in armor, his figure dwarfing her petite form. They clasped hands, no longer afraid to show the realm they belonged to one another.

"Hell of an entrance." I joked as they passed. "You always had a flare for the dramatic, Miranda."

She offered me a half smile, but I could see the underlying concern in her rich chocolate-brown eyes. "We thought it best to arrive prepared," she said quietly, her voice edged with an undertone of worry.

Eldric and Seraphine had arrived last. His wayward mop of reddish-brown curls and her long, straight silvery strands inspired a stark contrast to the glitter of the Citadel's crystals.

Two large figures were next to arrive. Farin's brown skin shone in the crystal light, his cropped black curly hair forming a halo around his head, was always a welcome sight. Ignis walked beside him. His light skin and auburn hair were a study in contrast. His presence burned with no less ferocity as the flames he controlled.

My jaw tightened involuntarily. "Farin, Ignis," I said, not quite hiding the edge of my voice. "Glad to see you."

A melodic voice filled the air as Farin spoke. "It's always good to see my grandson by marriage. But I'm happiest to see my granddaughters."

Olivia, Maya, and Miranda all rushed to him, hugging him tightly. That left Callie standing awkwardly alone.

"Farin, this is Callie," I said, beckoning her over. "This sweetheart could possibly be the one who helps save us all."

Farin bowed his head to her.

"The honor of meeting you is mine, Callie."

I barely heard him, but my eyes were fixed on Ignis, fury simmering just beneath the surface. This man, this king, had rejected Callie—our Callie. The mate bond between them was a tangible thread of tension.

My eye caught Ignis' eyes. "I trust you're prepared to face the challenges ahead," I said, the words dripping with veiled accusation. My hand twitched, longing to reach for Callie, to shield her from his gaze.

Ignis looked over our assembly, his face wearing a look of... regret? "Our troops have been working well with all those of other kingdoms. We are always prepared to defend our realm, Cade."

I felt Callie shift beside me, her discomfort obvious. My protective instincts flared, and I had to fight to keep from stepping in front of her.

"And what of those who need defending *within* those other kingdoms?" I asked, my voice low and dangerous. "Are you prepared for that, Ignis?"

The air crackled with unspoken friction. I watched as Callie's eyes flickered to Ignis, a mix of longing and pain evident in their emerald depths. I knew the mate bond tugged at her, an invisible force drawing her towards the man who had spurned her.

Ignis' jaw tightened, his own gaze drawn inexorably to Callie. For a moment, the mask of kingly indifference slipped, revealing a turmoil that mirrored Callie's own.

"We will protect all who dwell in Eldoria," Ignis said, his

voice rough with emotion he clearly tried to suppress.

I felt my anger rise, threatening to boil over. The air around us grew heavy, charged with the weight of unspoken words and suppressed desires. The crystal walls seemed to close in, amplifying the strain between us all.

Eldric's voice cut through the uneasiness, drawing our attention away from the simmering conflict. His tall frame seemed to fill the chamber as he stepped forward, his piercing green eyes scanning the assembled group.

"We have pressing matters to discuss," he said, his tone calm yet edged with urgency. The air around him seemed to shimmer, a reminder of the power that lurked beneath his controlled exterior.

Ignis jolted. "Why is this criminal within our midst?"

It was Olivia's turn to speak this time.

"Eldric freed our Callie from the Underworld. He has repented for the part he played in Magda's schemes, and at significant risk to his own life, he brings insight into how we can win this war. I was skeptical for a moment, as I am sure you must be. Rest assured, the Goddess herself has eased my mind and heart. He can be trusted. For delivering Callie alone is enough for me to be eternally grateful."

She locked arms with Callie and marched past Ignis, purposely knocking into his shoulder as she passed. Fuck. I loved my feisty mate.

The rest of our party followed my warrior mate and Callie into the large meeting room where we would all be able to see each other and better plan our strategies.

Eldric began again.

"The High Demons of the Underworld are on the move."

I felt a chill run down my spine, my senses instantly on high alert. The crystal walls of the Citadel suddenly felt less like protection and more like a fragile barrier against an encroaching darkness.

Eldric's words painted a grim picture. "New rifts will form at any moment. I expect they will make their moves throughout Eldoria, causing as much damage and chaos as possible. Every kingdom is vulnerable. Playing a defense superior to Magda's offense will do for a while, but we will need to come up with a definitive offensive plan if we are to lock her in the Underworld for good. I expect new and more ferocious creatures to come through the rifts next. Her demons are constantly creating monsters to send."

I could sense the fear in the room, an odorous, acrid tang that blended with the fresh mountain breeze filtering in from the open windows. My muscles tensed for a fight that wasn't yet here.

"What type of creatures are we talking about here?" Olivia's voice rang out. I turned to see her, hit again by the fire in her eyes. Despite all she'd faced, despite the sweet and docile personality she struggled against all this time, my mate stood strong and fearless.

Eldric had set his gaze on her. "Entities of absolute evil, each with the strength to decimate entire armies with their might."

Olivia clenched her lips, her jaw squared with resolve. "And their weaknesses? Every critter's got a weak spot."

I was filled with a combination of pride and concern for this woman. She was such a contradiction—perfectly willing to meet a monster on the battlefield, yet willing to forgive a person who made her life hell. This was the woman I adored —strong and unshakable. Yet, I still couldn't stop myself from wanting to protect her from all the horrors I knew we'd have to face.

"Their powers are of any number," Eldric continued in a low, grave voice. "Some can delve into the psyche, others can taint the earth itself with poisonous gas. Many feed on fear and chaos. Some can fly and have gaping jaws with rows of razor-sharp teeth that can rip a man into pieces. And there are those that Magda is still creating. In other words, we must be ready for any and everything."

Olivia's eyes narrowed, her mind clearly churning through the strategies. "Then we hit 'em over and over and over again 'til they stop comin'. Or until we get that heifer locked back in her hell hole where she belongs, for good."

I listened to her, amazed at her ability to make confronting demons from the very pit of hell sound like a cattle roundup. But underneath the bravado, I could feel a frisson of fear, smell the slight hint of trepidation she was trying so hard to hide.

As Eldric described more about the demons' power, my eyes drifted back to Olivia. In that instant, suffocated by kings and warriors, she sparkled like a beacon of hope and strength. Whatever darkness was approaching, whatever terrors would ensue, I knew for sure, without a doubt, that as long as Olivia was with me—with us—somehow we would find our way through.

"That leads us to talk about the latest development. It *does* get worse," he said, somberly. "We have reason to believe that Magda is going to target Callie specifically."

The air felt heavier inside the room now, bubbling up with rage at the thought of someone coming for one of us again. My eyes flicked to Ignis, gauging his reaction instinctively. The jaw of the Fire King grew tight as the knuckles of his hands turned white with the curling of fists on the table. It was as clear as day that his internal struggle was a tempest of pride, duty and the inevitable call of the mate bond.

Ignis' fierce and unyielding amber eyes now shone with something I had rarely seen in him; agony. His eyes fell on Callie much longer than he meant and had to quickly look away, as if even staring at her was too much. He felt their pain, their grief, as if he had plunged a blade deep into their hearts and twisted it for good measure.

I gritted my teeth, my frustration boiling. The bastard looked as if the decision was slaying him—and maybe it was —but that didn't absolve him of the risk his choice posed to Callie. I found it impossible to feel sorry for him. He had the power to fix this. To deny his mate bond was not only defiance; it was self-inflicted torture. It was Callie's feelings and safety that mattered to me.

Eldric coughed, refocusing our attention. His once-arrogant green eyes held a grave solemnity. "I've only just remembered one other serious threat we'll have to consider. Now, I know of only one of these creatures, but he could be deadly if he comes through a rift with a plan," he said, his voice low and urgent. "I'm referring to a shapeshifting demon, or a mimic. This demon is known as a morphiend."

The room went quiet as scenarios went through everyone's minds. A shiver went down my spine as long-buried memories of childhood stories bubbled up to the surface—monsters in the shape of family, friends, sewing chaos and distrust behind them.

"How can we fight somethin' we can't identify? What did you do?" Olivia asked, her voice firm even though I could feel the fear behind it.

Eldric surveyed us with a grim look in his eyes. "These demons are liars, the masters of deceit. They're capable of impersonating anyone—looks, voice, even idiosyncrasies. But there is a telltale sign we can look for."

I sat up a little straighter, my heart racing. "What is it?"

"The eyes," Eldric said in a low voice. "Their pupils always remain slitted, like a cat's, no matter how perfect the disguise."

A collective shudder went through the group. My heart sank as I pictured familiar faces with alien eyes, the insidious mistrust these creatures could plant between us. How could anyone possibly trust anyone in the heat of battle?

"We've got to have a verification system," Kaelen said, his voice all business. "Code words, perhaps, or—"

"Or we learn to look at each other in the eye," Seraphine added, her voice low but strong. "Really look. Look past the surface to the soul beneath."

I locked eyes with Olivia across the room; her face was

aflame with furious purpose. There was a spark between us, unvoiced but profoundly understood. We would not allow this demon, or any demon, to rip us apart.

"We stand together," I said, my voice ringing out loud and full. "Together for a common goal, having each other's backs. It's how we're going to win this fight."

Murmurs of agreement rippled through the room like a wave, and for the first time in what felt like ages, a glimmer of hope flickered to life inside me. Whatever horrors lay ahead, we would confront them together. And let the gods help any demon who's misguided enough to challenge us.

My eyes raked across the room, resting on the resolute faces of our allies. I felt the weight of our mission wrap around me like a heavy cloak, reassuring and comforting. My gaze fell back on Olivia, her unyielding strength shining like a beacon. Even now, after everything we'd overcome, the sight of her was breath-stealing.

I spoke to the room, my voice strong and stable.

"It sounds like we go on as we have, other than putting extra troops on the ground." What did we decide? Twenty-five more as quoted for each sub hub?

A chorus of ayes went up around the table.

Miranda stood. "Our generals will see it done." Her confidence was strong.

I agreed. "As we go back to our own kingdoms, let us be ever vigilant. If they outrun the troops, tap into the crystal communication network, we'll grab the Dragonia and head out. Don't try to be heroes. We are here to help. If anything seems strange alert us all. We must fight together, or we shall surely die separately."

We all drew swords and pointed them to the center of the table.

"For our kingdoms!" I roared, and the words echoed around the chamber.

"For Eldoria!" the group echoed, their voices swelling like a battle cry.

"For Goddess Vesperia!"

After my rallying cry was done fucking echoing, I sheathed my sword and felt the weight of what came next heavy on my shoulders.

"We should prepare for departure," I said, my voice low, yet able to carry through the tense quiet. "Every second that we delay gives Magda time to strengthen her position."

Even in the eye of this storm, Olivia's presence anchored me. The smell of her—stargazer lilies and sunshine—enveloped me, temporarily dulling the jagged edge of my anxiety.

"What's our next step, Cade?" she asked, her tone steady despite the current of anxiety I could sense rising from her.

I reached over and tucked a dark strand of hair behind her ear, giving myself this brief moment of tenderness. "We go home and strengthen the boundaries of the kingdom. Then we get Callie trained. And we wait for the call."

I looked back at Callie, who stood a few footsteps behind, looking a little lost, but no less determined. Her eyes still held shadows of what she'd survived, but beneath them, her spark of fire was untouched.

"Callie," Olivia called to her friend. "We need to get home and train you for battle. Are you ready?"

"Oh hell yeah, I am," she said, her face alight with a defiant fire. "I didn't go through Magda's torture to sit on the sidelines. I'm taking the fight to her."

Out of the corner of my eye, I saw Ignis' head turn at her words. For just a second, the mask of indifference he usually wore slipped, exposing his worry.

I thought bitterly, *"You stubborn fuck. Claim and protect her if you're so worried about her."* But there he stood with his impotent pride and tradition, his general Jorvahn beside him, looking as pissed at him as I felt. Damn fool. But we didn't have the luxury of time for inconveniences such as these. We had a war to win, and getting Callie trained was a huge part of that.

DEX HAVEN

We had to get back to Vesparra.

CHAPTER 11

Frayed Bonds and a Warrior's Heart

Callie

The Crystal Citadel glittered like a knife's blade in the afternoon sun, sharp and unforgiving. I stood there, my heart a frantic bird in my chest, as I steeled myself to leave the meeting that had everyone on edge. The cool breeze carried the scent of jasmine, a bittersweet reminder that its sweet aroma belied the dangers that awaited at every turn.

I closed my eyes, drawing in a shaky breath. Having to see Ignis everywhere I looked all afternoon—being reminded of his rejection—still burned. It was a wound that refused to heal. But I couldn't let it break me. I had to be strong, for Ollie, for myself, for this fight. My fingers curled into fists at my sides, nails biting into my palms.

"I can do this," I whispered, the words carried away by the wind. "I have to."

The soft scrape of boots on gravel made me stiffen. I felt him before I saw him. It drove me a little crazy that I knew his presence like that. He'd approached me and it caused my heart to stutter. My first inclination was to walk away, but I'd run away for the last time. So I sucked it up and turned to him.

I don't know what I expected when I looked at him. I guess I was praying he'd come to tell me he was wrong—that he couldn't live without me. Of course, what his body language said wasn't that. Oh, the look on his face said that he longed for me. Unfortunately, it battled with the familiar looks of regret and rejection. And in that battle, only rejection came out on top. My frustration rose as he searched for the right words to say.

He finally found his voice. "Callie." He reached for my hand and pulled me closer to the tree line. His touch sent a fire through my veins. That damn bond lit up every part of me. The bond he continued to ignore.

I yanked my hand away. "I'd prefer it if you didn't touch me." I fought to keep my voice steady. "You had a choice, Ignis, and it wasn't me."

He reached for me again, his fingers grazing mine, and I felt the same zap of electricity.

"Callie, you know it's not as easy as just making a choice." He looked away in frustration. "I have to consider my kingdom. But that doesn't mean I'm not worried about you."

At his words, I looked away. "Oh, I think I *do* understand, Ignis." I looked into his eyes. "I'm not worth fighting for. You couldn't make it anymore plain. But please, don't insult me— don't lie to me or yourself by saying you're worried about my safety. Where I'm from, we take care of the people we care about. We keep them close to us."

I saw a look of pain cross his face. And just for a second, I thought he might reach for me, might break through the chains of the damn prison of his kingdom's traditions that had him so bound. But he just couldn't let the mask of duty go.

"I can't," he said. The words almost sounded strangled leaving his lips. "Callie…"

I decided I'd had enough. "No. Thankfully, I *have* people in my life who love me and who will protect me. People who are not you." I forced a smile. "I'll see you around, Ignis."

I walked away, not feeling anywhere as powerful as I'd sounded. The further the distance I'd traveled from Ignis, the greater the hole in my soul. What kind of trick was the Goddess playing? I felt so broken inside. This was a sorrow like I'd never and I felt and it was tearing me apart.

Dammit, I felt that familiar burn in the back of my eyes. I would *not* cry. My vision might have blurred with unshed tears, but they would not fall. I swallowed the lump in my throat as I approached Olivia and the dragons.

"Hey y'all. Are we 'bout ready to fly home?" I did my best to sound like everything was good. I tried to not let on that Ignis had once again played kickball with my heart.

Vaelith lowered his majestic head and caught my gaze, his swirling turquoise eyes hypnotic. I felt like he must be giving Ollie a message to pass along to me. His silver scales glinted with iridescent rainbows in the dying light of the afternoon.

"Well Callie Girl, it seems The Big Guy here has a few more important words for you. Let's see, I want to get them right. He wants you to know:"

The very realm senses the goodness in you and stands ready to help you in your time of need. Don't worry about the things that you cannot control. Things have a way of happening when they are supposed to happen and in the time that you are waiting, you are growing into the person you are meant to be. Embrace the changes that are occurring in and around you. Become who you were born to be and let the Goddess take care of the rest.

"Holy crap! That's beautiful Vaelith. You are must have a silver tongue to go along with your scales." Olivia laughed.

I stood there and let the tears fall. I had to tell the Goddess I was sorry for accusing her of playing a trick on me. Wiping the tears, I walked to Vaelith and touched his neck. I thanked him for sharing such encouraging words and he gave a nod of his head in response.

Cade had joined us about the time Olivia had told me what Vaelith had wanted me to know. He let us know we needed to get in the air—it was time to head home and start training.

The dragons all waited a short way from the Citadel. The wyverns were already in the air. A fraction smaller, they were much more playful than the dragons. I heard Olivia banter with Skorn on more than one occasion. Honestly, with their tails having that poisonous barb on the end, they scared me a little. Ollie told me there was nothing to worry about, and I trusted her. Even so, when they buzzed us on the training grounds, I ducked just a little lower than everyone else.

I felt lighter as I was about to mount the saddle. Olivia gave me a knowing look.

"Everything good now, honey?" She was forever a mother hen to me.

"I'm ok." And I meant it.

She grabbed me and wrapped me in a big old Ollie hug, squeezing me tight. It was a hug that told me she was behind me no matter what happened and I was not alone. I had my family back, and we stood together.

"We've got this," Olivia told me. "Just like the old days. You and me, taking on the world. Or, well, the Underworld in this case."

I couldn't help but laugh. "Just another day for us, right?"

Her smile showed that pure Texas spirit we both carried in our veins. "You're dadgum right. Now, let's show these boys what a couple of country girls can do."

Standing beside her, with Vaelith's massive form towering above us, I felt a spark of hope in my heart. I still felt the emptiness of not having my mate in my life, that dull throb, I guess, might always be there. But the warmth of friendship helped. And the thought of the fight ahead gave me more than enough to think about.

"Ready to fly?" I asked.

Olivia nodded with a wide grin on her face. "Born ready, darlin'. Let's go save the world."

"Alright, let's saddle up," Olivia said, giving my hand a squeeze.

Gripping the rope with surprising ease, I pulled myself into the saddle and settled in behind Olivia. The movement was instinctive, my body remembering the motions from my first flight out here, though my heart still raced at the sheer enormity of the moment.

"You locked in?" Olivia asked, glancing over her shoulder with a grin that dared me not to be excited.

"Let's do it!" I hollered back, unable to hide my excitement.

I could feel Vaelith's muscles flex beneath us. Then, with a powerful surge, he took off into the sky. I felt my stomach drop with the sudden lift, but the thrill had me getting over the shock. Wind whipped at my face, and I never felt more alive.

"Woo-hoo!" I breathed, the exclamation tumbling out as I clung to Olivia. The world below stretched out like a quilt of greens and browns, the patchwork shrinking rapidly as we climbed higher and higher.

The cool, rushing air swept away the weight of everything—my doubts, my fears, even the lingering ache of Ignis' rejection. For the first time in what felt like forever, I felt free.

Olivia's laughter carried back to me. "It's better than any roller coaster, right?"

I absolutely agreed. There was nothing that possibly came close to the thrill of soaring through the air on the back of a freaking dragon! What even was my life? I'm was still coming to terms with the belief of the reality of it. It was best to just let reality go—live.

"It's magnificent," I yelled, my voice barely audible over the sound of the wind.

Olivia turned slightly and gave me a wink. Her hair whipped wildly. I'd never seen her look more alive. "It's the only way to fly!" she laughed.

I tore my gaze from the breathtaking view below. The patchwork forests and winding rivers had to be seen to be believed. I looked over at Cade. To watch him command Eryndor was like nothing else. His regal bearing was unmistakable. He moved with practiced ease, his movements fluid and sure as he settled into his ride.

"Cade looks like a dragon master," I told Olivia.

She glanced over at him. "That's my man. Gods, he's so fine."

He must have sensed that she was talking about him because he glanced her way. The look of adoration he wore was what every girl dreamed of. Not just that, even from across the sky, his expression one of protection. He was aware of every threat.

Olivia must have caught the message he sent through their mate bond because she turned back to me and passed it along, her tone losing some of its usual lightness. "He says we need to stay close."

I almost smiled. I knew the power that Olivia carried. There's no question she could protect Cade if it came down to it. But the Alpha in him instinctually longs to care for her. That we were always a moment away from danger still sent a chill up my spine.

He and Eryndor sped ahead of us on Eryndor's beautiful emerald wings.

We headed north, and the landscape began to change. The trees and vegetation of the forests turned to mountains, tall and rough. Their peaks reached the sky, disappearing into low clouds. The temperature dropped sharply, and the air grew thinner.

"It's a little different out here, huh?" Olivia called back over her shoulder, her voice hoarse from the wind hitting her face. "I'm getting a weird feeling."

I looked around, but didn't see anything unusual. Of course, I didn't really know what to look for.

"Define weird." I said, as I continued to scan the ground.

Olivia's voice lacked its usual lightness as she continued to glance around us. "By this feeling in my gut, I'd say weird, like, not good. But I'm sure whatever it is, between Cade, the dragons, and me, we can handle it."

She sounded confident, but I felt uneasy. I held onto the saddle a little tighter, braced for whatever might be hiding in the clouds ahead.

I closed my eyes, hoping that it would help calm my nerves. When I opened them, I glimpsed Cade. He looked like a man on a mission. Whatever Olivia had felt, he clearly felt it, too. He was in full on protection mode. His body language was rigid and carried an air of awareness. It honestly made me feel safer to know I had these two warriors on my side.

We flew deeper into what seemed to be an oncoming storm. I held on to Olivia a little tighter, hanging on just in case there was something waiting for us when we got to Vesparra.

A shrill chirping sound shattered the tension in the air. It emanated from Olivia's tunic, sharp and urgent. My heart jumped at the unexpected noise as Vaelith's massive form began his descent, his silver scales gleaming even in the eerie darkness surrounding Vesparra Castle.

Olivia reached into her pocket and pulled out the glowing communication crystal. "This is Olivia!" she answered as Vaelith touched down.

Farin's voice came through, grave and steady. "Granddaughter. A large rift is opening up just outside quadrant 561—close to the Ashenwild Forest. There's a sub-hub nearby, and troops are already on the move. But this... this is large. We need more help."

Olivia's reply was immediate, her coolness maintained despite the urgency of the call. "Grandpapa, we'll be on our way in just a few minutes. Hold tight."

"We'll see you soon," Farin replied before the crystal dimmed.

"Oh Goddess," I whispered as fear gripped my insides. My mind raced, trying to figure out what we might face.

Olivia caught my hands after we lowered from the saddle. Her grip was solid and anchoring. "Hey, no worries. We got this," she said, her deep purple eyes fixed on mine. "We're heading right back out. You need to stay here. The Twixits will protect you." Her voice was unfaltering with certainty, a steadying force in the turmoil.

"But I want to help!" I protested, feeling like a child. Panic and frustration did battle in my chest, as fear nagged at my insides.

Olivia held my face in her hands, her eyes met mine without hesitation. "Listen, Callie girl. Until you know how to control your magic, you're a liability. We'll be more worried about protecting you than fighting those uglies. You don't want that, and neither do I. Now, darlin', please wait in the castle. There's a crystal in the parlor, inside a small blue box on a side table. Francois knows where it is. Hold on to it. I'll call you on it when we're done kicking some demon butt, okay?"

Her words stung, but I knew she was right. The last thing I wanted was to jeopardize the fight. "You got it, Ollie," I said softly.

With a wink, Olivia turned to Cade, who had just joined us, his entire body radiating tension and authority. His piercing gaze swept the area, locking onto Olivia. "Where's Eldric and Seraphine? They used the portal to get back."

As if on cue, the two of them jogged up, looking slightly winded but ready.

Cade's eyes bore into both of them. "We're going to need both of you in this fight. Sera, are you up for it?"

Seraphine hesitated, glancing at Eldric before squaring her shoulders. She drew in a deep breath, determination flickering in her silver eyes. "Brother, I'm up for the fight," she said firmly.

Eldric's worry was written across his face as he looked down at her, his jaw tightening.

Cade nodded once before continuing. "We're headed to Ashenwild Forest. I've spoken to Zarvyn; he'll take you both. Think you can hold a dragon saddle?"

Eldric, always the picture of calm and control, responded immediately. "I can do it. I'll keep her in the saddle."

Seraphine's incredulous look was nothing short of priceless. She placed her hands on her hips, leveling him with an exasperated glare. "I'm an accomplished rider, I'll have you know. Not of dragons, but of several other creatures."

Eldric glanced at Cade, one brow raised in silent commentary.

Cade's sharp reply cut through the brewing argument like a blade. "Not a word, Eldric. Not. One. Word."

The corner of Eldric's mouth twitched, but he wisely held his tongue, while Seraphine shot him a triumphant look. Cade's no-nonsense tone left no room for discussion.

"Good," Cade added, turning his attention back to the mission. "Let's move."

CHAPTER 12

The Agony of Victory

Olivia

As we crossed over from the tree line, the acrid sting of smoke and sulfur entered my nostrils. The Ashenwild Forest gave way to utter chaos. Menacing wild growls and snarls mixed with the sounds of clashing weapons and crackling magic filled the air. The chasm in the ground roared open and spewed forth twisted and grotesque creatures as the earth trembled.

My eye flew from one point of conflict to the next as my heart raced taking in the battlefield. The sky was lit with red streaks of magic spells, exploding with churning lightning that painted the sky in an eerie haze. The wind blew through the trees carrying with it cries of pain and fury.

"Sweet baby Jesus," I said, speaking through a throat tightened with tension. "Well, this is a right mess we've gotten ourselves into."

Cade was a steady anchor to my left. Wisps of his midnight hair slipped loose from the leather strap he'd used to tie it back from his face. He took at the carnage around him, eyes burning with fire, knuckles white from how tightly he gripped his sword.

"We have to move fast, Olivia," he told me through our bond. *"The rift is widening by the minute."*

"Yes," I replied, the gravity of the destruction looming over

me. The power of the Goddess Star throbbed beneath my skin, waiting to be released. Its energy coursed through me, mixing with my determination and resolve. My outrage flared like fire.

I winked at Cade, then turned to our allies. "Y'all ready?" I shouted out to our little band, my voice rising above the fray. "Time to give these bullies a taste of what happens when you mess with Eldoria."

Our dragons—Vaelith, Eryndor, and Zarvyn—touched down with earth trembling thuds, their enormous bodies forming a shield between us and the battlefield. They were a part of this war, their thoughts brushing mine through our telepathic link, and as I dismounted, I could sense their eagerness to enter the fray.

"Vaelith," I said, as I met the eye of my magnificent friend, "I need you and the others to get to flyin'. Y'all can give us an aerial view of the battlefield and take out any of these mofos trying to escape us. We cannot allow them to squeeze through the land we hold."

His turquoise eyes flashed. *"The mofos won't get past us, StarHeart."*

His wings expanded, and I was suddenly filled with such love for this creature who had come to mean so much to me. As the rest of Dragonia took flight, I turned to face our party.

"Cade, Eldric, Seraphine—we gotta push toward that rift," I told them. I'd never been more assertive in my life. "Whatever's comin' through, we gotta shut it down fast."

I felt Cade grab my hand. Just his presence lifted my confidence. "We are with you, my love. Lead on."

We moved forward with purpose. As we neared the sounds of steel on steel and the roars of creatures unknown, my pulse rose. But I knew we could do this. I was no longer that scared little girl from Texas. I was leading a charge against monsters who were far greater than the one I'd faced then. The scars on my back suddenly flared with pain as a reminder of who I once was. Not today.

Our magic surged with each step. Cade's rune sword glowed at his side. My hands shone with a faint purple light. Sera wore a look of fierce determination I'd never seen before. And I never had to doubt the power that Eldric carried. I'd certainly seen it in action.

The dragons fought winged creatures, using their fire and ice. They opened up a barrage of power yet seen as they destroyed Underworld monsters left and right. With every hideous creature killed, Eldoria's forces got a little stronger.

I began flinging mist orbs and shooting magic from my fingertips at creatures who'd gotten past the first lines of defense. Sera dispatched creatures using powerful shadow magic. Eldric joined her. His shadows were different, even more powerful.

We'd made it to the heart of the battled where Grandpapa had transformed into a hardened warrior. He wielded his Moonstone blade with deadly precision. Its blade of silvery metal arced through the air, slicing the flesh of a creature that was more insect than reptile, but was definitely an ungodly combination of the two.

As quickly as he destroyed one, he was on to the next.

To his left, Miranda looked like she had choreographed her movements. She was so graceful and precise. Her Water Whip was simply an extension of her arm, its high-pressure steam simply sliced through abominations like a hot knife through butter. Geez, but that girl was elegant in the way she massacred the bad guys.

"Majesty!" Thorne's booming voice cut through the madness. Cade's towering general stood like a fortress against the chaos. "We've got more coming from the east! Thalassan troops are holding the line, but they need support!"

I nodded, my mind racing with strategies. "Miranda!" I called out. "Take a squad and reinforce the eastern flank. Use those Mist Orbs to confuse and disorient!"

As Miranda headed that way with a group of warriors, I felt

a presence at my side. Seraphine, her silver blowing around her face, nodded at me. "We'll take the western side," she said, her voice sure and clear. "Eldric and I can create a bottleneck. I believe we can funnel them into a killing field."

"Do it," I agreed. "But be careful. These creatures are freakin' nightmares."

Seraphine gave me a wicked little smile. "Don't worry about us, sister. We've got a few tricks up our sleeves."

She moved away, looking more like a trained assassin than my sister-in-law. Eldric moved right into lock-step beside her. Those two had an undeniable chemistry between them. Their silent communication would make up for their lack of training together. Cade was going to have to get over his misgivings.

They worked great together as a team. Seraphine had a natural calmness about her—always able to keep her cool, even when things got dicey. I saw her send Eldric a group of Vesparran soldiers several hand signals, getting them into position. Amazing.

Eldric summoned his dark magic, mixing it with Sera's own unique magic. They created some kind of funnel shadow illusion, herding monstrous creatures into a corridor of death.

I felt such admiration for my sister-in-law. I hoped Cade could square with her newfound relationship. I shook my head, focusing on the battle at hand. There would be time for warm fuzzies later—if we survived this hellish day.

I was at the rift doing everything I could to shut it down. This rift was stubborn. My mind raced as to how I could get it closed. Of course, I had to fight off creatures at the same time. This was multi-tasking to the nth degree.

The sounds of steel against monstrous flesh filled the air. A mix of unholy screeches and the smell of burned flesh was everywhere. I saw a group of Therionis shifters move forward. They changed instantly. I saw men and women suddenly transform from humans to giant wolves, bears, and birds of prey. There was even an alligator! Then it was just teeth and claws.

"Geez Alou," I breathed. "Freakin' awesome."

The shifters moved with frightening coordination. One particularly massive wolf—was that Kaelen's beta? — leapt onto the back of something straight out of a nightmare. His jaws clamped down on its neck while the others joined in, slashing at its legs again, biting, and ripping flesh.

The creature emitted an otherworldly screech that sent shivers down my spine, but I couldn't tear my gaze away from the intense battle unfolding before me. This was an unnatural war—brutal and unforgiving. There was no room for squeamishness or hesitation.

"Olivia!" Cade's urgent voice cut through the chaos, snapping me back to attention. "Look!"

I followed his gaze skyward and felt my heart drop. Winged monstrosities were pouring from the rift now, their leathery wings blocking out the afternoon sun. Terror gripped my chest as I realized these creatures would have the advantage of air attacks if we didn't act swiftly.

"Oh, heck no," I muttered under my breath, feeling the familiar tingle of magic surging through my veins. "We ain't lettin' those uglies have free rein of our skies."

Taking a deep breath, I reached out with my mind, searching for the familiar presence of our dragons. "Vaelith! Eryndor! Zarvyn!" I called out. "We need you, now!"

The ground trembled beneath us as three massive forms landed nearby. Vaelith, with his swirling turquoise eyes, lowered his head to my level. Determination burned in his gaze.

"Ready to barbecue some baddies, Big Guy?" I asked.

Vaelith's voice rumbled through my bones. *"Always, Little One,"* he replied in my mind.

As Cade and I prepared to mount our dragons, I caught sight of Seraphine and Eldric in the middle of the chaos. Countless creatures surrounded them. They still wielded their magic with deadly precision, using their silent communication.

I couldn't help but worry about them, as so many creatures kept coming their way. I gave a plea for their safety under my breath.

I swung onto Vaelith's back, feeling the familiar heat of his scales beneath my thighs. Beside us, Cade mounted Eryndor with his muscular form rigid with worry. As we took to the air, the wind whipped around us, carrying with it the acrid scent of smoke and blood.

"Let's finish this!" I shouted to Cade. The rush of adrenaline coursed through my veins. I was filled with a strange mix of adrenaline and an edge of fear.

Cade looked at me as we took to the sky. His love and fear for me flowed through our bond. *"You are my badass queen. But please be careful, my love,"* he told me. His voice a blend of admiration and pride.

Together with our dragons, we were an unstoppable force. Carving through the chaos of the battlefield. Vaelith's silver wings sliced through the smoke-filled sky, each beat sending tremors of raw power through the air. Beside me, Cade and Eryndor were a storm of emerald and flame, their combined magic illuminating the smoky air.

As the aerial battlefield came into full view, winged monstrosities filled the skies, ghastly forms barely able to fly, their wings like twisted nightmares. Their talons were sharp enough to tear through human flesh, and I mean, they could rip a person in half. Some of them had multiple eyes that seemed to work independently of each other. They flew in erratic patterns, like massive ink-stained deranged butterflies. I just knew we had to reach out with our weapons and magic and knock them out of the sky.

"We gotta kill these things," I muttered under my breath, gripping the saddle tighter. The magic of the five kingdoms heated in my veins. I felt the Goddess' Star vibrate in my chest.

"Vaelith, on your left!" I shouted, twisting to release a fiery blast. The flames roared to life, engulfing the closest creature. Its shriek was an unholy sound as its wings ignited, turning to ash before it spiraled to the ground below.

Another shriek tore through the chaos. Vaelith snarled in response. He made a hard turn, barely missing being slashed on his left flank. My stomach dropped as I fought to stay seated. I felt Vaelith's fury burning beneath me as his words floated in my mind. *"I've got you, Little One."*

Then a massive shot of fire poured from his throat and consumed the creature who had taken the swipe at us. Its ashes floated through that air.

"Cade!" I shouted through our bond, pointing toward the rift where creatures continued to pour out like ants from a disturbed anthill.. *"Take the ones near the rift! Eryndor, cover their flank!"*

Cade responded immediately, his voice booming over the chaos. *"You focus on shutting that thing down, Starlight. I'll clear your way!"*

My heart clenched. I hated this—putting him in danger—but I trusted him with everything I had. *"Vaelith,"* I murmured, leaning close to his silver neck. *"Think you can get me closer, Big Guy? We've got a date with that rift."*

"Hold on tight, Little One." His deep voice rumbled in my mind. He gave a powerful flap of his massive wings, picking up speed. We dove toward the rift. In no time, we neared the large opening in the ground. It pulsed with an eerie energy, like it was alive itself. My magic built. I knew it would take a tremendous amount of energy directed at this thing if I even hoped to close it.

Before I could act, a flash of silver caught my eye below. Seraphine. Her hair gleamed like moonlight as delivered blow after magical blow, killing creatures that never seemed to stop coming for her. A pair of creatures lunged at her, but she reached for her twin blades and cut them down at the last second. That was close. Good grief, she was a warrior.

But then I saw it—the thing behind her.

It was like nothing I'd ever seen. A monstrous fusion of shadow and bone, its body writhing as if it were constantly shifting. Its glowing head had its eyes locked on her. Its claws stretched forward. I was sure they could cut through steel.

"Seraphine!" I screamed, panic ripping through me. The wind stole my words, carrying them away before they could reach her.

Time slowed, Goddess, that thing was going to kill her. The creature lunged, its claws aiming straight for her back. I tensed, ready to leap from Vaelith's back—ready to do anything.

But then, a blur of motion. Eldric.

He appeared out of nowhere, his sword slashing upward to intercept the creature. His reddish-brown curls whipped in the wind as he moved.

"No!" I screamed as the creature's claws struck.

The world seemed to shatter as Eldric's body jerked; the impact sending a spray of crimson into the air. He stumbled, his sword slipping from his grasp as blood blossomed across his chest.

Seraphine whirled, her eyes wide with horror as she saw what had just happened. "Eldric!" her voice sounded inhuman as she screamed. She lunged for him, her blades forgotten as she caught him just before he collapsed.

"Eldric, no—" She was anguished as she knelt in the blood-soaked dirt, her arms cradling him.

The creature reared back, ready to strike again. My heart pounded, and magic surged in my veins. "Vaelith, dive!" I commanded.

The dragon obeyed, his wings folding as we plummeted toward them like a missile. I gritted my teeth, flames sparking at my fingertips as we closed the distance.

"Eryndor, Cade, toward Sera! Now!" I shouted, my voice raw.

Eryndor roared, unleashing a torrent of emerald fire that

engulfed the beast. It shrieked, its body writhing as Cade and Eryndor drove it back.

I leapt from Vaelith's back before we'd fully landed, rolling as I hit the ground. Pain lanced through my shoulder, but I ignored it, scrambling to my feet. My gaze locked on Seraphine and Eldric.

Blood pooled beneath him, staining the dirt. Seraphine's silver hair was matted with it as she pressed her hands to his wound, tears streaming down her face.

"Eldric, stay with me," she pleaded, her voice trembling. "Don't you dare leave me!"

My magic surged, desperate to help, but I knew I couldn't spare the energy. The rift was still open, and every second we delayed meant more creatures spilled through.

Cade landed beside me, his expression grim. "Go," he said, his voice low. "Close that damn rift. I'll protect them."

I hesitated, torn between the battle raging around us and the bleeding man before me. But Cade's fierce gaze left no room for argument.

"Go, Olivia," he growled. "Save the rest of us."

I nodded, steeling myself. "Vaelith, let's end this."

As we launched back into the sky, my heart ached for Seraphine and Eldric. But there was no time for grief—not yet. The rift pulsed, a wound in the world that demanded to be sealed. And I was the only one who could do it.

Drawing on the power of the Goddess Vesperia, I felt the familiar surge of magic coursing through my veins. This time, it was different—wilder, more insistent. This felt very much like the day I'd almost lost Cade. The purple glow of my hands intensified, reflecting off Vaelith's shimmering silver scales.

"Come on, Big Guy," I whispered to my dragon. *"Let's seal this sucker."*

Vaelith nodded his colossal head, telling me he was ready. His wings cut through the air with speed. We neared the rift as my magic seemed to build in its intensity. Dark energy continued to pour out of the ground, a force trying to push me back.

Vaelith swooped closer, his eyes locked on his target. I was so tired of Magda's hold on this realm. I felt the Goddess's power flowing through my veins as righteous fury pooled inside of me. I raised my hands, channeling every ounce of that power. I called the elements of the kingdoms of Eldoria to me. The untamed force of Wyldcaster magic became one with the other elements.

"By the Goddess," my voice rose with a force I'd never heard before as I raised my hands toward the rift.

Magic burst from my fingertips, threads of light of every color shot across the rift. It pulsed and pushed and tried to resist. Sweat poured down my face as I pushed magic against the darkness. Then I got downright angry as the rift tried to defy me.

I caught Elric being cradled in Seraphine's lap, her tears pouring down her face. "NO. You don't get to win today." I growled. "NOT TODAY!" And with a final push of power, I poured everything I had into sealing the rift.

"Keep going, baby!" Cade shouted. He had moved near the rift and was pouring his shadows into it as well.

It began to shrink, its edges fraying as mine and Cade's magic overwhelmed it. It shrank smaller and smaller until its resistance had nothing more to give. Finally, with the sound like thunder, the earth closed tight.

There was what seemed like an unnatural silence that followed. The battlefield lay eerily still, broken only by the distant cries of the wounded and the labored breathing of dragons. Vaelith landed with hardly a sound. All at once, exhaustion crashed into me like a tidal wave. My vision blurred, my strength evaporating as I slumped forward against the saddle. Cade was there instantly. Somewhere nearby, I saw Seraphine, still clutching Eldric's bloodied form, her shoulders trembling with silent sobs.

"We did it," I whispered, though my voice sounded distant, barely my own. I managed the ghost of a smile. "But Eldric"

Cade pulled me from the saddle.

Darkness ripped me from my consciousness, pulling me under. The last thing I saw was Seraphine's tear-streaked face. Her lips formed words I couldn't hear. Her pain seared itself into my mind. The battle ended, but at what cost? It was a hollow victory. As the world faded, I kept thinking, the cost had been too great.

CHAPTER 13

In the Arms of Sacrifice

Seraphine

The smell of blood was everywhere, its metallic tang filled my nostrils. Eldric's body lay limp in my arms. The tremendous gash left by a monstrous claw was determined to steal every drop of his precious life's blood. My hands trembled as I fruitlessly tried to stop the flow of blood.

"Stay with me, please." I pleaded. "Don't you dare leave me, Eldric."

His eyes gave a small flutter and opened slightly. I could see in his beautiful green eyes that he was in so much pain. His voice was barely above a whisper.

"Sera... you're alive." He had the audacity to sound relieved. Then his eyes slipped closed again, as if he didn't have the strength to keep them open.

I could not stop my tears. "You listen to me, Eldric. You're going to stay alive. I won't let you die." My tears created small crimson rivers when they mixed with the blood and traced the contours of his face.

I focused all of my attention on Eldric, causing the battlefield around us to disappear. The coppery scent of blood and smoke faded into the background. Maybe it was shock. Things seemed dreamlike.

"Seraphine!" Cade's deep voice cut through the odd state I was in. I glanced up to see he had an unconscious Olivia cradled in his arms, her dark hair trailing behind her, a silken sail.

"Is she...?" The thought of her being seriously injured was almost too much to bear.

"She lives," Cade said quietly as he looked at Eldric in my arms. He gently laid her next to me. "And she will be fine. The burst of magic drained her. What about Eldric?"

I brushed the hair from Eldric's forehead. "I don't know, Cade. It's about as bad as it can be. I don't know if I can save him."

Cade's jaw clenched, his normal, calm demeanor faltering. He knelt beside me, his hand instinctively hovered over Olivia as though even unconscious, she anchored him. His gaze dropped to Eldric's wound, his expression grim. "I'm sorry, Sera. I saw what he did. It's because of him that you breathe now," he murmured, the rough edge of vulnerability in his voice unfamiliar.

I was absolutely determined that I would not let this man die. "I will not let him die because of me." I vowed even as I felt the tears threatening to fall. "I won't."

I went over every spell, every story I'd ever heard that might help me save Eldric's life. I knew there had to be a way. I would not let him die like this. Not for me.

Eldric's eyes slowly opened as though he sensed my desperation. They locked onto mine with an intensity that cut through his haze of death. "Sera..." he rasped, his hand gripping my arm.

"I'm here Eldric. I need for you to just hold on. I'm going to save you. I swear it. Please, just hold on."

A tiny smile graced his lips, just a brief moment of warmth before his eyes rolled back and his body went slack in my arms. Panic, like I've never felt gripped my heart. I felt for a pulse.

"No." I felt almost feral. I would not accept this. My sobs were uncontrollable. "You don't get to leave me. I don't want to be alone again. Please..."

Cade's hand rested on my shoulder. He's my brother, the fixer. "Seraphine," he began. "I don't know if it's safe here."

"Then leave! I'm not leaving without him! I know there's a way to save him. We're Vesparran, we carry the Goddess blood!" And that's when it hit me.

Cade clearly saw what I was thinking.

"Sera, you can't be serious."

"Oh, you better believe I'm serious. I've never been more serious about anything in my life."

"You can't," he warned. I could hear the uncertainty in his voice, the fear of what I might do.

"Watch me," I replied, daring him to try to stop me.

Olivia had woken up and asked Cade what was happening. He took her to the side and explained my plan. She must have agreed with me, because Cade was very animated for a moment.

Oliva and Cade came back to me when our other friends made their way to us. Farin, Miranda, and Thorne had gathered. I could feel all eyes on me, and on Eldric's limp form in my arms. I knew I was running out of time. He had to have life left in his body for this to work.

"By the Goddess," Miranda gasped, her voice little more than a whisper. "Is he…?"

Thorne's deep voice honored Eldric's bravery. "He sacrificed himself for Seraphine. Threw himself in front of a killing blow meant for her."

The sweet timbre of Farin's voice broke through. "Is there anything we can do to save him?"

I looked at Farin. "There *is* something. My blood, the blood of Vesparra."

Protests erupted all around, but I tuned them out. I focused on Eldric's face—the face of a man who'd been given a second chance, who'd chosen redemption over power, who'd saved my life at the cost of his own.

My heart raced, a tempest of hope and fear. What if it didn't work? What if it changed him in ways we couldn't predict? The risks swirled in my mind, two possibilities. A path of either damnation or salvation.

But as I looked at Eldric, remembering the warmth of his smile, the depth of his remorse, I knew I had to try. For me, there was only a singular choice.

"I won't let him die," I declared, my voice settling it. "Not when I have the power to save him."

With trembling fingers, I brought my wrist to my mouth, hesitating for just a moment before sinking my fangs into my flesh. The taste of my blood, rich and potent with the power of Vesparra, flooded my senses, metallic and life-affirming.

As I lowered my bleeding wrist to Eldric's lips, I whispered a silent prayer to the Goddess. "Please," I breathed, "let this work. Let him live."

The world seemed to hold its breath, the air thick with anticipation, hope, and fear intertwining in the charged silence.

I could feel Cade's gaze boring into me, his disapproval boring into me.

"Seraphine, stop!" His voice cut through the silence. "You don't know what this could do to him... or to you." He glanced at. Olivia. She gave him a reassuring smile as she squeezed his hand. Her touch was like a magic balm.

I lifted my eyes to meet his, knowing that Olivia was in my corner helped immensely.

"I have to try, Cade," I replied, my voice soft but unyielding, willing him to understand. "He sacrificed himself for me. I can't just let him die."

Cade's jaw clenched. He gripped Olivia's hand tighter. "And what if this turns him into something we can't control? What if it drains you beyond recovery? Have you thought about the consequences?"

I felt a flicker of doubt, like a shadow crossing my heart, but I pushed it aside with the force of my conviction. "I have," I said, my voice growing stronger, resonating with the power of my choice. "And I've decided it's worth the risk."

Without waiting for a response, I pressed my bleeding wrist to Eldric's pale lips. I tried to will him to drink. Warm droplets trickled down his pale chin, stark crimson, the contrast macabre. The metallic scent of blood filled the air.

"Come on, Eldric," I murmured, my free hand caressing his face, trying to coax life back into his features. "Fight. Live."

My heart pounded in my chest as I said a silent prayer. Please, let this work. Let him come back to me. I knew this was a risk, but I was out of choices. I believed the Goddess had sent Eldric into my life, into all our lives, and I had to trust my gut that she would be here to help him through this. Still, as I watched, no hint of color returned to Eldric's cheeks. It felt like my heart would break.

No matter what I wouldn't let him go. Not now. Not ever.

Minutes passed and as I waited, hope faded. But I refused to give up. Eldric remained still, his chest barely rising. Each breath, proof that his life was hanging by a thread. The battlefield around ceased to exist. My entire world narrowed to the man in my arms and the steady drip of my blood into his unresponsive mouth.

I couldn't understand why it wasn't working. "Why isn't it working?"

The puncture wound on my wrist had started to close. The magic of my healing was going to make this difficult if he didn't drink. But I would not be defeated. I pulled my wrist away, ignoring the sting as I bit down again, harder this time, the pain a sharp reminder of the stakes. The fresh bite made more blood well up. I hoped this would make it easier for him to start drinking.

"Please," I begged, my voice breaking. "Please, Eldric. Don't leave me."

I felt myself getting lightheaded. But I wouldn't give up. I couldn't. Eldric had changed. I knew he had. He had become someone worthy of redemption. Someone I... cared for deeply.

Just as I was about to try a third time, I felt it. I felt the smallest flutter of movement against my wrist, just a twinge where none had been before. Then, suddenly, Eldric's hands shot up, and he grasped my arm with a surprising strength. His lips sealed around my bite, and he drank.

"Finally, it's working," I breathed, watching as the large wound in Eldric's chest started to close, mending itself with a supernatural speed. "By the Goddess, it's really working!"

I knew it would work. I just knew it. Eldric's head rested in the cradle of my arm as my fingers of my free hand ran through his tangled curls. Although his eyes were still closed, the color was returning to his face.

I told him to keep drinking. "That's it, Eldric. Come back to me."

At that moment, his eyes snapped open, and he stopped. He let go of my wrist. The look of shame and regret was all over his face.

"Seraphine." He sat up and looked at me. "I'm so sorry. I didn't mean to—"

I pressed a finger to his lips, telling him to be quiet. "Eldric, it's ok. All that matters is that you're alive." Tears poured down my face. I'd never been so relieved in all of my life.

The wound in his chest had healed completely. Strength had returned to his limbs, but he looked like a man who was consumed by the shame of his past sins.

He looked stricken. "I didn't deserve this. After everything I've done... You should've let me die."

I caressed his cheek, offering a vow of forgiveness and understanding. "You protected me. You didn't have to do that. Everyone can see that you've changed. You're no longer the man you used to be. Redemption exists for those who can acknowledge the things that they've done wrong and have a desire and will to correct them. This is your redemption story, Eldric, This is your second chance. Don't waste it."

He took my face in his hands. "I won't," he promised. It was a promise that sounded like it came from his soul.

Magda

The latest rift I managed to open in Eldoria released a torrent of the most delightfully horrific monstrosities I've created to date. If all went well, they would have left a path of death and destruction in their wake, painting the landscape with the blood of the foolish Eldorian inhabitants.

"Well?" My sniveling demon captain cowered before me, his form trembling like a leaf in a storm. Seriously, how difficult is it to find commanders who didn't shit themselves when I spoke to them? "What news of the attack, Vexus? Please tell me there were mass casualties."

The demon cowered like an abused animal, his leathery wings rustling nervously, each movement a testament to his fear. "My Queen, initial reports indicate that many soldiers from several kingdoms suffered catastrophic injuries. They seemed to be well-prepared for our attack, but we made progress. There was one significant blow struck today, however."

Now, this was intriguing.

"Tell me."

His face twisted into a sadistic grin, the corners of his mouth curling with malevolent glee. "A particularly gruesome direct strike felled the traitor Eldric Alinar in today's battle. He made the mistake of getting between a *malgrith* and the Vesparran princess. Even the mighty sorcerer was no match for the creature's great claws."

I could not help the cruel smile that crossed my lips, the joy of vengeance sweet and sharp. "Defending her, was he? How deliciously ironic." I laughed, the sound echoing off the cavernous walls of the Underworld. "I always knew his weakness for pretty faces would be his undoing."

I strolled to a nearby window, gazing out at the fires of

the Underworld, the flames licking at the black sky like eager tongues. "At last, that thorn in my side has been removed. With Eldric gone, Eldoria's defenses will more easily crumble." I tapped my talon-sharp nails against the windowsill, each tap a note in the symphony of my impending victory.

"What about the second part of this mission? Did our *morfiend* deploy as planned?"

Vexus' self-satisfied look was quite irritating. I thought of knocking it off his face, but let him continue, curiosity outweighing my annoyance.

"Drakhar made it out in the first wave, before the Draconia arrived on the scene. He should be in Thalassa as we speak, my queen."

My nails continued tapping, the rhythm a meditation on the chaos I had sown. With Eldric out of the picture and my plan in motion, I felt with certainty that the realm of Eldoria was within my grasp, ready to be crushed like a butterfly in my fist.

Eldric

I inhaled deeply, savoring the scent of damp earth and wildflowers that clung to Seraphine's skin, the aroma grounding me in this new reality. My body hummed with newfound strength, every nerve ending alive and tingling, like a symphony of sensation playing just beneath my skin. It was as if I'd been reborn, my senses heightened to an almost painful degree, each breath a revelation.

"How do you feel?" Seraphine asked, her navy eyes searching mine with a depth that seemed to reach into my very soul.

"Like I could move mountains," I replied, flexing my fingers, feeling the power surge through them. The wound in my chest had vanished, leaving only smooth, unmarred skin where death had once marked its claim. "Seraphine, I—"

She pressed a finger to my lips, silencing me, her touch gentle yet firm. "We can talk later. Right now, we need to regroup and assess the damage."

As we rose to our feet, I couldn't help but marvel at the woman before me. Her silver hair caught the fading sunlight, creating a halo around her face that seemed to defy the darkness we were surrounded by. In that moment, I realized how deeply I cared for her—not just for her ethereal beauty, but for her strength, her compassion, her unwavering spirit.

"Thank you," I murmured, grasping her hand, feeling the warmth of her skin against mine, a testament to life and connection. "For everything."

Despite the warmth of Seraphine's touch, a chill ran down my spine, an ominous whisper of foreboding. Something dark was coming. I could feel it in my bones, a shadow on the horizon of my newly sharpened senses.

Olivia had roused completely from the tremendous energy she'd expended closing the rift, her eyes regaining their spark as she stood with Cade and the others, her presence commanding even in her weariness.

"You scared the bejesus outa me, Eldric. I thought for sure you were a goner." I still marveled at how this woman had such capacity for forgiveness, her spirit as resilient as the land she fought to protect.

"Thank you, Majesty, if you hadn't gotten here in time, that creature would surely have killed Sera. I'm so grateful to..." I looked around at all who had gathered, their faces etched with relief and fatigue. "Everyone."

Cade cleared his throat, his voice breaking through the aftermath's quiet. "Alright. It appears you are feeling fine to travel now?"

"Yes. I feel better than ever," I told him, amazed at the vitality coursing through me like a river.

He clapped his hands twice, the sound sharp in the air. "We need to get back to Vesparra. Farin, do you have this area in hand?"

"I do. I'll get the commanders squared away. Medical will triage the injured and get them to the healer's tents.

Fortunately, we had no loss of life today. Once that is done, I have business back in Thalassa that I must attend to."

Miranda looked like she was dead on her feet, her vitality drained from the effort of the battle. Thorne's concern for her showed clearly on his face, his expression a mix of love and worry. He looked to Cade.

"Your Majesty. I'd like to accompany Queen Miranda back to Ilyndor."

Cade's smile showed his realization he's likely lost his general, a hint of understanding in his eyes. "Of course, General. We need to talk soon."

Thorne straightened, heels clicked together, his right fist pounding his chest plate over his heart in salute. Then they turned to the portal, their figures silhouetted against its shimmering light.

Cade sighed, the weight of leadership clear in the set of his shoulders. "Let's head home. Olivia is riding with me. We'll be on Vaelith. Eldric, I know you say you're feeling better than ever, but I'm not sure I trust that to last. To be on the safe side, I'd appreciate it if you and Seraphine rode tandem on Eryndor. The other Dragonia will accompany us in formation."

I nodded my agreement, the prospect of flight with Seraphine both comforting and exhilarating. Together, we all mounted up, our dragons taking to the sky, their wings beating a rhythm of hope and determination as we headed for Vesparra.

Drakhar (the morphiend)

Making my way into Thalassa could not have been easier. Being able to hide in the shadows has its advantages, like slipping through a keyhole in the dark. Getting into the castle, though, is a bit more of a challenge. Yet again, being able to step out from the shadows allows me the element of surprise. Someone clearly warned them about me; they're on high alert, their eyes darting, hands twitching near weapons. They didn't think it all the way through, however. More than guards have run of the castle. A variety of ladies' maids, even more so, flit here and there like nervous butterflies.

Oh, this is too easy. I've only waited in this alcove for mere minutes and here comes a little beauty. One…two…three! "Gotcha!" My shadows muffle her delicious screams, wrapping around her like a dark blanket. One little twist and no more noise. Now, I'll just drag her body into this empty bed chamber closet. It's too easy.

I do not enjoy wearing a woman's skin. Too many soft areas, too many lumps. Not nearly enough muscle. I'm startled as I exit the room, my new form feeling alien.

"Millicent, why were you in that chamber? Queen Olivia is not currently in residence. There would be no need to go in there," another maid queries, her voice echoing slightly in the stone corridor.

Fuck. This room belongs to that bitch.

"Yes, I know, but I thought I'd heard something in there. I quickly took a peek to be certain nothing was amiss," I respond, trying to mimic the cadence of a nervous maid.

The other maid raised a brow, her skepticism as clear as the daylight through the castle's tall windows.

"Very well. Please continue your work."

I nodded, feigning deference, and ventured past her. That was close. Now to make my way to the dungeon, my heart beating with the thrill of the hunt, every step forward, a step closer to my dark purpose.

This is odd. I guess they figured the dungeons would be ignored during an attack. I've only counted six guards down here. Then again, there is only one prisoner. That made her well-guarded by any standard. My illusion wore off moments ago, so I needed to be careful to stick to the shadows, which are plentiful down here. I moved, hidden like ink spilled across the stone. The first guard sensed my presence, his head tilting slightly, a dog catching a scent. I needed to decide where I'd put his body before I took him down. A uniform closet. Perfect.

"I see you looking around," I said to myself as I watched him for a moment, his eyes scanning the darkness. *"By the time you realize where I am, it will be too late."*

I stepped out of the shadows behind him and whispered in his ear, my breath a cold promise. "Looking for me?"

His head whipped around to the left. I helped it keep on its trajectory in that direction. Sadly for this fellow, your head is not meant to keep going in that direction. His body crumpled like his bones had turned to dust. I caught him beneath his arms and quickly dragged him to the closet. Yes. This is more like it. A nice, powerful male body—made for destruction.

I walked with purpose, further into the dungeon, wearing my new body. The key to not raising suspicion is to act like you belong exactly where you are, moving with the confidence of one who owns the shadows. Guards chatted with each other, their voices echoing off the cold walls, barely giving me a second glance. There was only one guard stationed at the cell of the former queen of Thalassa. There she sat, looking nothing like the beauty she was reported to be. No, this woman was haggard and tired, her once radiant aura dimmed by captivity. But she was unquestionably Nerissa Thalassa, a most powerful wielder of magic, now stripped of her power by the suppression shackles that bound her.

The guard looked at me, a bit surprised but not alarmed. "Naharo, you aren't usually on cell duty. Did you draw the short straw today?"

I lowered my head so he couldn't get a look at my eyes, feigning sheepishness. "It finally has fallen to me." I edged a bit closer to him.

He laughed, the sound hollow in this place of despair. "It's not so bad, brother. She has nothing good to say, that's for sure. Just get ready to be continually dressed down."

I took a small step closer to him. "She likely realizes how

superior she is to all of you and that she should be the one on the throne when Magda finally destroys the Chosen One."

I was nose to nose with him now. Terror marked his features, the realization of death dawning like a dark sun. He got the same treatment as the others and fell limp to the floor. I took on his form in case I encountered anyone new. I dragged his body to a dark corner; the shadows swallowing the evidence of my passage.

The queen arose, her movements slow from disuse, gripping the bars of her cell with hands that once commanded respect and fear.

"What is happening?" Her voice was hoarse, tinged with the desperation of one long confined.

A feral grin split my face, the thrill of the hunt culminating in this moment. "I'm retrieving you, Highness. You have an appointment with a goddess." I had one spell at my disposal, a dark whisper of magic that would open a one-way portal to the Underworld, fleeting in its existence. I recited the spell, the words ancient and harsh, and the portal appeared with a sound like the tearing of reality itself. The queen took a few steps backward, her eyes wide with terror.

"No, ma'am. You are coming with me, Highness." I grabbed her around the waist, her body tensing in my grasp, and yanked her through the portal only moments before it vanished, the edges of the world knitting back together in its wake. And just like that, the cell that had held the one prisoner of Thalassa was empty, the silence of the dungeon now echoing the absence of its once formidable occupant.

CHAPTER 14

Blood of my Soul

Eldric

After arriving back at Vesparra Castle, we gathered in the dining room, the air thick with the scent of fresh bread and the lingering tension of battle. Cade's Circle had assembled to dine and debrief, the room a mix of relief and urgency. Amaya was unhappy, her displeasure evident because she and Kaelen had not been informed of the attack. She was, in fact, livid.

She stormed back and forth in the dining room, her movements like a tempest contained within the stone walls. "This little system is not working for me! How is it that my Alpha and I were in the same company as that jackass Ignis and excluded from a major battle?" She winced a bit and looked at Callie. "Sorry, Callie girl." I could only imagine that was for calling Ignis a jackass.

Callie chuckled, her laughter a brief light in the tense atmosphere. "No need to apologize, Maya. Truth hurts."

Maya was not finished, her voice rising like the tide. "So, who is going to explain this to me? There were Therionis troops there fighting their asses off. And yet their Alpha and Luna were none the wiser? Cade? Explanation?"

"LUNA. Enough." Kaelen's Alpha tone was almost enough to cower me, his voice echoing with command, vibrating through the room like thunder.

She immediately stopped her tirade, her body posture

changing as she lowered her head, still fuming but unwilling to defy her Alpha.

Kaelen walked up to her, his steps measured, knowing it wasn't anger she was feeling, but fear. She could have lost her sister today without being there to protect her. He wrapped her in his arms, his Alpha growl a soothing rumble that had her melting into him. He was clearly speaking to her through their bond, his words silent but their effect palpable. She nodded and turned from him, her expression softening.

She addressed Cade, her voice now subdued, the fire in her eyes replaced by regret. "I'm sorry I spoke to you with such disrespect in your own home, Cade. I had no right. I should have addressed any concerns I had when we assembled in our war council. Forgive me." A single tear traced a path down her cheek, shining like crystal under the chandelier's light.

Olivia ran to her, enveloping Amaya in a crushing hug, her arms like steel bands around her little sister.

"Itty Bitty. I understand why you're pissed, I do. We just got the call and had Sera and Eldric with us. It wasn't a slight. We were just closest. I know you are a badass wolf. Listen to me. I love having you fight beside me, no matter the monsters." She cupped her face in her hands, her touch gentle yet firm. "You hear me? But we can't think of these situations like this. Anybody can get the call or not get the call at any time. It's never because of a slight. Not one of us is more capable than the next—except for me—cuz, you know… the Goddess made me a superstar and all."

Olivia tried to hold on to her laughter but failed, her giggles breaking through like sunlight through storm clouds.

"Oooh girlfriend, the look on your face! Now, sit down and eat something. I'm so freakin' tired. And Eldric basically died today, so give us all a break."

Amaya's head jerked towards me, her eyes wide with shock. I just shrugged my shoulders and nodded, then turned my attention back to my meal, the flavors dull compared to the day's events. What a fucking day.

Everyone ate with what I assume is normal chatter for this group, the clink of cutlery and murmur of voices filling the room like any other night, masking the undercurrents of the day's battle. Then we all went up to our rooms for the night. I dropped Sera at her chamber door, the urge to follow her inside like a physical pull. I wanted to take her in my arms, toss her onto her bed, and ravage her, to feel the life we'd both almost lost. But I settled for a small kiss on her forehead, a last "thank you" for saving me, my words a whisper of gratitude and longing in the quiet hallway.

After a hot shower, I put on a pair of silk sleep pants and sat in a large armchair in the living area of my room, the fabric cool against my heated skin. The fireplace crackled, its flames casting shadows that danced across the walls, reflecting the raging inferno in my blood. Seraphine filled every empty space in my mind, body, and soul. I'd had no one who'd ever cared enough to fight for me. My little warrior would not let me go, and the feelings this evoked swelled in my chest like a storm gathering force.

The taste of her blood on my tongue was like the sweetest sugar and cinnamon, a nectar that had brought me back from the brink. The power that surged as a result was as intoxicating as it was sweet. But the shame that followed was like a boat crashing against the rocks, each wave of guilt threatening to pull me under. The love in her eyes made it better and worse. I was not worthy of her. How could I ever be? A good man, I was not. But I would prove to her I could be better.

There was no way I could sleep tonight. I was not even slightly sleepy. My blood was buzzing in my veins like a hive awakened.

A soft knock drew me from my revelry. The door opened, and in walked Seraphine. She shut the door, pressing her back to it, looking every bit like a goddess. Her unbound silver hair hung loose around her shoulders, cascading like rays of moonlight well past her waist. The long, black satin robe she wore flowed like liquid onyx around her generous curves, each movement a testament to her grace.

Neither one of us spoke.

I couldn't tear my eyes away from her. The silver flecks in her navy eyes seemed to swirl in the fading firelight, hypnotizing me, pulling me into their depths. My heart raced. Each beat a thunderous reminder of how close I'd come to losing everything today—and how she'd saved me.

She finally spoke as she walked towards me, her steps silent on the plush carpet. "Eldric," she whispered, her voice like silk against my skin. "I want—"

I stood and met her then silenced her with a kiss, urgent and passionate, our lips meeting like the crashing waves. The taste of her lips, a mix of honey and brandy, intoxicated me, filling my senses with her essence. My hands found her waist, pulling her closer until I could feel the heat of her body through the thin robe she wore. Did she have anything on under it?

Seraphine responded with all of herself. Her fingers tangled in my hair and pulled closer to her. We were breathless when we finally broke apart. I rested my forehead against hers, breathing in her essence, enjoying her closeness.

She dropped her head to my chest. "I thought I'd lost you," her words sounded muffled against my chest.

"I *was* lost, Sera." I couldn't hide the emotion in my voice. "You gave my life back to me."

The look she gave me took my breath away. I stood there trying to figure out why this woman chose me. When she spoke, "Eldric, I—"

This time, when she kissed me I lost myself in the taste of her, savoring every moment. The aftermath of everything that had happened faded away and had it come down to just the two of us in this moment.

I ran my hands through her silky hair and tilted her head back as I as I deepened the kiss. I wanted to feel the softness of her lips, taste her tongue against mine, consume every part of her. Her tongue moved against mine, exploring, sucking and pulling against it. Her desire coursed through my veins.

When she pulled back, her eyes shone with desire. She looked away just for a moment. I didn't know if she felt embarrassed or what if I had done something.

She explained, and then I understood.

"When your mouth responded, it was a sensation that I'd never felt before. As a royal vampire, I'm always the one to give the euphoric sensation of my bite. I understand now what people feel. I knew that I wanted you before then. But having received the same feeling, I get it. And somehow the bond that I'd already felt with you somehow became stronger. Please tell me you felt it too."

"I felt that, and so much more for you. When I saw you in the hallway, the night I arrived, I felt the Goddess had sent you to me. But I also felt so unworthy of you."

"Eldric, you're not. Please. Don't keep me waiting."

She stepped back and untied the robe she was wearing, letting it fall to the floor in a pool of liquid fabric around her feet, revealing her vulnerability and strength in one breathtaking moment.

There was the answer to my question. No. She had nothing on beneath that robe. Nothing but the most exquisite body I'd ever laid my eyes on. She was flawless, sculpted and glowing, with soft curves that called to me like a siren's song. Perfect. Every inch of her, perfection. She suddenly seemed shy at exposing herself to me so completely, her vulnerability a stark contrast to her usual strength.

"Come here," I whispered, my voice barely more than a breath, heavy with desire.

She stepped into my embrace without hesitation, our bodies pressed together. I ran my hands down her sides, reveling in the feel of smooth skin under my fingertips, each touch an exploration. Lowering my head, I kissed a path up her neck, stopping at her earlobe to tease it lightly with my teeth. A soft gasp escaped from her throat, sending shivers down my spine like ripples on water.

"This is not something I take lightly, Sera. I won't do this without your commitment to us."

I stepped back, creating some small distance, the space between us charged with anticipation. Slowly, I lifted one perfect breast into my mouth, giving it a tender caress with my tongue, savoring the taste of her. As I kneaded the soft flesh between my fingers, Seraphine threw her head back in pleasure, her long silver hair cascading down her back. Her fingers raked through my hair, urging me on as she arched into me even more. My other hand drifted lower, tracing the outline of her hip before sliding lower still until it came to rest on her warm thigh, the heat of her skin a radiating through me.

Her head lowered, her gaze honing into mine, her eyes alight with emotion. "Eldric, what is between us is not an accident. We are meant to be together. I felt it the night I passed you in the hall. I feel it now. Tell me you feel it too. It's more than an infatuation. It's a bond," she breathed out, sounding both surprised and delighted by the sensations coursing through her body.

I continued to caress her thigh, my touch deliberate. "I know without hesitation or doubt, Sera, the Goddess gave you to me. And you are so much more than I deserve."

Without breaking the rhythm of gentle touches and eager gasps for air, we moved towards the bed together, our bodies intertwined like two dancers lost in each other's arms. I removed my sleep pants along the way, my desire for her growing with each passing moment, my erection almost painful in its need for her touch.

I sank into the mattress next to her and pulled her close once more, the silk sheets cool against our heated skin. It was unbelievable that she lay here with me in all her naked glory, a goddess in her own right. I reached for her leg, pulling it across my body, pressing her even closer, our hearts beating in sync. My hands cupped her face as my tongue assaulted her mouth in a torrent of kisses, sucking, licking, and exploring every inch. My little warrior returned the kisses with as much fervor and desire, her passion igniting mine. I was lost in the taste of her, the delicacy of her essence.

She reached between us, taking my cock in her hand, moving up and down the shaft with slow and deliberate movements, her touch like silk.

"Fuck, your hand is perfect on me, my Sanguis Anima."

Her beautiful eyes held mine, a universe of emotion swirling within them.

"This may be a challenge for me. You are quite large." Her words were barely a whisper, tinged with both excitement and apprehension.

I moved her leg back and leaned back some, my hand joining hers. I swear my cock grew with both of our movements, the anticipation building.

"No, my sweet. Your beautiful pussy will take all of me. You were made for me."

I let go of my erection and reached between her creamy thighs to her dripping core, running my fingers through her wetness, feeling the readiness of her body.

"Oh, see, my love. See the way you drip? Your body readies itself for your mate."

I drew my fingers through her wetness, then entered her opening with two.

"Ahh, Eldric. That is... mmm." Her body writhed against my hand, her pleasure palpable. Then she looked at me, her eyes clouded with desire.

"Yes," she moaned. "My body recognizes its mate."

While my fingers were still inside her, she leaned up, grabbed me around the neck, and kissed me with all of herself, moaning into my mouth. I pulled her to me with my free arm, keeping up the invasion of her pussy with my other hand, my fingers pounding into her with the same rhythm as my tongue moving in and out of her mouth.

"Mmm," she pulled back, her body moving with the tempo of my fingers. "Eldric, please, more. I need…"

I moved my fingers from inside her and traced up to her swollen clit, rubbing rapidly, never taking my eyes from her exquisite face. She was lost in the throes of her ecstasy, her expressions a canvas of pleasure, and I'd seen nothing more stunning.

After a moment, she shattered.

"Yes, there, that's…. I… Gods!"

Her body shuddered with her moans as she came, waves of pleasure washing over her. After her release, her eyes hazy with lust, I moved my fingers to my mouth and sucked them clean of her essence, the taste of her like a forbidden fruit. Her grin was adorable, a mix of satisfaction and anticipation.

"Now, my Sanguis Anima, I'm going to ravish you."

Her eyes widened, but only for a moment, a flicker of excitement.

"Please do, my mate. Please do."

"Make no mistake, I'm going to take my time."

I moved my body over hers, careful to use my arms to hold my massive weight off of her, my muscles taut with restraint. She held my gaze as I began to rain kisses across her beautiful face, each one a whisper of my devotion. I reached for her perfect mouth, sinking my tongue once more, unable to get enough of the taste of her.

I continued down the slim column of her neck, kissing, sucking, and nibbling my way to her collarbone, her skin glowing with an ethereal light as if kissed by moonlight. Her breasts were beautiful and heavy in my hands, the perfect size.

"There is not a more beautiful woman in this realm or any other, my Sanguis Anima."

I took one of her breasts in my mouth and sucked as she writhed beneath me, her body arching with each sensation.

"Eldric." Her hands were in my hair, pulling me closer.

I released with a pop and licked and kissed the other with the same care. My hands replaced my lips as I kneaded both, loving the feel of the softness of each against the hardness of each nipple, the contrast intoxicating.

My mouth continued the journey down her body, stopping to add small bites to her gorgeous flesh, each one a whisper of desire. Not enough to mar, never enough to mark, just enough to elicit the reactions I wanted. Her body rocked from side to side, her moans and gasps the most beautiful sounds I've heard, a symphony of pleasure.

I slightly leaned back and rubbed my left hand along her beautiful creamy thigh, my touch light. "Sera, your body is a treasure. The Goddess has kissed you." I lightly moved my hand up until I reached her dripping core.

"But this," I said as I brushed my fingers over her sopping pussy, "this is what dreams are made of."

"Ahh, yes!" Her hips rose from the bed, seeking more of my touch.

"That's my girl. You are a fountain for me, Sanguis Anima. And I've never been more thirsty for a drink."

I leaned in and gave her a long, slow lick, starting at the bottom of her opening, drifting to her clit. Her hips rose to meet my tongue as I pressed in, moving it around and up and down, the taste of her a sweet elixir. Her hands were suddenly in my hair, willing me to let her finish, her urgency palpable. I was eager to be inside her, so I was ready as well. A few more passes and her body shivered with the orgasm that tore through her, like a storm breaking.

"Ahh...it's so good. So good..." Her body was almost spent, but we were not finished.

I made my way up her body with slow, deliberate movements, each kiss a promise of more.

"Oh my love, you are so beautiful when you come. You make me weak. But now you will see how you were truly made for me."

I lined myself up at her entrance, stroking myself several times as she watched. I entered her inch at a time, her body welcoming me. The look on her face told me she took my size with no problems. Her hooded navy eyes, lost in ecstasy, held my gaze.

"How are you, beautiful girl?"

"I'm amazing, my love."

I looked down between us, watching her pussy swallow my cock an inch at a time.

"I'm struggling to hold back, sweetheart."

Her head was tossing back and forth, her need clear.

"Please, I need you! I'm a vampire, Eldric! Fuck me, now!"

It was like she'd turned a switch on inside of me. It was all systems go. I slammed into her body, and I swore I could see faint wisps of silver and emerald light dancing around our entwined forms, our connection transcending the physical.

"Do you feel that?" Seraphine gasped, her voice a mixture of awe and pleasure.

I nodded, as I continued to thrust in and out of her, unable to speak words to describe the sensation. It was as if every cell in my body was singing, resonating with a frequency that matched Seraphine's perfectly.

I was getting close.

"I want you to come one more time for me, love."

She had an odd look on her face, a mixture of desire and hesitation.

"I want to bite you. Will you let me?"

We hadn't discussed this, but I'd love nothing more.

"Please."

I leaned over her as I continued to move in and out of her, our bodies synchronized in a dance as old as time. She leaned up, wrapping one arm around my neck, and without preamble, she struck. Her fangs sank into the area where my neck and shoulder meet, a sharp, sweet sting that sent me over the edge. Instantly, I came with a euphoric force that was indescribable, my climax mingling with the sensation of her feeding.

"Ahh Fuck, Gods," I grunted, and moaned. I almost lost control of my body with the force of my release.

She drank for several seconds, moaning and writhing against me until she let go and sealed the wound with a gentle lick. We both crashed to the bed, entangled in each other's arms, our panting. Our breaths mingling in the aftermath.

I held her to my chest, breathless, feeling the beat of our hearts.

Her gaze held mine, searching, hopeful.

"Why do you call me Sanguis Anima?"

"Because you are the blood of my soul," I whispered, the words heavy with meaning.

I gently wiped the tear that fell from the corner of her eye, the droplet carrying the weight of our connection.

She finally spoke, her voice soft, laden with emotion. "I thank the Goddess she has given you to me."

I had no right to speak to the Goddess, but I was thankful to her as well.

CHAPTER 15

A Fractured Crown

Magda

The acrid stench of sulfur assaulted my nostrils as I watched Drakhar drag Nerissa into my domain, her feet scraping the dark stone. Shadows clung to her like a second skin, writhing and pulsing in the oppressive darkness, a stark contrast to the once-proud queen. The air hung heavy, each breath a struggle against the frigid murkiness that permeated the Underworld, thick with the promise of despair.

I plastered on my most beguiling smile, allowing a hint of fang to peek through, the points sharp against my lips. "Darling Nerissa! How nice to see you finally."

Nerissa's eyes darted wildly, seeking an escape that didn't exist. Her demeanor, that I'm sure was typically flawless, had cracked, fear etching lines into her barely aged face. These past weeks had apparently taken its toll. Her once vibrant hair now hung limp around her sallow face, dressed in all but rags.

"My, my, you certainly are not looking much like a queen these days, are you?" They had really done a number on her up in the land of sunshine and happiness.

"Magda?" she managed. Her voice was barely louder than a whisper in the vast emptiness.

"Oh, come now Nerissa, don't tell me you're surprised." I clasped her dirty hands in mine. I just loved the way she recoiled at my touch, her skin cold and clammy. "There's no way you didn't suspect that I'd be bringing you here one day."

She stared at me wide-eyed as my fingers traced idle patterns across her skin.

"Well, come on. We have matters to discuss and plans to make." I pulled her along, deeper into the cavernous darkness. Each step echoed ominously. My demons kept poking their heads around corners, trying to catch a peek at the fallen queen. She stumbled several times, her bare feet slapping on the rough stone floors as pools of shadows slid in and around her legs like curious, malicious cats.

"I have to say, it really was quite a challenge freeing you from your prison, darling," I sang, as I guided her to a throne of polished bones. I thought it only fair that a queen sit on a throne after all. Even one made of the bones of my enemies. "Please, do try to make yourself comfortable. My throne is your throne, as they say." She didn't join me in my laughter. Some people lack a sense of humor, I guess.

NO. Nerissa just sat perched near the edge of the throne. I can't say if her trembling was because she was cold or terrified. Although, I could taste a good bit of fear coming from her, and it was delicious. Her dull blue eyes never left mine. They seemed to search for some hint of mercy she would not find in this world. Finally, she found the courage to speak.

"Why have you brought me here, Magda?"

I laughed, the sound sharp enough to cut glass, a harsh melody in the silence. "Why, just to chat about how everything managed to become fucked up so badly," I gritted out, each word dripping with disdain. "I thought I had set things up so perfectly for you. You just needed to execute the plan. It seemed easy enough. A simple plan. Yet. You. Couldn't. Even. Do. That."

She clenched as I circled her throne, a predator toying with its prey. I loved in the way she caught her breath the closer I got to her. When my fingers trailed along the back of her throne, they glanced off her tangled dirty hair and I felt her flinch.

Mmm, the fear that rolled off her was what I craved. To see the arrogant fall so completely is its own reward.

"I imagine you used to dress in much more lavish gowns," I murmured, leaning in close enough that my lips grazed her ear, my breath hot against her cold skin. "I wonder, did your darling husband know the depths of your ambition? The things you were willing to do for power?"

Nerissa stiffened, her voice barely audible, a whisper against the howling winds of the Underworld. "He did not. But, he does now."

"That must have been terribly awkward for you." I pulled back, studying her with faux concern, my gaze piercing through her defenses. "Or did you even care? Perhaps not. You can go so far until you can't see past your own... evil." My laughter echoed through the chamber, bouncing off the walls, a cacophony of doom. "Oh, this will be such fun, won't it? You're about to get a taste of what real evil feels like."

I sank into my obsidian throne, the cool stone a stark contrast to the fire burning within me, its chill seeping into my bones. My lips curled into a smirk as I regarded Nerissa, trying to hold a regal posture belying the alarm in her eyes.

"Now, Nerissa, about those plans," I purred. "We must discuss your... unique talents."

My mind was filled with possibilities. Nerissa's water and ice powers were ancient. She could do more than just control tides and create little ice spears. Her power was vast, and combined with my own, could be part of a combination that could rip open a portal between worlds. The thought sent tingles of anticipation down my spine.

"Your ability to manipulate your elements is well known and unsurpassed," I mused aloud, careful to gauge her reactions. "Water, ice, and something infinitely darker."

Nerissa sat silently, but I did not miss the way she clenched her jaw.

I leaned forward to the point to where she could feel

my breath on her face. "Together," I told her, adding a seductive edge to my voice, "we could produce something... extraordinary. Think of it, Nerissa. A gateway of sorts between realms. The possibilities are endless."

I knew she was a greedy bitch. She craved power above all else. Stupid fool. She remained silent, but she couldn't hide the intrigue from her eyes.

As I spoke, I weighed my options. Nerissa alone wouldn't be enough. We needed a catalyst, someone with a connection to both worlds. Someone like...

"Tell me," I asked, a slow smile spreading across my face, "how is your dear husband these days?"

Nerissa's eyes widened in horror, and I knew I'd struck gold. Farin, the noble king of Thalassa. Oh yes, he would do nicely.

Farin

The salty breeze brushed across my face the moment I stepped onto the shores of Thalassa. The scent of the sea brought the usual promise of home. Relief washed over me, like the gentle waves lapping at the golden shores I loved so much. Home, there was really no place like it.

I walked through the village on my way to the castle. Even in the midst of having troops stationed away from home and battles being fought, daily life had continued. Gardens had been tended, markets were opened, and children still attended school. As I walked, I was glad to see the market was opened and vendors were still in business.

My reverie was broken as I walked into the palace courtyard. The captain of my palace guards hurried my direction. His weathered face was heavy with worry.

"Your Majesty," He said, his voice low so no passersby could hear what he was saying. "I'm afraid I bring dire news."

I was immediately filled with dread at whatever news he had to share. "Speak, Captain. What's happened?"

He walked with me up the palace steps as he broke the news.

"There have been... deaths, sire. A maid in the residence wing and two guards found in the dungeon. And... Sire... Queen Nerissa... she's vanished without a trace."

The words hit me like a physical blow, my heart faltering in my chest. I stopped in my tracks. "Nerissa? Gone? That's impossible. She was secure in her cell? Was she not? When did this happen?"

"Details are still sketchy at this point, Sire. But it seems it happened sometime last night or in the very early morning hours." He replied. "The bodies we discovered a few hours ago. As for the queen... We found her cell empty, but her cell door was locked up tight and her guard's body was in the shadows."

This entire thing made no sense. A maid in the residence wing? And then two guards? It was a puzzle with pieces that seemed to not fit.

"Show me," I commanded. I dreaded what I'd find. "Take me to the dungeon now."

Without waiting for a response, I strode forward, my legs carrying me swiftly through the palace.

My mind was racing with questions and possibilities. Could Nerissa have been behind this? She had done horrific things before. Just the thought of her past sins sent chills down my spine. A woman who would have her own daughter murdered by her other daughter is the very definition of soulless. She could have done this.

We ran down the cool damp stairs to the dungeons, taking two at a time. My heart pounded in my chest, honestly afraid of what I'd find. Lately, it seemed to be one grim thing after another. This was just another in a long list of tragedies to befall Thalassa in the past several years.

At the top of the stairs, in a uniform closet, lay the first body, his head twisted at an odd angle, like a macabre sculpture. Erik spoke, his voice somber.

"We left the bodies so you could see, Highness. We thought

you might have some insight."

He'd clearly had his neck broken.

"My guess is that the murderer snuck up behind him somehow and broke his neck. This would be the quickest, cleanest, and most quiet way to get him out of the way. Clearly, he was dragged into this closet."

The scent of salt and seawater gave way to something darker, the unmistakable smell of something otherworldly. What could that gods awful odor be?

I pressed on through the corridor; the torchlights adding to the unease by casting eerie shadows along the damp stone walls. As we neared Nerissa's cell, I noticed how difficult it was to see down here. It would actually be fairly easy for someone to slip in here unnoticed. Dammit, I should have paid more attention to the conditions here.

The silence was deafening. A steady drip of water and the scratching and scurrying of unseen creatures were the only sounds. I checked the nearby cells just to be sure she didn't somehow wind up in one of them. Dread was slowly sinking into my bones.

There her cell sat, empty. The cell door was shut and locked. I did not enter it. I thought it best to observe first. Looking inside, I saw footprints on the dirt on the floor. Two sets. One bare footed and one wearing boots.

"Do guards enter her cell often?" I asked, my voice echoing slightly in the hollow space.

The guard looked surprised, his forehead wrinkled. "No, Your Highness. Never!"

I looked back at the cell floor and pointed to it, my finger moving in a circular motion.

"Well, it appears a person wearing guards' boots went into her cell at some point. Other than the prints from her bare feet, those boot prints tell the tale. They must be fresh because there are no other prints on top of those."

The guard's face paled. He yelled for the guards who were on duty overnight, his voice echoing through the dungeon.

"Who guarded this cell last night?"

They pointed to the dead man in the shadows, his body a frightening reminder of the night's events. I looked at his boots. The left heel had a small triangular notch on the right side, like it had gotten caught on a nail at some point. The boot print in the cell had a matching notch on the same heel.

"By the Goddess," I whispered. I reached out to the dead soldier's face and closed his eyes, a gesture of respect for the fallen. I knew who had taken her.

"I need to contact Olivia," I muttered to myself, the idea settling in my mind. "She needs to know."

My hands shook as I pulled out the small crystal from my pocket. I activated it by channeling a bit of my energy into it and repeating the incantation for Vesparra, praying that Olivia would answer. Each second felt like an eternity.

"Olivia," I said as soon as the connection was made. "It's Grandpapa. Something terrible has happened. Your grandmother... she's missing. And there have been deaths. I need your help, my dear. Please, come quickly."

As I ended the communication, I slumped against the wall, the weight of my fear and desperation threatening to crush me, the cold stone offering no comfort. If what I thought was true, how could I protect my kingdom from a threat I couldn't even see?

Olivia

I was jolted awake by the pulsing of the crystal on my nightstand. Its magic and bright energy had me wide awake in an instant. Grandpapa's voice sounded weak and worried. I needed to get to him quickly.

"Cade," I whisper-shouted at him, shaking his shoulder. "Wake up. Grandpapa needs us."

His eyes snapped opened, instantly alert, like some kind of

sentinel programmed for war. "What is it Starlight? Another rift?"

"No, thank the Goddess. But it's bad. Grandpapa said Nerissa's missin', and people have died or somethin.'"

I jumped out of bed, and the cool morning air gave me chill bumps. I ran to the washroom and quickly threw on my clothes. I was dragging a brush through my hair, getting it braided, when I walked back in the bedroom.

Cade headed to the washroom to get himself dressed as I was putting my boots on. He gave me a quick kiss as he passed. "I'll get dressed."

My mind ran wild as I finished getting dressed. My Grandmother Nerissa, cruel old heifer she was, was still family. And Grandpapa is the sweetest man alive. I think he was more worried about Thalassa than he was Nerissa, if I'm being honest.

"Ready?" I asked, turning to Cade. He nodded. That man is my pillar of strength and peace.

We hurried down the corridor, the stone walls seeming to close in around us, each step echoing our haste. When we reached Eldric's room, I raised my hand to knock, but Cade beat me to it, his fist pounding on the heavy oak door a herald of doom.

"Eldric! We need to—" Cade's words died on his lips as the door swung open, revealing a scene that momentarily stalled our momentum.

Eldric stood there, his reddish-brown curls in disarray. But it was the figure behind him that made my breath catch. Seraphine, Cade's sister, her silver hair gleaming, eyes wide with surprise, a deer in headlights.

"Seraphine?" Cade's voice was a mix of confusion and dawning realization. "What are you...?"

I felt the tension sparking between them, a storm of unspoken questions, electric and palpable. But there wasn't time for this now.

"We can discuss this later," I said, my voice sharper than I intended, cutting through the charged air. "Grandpapa needs us. Now."

Eldric's green eyes narrowed, his usual confidence wavering a bit. "What's happened?"

As I explained the situation, I watched the play of emotions across their faces - concern, fear, determination, each one painting a vivid picture of the storm brewing within. The air grew thick with the weight of unspoken worries, almost tangible in its intensity.

As we prepared to leave, I caught Seraphine and Eldric exchanging a loaded glance, their eyes windows to a world of secrets. Whatever was between them, it would have to wait. For now, we had bigger fish to fry.

"I'm gonna go get Callie. She'll have my hiney if we leave her behind."

I dragged Callie to the war room with me, and we both filled packs with weapons. My Gale Blade hummed softly as I strapped it to my hip. Its invisible edge always made me feel like kind of a badass with it singing the promise of protection. Across the room, Cade was a blur of motion, as he packed, each item chosen with the care of a warrior preparing for battle.

"Starlight," he looked at me with concern. "Are you ready for this?"

I paused, meeting his intense gaze, feeling the weight of the moment. Goddess love him. We've battled the worst monsters from the Underworld and he still treats me like I'm fragile. He's such a sweetheart. I gave him a wink. "You betcha," I replied. "No use frettin' over spilled milk when the whole dang barn's on fire. Plus, it may just be an information gatherin' session at this point."

A ghost of a smile touched his lips, but his eyes remained serious. "You're right, my love. We'll just assess and get a handle on things."

Things felt a little tense when Eldric and Seraphine joined

us. Sheer grit replaced their earlier awkwardness. Seraphine's moonsteel blade glinted in the dim light, a reminder of the danger we could be walking into, its silver sheen almost luminescent.

"Time to go," I announced. My heart pounded like it wanted to escape my chest as we walked out into the courtyard.

I looked at our little team of warriors. "Cade and I are going to shadow mist over. Y'all use the portal and we should all arrive at about the same time."

Eldric, Seraphine, and Callie gathered around the shimmering portal. I was happy to have them with us. The light from the portal cast shadows across their features. The swirling energy pulsed with an otherworldly light.

"Ready?" Eldric's voice was low as he looked at Sera.

She nodded. "Ready."

Callie, her once-vibrant appearance now marred by Magda's cruelty, squared her shoulders, her resolve hardening. "Let's do this."

They stepped forward as one, the portal's energy enveloping them. I held my breath, watching as they disappeared into the swirling light. In a flash, they were gone.

I turned and caught the eyes of the man that had become so much more than my mate. He was my Iron Heart in every way.

"Are you ready, my love?"

He nodded, extending his hand. The surrounding shadows began to writhe and coalesce, forming a swirling vortex of inky blackness.

"Hold on baby," Cade said.

I gripped his hand tightly as the shadowy mist overcame us. The world blurred, reality melting away like as we drifted into the void. My skin tingled, every nerve ending alive with the sensation of magic, the feeling of being pulled through the very fabric of existence.

Moments later, we all materialized at the edge of a sun-drenched beach. The abrupt transition from shadow to light left me dizzy, my senses reeling. The salty breeze of Thalassa whipped around us, carrying the scent of brine and blooming flowers.

Seraphine looked around. "It's so beautiful here. You forget when you haven't been here in a while." Eldric reached around her waist and gave her a small squeeze.

I took in our surroundings, looking at the lush gardens and forests that bordered the coastline. The spires of the castle gleamed under the sun. But an undercurrent of panic shattered the usual tranquility of Thalassa.

People rushed about, their voices raised in worry and confusion, creating an atmosphere of distress. Guards marched purposefully through the streets, their armor glinting in the sunlight, a parade of urgency. Although the people went about their everyday business, there was still an underlying feeling that they were waiting for something big to happen.

"Oh yeah, somethin' is definitely wonky around here," I murmured. "We need to find Grandpapa."

He met us at the castle doors, his face etched with concern, as he quickly escorted us to the dungeon.

"She disappeared right out of her cell. Everything is exactly as the guards found it. It's my understanding they never enter her cell. Check out the dirt on the floor."

It was very clear there were two sets of footprints. One were tiny female bare feet, marking the ground like whispers of her presence. The other looked like soldier's boots, heavy and purposeful. Grandpapa pointed out the heel anomaly. Then he directed our gaze to the boots on the dead soldier in the shadows. A perfect match.

"I'm positive it was the morphiend that took her. Nerissa is in the Underworld."

CHAPTER 16

Throwing Caution to the Wind

Ignis

The polished mahogany table reflected the flickering candle lights of the chandelier in my council chamber. It would also reflect the simpering faces of the nobles who would sit here tonight whining about the part Aurelion must play in this war against the Underworld. Godsdamn fools. I turned to Jorvahn as we waited for them all to assemble for this meeting.

"Maybe I could just have them all executed."

His rumbling laughter filled the space. "If only that weer an option, Highness." He said his Aurelion brogue in full force as he wiped a tear from his sudden outburst. "No, friend. You'll handle them with the same diplomacy you've always used to convince them. If not, simply pull rank on them."

They'd finally all taken their seats, and it quickly began.

"Your Majesty," the grating voice of Lord Vanth plagued my ears, "this mixing of our troops with those of lesser kingdoms is simply intolerable. The Aurelion army has stood alone forever, ever a beacon of strength and pride."

I stifled a sharp retort, my face a wooden mask even though frustration boiled inside me. "Lord Vanth, the simple truth is we would have been absolutely decimated in the latest battle, had we not been blessed with the combined magical might of our allies. The challenges we face call for solidarity, not isolation."

Oh, the arrogant fool scoffed, as if it was an idea too preposterous.

These people cannot see beyond their prejudices. "We will not be seen as a kingdom of cowards. I won't have us hide behind our walls while other kingdoms bleed for this cause. Aurelion warriors are as brave as any in Eldoria. We *will* fight alongside the other kingdoms for the survival of this realm."

Lady Mira leveled me with a sidelong glare, her green eyes throwing daggers. Gods, her voice could cause Aurelion grapes to shrivel. "But your Majesty, how can we trust these, eh... foreigners? With their odd magic? It's so vastly different from ours. I fear they could turn on us at any moment."

The scent of hatred hung heavy in the air, cloying and suffocating. It was simply born of their prejudice. "Lady Mira, there has never been a single incident that could give you cause for this fear. I am well acquainted with every sovereign from each kingdom. I know them all to be honorable. Our troops have been stationed with theirs for weeks now, and not *one* has come to harm of any kind. I find your accusation to be unfounded and inflammatory."

The council members continued to protest. Each one ranted about the reasons it's wrong for us to take part in this war. I don't know how I could have made it more clear. They simply could not see further than their own noses.

As they rambled their incoherent arguments, my mind wandered unbidden to the only place it longed to be—with Callie. My absence from her had become a problem. Most of my thoughts were consumed with her. I realized I was content just to be near her. To be allowed to bask in the warmth of her smile. That beautiful smile so freely given. To hear her laughter when she was with the people she loved. It was a symphony. I wanted her to give me those smiles. I wanted her laughter. I wanted everything.

"Your Majesty?" It was Lady Mira's sharp tone that brought me back to the present. Her words slicing through my remembrance like an icy wind. "What say you to our concerns?"

I straightened and put my thoughts of Callie aside. I felt the familiar guilt that always came along with most of my thoughts about her. She deserved the world. Not a king who was being ruled by his council. "Your concerns have been noted, my lords and ladies. Nevertheless, I do not regret the choice. If we are to withstand the storm ahead, we must adapt."

The crown on my head felt so heavy, each stone a reminder of every responsibility associated with the wearing of it. Sometimes the weight pressed down unbearably, threatening to crush my skull.

"We will continue as we have and pray to the Goddess for a quick end to this was. This meeting is adjourned," I declared, rising from my seat. The scraping of chairs filled the room as the council members stood, bowing stiffly before filing out, their movements like the closing of a heavy book.

I looked at Jorvahn. "I have a feeling I have not heard the last of this."

"Oh, ye most assuredly have not." He huffed in exasperation as he trailed out behind the council.

Alone in the chamber, I allowed my mask to slip for just a moment. I traced the carvings that edged the table, each one a representation of Aurelion's proud history. I could almost feel the heat under my touch. My pride and issuing commands would not be enough to weather the coming storm.

I closed my eyes and pictured Callie's face once more. I ached for her until the pain in my chest was a physical reminder of all that I'd given up for the sake of my crown. And as much as I wanted to be by her side, I knew that every choice I made would affect more than the two of us.

I shook my head and took a deep breath. The path ahead had never been more uncertain, but I had to face it head on, not just for Aurelion, but for Callie and Eldoria. With determination, I headed out the door.

Jorvahn was waiting for me. His freckled face and open smile always grounded me. "I thought ye weer right behind me."

"I had to calm myself before stepping out the door."

"Don't let those ol' buzzards get to ye, Iggy," he murmured, his voice low enough that only I could hear him. I was glad to have someone in my life who was always honest with me. "You're doing the right thing, they're just too blind to see it."

Even a king needs to hear reassuring words sometimes, and I was glad to hear them.

"Thanks for that, Jor," I told him. "Sometimes I wonder if I'm fighting a losing battle."

My oldest friend and general looked at me as serious as he could, "Then we'll lose it together and go down in a blaze o' glory."

"Always the optimist." I laughed and hit him on the shoulder.

Lady Rovelle's voice cut through the air and ended our moment.

"Your Majesty," she said. She tried to sound sincere and failed miserably. "Surely you can't be serious about this... integration. It goes against everything Aurelion stands for."

I turned to her and noticed Lord Caldor was with her. "Oh, I can assure you, I am quite serious, Aunt," I replied. I hoped she caught my irritation. "Times are changing, and we must change with them if we hope to survive."

Lord Caldor stepped forward. He tried hard to look concerned. "We only have your best interests at heart, nephew. And... um... the best interests of the kingdom, of course."

That weasel was trying to intimidate me. I knew Jorvahn felt it too when I saw his hand slide over to the hilt of his sword.

"I appreciate your... concern." I said carefully, meeting Caldor's eyes. "But, as you know, I carry the power of generations of Aurelion kings. There is no one in this kingdom who can match my power. Are you aware of any who've grown the balls who'd like to try?"

My mother's brother sputtered around. "No Highness, of course not."

"I can assure you, Uncle, I am more than up to the task. I am the king of this kingdom and I rule as I see fit for what is best for my people, *all* of my people. Not just you nobles. You'd do well to remember that. The decision has been made. Aurelion will no longer stand alone."

As I spoke, I couldn't help but think of Callie, wondering if she could feel the turmoil within me through our bond. The thought of her gave me strength, even as it made my heart ache with longing.

Lady Rovelle's wasn't quite finished. "You play a dangerous game, Your Majesty. One that could cost you everything."

"Then it's a good thing I've never been one to shy away from danger. Or veiled threats in front of my most trusted general. Maybe it's *you* who plays a dangerous game, Aunt." I replied. "Now, if you'll excuse me, I have a kingdom to run."

As I turned to leave with Jorvahn at my side, I could feel their eyes boring holes through us. I don't know what game they thought they're playing, but it's one I intended to win.

I turned to Jorvahn to let him know what I was about to do.

"I'm going to get Callie."

Jorvahn responded, his smile wide. "You decided to throw caution to the wind and risk it all? Look at ye! My renegade king!"

I glanced at him, holding my own smile. "Did you expect anything less?"

He shook his head, his laughter a brief light in the dark. "No, I suppose not. You've always been an ornery bastard."

"It's part of my charm," I laughed. I felt like a burden had been lifted from my shoulders, knowing I was going to make things right with Callie. The shadow of my crown still weighed heavily on my mind, but I'd take things one step at a time.

"I know. Just... be careful, yeah? I don't think you're at the top of Cade Vesparra's favorite list."

I nodded, "Cade and I are friends. Things might be frosty between us at the moment, but he's fair and honorable. If he knows why I'm there and I come it with the right intensions, he'll understand and hopefully help me make things right."

As we reached the palace gates, I paused, looking out over the sprawling city. The late afternoon sun painted the sky in hues of orange and pink, turning the horizon into a canvas of fire. In just a bit, I'd be in Vesparra, surrounded by angry faces. But none of that mattered. Not when Callie was waiting.

"Keep things running smoothly while I'm gone and watch your back." I told Jorvahn, clasping his shoulder. I couldn't help but worry with the council in such an uproar.

He nodded. "Just come back in one piece, ye hear me?"

I grinned, feeling a surge of affection for my oldest friend, the bond of years shared in that single look. "I always do."

With one last look at my kingdom, I stepped through the gates. My heart raced with anticipation and fear. Callie, I thought, sending the feeling through our bond, a silent call across the distance as I walked toward the portal.

***

I felt the magic of ancient power in the air as I approached the training field of Vesparra. Dragonia circled overhead with scales that glimmered in the fading sunlight in an array of sparkling colors of greens, golds, and reds. Echos of roars across the sky resonated like an ancient song that sent a chill down my spine.

I took a deep breath and let my lungs fill with the scent of the magic filled earth. The power here felt intoxicating. Everything felt alive and charged with power. My eyes scanned the area. People were training with a variety of magical weapons. Friendships and laughter gave every acre a feeling of warmth, in spite of the cool temperatures. Even though fear lingered just under the surface, everyone trained with a feeling of hopefulness. I still hadn't found what I search for though. So I continued to scan the fields.

Then I saw her.

In the center of a large field stood Callie. Her soft layered blond hair whipped around her face. She moved through several complex movements—a dance of magical power. From this distance, I could still see the determination carved in the features of her face. Her eyes held extreme concentration. My heart pinched in my chest.

Gods, she was perfection. And I had no right to be here in her presence. I hadn't even realized it, but I'd been moving in her direction before I stopped just feet away from her.

Hesitantly, I took another step forward. The energy of the entire field suddenly shifted, as if the land somehow knew I was there. Callie's head snapped up, and her movements faltered. Her eyes were immediately drawn to mine. I had moved close enough to touch her. The air was charged with electricity between us. Words I wanted to say hovered on my tongue. Damn, I didn't want to fuck this up.

She finally spoke. breathlessly "Ignis?" I barely heard her over the pounding of my heart in my ears. "What are you doing here?"

I had to fight to keep from closing the rest of the distance between us.

I swallowed hard, trying to get any words out. "I... I needed to see you." I hated how vulnerable I sounded. "I need to talk to you."

A spark of anger flashed in her narrowed eyes. "*Now* you want to talk? After all the pain you caused?" She crossed her arms over her chest.

Her anger is what I deserve, and nothing less, but I still flinched at her harsh words. "I deserve every ounce of your anger for the horrible mistakes I've made." I said softly. "But,

Callie, please. Give me a chance to try to explain."

She worried her bottom lip between her teeth in hesitation. Gods, I wanted to cradle her in my arms, to erase every time I caused her pain, to take away her worry and shield her from the world. But she wouldn't want that. And fuck if that didn't sting.

She gave a heavy sigh, resolved to hear what I had to say. It wasn't an enthusiastic sigh, either. And I don't blame her.

"Fine," she said finally, her voice guarded. "You got five minutes. That's it."

I nodded. Five minutes was better than nothing.

I stepped closer, the scent of jasmine and sunshine filled my senses. Damn, I wanted to bathe in the very essence of her. All I wanted to do was claim her.

Right when I'd open my mouth to speak, the dragons about let loose a deafening roar, as if understanding the storm that was raging in my heart. I took a deep breath, trying to calm myself. I had to face the consequences of my actions.

Just as I'd begun to speak, I met Callie's gaze. Her eyes were a mirror to my soul. I felt the bond between us surge to life. It stole the breath from my lungs. She looked at me with a wariness that almost broke me. I was a testament to how I had wounded her. Her entire body had started to tremble.

"Callie, I—" my voice was hoarse with emotion.

"Don't," she whispered as she raised her hand to silence me. Her voice was raw with emotion. "I can't... do this right now."

I felt the weight of her hurt. Her torment was tangible. Even though we hadn't completed our bond, I felt her pain and confusion. It was a physical ache even in our separation. But I couldn't move. I stood rooted to where I was.

All at once, a blue of motion flashed before my eye. Olivia's dark hair whipped into view. Her purple eyes blazed with barely contained fury. "Back off, Ignis," she snarled, putting herself between Callie and me. "Haven't you hurt her enough?"

Her words were like a slap. What's worse—I deserved them.

Before I could respond, Cade was at Olivia's side. His presence was a port in Olivia's storm.

"Starlight, my love," he murmured, his hand gentle, but firm on her forearm a silent command in his touch. "Maybe we should give them some space?"

Olivia whirled on him. Her anger was still palpable. "Are you kiddin' me? After everything he's put her through?"

I was intrigued as I watched how Cade whispered words in Olivia's ear. Her face relaxed, but the glare she shot me, well, it scared me a little.

After Cade lead Olivia away, I turned back to Callie. I could still see the hurt on her face. I had to say something quickly. So I started with what I thought were the most important words I knew for all I had done.

"I'm sorry," I whispered, the words feeling completely inadequate. "For everything."

The next person coming in our Callie and Ignis parade was Eldric. I watched him approach, his curls tossed by the wind, his eyes fixed on me. The tension in the air rose as he drew near.

"King Ignis," Eldric's voice was low and respectful. "A moment if you please."

I gave him a small nod. "Of course."

We moved a short ways away from Callie. I still marveled at the changes in Eldric. The man who stood before me was no longer the arrogant, power-hungry man I'd known before. He'd undergone a profound change, that is certain.

"I'll be brief," he began. "Please understand. I acknowledge that you are a king of a powerful kingdom. But Callie is… my family. I need to make it known to you that I will not sit idly by if you hurt her again."

I'm not used to men threatening me. But in this case, he had every right.

"I never meant to—"

"Intentions mean little when weighed against actions,"

Eldric reminded me.

His words cut me to my core.

He continued. "I understand that as king you have a responsibility to your kingdom. It must be an incredible burden. But your relationship with Callie cannot be controlled by the whims of kingdom politics."

Eldric's words struck deep. And I agreed totally.

"Eldric, you are right. I told my council just today that they should expect Aurelion to be integrated. We will no longer be a kingdom in isolation. I knew that I could not possibly live in a world that didn't have Callie in it. If she will have me, that is. She means more to me than my crown and my kingdom. That is why I'm here. To try to make things right."

Eldric's expression changed ever so slightly. "Then prove it, Highness. Not with grand gestures or pretty words, but with consistent actions. Show her—show all of us—that you are worthy of her trust."

"I will," I vowed. "Whatever it takes. I'll prove myself to Callie, to you, to everyone."

Eldric looked at me as though I were a study in honesty. "See that you do." He said. "For all our sakes."

As he walked away, I thought about how thankful I was that Callie had such amazing people in her life.

I turned back to the training field and refocused myself on this moment. I allowed the crisp air and the magic of this place to fill me up. Then I made my way back to Callie.

Callie

"Again," I muttered to myself, clenching my fists at my sides, feeling the resolve harden within me. I closed my eyes, drawing deep from the well of magic within me. It surged through my veins, a torrent of raw energy that made my skin tingle, alive with potential.

When I opened my eyes, the world around me seemed

sharper, more vivid, as if I could see the very threads of magic weaving through the air. I raised my hands, palms outward, and felt the earth respond. A tremor ran through the ground, like the heartbeat of the world itself.

"That's it, Callie," Cade's voice called out, encouragement laced with a hint of pride, his voice a beacon in the storm of my concentration. "Now, this will seem really uncomfortable, but try to call forth any small, deceased creature whose bones are underground and near here."

I nodded, sweat beading on my brow as I concentrated, the task both daunting and exhilarating. I was a little afraid that I'd accidentally bring up some kind of zombie. My brow furrowed as I thought of small animals—rabbits, squirrels, and the like. Suddenly, I sensed movement to my right. The ground began to open up, and through the crack came a really scary-looking little skeletal creature. I think it was a squirrel.

"Oh crap! Ollie! Get over here!"

She was there at a moment's notice, her presence like a whirlwind.

"My stars and garters, girl. What did you wake up? That thing's as creepy as all get out!"

Ignis, Cade, and Eldric were all by my side in an instant as well. Shit, Ignis hadn't gotten the memo about what I was.

Eldric started giving instructions while Ignis watched on in wonder, his eyes wide with a mix of fascination and surprise.

"Ok, Callie. You can control the little monster with your mind. Just tell it to walk towards the wyverns."

All the Dragonia had gathered on the training grounds to watch and give me pointers, their massive forms a wall of scales and wings. I concentrated my thoughts toward the decaying bones of the squirrel, feeling the connection form like a thread between us.

"Hey you, little dead guy." I was startled when it suddenly looked at me, its empty sockets fixing on me with an unnatural alertness. *"Uh yeah you. Umm. Please walk toward the red wyvern*

near the tree line. That's the enormous creature with the wings and long tail." As soon as I gave the command, he began walking, his bones clattering softly against the earth.

I was astonished, my heart racing with the thrill of success.

"It's working!" I grabbed Olivia's arm, my excitement palpable.

She gave a small laugh, her eyes twinkling with amusement. "Well, look at you, our little zombie whisperer."

I looked at Eldric, seeking guidance. "Uhh, ok, so how do I get him back in the ground?"

He looked a bit thoughtful for a second, his brow furrowing in contemplation.

"Come on cousin, tell me you know how I send him back to peaceful deathly rest."

I looked at the zombie squirrel. *"Hey, squirrel. Stop."* He immediately stopped, his skeletal body still as death should be.

Vaelith lumbered in our direction, his presence like a moving mountain. He clearly was speaking to Ollie and Cade telepathically.

Olivia caught my gaze, her expression one of understanding. "Vaelith says you simply need to tell him to go back to the resting place of his death, not to stir again."

I looked at Vaelith and gave him a nod of understanding, appreciating his wisdom. Then I spoke to the zombie squirrel, my voice gentle yet firm.

"Thanks, little dead squirrel. Now I want you to return to the resting place of your death. You will remain in that place and not stir again."

Upon my command, he burrowed back into the ground until it collapsed on top of him; the earth reclaiming its own. I felt the magic settle, a wave of calmness washing over the area, but suddenly a wave of exhaustion washed over me and I nearly dropped to my knees, my legs trembling with the effort.

Ignis was there in a moment, his arms wrapping around me to keep me upright, his touch a grounding force. Nothing had ever felt so right in my life. His warmth was a stark contrast to the chill of the magic I had just wielded.

CHAPTER 17

The Sun King Takes a Mate

Callie

The eerie green glow faded from my hands as the last wisps of necromantic energy dissipated into the air, like smoke vanishing into the ether. My legs buckled beneath me, strength draining away like water through cupped fingers. But before I could hit the ground, powerful arms caught me, pulling me against a solid chest, a fortress in my moment of weakness.

I looked up into Ignis' face, expecting revulsion or fear, bracing for the judgment I'd seen in so many others' eyes. Instead, his eyes shone with awe, lips parted in wonder as he gazed down at me. My breath caught in my throat, a silent gasp.

"That was," he whispered, his voice husky, filled with a reverence that surprised me. "Incredible. I've never seen anything like it."

His fingers traced delicate patterns on my arm, sending shivers down my spine, each touch a whisper of acceptance. The warmth of his touch seemed to chase away the lingering chill of death magic, banishing the cold that clung to my soul.

"You're not...disgusted?" I asked hesitantly, searching his face for any sign of rejection, my heart pounding with the fear of his answer.

Ignis shook his head, a crooked smile playing at the corners of his mouth, his expression one of genuine amazement.

"Disgusted? Hardly. Though I have to say, your powers are to die for."

A startled laugh bubbled up from my chest before I could stop it, the sound breaking the tension. The pun was terrible, but the playful glint in his eyes melted away the knot of anxiety in my stomach. For the first time since discovering my abilities, I felt a flicker of pride rather than shame, a small flame of self-acceptance igniting within me.

"That was awful," I said, unable to keep the grin off my face, feeling the weight of my fears lighten.

Ignis' answering chuckle rumbled through his chest, a comforting vibration against my ear. "Perhaps. But it made you smile."

His hand came up to cup my cheek, thumb brushing away a stray tear I hadn't realized had fallen, his touch as gentle as the first light of dawn. The tender gesture made my heart skip a beat, a moment of pure connection. In that moment, basking in the warmth of his acceptance, I allowed myself to hope that maybe—just maybe—I wasn't the monster I'd feared I'd become.

Olivia and Cade had been standing in the distance as if to give Ignis and me a few moments alone, but there was no way she could let this moment pass. She broke away from Cade at a little jog so she could gush over my accomplishment, enveloping me in an enormous hug.

"Callie Girl! I'm so proud of you! That was re-gosh-darn-diculous! You hauled that little dude right up out of the ground. You are a wonder."

"Ollie, you're always my number one fan."

Then, in typical Ollie style, she awkwardly noticed she had interrupted mine and Ignis' moment.

"Aww, dang, sorry y'all. I'll just go over there with Cade and the Dragonia. Resume. Um, love you, bye."

I cracked up laughing. For her to be the Chosen One, she sure was a doofus.

Even though the tender moment had passed, we easily fell right back into the same familiar feeling with each other. The sun was setting, casting long shadows across the field, and I was hopeful he'd stay a while longer.

"Would you like to head up to the castle?"

"I was hoping you might join me for dinner. In your quarters, if that's agreeable."

He looked a little sheepish, his usual confidence giving way to a more vulnerable expression.

My breath hitched. "I'd like that."

Ignis' eyes met mine, and I saw a flash of something deep and primal there, a look that promised more than just dinner. "Good," he murmured. "I think we have much to discuss."

As we made our way to my chambers, the lighthearted conversation turned serious, the air between us thickening with anticipation and unspoken words.

I hated we had to have this conversation, but I had to explain the depths of my powers—what I was. As much as it would break me, he had to know everything so he could decide if he would even want to be with me.

"Listen, Ignis, I feel like it's only fair that I share with you the origins of my magic. You think you want to be with me..." I cast my eyes towards the ground as my voice faltered, then slowly looked back up at his beautiful face. "But you may change your mind once you know everything."

The movement of his throat told me he was prepared for bad news, his Adam's apple bobbing with a nervous swallow.

"Let's not do this in the hall, huh?"

I nodded and opened the door, thankful that my room was as large as a small apartment, complete with a living and dining area. He took my hand, guiding me to the velvet tufted sofa that sat against the wall, its plush surface welcoming us.

"Callie, please don't be afraid to talk to me."

There, I gave him the details of my life and the bizarre journey it had taken for me to get to this point. The hardest part was telling him I was a creature of the Underworld—a monster. The words felt like shards of glass in my mouth, each one cutting deeper into my resolve.

Ignis' face hardened, and I thought this was it. Here is the point at which he was going to tell me he could never accept, much less mate with someone who is clearly innately evil. I looked down at our joined hands as a tear escaped my eye, tracing a path down my cheek.

"Callie." His voice was rough with frustration, pulling me back from the brink of despair. "Look at me. I never, ever, want to hear you refer to yourself as a monster again. You are anything but a monster. I have only observed you to be a beautiful, caring, unselfish woman who loves her friends and wants to protect them and this realm at all costs. These are not the characteristics of monsters, my love. This information does nothing to diminish my feelings for you. If you had evil intent, you'd have stayed in the Underworld. And I know without doubting, the Goddess would not have made us mates unless you were good, and pure, and true."

I gazed into Ignis' eyes, basking in the warmth of his acceptance, feeling the weight of my fears lift like a fog in the morning sun. But as I studied his face, I noticed a flicker of something else behind his tender expression—a shadow of worry that creased his brow, a hint that all was not entirely settled.

Something troubled Ignis, I could tell. I hoped this wasn't the other shoe dropping situation.

"Tell me what the problem is. I know something is worrying you." I told him.

I touched his face gently. "Tell me."

His shoulder sagged just a little. "My council," he sighed. "They are a group of close-minded purist. I had a face off with them today and told them on no uncertain terms that the days of Aurelion being closed off from the rest of the realm were over. Needless to say, I got some push back. Especially from two in particular. The two who made the most noise happen to be an aunt and uncle. They may give us some trouble. I wanted to be honest with you."

I had heard that Aurelion was an isolationist kingdom. I knew that's why he had rejected our bond in the first place. But even though my stomach was tangled up in knots, I would be strong for him.

He continued, "I will not let them hurt you, Callie. You're under my protection now."

Even as his words warmed me, I was still unsure.

I gave him a small smile. "Your people are going to have a difficult time accepting a necromancer being mated to their glorious Sun King. I don't see how they could think that is a good thing."

He cupped my face. "They will accept you, Callie. You're so loveable."

I bit my lip with worry. "But what if they don't?"

His eyes had fire in them. "Then they will answer to me."

"Ignis, you can't risk your crown for me." I told him quietly.

He held my gaze. "I'd risk so much more than that for you, Callie."

My mind was a storm of hope and worry. But the look on Ignis' face told me how much he cared, and that meant everything to me.

"I need to talk to Cade," he said, his voice sounding every bit the king that he was. "He'll understand the complexities of our situation."

"What will you tell him?" I asked, curious about how this conversation would go.

Ignis' eyes were filled with love when he spoke. "The truth. That I've found my mate and I intend to move mountains to keep her safe."

I nodded. "Well, if there is anyone is this realm I trust to give me sound advice, it's Cade Vesparra. While you're gone, I'll shower and order us that dinner we spoke about. When you come back, we can eat, and you can tell me the grand advice he and probably Ollie had to give you. Forgive her if she has anything mean to say. She's a bit over-protective of me." I gave him a wide grin, imagining the grief Olivia was likely to give him, her protective nature like a dragon guarding its treasure.

I watched Ignis leave, my heart pounding with a mix of fear and longing. Each step he took away from me felt like a piece of my soul was being pulled. The room felt colder without his presence, and I wrapped my arms around myself, trying to hold on to the warmth of his touch, the ghost of his embrace.

I ordered dinner to be brought to my room while I showered and changed into something more comfortable than battle leathers; the water washing away the remnants of the day's strain. Ignis' timing was perfect, as he'd arrived just as my lady's maid had left. A delicious meal for two had been prepared and set on my small dining table, the aroma filling the room with promises of comfort.

He pulled my chair out for me, an act of chivalry that felt as foreign as it was comforting. I'd never been treated with such care and courtesy, each gesture from him like a brushstroke painting me into a life I'd never dared to dream of. He sat in the chair next to me at the round table, our closeness a silent promise of intimacy.

"Ignis," I began, my voice barely above a whisper, filled with trepidation, my heart in my throat. "Did Cade offer valuable insights?"

He took my hand in his, his touch grounding me. "He did. I've known him for many years, so his advice was not a surprise. Basically, he reminded me I am the sovereign of Aurelion. And while I take my council's advice, I ultimately am the law. I know what is best for my kingdom, and isolation is not it. We can no longer live in a vacuum. I will make a proclamation that will free the kingdom and my people, which will, in turn, free me."

I must have had a worried look, my brow furrowed with

concern.

"Won't that be dangerous?"

He gave a humorless laugh, his eyes darkening with the shadow of responsibility. "No more than the dangers we're facing every day, my dear. Now let us eat this lovely meal before it gets cold. No more talk of danger or war this night." He took a bite, the act simple yet symbolic of his desire to escape into this moment with me. "I'd rather bask in the glow of your radiance. You look beautiful tonight, Callie."

I barely swallowed the bite I'd just taken, my emotions making it hard to eat. I took a drink of the wine before me; the liquid soothing my throat.

"You are the handsomest man I've ever seen, Ignis. Truly, you should grace the covers of mortal magazines." I smiled, the compliment slipping out with an ease that surprised me.

He stood and took my hand, raising me from my chair with a gentle pull.

"I can't fight this anymore, Callie," he said, his voice rough with emotion, breaking through the facade of calm. "I know it sounds absurd, because it's only been a few weeks. But, I love you. Despite every obstacle, I love you with every fiber of my being."

My heart soared and shattered simultaneously, overwhelmed by the sincerity in his eyes and the weight of his words, like a dam breaking. Tears spilled down my cheeks as I toyed with his hand in mine, feeling the warmth of his skin.

I closed my eyes, letting his words wash over me, a warmth that seeped into my very soul. When I opened them again, I saw my own love and longing reflected in his gaze, a mirror of our shared heart.

"I love you too," I whispered, my voice thick with emotion, each word a testament to the truth of my feelings. "More than I ever thought possible."

Ignis gathered me in his arms, dinner forgotten. I felt something shift inside of me. It seemed like a new beginning.

Danger and uncertainty might surround us, but here and now, I knew I was home.

Nestled in his embrace, I breathed in his delicious scent of burning oak. I reminded me of warmth and safety.

Ignis I murmured, as I pulled back just enough to meet his eyes. "How... how does this work? The mate bond, I mean. With our different magical backgrounds, I don't know what to expect."

He tilted his head a bit, as he thought a moment. "Truthfully, I'm not entirely sure," he admitted. "For fire and sun magic wielders like me, we don't have the traditional mate bite that other kingdoms use."

I don't know why that disappointed me a little. I guess maybe I wanted a tangible sign.

"But that doesn't mean our bond is any less real," he continued. His voice was low and intense. "I can feel it, Callie. It's like... a warmth in my chest, pulling me towards you. I think our bond might manifest differently, perhaps through our magic intertwining. The Goddess chose you for me. We are Fated Mates. Our bond will lock into place like other fated pairs. You are a part of me."

I became acutely aware of the thrum of energy between us the more he spoke. It felt like two flames, moving closer and closer together. "I feel it too." I whispered, placing my hand over my heart. "I don't know exactly what it *should* feel like. But I know I've never felt anything close to what *this* feels like."

His amber eyes lit with an internal fire. "Tell me," he urged gently.

I took a shaky breath. "No one has ever made me feel the way you do, Ignis. It's like... like I've been living in a world of shadows, and you're the first ray of sunlight to break through."

My vulnerability made me feel awkward about admitting this, but I continued. "When I'm with you, I feel... whole. Seen. Like all the broken pieces of me are finally coming together. Pieces I didn't even realize were broken."

His arms tightened around me. "My beautiful, brave Callie." He pressed his forehead to mine, our breaths mingling. "You've awakened something in me I never dared to wish for."

I felt the last of my walls crumbling as I stood there wrapped in his arms. I lost myself in his eyes. His thumb traced the curve of my jaw in a tender, reverent caress.

"Callie," he breathed. "I swear to you, I will fight for us. For our love. The prejudices of my kingdom, the expectations of my council—none of it matters. You are my future." His expression grew serious again. "You are my mate, Callie. My equal. My queen, if you'll have me."

The words were filled with promise and felt like a binding spell. I felt a heat that started low in my belly and radiated outward. Ignis must have felt it too, because his pupils dilated, darkening his eyes to pools of night.

"Yes," I whispered, barely audible. "Yes, I'll have you."

Ignis growled and shivers crawled down my spine. Then he claimed my mouth with an all-consuming kiss. This differed from our previous embraces. It was hungrier, more urgent. I tasted smoke and sunlight on his tongue, felt the barely contained inferno of his power just beneath the surface of his skin. This defined all the ways he was the fire king.

My own magic responded, humming beneath my skin, intertwining with his flames, our powers coming together. The air was scented with wood smoke and night-blooming flowers, creating an intoxicating blend of our essences. As his hands roamed my body, leaving trails of delicious heat in their wake, I felt our energies begin to merge and meld, rising higher between us.

His eyes widened in wonder, a new light in them. "I feel it too. Gods, Callie, you're magnificent."

I had my hands in his thick dark auburn hair, needing something to ground myself as he walked me backwards towards my large king-sized bed, each step deliberate, each moment stretching into eternity.

"Are you sure you want this, Callie? There's no going back."

I opened my eyes and I swear I could see flames dancing in the large dark pupils of his eyes, a fire that promised more than warmth.

"I've never been more certain of anything in my life."

He took two steps back and started unbuttoning his shirt, his movements deliberate and mesmerizing. My god, his body was perfection, each muscle sculpted as if by the hands of the Goddess herself. I stood, so hypnotized, watching his beautiful, deft fingers at work, each button revealing more of the treasure beneath. I was almost startled when he spoke.

"Callie. I need for you to strip for me, baby. I need to see all of you."

I was wearing a loose pair of drawstring pants and a button shirt. My instinct was to rip them off as quickly as I could, but I forced myself to go slowly. I wanted to look sexy for him. He was already completely naked before me, and stars, what a sight. He was stroking his cock, standing fully erect. I surely had died and gone to heaven.

Slowly and seductively, I managed to undress without falling. I had one goal in mind: to have the length of him in my mouth as quickly as humanly, or "revenantly" possible. I quickly was on my knees in front of him, both of my hands on the beautiful length of him. He hissed as I leaned up and spread small kisses across the substantial tip.

"Callie, Goddess, fuck!"

His fingers were gripping my short hair as tightly as the length allowed as I licked up and down his length, each stroke of my tongue drawing out sounds from him that were a concerto to my ears, notes of pleasure that resonated deep within me.

When I got back to the tip of him, I allowed a good amount of saliva to run down the length of him, so my hands could move around the base of the base as I took his length deep into my mouth. My tongue massaged, and my lips, which had covered my teeth, gently tightened as I moved up and down, each motion a dance of desire.

"Baby, you're magnificent. So. Fucking. Good. Yes, Like that."

Then I moved one of my hands from his erection of velvet steel and tickled his balls, the sensation making his knees almost buckle. I looked up at him and grinned, the power of my effect on him a thrill that surged through me.

"You're a naughty fucking girl. But I don't mind when it feels so good. I'm going to come down your gorgeous throat in a moment if you don't stop, Solmia."

This only made me lick and suck harder, driven by the primal urge to unravel him. I swirled my tongue around the tip and ran my hands up and down his shaft, then one last time I took him as far down my throat as I could, swallowing him down. And that did it.

His hips juddered forward, and he released with a shout, the most masculine sounds I'd ever heard echoing in the room. Ropes of his come shot down my throat, tasting of fire and smoke, a flavor uniquely his. I drank every drop, savoring it like the finest wine. I pulled back slightly so I could be sure I licked and cleaned every trace of him off his glorious length. The bonus in doing so, he was already getting hard again, his body responding to my touch with eager readiness.

He reached down and hauled me into his arms, lifting me as if I weighed nothing, and swiftly deposited me onto the bed. His mouth was on mine in seconds, his tongue exploring every inch of my mouth, licking, tasting, devouring, the kiss a wild, claiming dance.

Ignis

I have experienced nothing, never come as hard as I just had, when my cock was inside my Solmia's mouth. I could feel the blood heat in my veins, a fire that only she could stoke. This woman was perfect for me. I wanted to build an altar and sacrifice to the Goddess for her.

But it was now my turn to take my fill of her. Callie's lust-filled eyes were fixed on me as I held her wrists over her head with one of my hands, her pulse quickening under my touch. I rubbed my nose down her face, taking in her fragrance of sunshine and smoke, a scent that was uniquely hers.

"You are exquisite, my Solmia."

I rained kisses down her neck, releasing her hands, so I now had two of my own to explore her perfect body. Reaching her round and heavy breasts, I brought them together, alternating between each dusky nipple, licking and sucking until they stood erect, begging for my touch. She arched her back, pressing into me for more. I simultaneously massaged them with my calloused hands as I gently assaulted them with my tongue and teeth. I nipped and kissed them first one then the other, loving the taste and feel of them against my tongue, each sensation a delight.

"Ignis, that feels so good."

I squeezed them both in my hands, marveling at their perfection. Everything about her was amazing.

Continuing my worship of her body, I licked further down to the prize that rested between her creamy thighs. I reached down with a hand and ran my fingers through her wetness, the slickness a testament to her desire.

"By the Goddess, you are dripping, aren't you, my love?"

I continued to tease her opening, each stroke deliberate, drawing out her pleasure.

"Yes! That's because I want you! And need you!"

Her body was writhing back and forth across the satin sheets, the fabric whispering with her movements.

"But what if I wanted to put my mouth on you—to taste you? You smell divine."

She held my eyes, her gaze intense, and leaned up on her elbows. Her eyes were glowing, a light from within her soul.

"But I need you inside me, now!"

I laughed, the sound rich with affection. "Alright, my little necromancer. As you wish."

I crawled up the length of her beautiful body, my gaze never leaving hers except for the moment when I watched her take my cock in her small hand and line it up with her gorgeous pussy. Then I eased myself in, the sensation overwhelming.

"My Solmia, I'm going in slowly at first. Tell me if it's fine and I'll go faster."

When I was halfway in, I felt the bond start to hum, a vibration deep within us both. Her eyes widened, reflecting the wonder of this connection.

"Ignis, do you feel that?"

"Yes, my love. It's the bond."

Her hips started to move, an invitation to deepen our union.

"I need more. Mmm. Please."

That's all it took. In one thrust, I was fully seated. She threw her head back and moaned the most beautiful moan I'd ever heard, a sound that seemed to echo through my very soul.

"Ignis! More!" She yelled as she moved her hips, our bodies finding a rhythm as old as time.

And then we began the ancient dance. The more I thrust, the more her hips rose to meet mine, our movements a symphony of passion.

I could not hold back my hips or my voice, each thrust accompanied by a declaration.

"Gods, Callie! You're beautiful!"

I reached down and started to rub her clit, her eyes glowing as she got closer to her release, the light within her a beacon of her pleasure.

"Sweetheart, I'm close. I want you to come with me."

"Ignis! I love you."

"My Callie, I love you."

As we both hit our climaxes simultaneously, I felt like my body was on fire, a physical change happening inside of me, our connection forging something new. I continued to move inside of her, slowing my thrusts until I was entirely spent and her breathing slowed.

I fell beside her, holding her to my chest, our breaths ragged. The air around us was still charged with residual magic, tiny sparks of fire and wisps of shadow dancing in the dim light of the room, a testament to our union.

"I never knew it could be like this," she murmured, breaking the comfortable silence.

My fingers combed through her short hair, the strands soft under my touch. "Like what, Solmia?"

She smiled at the Aurelion endearment, her eyes softening. "So... complete. Like I've found a piece of myself I didn't even know was missing."

I tilted her chin up, my eyes meeting hers, seeing the universe in her gaze. "That's exactly what it is. We're two halves of a whole, Callie. No matter what challenges we face, we'll face them together."

CHAPTER 18

Betrayal Inside the Gates

Callie

The heat of Ignis' body lingered on my skin. His warmth seeped into my skin, my bones, my very being. I nestled in closer to him, not wanting to break the spell by having to face the day. I took a peek at his beautiful chest under my fingers as I felt the slow and steady rise and fall of his breathing. It felt so perfect lying next to him. Our bodies fit perfectly together, two pieces of the same puzzle.

"Callie," he murmured, his voice rough with sleep. "Are you alright?"

I nodded against his shoulder. "More than alright." The words were inadequate to relay the depth of what I was feeling. Our connection—this mate bond was something no one could have prepared me for. It was an experience unlike any other. It went beyond the physical, although the physical was earth shattering. And saying there was an emotional connection sells it far short. It was as if our souls had merged, creating a "oneness" that hadn't existed before.

I felt Ignis' hand in my hair, his gentle touch a reminder of his nearness. "We should prepare to leave soon," he said tenderly. "But I find myself reluctant to leave this bed."

A small bloom of happiness filled my chest. "Then don't," I purred, my voice barely more than a breath. "Not yet."

A few more moments passed, but reality couldn't be held

at bay forever. With a sigh, I disentangled myself from Ignis' embrace and sat up. I ran a hand through the uneven layers of my hair, trying to fully awaken.

"You're right." I said, sounding more chipper than I felt. "We need to head out soon."

As we dressed, I caught Ignis watching me, his gaze intense, filled with a mixture of pride and desire. "What is it?" I asked, smoothing down the fabric of the gown I chose. "I thought wearing a gown would be most appropriate to meet your people."

He crossed the room to me, his movements graceful yet purposeful, taking my hands, his touch grounding me. *"Our* people. And you look stunning." He said as he gently kissed me, the kiss a seal of his approval. "I want you to know," he said solemnly, his voice deepening with conviction, "that whatever challenges we face in Aurelion, we face them together. It's you and me, Callie. You are not alone."

My heart bloomed with emotion. "I know," I replied, our fingers intertwining. "And neither are you."

Olivia and Cade were waiting for us in the castle's main hall. Saying goodbye to my best friend wasn't easy. We hadn't had to say very many goodbyes to each other over the years, and this goodbye seemed like a big one.

"Be careful," Olivia said as she pulled me into a tight hug. "Aurelion isn't like Vesparra. The people there are... well," she glanced at Ignis. "Sorry Ignis. The people there are dicks. Well... that's not fair, cuz I haven't met all the people. Mostly just him." She motioned with her thumb back at Ignis. "Sorry again, Ignis." Cade just shook his head. "So, anyways, just be safe and just be yourself. There is no way those people won't adore you." She looked away with tears in her eyes. "And... dadgummit, I just got you back, Cal. But I'm so proud for you. I'm happy you found your forever mate and I love more than you could know."

I nodded, trying not to cry. "I'll be careful, I promise."

Cade stepped forward, "Take care of each other," he told us, and patted Ignis on the back. Then he turned to me and gave me a brotherly kiss on the forehead. "Remember, you're stronger than you know, Callie."

I blinked back tears, touched by his words, feeling strength from his belief in me. "Thank you, Cade."

Seraphine and Eldric hurriedly made their way down the stairs, their steps echoing through the hall. Eldric looked was a man on a mission, his face locked on us.

He stepped between Ignis and me, his presence sure.

"Pardon me, Ignis." Ignis gave him a look of understanding as Eldric took my hands in his, his touch warm and familiar.

We stood there silent for a moment. His face conveyed a world of emotions—regret, pain, and yes, even love.

I swallowed hard and uttered, "I know, Eldric."

He leaned in toward my ear and quietly said, "Thank you, Callie."

He also lightly kissed my forehead, a gesture full of respect and affection, then turned and walked back to Sera. She gave me a sweet smile and a tiny wave, her expression filled with encouragement.

As Ignis and I moved towards the portal that would take us to Aurelion, I felt a mix of anticipation and trepidation.

The portal's shimmering surface rippled as we stepped through.

When we exited the portal, we were greeted with a world of rolling hills and lush vineyards bathed in the morning light's glow. The sky was so vast and blue that I could almost swear I was back in Texas.

"Wow, it looks so different from what I remember." I uttered, as I tried to take in every detail.

Ignis' hand found mine. "Welcome home, Solmia," he responded, his Aurelion brogue more pronounced in the emotion of the moment.

"Why do you call me that? Solmia?"

He looked down at me, love in his eyes. "It's old Aurelion for 'My Sun.' That's what you are to me."

"It's beautiful."

He squeezed my hand, and crooned, "Not nearly as beautiful as you."

As we approached the city gates, I was floored by the architecture. I felt like we'd entered El Dorado. The buildings shone in colors of rose-gold stone with tall spires that seemed to sparkle in the sunlight.

A palace guard shattered our moment of peace by bringing Ignis urgent news.

"Your Majesty! It's General Jorvahn. He's gravely ill!"

Oh no! I remembered him. He was with Ignis the night I went to the portal. He seemed very kind..

"What happened?" Ignis demanded.

The soldier shook his head, looking helpless. "We're not sure, Your Majesty. He was found in his chambers, unconscious and barely breathing."

Ignis turned to me, worry in his eyes. "Callie, I—"

"Go!" I gave him a small push. "I'm right behind you."

We rushed through the city streets, hurrying to the castle.

Jorvahn's quarters were in the west wing of the castle. They were as I would have imagined—masculine, with sparse decor and dark furnishings. The room smelled of medicinal herbs and fear, the cloying mixture made it hard to breathe.

Jorvahn lay pale and still in his bed and I felt Ignis' worry for his friend pouring through our bond. I looked to Ignis for permission to move everyone back from the bed. He nodded.

"Please, everyone step back," I requested. I was glad when the worried attendants followed my directions.

I took a breath then closed my eyes and reached out with my revenant powers. A familiar chill ran up my spine as I connected to the ethereal plane. I stretched my senses out and hovered my hands over Jorvahn's body.

"What do you see?" Ignis whispered. His voice was filled with concern.

My brow furrowed as I concentrated on what I was feeling. "I feel his life force weakening. There's a... darkness. It's spreading through his body, like ink in water. It's definitely foreign to his system." My fingers hovered over Jorvahn's chest, tracing the invisible trail of poison. "It's not natural, but was deliberately made to look natural."

As I looked deeper, a flash of metal caught my eye in the spiritual realm. "There, I see it." My eyes flew open. "In his side. His left side. There will be a wound."

Ignis gently lifted his shirt and there on his side right at his waistline, was an irritated puncture mark. The skin around it was inflamed.

Ignis looked furious. "This is a knife wound," he said through gritted teeth.

I nodded at the implication. "A poisoned one. But this poison was created with dark magic. Only someone very powerful could have created a poison like this. Ignis, do you know of such a person?"

His eyes met mine, realization suddenly dawning. "Aunt Rovelle." He hissed. "She is on my council, and is adamantly opposed to my opening our borders. She all but threatened me before I went to you."

"I'm so sorry, Ignis. But there is a magical signature... it's unmistakable."

He looked at me once more. "And you're certain?"

I swallowed hard, wishing it wasn't true. "Yes. The poison, the magic... it is definitely dark magic. If her abilities include wielding that magic, then I'm afraid it points to her. Ignis, this wasn't just an attack on Jorvahn. It's an attack on you, on the throne itself. It must be some kind of warning. She's showing that unless you do as she says, she can touch those you love the most."

He stood abruptly, pacing the room. "How could she? After

everything"

I reached out, catching his hand. "We'll figure this out," I promised, even as doubt gnawed at me, my voice a tether in his storm. "But first, we need to help Jorvahn. I think I can slow the poison, buy us some time."

Ignis nodded, his eyes softening. "What do you need?"

"Just... stay close," I murmured, drawing strength from his presence.

***

The throne room was filled with people. When we entered, Aunt Rovelle was chatting with several nobles, as though she had not a care in the world. Her amber eyes, so like Ignis', widened in phony shock as we stepped in. It seemed like the entire room could sense the betrayal.

"Nephew," Rovelle purred, her voice dripping honey. "And... an outsider? When did you two arrive back in the kingdom?"

I bristled at her dismissive tone, her words clearly an insult. I was glad for Ignis' hand on my lower back. It somehow calmed me. I'd hate it if my magic went rogue and I sucked the life out of that bitch. Ignis gave my back a slight squeeze. I hoped he couldn't read my thoughts.

"Enough games, Aunt," Ignis growled. "We know what you've done to Jorvahn."

Rovelle's mask slipped for just a moment. A flicker of fear ran across her face before she recovered. "I'm sure I don't know what you mean."

"The poison that currently threatens his life," I interjected, my voice rang strong, "It bears your magical signature."

A chorus of murmurs arose across the room.

She turned to me; her gaze accusing. "And we're to take the word of an outsider? And..." She paused, looking at me as if I was no better than gum stuck to the bottom of her shoe. "If the rumors I'm hearing are true...a revenant? I thought they only existed in the Underworld! What have you unleashed on our kingdom, nephew? They are creatures supposedly more dead than alive, with powers we have no knowledge of! Maybe she hurt Jorvahn!"

I felt the weight of her words, the implied threat, like a stone around my neck. My fists clenched at my sides, my powers still new, still frightening, even to me. But I refused to back down, standing firm in my truth.

"I know exactly what I felt," I kept my voice calm and measured. "Dark magic. Betrayal."

Rovelle's lip curled, her expression one of scorn. "Ignis, surely you can't believe this... this outsider, this *monster*, over your own blood? She's bewitched you, turned you against your family, your kingdom!"

I felt a ripple of unease through the room, like a current of doubt passing through the crowd. The guards shifted, exchanging uncertain glances, the tide of support wavering. Ignis tensed beside me, and I felt his confidence and love flow to me through the bond, a steadfast stream in this sea of mistrust.

"I. Said. Enough. Rovelle! You're the one who's turned against us," Ignis said, his voice low and dangerous, each word a sentence in itself. "Against everything Aurelion stands for."

Rovelle's eyes flashed, a spark of defiance in them. "Everything I've done has been for Aurelion! To keep us strong, to protect us from those who would weaken us." Her gaze fell on me, filled with contempt, as if I were a blight upon her world. "Like her."

I felt a surge of anger, of hurt, like a wave crashing against me. But beneath it, a flicker of understanding. Rovelle truly believed she was protecting her kingdom. It didn't excuse her actions, but it made them... slightly more understandable.

"I'm not here to weaken anyone," I said softly, my voice as calm as I could make it. "I'm here because fate brought me to Ignis. If you're upset at my being here, you'll need to take it up with the Goddess. And the last time I checked, she does not make mistakes. My being here will only strengthen us."

Rovelle scoffed, her laughter sharp and bitter. "Pretty words from a pretty mouth. But what do you truly know of our ways, our struggles? You're nothing but a liability, a distraction when we need strength most."

I felt the weight of her words, saw the doubt creeping into the eyes of those around us. For a moment, I wondered if she was right—if I was truly meant to be here, in this world, so different from my own.

But then I felt Ignis' hand tighten on my back, his fierce protectiveness flooding our bond. And I knew, with a certainty that this went beyond logic, that this was exactly where I belonged, where my heart was meant to be.

I took a deep breath, drawing on a courage I didn't know I possessed, feeling it rise within me. "You're right, Rovelle. I'm not from here. I don't know all your ways." The room fell silent, every eye on me, the atmosphere tense with anticipation. "But I know right from wrong. And I know what it means to fight for those you love."

My hand trembled as I reached into my pocket, pulling out the vial of poison that was discovered earlier, its contents dark and deadly. The same poison that had nearly killed Jorvahn. "This was found in your chambers, Rovelle. The same poison used on Jorvahn."

Gasps echoed through the room. Rovelle's face paled, her composure cracking. "That's... that's impossible. I've been framed!"

I shook my head, my voice growing stronger. "My revenant abilities don't lie. I can sense the traces of your touch on this vial, feel the intent behind it." I turned to the gathered crowd, my heart pounding like a drum in my chest. "I may be an outsider, but I care deeply for Aurelion and its people. I would never betray you—or Ignis. Plus, your king is no fool. When I sensed the poison was in your wing of the castle, we called several guards to search your room."

Rovelle's face paled.

"Ignis, would you like to call your guards to testify?"

His smug smile said it all, a silent victory. "Absolutely, my dear. Javen, Mishal, please step forth."

His guards stepped out of the assembly of guards that were lined up around the throne room.

"Please tell this congregation of people what happened when you searched Lady Rovelle's room. Javen, you can speak for the two of you."

Javen cleared his throat, his voice steady as he recounted the events.

"We accompanied Your Majesty and Lady Callie to Lady Rovelle's wing and entered her chamber. We searched, and after a few moments, I came across a small stone box. Upon opening, I discovered a small vial of what appeared to be poison. I gave it to Lady Callie, and she confirmed my suspicion."

A murmur rippled through the crowd. I saw confusion in their eyes, but also a glimmer of something else—anger, for sure. Respect, perhaps. Hopefully, the beginnings of acceptance.

Ignis stepped forward, his presence commanding the room, his stature that of a true king. "Thank you, gentlemen. Now, please guard my aunt. As you can see, Lady Callie speaks the truth. She not only diagnosed the problem with Jorvahn, but she also slowed the poison enough to ensure he'll recover. Discovering the origin of the poison was pivotal in assuring the safety of our kingdom. Lady Callie loves Aurelion. And I love her. As your king, I ask that you embrace her as one of our own."

To my astonishment, a cheer went up from the crowd. Faces that had been wary now looked at me with warmth, even admiration. Rovelle was led away, her protests fading as the truth of her betrayal sank in.

Ignis addressed the crowd once more, his voice carrying the weight of his authority and the promise of change.

"Please! Everyone! As your king, let it be known that I am preparing a proclamation that will officially open Aurelion's borders. We will no longer be a kingdom in isolation. Our armies will continue to fight the war against the Underworld alongside all other kingdoms of Eldoria. Once we are victorious, and we *shall* be victorious, all citizens are free to travel to any kingdom of their choosing. You will be free to love who you choose, regardless of the magical order they belong to. Consider today Aurelion liberation day!" A thunderous cheer arose around the room. It was clear the people had longed for this day.

I made my way to Ignis and whispered in his ear. "I don't know much about kings and kingdoms, but it seemed clear you've accomplished something great today."

He squeezed my hand, a rare smile gracing his lovely features. "I think you may be right."

CHAPTER 19

We Fight Together

Olivia

As much as I loved seeing Callie's dreams of happiness come true, I sure hated to see her go. I was just getting used to having her back in my life, feeling the warmth of her presence like sunlight after a long winter.

I spoke as the door closed behind them, the sound echoing like the sealing of a chapter. "She looked so in love and beautiful." My voice was barely above a whisper. It felt weird to be so happy and so sad all at the same time.

Cade's expression softened. "As do you, Olivia." His thumb traced my cheekbone, a tender gesture at odds with the gravity in his voice. "But I'm afraid our reprieve is at an end. We must leave for the Crystal Citadel in a short while."

Reality crashed back down, and I squared my shoulders, ready to fight another day. "Right. Time to face the music and figure out how to keep Magda from turning our world into her personal playground."

"Your way with words never fails to astound me," Cade said dryly.

I smirked, "What can I say? It's part of my charm."

Cade looked at me like he wanted to eat me whole and boy I gotta say, I was tempted to run right back up to our chambers and let him make a meal out of me. But the weight of my Goddess's Star mark was a constant reminder of the battles to come.

"As much as I'd love to ravish you, Highness. We should prepare." I stepped back. A little physical distance would help keep me on task. "We're not gonna want to keep the other leaders waiting."

Cade nodded. He needed to meet with Darius this morning to check on how the kingdom was running. We've spent so much time at the Citadel that the running of Vesparra had been an afterthought. Thank the Goddess that Darius is so capable of keeping the day to day on track.

I had made my way to the armory to add more weapons to our packs. After about twenty minutes, I sat for just a moment. I was so tired these days. It seemed while in battle I was fine. My energy never waned until battle's end. But then I crashed and crashed hard. Getting up most days was increasingly more difficult. I think the stress of this war was catching up with me. I heard Cade's footsteps, so I jumped up. I didn't want to worry him.

"Starlight? Are you ok?" Dang it. I wasn't fast enough.

"Right as rain." I answered him brightly. "I had just packed several bags with weapons and thought I'd catch my breath until you were ready to go. We just never get a minute to stop. I thought I'd take some time while I had it." I gave him a sweet kiss and grabbed my gale sword and a smaller bag of gear.

"That's a good idea, sweetheart. I know how hard you have pushed yourself, especially when closing those rifts. I want you resting every chance you get. On our way to the courtyard, I'll send a soldier in here to grab all this gear so they can portal it to the Citadel."

Cade and I gathered in the open field, with Eldric and Seraphine by our side. I was thrilled to have her as part of our fighting team. She had been hesitant when I'd first asked her to don battle gear and join us, but my gut told me she'd be a fierce warrior, and she had not let me down. Her mind for strategy translated into her fighting style. The girl could hold her own in battle. I'd be happy to have her at my back any day, her presence a silent promise of protection.

Of course, the most amazing transformation I'd ever witnessed was what had become of Eldric. You know what was said about the love of a good woman? But it was definitely more than that. A man who searched for redemption was an awe-inspiring sight. His eyes now held a light that spoke of second chances. Accepting forgiveness seemed to be the biggest hurdle for him. But amazingly, my capacity to forgive him somehow came easily to me. Chalk it up to the miraculous, I guess.

Cade had called the Dragonia to meet us, their massive forms a testament to the raw power at our command. We'd decided flying to the Citadel was the best option, the urgency in our bones echoing the call to action. My "Spidey" senses were on overload, the air thick with anticipation, and we needed all our fighting forces ready to go.

We mounted up as usual. Our dragons were primed and ready to go. Vaelith greeted me with enthusiasm today. *"Little One, you look bright and ready to fly this early afternoon."*

I gave him a sideways look. That was unusual. "Umm. "Well, hello there, Big Guy. Thank you. And you're looking rather dapper yourself... I guess.? But, yes, I'm ready to fly today. Let's get this party started!"

Cade hopped on Eryndor. His emerald scales glinted under the bright sunlight. Finally Eldric and Sera hauled themselves up on Zarvyn's back and rode tandem. His dark scales always cut a dynamic glow in against the blue sky.

Vaelith and I rode in the back.. Thyra and Ariaxom flanked us. This was a new formation. The wyverns flanked Eryndor and Zarvyn and Skorn had our "six" so they say. I'm sure we were a sight to anyone on the ground.

Cade looked over his shoulder to see me. I gave him a little wave. He seemed satisfied to see me cradled between all the Dragonia.

"Not sure what's up, but they've got me covered!" I spoke to him through our bond, the wind a wild companion around us.

Cade's deep voice came back to me. *"Indeed, they do. Thank you all for keeping our Starlight so safe."*

I heard rumbles across the sky, but Vaelith's voice who spoke. *"It is our joy to keep the little one safe and ready for whatever comes her way.."*

How I loved these creatures.

***

The sight of the Citadel always took my breath away. Its crystalline spires pierced the clouds like spears of light. The gravity of our situation weighed heavily, with its cloak of responsibility, but the joining of our allies bolstered my resolve. We had a war to fight, and by gosh, we were gonna fight it. And we were gonna win.

We landed in a flurry of wings and scales, the ground trembling beneath the might of our arrival. Dismounting onto the sunny field nearby, the earth seemed to welcome us back with open arms. The other leaders had already gathered— Amaya and Kaelen, their presence as wild and untamed as their kingdom; Miranda and Thorne, their love a visible force; Farin, his wisdom etched into the lines of his face; and Ignis and Callie were just approaching, their silhouettes against the horizon a picture of new beginnings.

The startled look on the others' faces was priceless. The change in Ignis was stunning. Gone was the perpetual scowl, replaced by a softness never seen before, his features like a landscape after the first rain of spring. His fingers were intertwined with Callie's, and the way he looked at her—it was like she'd hung the moon and stars, his gaze a silent hymn of devotion.

"Olivia!" Callie called out, her green eyes sparkling with life I feared I'd never see again. "We made it!"

I embraced her, feeling the strength returning to her frame, like iron reforged. "How'd it go?"

A worried look crossed her face, a shadow fleeting across a sunny day. "Girl, it was dicey at first. I'll give the deets later. But it turned out fine. And here we are!" A radiant smile crossed her face, that made my heart sing.

"That's so good, Callie Girl. So good." I gave her one last hug, feeling the warmth of her spirit.

Ignis actually smiled—a genuine, warm expression that transformed his entire face. It was like a weight had been lifted from his shoulders.

As the group converged, I felt the shift in energy. An urgency had fallen. The joy of reuniting quickly gave way to the seriousness of our purpose. We made our way into the war room; the walls echoing with the weight of our shared destiny. Cade's commanding presence drew everyone's attention as he stepped forward, his form a pillar of strength.

"My friends," he began, his voice resonating with authority, cutting through the silence like a beacon, "we face the same threat as before."

I surveyed the surrounding faces — determination, fear, hope all mingled together. My fingers unconsciously traced the outline of the Goddess' Star mark over my heart, its warmth a reminder of our sacred duty.

Cade's voice cut through the tension, commanding and resolute, each word a hammer strike on an anvil. "We must address the most pressing matter at hand," he said, his piercing gaze sweeping across the room. "Nerissa's disappearance."

A chill ran down my spine at the mention of my grandmother's name, the icy dread settling like frost on my heart. The weight of her absence pressed against my chest, a mixture of worry and suspicion churning in my gut..

Miranda, her black curls gleaming in the crystal-refracted light, leaned forward, her eyes sharp with focus. "What do we know for certain?"

Cades clenched his jaw slightly. "Precious little. She basically vanished without a trace. But there is every sign that the mimic took her. There were only two sets of footprints in her cell. Small bare feet and a guard's boot prints. Boot prints that matched the deceased guard outside her cell."

That sent the room into a whirlwind of theories. But the mimic theory is the only one that had legs. I glanced over at Farin. His face looked impassive.

Amaya interrupted the sea of voices. "We must consider the worst. She said, her voice worried. If Nerissa was taken by the mimic, we have to assume she's in the Underworld and Magda plans on using her power to open a breach between realms."

I gotta give my baby sister props. We were all thinkin' that. She just came right out and said it. The idea of that made my stomach lurch—like seriously made it a little nauseous.

Ignis slammed his hand on the table, making us all jump. "We can't just sit here speculating," he growled. "We need a plan of action."

I watched as Callie placed a gentle hand on his arm, her touch visibly calming him. The change in Ignis was still jarring, but in that moment, I was grateful for it.

"Ignis is right." I found myself saying. "If it was the mimic, it's likely that Nerissa is in the Underworld and Magda is trying to harness her power so she can use it to breach Eldoria. So that means we better get our ducks in a row and be dang sure we're ready to meet her on the field of battle."

Cade's eyes met mine. "Indeed," he agreed, his voice a steady. "We must fortify our defenses, strengthen our magical barriers, and—"

A sudden tremor shook the Citadel, cutting off Cade's words.

"By the Goddess," Miranda gasped, her eyes widened.

Cade's voice called out. "We must be prepared for battle. We have no idea what creatures we'll face this time."

Miranda stood tall, a queen in every way. "Ilyndor's troops are ready. Our magic combined with the magic of the other kingdoms in Eldoria along with Olivia's and Callie's magic, we'll be ready. And with the help of the Dragonia—we are well-equipped!"

Ignis barked out, "The fires of Aurelion are ready to fight beside all others in the war."

Callie stood next to Ignis, the look of pride on her face.

"And Thalassa's warriors will crush the enemy," Farin added, his voice steady.

Suddenly, a familiar presence touched my mind. Vaelith's voice echoed in my thoughts, urgent and clear. *"Little One, south of the Citadel is under attack near Therionis. Dark creatures pour through a rift, unlike anything we've seen before."*

I locked eyes with Cade. He had heard Vaelith as well. "Farin," he shouted. "Activate the crystal network. Now! We need troops moving—south, near Therionis!"

The air crackled with energy as Farin's crystals pulsed, sending out waves of iridescent light.

"Vaelith says that the breach is only a few miles south of here, and it's big. Creatures we've never seen before." I said, urgency lacing my words. "Every second we waste is another monster crossin' over."

Cade nodded. "Miranda, can your mages open temporary portals? We need to move troops fast."

"Consider it done. My air elementals can create vortexes to transport our warriors directly to the breach site."

Immediately, she used her crystal to contact her mages.

Everyone headed outside. It was time to meet the enemy head on, once more.

"Ready to kick some creepy creatures, booties?" I murmured, running my hand along his muscular neck.

Vaelith snorted, a plume of smoke curling from his nostrils.

As I mounted, I caught sight of Cade doing the same. His jet-black hair whipped in the wind. Our eyes met, a wordless understanding passing between us, a silent vow in the chaos.

"We ride together," he said, his voice low and intense. *"No*

matter what happens, we face it as one."

I nodded, my throat suddenly tight. *"Together,"* I echoed.

From the corner of my eye, I spotted movement. Eldric and Seraphine were hurrying towards us.

"Were you leaving without us?" Seraphine asked.

I gave her a smile. "Hey girl, you snooze you lose. Let's get it and go!"

Eldric nodded, his usual arrogance replaced by a quiet resolve. "We've got this. That Goddess Star you wear evens the score, Highness."

"Ready?" I asked, my gaze lingering on Eldric.

He met my eyes, unflinching, his gaze like steel. "All a part of my redemption."

Cade's voice cut through the moment. "Time's wasting. Mount up, both of you. We fly now."

As Eldric and Seraphine scrambled onto their mounts, I felt a strange mix of emotions churning inside me. And a burning question: are we enough?

"Goddess, guide us," I whispered, a prayer into the wind, and then we soared towards an uncertain fate.

The lush forests of Therionis sprawled beneath us. As we approached, the acrid scent of smoke assaulted my nostrils, a stark contrast to the usual earthy aroma of the shifter kingdom.

"There!" Cade's voice carried over the wind, his arm extended pointed at a writhing mass of darkness at the forest's edge, where the very fabric of the world was being torn apart.

My stomach clenched as I took in the scene below. A seething tide of nightmarish creatures that seemed to devour the very light around them. Against this darkness stood the proud shifters of Therionis, many already transformed into their animal forms.

I spotted Kaelen at the forefront, his massive dire wolf leading the charge. His howl pierced the air, a rallying cry that echoed through the trees, rallying his troops even as he tore through the enemy ranks with a terrifying efficiency, his jaws snapping with deadly precision.

Aurelion warriors emerged with flames dancing along their blades. Thalassan troops materialized in shimmering cascades of water, their movements fluid as the sea. Ilyndor's forces rode gusts of wind, their speed and grace a testament to the air they commanded. Therionis shifters bounded through the battlefield in their animal forms, their fur bristling with anticipation, each step a declaration of their resolve.

"It's like watchin' the most badass parade in history," I muttered, as I watched the coordinated chaos of our troops deploying.

"We need to close that portal," I told Cade through our bond, the din of battle roaring around us. *"If we don't stem the flow—"*

"I know," he cut me off, his expression grim. *"But look."*

Following his gaze, I saw another massive beast, its power radiating in palpable waves, the air around it shimmering with dark energy.

We dove into the action, dragon-fire blazing, burning a path through the enemy ranks. Each burst of flame was a message showing we meant business. The sound of the battle engulfed us—the clash of steel rang everywhere around us. Snarls of shifters mixed with the unholy shrieks of Magda's monsters. The sounds were things of nightmares.

As I raised my hands, magic crackled at my fingertips —lightning ready to strike. I whispered a silent prayer to Vesperia. "Please keep us strong," I pleaded, my voice lost in the wind. "For all our sakes."

And then I hurled myself into the heart of the battle, towards the creature who threatened hundreds of troops. I was gonna do my dead level best to keep them alive.

CHAPTER 20

The High Price of Battle

Cade

I gripped Eryndor's reins tightly, feeling the dragon's powerful muscles ripple beneath me. The acrid stench of smoke and otherworldly blood filled my nostrils. Below, an endless sea of writhing shadows poured from the pulsing rift —monstrous creatures with razor-sharp claws and gnashing teeth, their monstrous shrieks pierced the air.

The sounds of steel hitting bone could be heard across the valley. Fire and ice exploded from the dragons' mouths, melting hideous creatures that had no business breathing the same air that we did. The scents burned my nostrils as we flew and the sight of the carnage turned my stomach.

As we flew, I desperately scanned the battlefield, looking for Olivia. I couldn't help but fear for her safety amidst the extreme bloodbath unfolding before me. *"Hold steady, friend,"* I murmured to Eryndor. My hand stroked his emerald scales as we flew lower. I knew she was more capable than any of us in battle, but I still wanted my eyes on her. Especially since this battle was like none we'd fought before. It was a living hell.

This rift sent an endless stream of the deadliest creatures we've ever encountered. The more we killed, the more there were to kill. *"We cannot let them win."* I made a solemn vow. *"No matter the cost, we must protect this realm—and Starlight."* The dragon roared in agreement as we flew and continued to search for weak points in the enemy's ranks.

"Get ready, Eryndor," I told him. I drew my rune sword. Its obsidian blade gleamed. *"It's time we remind these abominations why they should fear the children of Vesperia."* With a great roar that echoed across the battlefield, we dove into the heart of the battle. I extended my hand as tendrils of darkness erupted from my fingertips, writhing like dark serpents. They searched for the enemy. The inky strands coiled around a group of winged creatures and ensnared them.

"Now Eryndor!" I shouted, and guided the dragon into a steep dive as I swung my rune sword in a high arc, shadows trailing behind. With precision, I severed wings and claws, ending creatures left and right.

"We need to push them back from the rift," I told Eryndor, my mind already racing with strategy. *"If we can bottleneck their forces,"*

A flash of brilliant light caught my eye. Through the chaos, Vaelith appeared, Olivia glorious upon his back. Her dark hair whipped behind her, a dark sail. My queen of war.

"Goddess, but she is magnificent," I breathed, as a surge of love and pride filled my soul.

As I watched, Olivia raised her arms, her eyes glowed with purple light as she gathered energy, then she unleashed a torrent of lightning rays at a mass of unholy creatures that had crawled out of the rift. Vaelith then opened his massive jaws and unleashed a devastating deluge of fire and ice on another group of writhing masses of teeth and claws.

There were screams and shrieks across the battlefield from Olivia's and Vaelith's destruction. My mate was a force to be reckoned with.

"Let's go Eryndor," I said. *"We can't let them have all the glory."*

Eryndor and I banked towards the ground, searching for our allies amid the chaos. A thunderous roar cut through the sounds of battle. I spotted a massive dark form tearing through the enemy lines with a savagery that gave me pause.

Kaelen. His Dire Wolf's teeth flashed in the dim light as he ripped into a grotesque rift creature. In his wolf form, Kaelen operated on instinct alone. He was a precision killing machine, his bone crushing jaws, the perfect tools for the job.

A blur of white fur fought beside him. His Luna, my sister-in-law. Amaya. Her Arctic Wolf was smaller than Kaelen's wolf, but what she lacked in size, she made up for in agility. Together, they were a force to be reckoned with.

I noticed a group of several creatures coming toward Kaelen and Maya's position. While there were other troops nearby, they would be outnumbered. They needed to retreat to another position. "Look out!" I shouted, though I knew she couldn't hear me over the din of battle.

Just then, Amaya shifted back into her human form. As a hybrid, Amaya carries both elemental magic along with being able to shift. She put her hands on the ground and worked her strong elemental magic. The ground rumbled and suddenly erupted. A wall of stone and soil shot upward, creating a barrier between our forces and the advancing horde, a natural fortification against the tide of darkness. The creatures slammed into the barrier she had created.

But she wasn't finished yet. Using her wind magic, she created a whirlwind large enough to tear through enemy ranks. Flying debris maimed and scattered the enemy and also distracted the creatures so our soldiers could move on them without detection. She bought time for our troops.

"Good strategy, Maya," I murmured, impressed by her quick thinking.

"Cade!" Kaelen's deep voice carried to me as he shifted back to his human form, his eyes fierce with battle-rage. "We need support on the eastern flank!"

I nodded, guiding Eryndor higher towards their position. As we descended, I caught sight of Miranda and Thorne coordinating their efforts near the northern ridge. The unlikely pair moved in perfect sync, their contrasting magics weaving together in a deadly dance.

Miranda's elemental control over water was unsurpassed. She summoned river water to create a massive tidal wave. Working with Thorne's shadow magic, his hands thrust forward and stopped the wave mid-crash, making it solid. Creatures ran into the wave trying to get to our troops, which gave Miranda the opportunity to freeze the water solid, turning to it to a shadowy ice wall capturing countless rift monsters in its icy grip, their forms dark masses encased in crystal.

As Eryndor touched down, the ground trembling beneath his weight, I leapt from his back, my rune sword at the ready, the blade whispering promises of shadow. "Nice work with the barrier," I called to Amaya, who tossed me a quick, tired smile amidst the chaos. She had quickly adjusted to the fact that nakedness was a part of being a shifter. All thoughts of modesty were easily forgotten in the heat of battle.

"It won't hold forever," she panted, her eyes wild with a mix of fear and determination, her breath coming in ragged gasps. "There's just so many of them, Cade. How can we possibly—"

A deafening screech cut her off as a winged monstrosity dive-bombed our position. I raised my sword, channeling shadow magic through the blade, the darkness coiling around it like a serpent. "We hold the line," I growled, meeting Kaelen's steely gaze, as he nodded, a tower of strength. "No matter the cost."

I felt the air grow heavy, charged with power as a blinding light erupted to my left. Squinting against the glare, I saw Ignis materialize.

He turned, his piercing gaze finding mine. "Where is she, Cade?" he demanded, his voice tight. "Where's Callie?"

Before I could answer, a wave of plasma erupted from his outstretched hands, incinerating a group of rift creatures that had been advancing on our position. The air crackled with heat, and I felt sweat beading on my forehead.

"I… I don't know," I admitted, guilt twisting in my gut. "But we'll find her, I swear it."

Ignis' jaw clenched, a muscle twitching beneath his skin. "I can feel her," he murmured, almost to himself. "She's close, and she's in danger."

As if in response to his words, an eerie chill swept across the battlefield, the air turning cold as the grave. The hairs on the back of my neck stood on end.

"By the goddess," I breathed. "Callie."

From the fissures in the ground, skeletal hands clawed their way to the surface, the earth giving birth to the dead. Corpses in various states of decay rose, their hollow eyes glowing with an unnatural, baleful light. At the center of this macabre army stood Callie, her ragged blonde hair floating around her gaunt face as if suspended in water, an ethereal ghost amidst the living.

"Callie, no," Ignis whispered, his voice breaking.

I watched, my breath caught in my throat, as Callie raised her arms, her movements graceful yet unsettling, a conductor of death. The dead surged forward, tearing into the rift creatures with ruthless efficiency, their movements jerky and unnatural. But with each command, I saw Callie's frame shudder, the toll of her power clear in the pallor of her skin, the trembling of her hands, each gesture a sign of her struggle.

"We have to get to her," I said, gripping Ignis' arm, feeling the heat of his fire through his skin. "Before she loses control."

Ignis nodded, his eyes never leaving Callie's distant figure, his gaze a lifeline he was trying to cast. Flames dancing along his skin, ready to ignite. "I've got this Cade. Go!"

I ran for Eryndor, my boots pounding the earth with each desperate step. We took to the sky, the dragon's wings beating with the urgency. Bodies were scattered across the scorched earth. Faces I recognized, friends I'd shared drinks with on more than one occasion, now lay lifeless and still, their silence a loud lament in the air. My hope was that they still breathed, that some spark of life lingered.

"Cade," Olivia's voice crackled through our mental link. *"We're losing too many."*

I swallowed hard, fighting back the wave of grief threatening to overwhelm me. *"I know, Starlight. But we must keep fighting."*

A piercing scream tore through the air and I whipped my head around to see a young Thalassan warrior fall, her water whip dissolving as life left her body. My mind immediately went back to watching her train. Her love for this realm drove her to duty. She wanted desperately to fight for the Goddess. And now her life was gone.

"Damn it all," I growled. "Eryndor, dive!"

As we plummeted towards the fight, the rift pulsed with malevolent energy. More creatures poured forth—each one more horrific than the last.

I leapt from Eryndor's back, landing in the middle of a group of beleaguered Vesparra warriors. My rune sword glowed as I cut through the nearest monster, its acidic blood sizzling against the enchanted metal.

"My King," a bloodied soldier rasped. I could see his relief at my presence. But some fear remained. "We can't... there's too many."

I put my hand on his shoulder, pouring strength into my words. "We stand together, or we fall alone. Remember who you are—children of Vesperia herself. Now fight!"

I felt a small amount of confidence return to my ranks. With my sword raised high, I channeled all the power I had into the shadows I controlled. At once, inky darkness spread across the ground and engulfed a countless number of creatures that had gathered and were moving toward me and my troops. With a shout, I willed the shadow to consume them all at once.

The sound of crushing bone and squelching flesh mixed with shrieks and wails of the creatures came as they all fell. But it wasn't enough as more creature rose from the rift dark and hungry.

"*Olivia*," I called out, desperation taking hold.

Her reply came tinged with exhaustion. "*I'm trying, Cade. But it's… it's like nothing I've ever faced before.*"

I gritted my teeth and pushed back another wave of monsters. My muscles screamed in protest. "*Whatever it takes, Starlight. The fate of Eldoria hangs in the balance.*"

As I fought, I couldn't shake the gnawing fear that this might be our last stand. And if it were, I'd damn sure go down fighting.

Olivia

I soared above the chaos as Vaelith's mighty wings cut through the sky. The combined magic of the five kingdoms surged through me. My hands shook as I clung to the saddle. I felt my magic weakening ever so slightly.

"Just a little more," I whispered to myself. The rift still loomed, a gaping wound in reality that continually spewed its nightmares into our world.

I reached out with my magic and felt energy weaving together, creating the fiery wave and wind I'd pelt them with next. It was amazing that I still had such powerful magic at my fingertips. I'd expended so much already. And yet these freakin' monsters just kept coming. Frustrated doesn't begin to explain how I felt. I needed to close that rift, but I didn't know how I could. Trying to keep my people alive and close the rift was just too much.

"*Olivia!*" Cade's voice echoed in my mind, laced with desperation. "*We can't hold them much longer!*"

I gritted my teeth and pushed harder. "*I know, I know. I'm tryin' to close that rift. It's just… it's fightin' back.*"

I patted Vaelith's neck. "*Let's try gettin' a little closer Big Guy.*" He slowly flew us in a pattern several feet above the rift.

As if it sensed my efforts, the rift lashed out with tendrils of its own. I gasped as a tendril grazed my cheek, leaving a trail of ice-cold fire in its wake.

"Dadgummit," I hissed.. "This ain't exactly like closin' a barn door."

I closed my eyes and pulled from the well of power within me. The scars on my back burned, a reminder of all I'd endured to be here. I was Olivia Ilyndor Vesparra, The Chosen One of the Goddess herself. I would not fail.

With everything in me, I poured my essence into sealing the rift. Suddenly, a chill ran down my spine, a wrongness. Someone was missing.

"*Cade!*" I called out, fear in my voice. I knew whose presence was no longer here. "*Where's Grandpapa?*"

The silence that followed was deafening. I scanned the battlefield below with frantic eyes, searching for the familiar sight of his dark skin, his curly hair. But there was nothing.

"No," I whispered, my heart shattering into a thousand pieces. "No, no, no."

Grief surged within me. I felt the control of my magic falter for a moment. Grandpapa, with his gentle smile and melodic voice. The man who'd shown me kindness when I was lost in this strange world. The first person to ever to say the words, "I love you." Gone.

A sob tore from my throat, raw and primal. My magic soared within me, my rage a driving force.

"*Olivia,*" Cade's voice was thick with concern. "*I'm so sorry. But we can't*"

"*I know,*" I cut him off, my reply concrete, despite the tears that streamed down my face. A new fire kindled in my chest. "*We finish this. For Grandpapa. For everyone we've lost.*"

With a scream that reverberated across the battlefield, I unleashed the full brunt of my power. The magic of the five kingdoms erupted in a blinding display and slammed into the rift with a force that rocked the creatures trying to escape.

Energy coursed through me like liquid fire in my veins. I

gritted my teeth as the rift pulsed, trying to resist my assault, but I refused to relent. Not now, not with so much at stake.

"Come on, you son of a biscuit eater," I snarled. I poured every ounce of my Texas stubbornness into my efforts.

And then, with a sound that cracked like lightning, the rift collapsed upon itself. A blinding flash of light forced me to squeeze my eyes shut. When I opened them, the sky was clear, and the rift was gone.

I slumped in Vaelith's saddle, suddenly boneless with exhaustion. "We did it, Big Guy," I whispered, patting the dragon's scales. He rumbled in response, his own weariness evident in the sluggish beat of his wings.

As we descended, the full weight of what we'd just endured struck me. The battlefield below was dotted with bodies, most assessing their damage. Others as still as... well, you know. The awful stench of smoke and blood made me want to throw up.

"Vaelith, what if I was gonna be sick? I wouldn't be able to clear your scales."

I felt his chest rumble with a laugh. *"Oh, Little One, if you needed to empty your stomach's contents and it got on my scales, it would not be the worst thing I've ever endured. It would be for a good cause."*

Talking to him helped the momentary nausea to pass, thankfully. I slumped forward on the saddle and held on until he gently landed.

"Olivia!" Cade's voice pierced through the fog of my exhaustion. He sprinted towards us.

I slid off Vaelith. My legs gave way as soon as they touched the ground. Cade caught me. His powerful arms wrapped me up in a tight embrace. I buried my face into his chest. I could stay right here forever.

"You okay, love?" he murmured, giving me a light kiss on my forehead.

I huffed out a laugh that teetered on the edge of hysteria. "Define okay," I said, pulling back to look into his concerned eyes. "We're alive. That's somethin', I guess."

Around us, survivors slowly congregated. I spotted Miranda, her water-blade still faintly glowing as she aided a wounded Thalassan soldier. Kaelen limped up, and Callie stood nearby. Her face haunted as she took in the devastation.

"How many?" I asked and braced for the grim tally.

Cade's jaw clenched. "Too many," he replied softly. "We're still counting."

The burden of our losses pressed down on me, threatening to overwhelm. I closed my eyes, seeking solace in Cade's embrace. "What now?" I asked quietly.

He was silent for a moment as his hand drew soothing circles on my back. "Now," he said at last, "we honor our dead. We tend our wounded. And we prepare for whatever comes next."

I nodded, inhaling a shaky breath. The atmosphere was heavy with sorrow, the mood somber as the reality settled in. Yet, beneath the grief, I sensed something else stirring—a spark of determination, a flicker of hope. We had survived this battle. Together, we would face whatever followed.

I opened my eyes and looked around at all of us. "Alright, folks," I said, my voice gained strength with every word. "Let's get to work."

"Cade," I murmured, a chill racing down my spine. "This rift… it was bigger than anything we've seen before. What if —"

"Magda," he finished. His eyes met mine. "You're thinking she's getting closer to breaching the barrier between Eldoria and the Underworld?"

I nodded, swallowing hard. "We know it will take a butt ton of power. But it looks like now she's got it."

Ignis approached. "I fear you're right," he said, his gaze swept across the devastated landscape. "This battle was merely a prelude."

"A test of our defenses," Cade growled.

"She's comin' for Eldoria. That's always been her plan. She won't rest until she occupies both worlds." Just thinking about that haint made my blood boil.

Cade pulled me close. "Then we won't rest either," he said. "We'll find a way to stop her."

I looked up at him. "Well, we're gonna have to do better than this. We barely got outa this fight alive. We gotta come up with some kind of strategy to beat her. How we gonna do that?"

Ignis stepped closer. I'll be danged if he didn't look more determined than ever.

"We adapt. We learn. And we stand together against the darkness." Wow, Callie sure did a number on that guy!

I nodded, straightening my shoulders. Just the thought of Magda made me shiver. How could someone so beautiful be so cruel and filled with hatred?

I guess it didn't matter why. What mattered was how we were gonna stop her. My guess was we'd find out soon. She had Nerissa and now poor Grandpapa. She'd be breachin' that barrier soon. We just had to be ready for her when she did.

CHAPTER 21

Keeping up the Fight

Olivia

After our quick meet up, we moved out to survey the aftermath of the horrific battle we'd just fought. The scents of blood and burned flesh still hovered in the air, but thank the Goddess it was dispersing in the wind somewhat. Healers from each kingdom moved in and out of the wounded, tending to wounds of every shape and size. I saw a Thalassan healer use crystal droplets of water to wash over a gash on a Vesparran soldier's arm. After a short incantation the droplets coalesced and pulled the wound closed. Amazing. An Aurelion healer worked similar magic with glowing palms.

The Goddess blessed healers offered kindness and comfort for every patient they tended as well. Thankfully, most of the wounded had smaller injuries, but there were some whose injuries were more serious. We had them moved to the healers' tents.

"It could have been much worse," Miranda murmured, joining me. Her dark eyes were haunted—dark curls matted with dirt and blood.

I nodded, my throat tight with emotion. "Fourteen souls lost are still fourteen too many."

The weight of those deaths bore down on me. Yet, as I looked out over the field where so many of our allies lay, injured but alive, a flicker of hope sparked within me.

Callie approached, her eyes bloodshot, her expression dazed. "We should say our farewells to the fallen," she said softly.

I followed as all our friends, the sovereigns of each kingdom, gathered around the shrouded forms of our lost subjects. Kaelen stood tall beside his Luna, both still dressed in robes from a day spent shifting between human and wolf. Thorne had a protective arm around Miranda near Ilyndor's fallen, her face stoic, her eyes shimmering with unshed tears. Callie clung to Ignis, still grappling with the part she had played today. Ignis held her close, as if he could shield her from the haunting memories. Sera and Eldric were the last to arrive, leaning on each other, covered in blood and dirt like the rest of us. They kept their distance, allowing the monarchs space to pay their respects.

Cade appeared at my side, his strong hand finding mine. I leaned into him, drawing strength from his presence.

"They died with honor," Cade intoned, his deep voice resonating across the hushed gathering. "Their sacrifices will not be forgotten."

One by one, the leaders stepped forward to pay their respects. I watched as even the most hardened warriors struggled under the weight of their grief. Each loss felt so acutely.

"It's as horrible a thing as I've ever seen," I murmured to Cade.

Cade's thumb traced soothing circles on my palm. "We'll make sure their names are not forgotten."

As each queen bent to place a kiss on each shroud, I felt a swell of determination. We had weathered this storm together. Whatever challenges lay ahead, we would face them united.

I closed my eyes. My bones ached, and muscles were sore. The power of the Goddess Vesperia still hummed inside me.

"You okay, my sweet?" Cade asked.

I forced a smile. "Just peachy. Nothin' a week-long nap won't fix."

But even as the words left my lips, I felt my knees buckle. Cade's arm swiftly wrapped around my waist, supporting me.

"I can feel you trembling, Starlight," he murmured. "You gave so much of yourself today."

I leaned into him, breathing in his familiar scent. "Had to," I whispered. "Chosen One and all"

A presence brushed against my mind, *"Olivia,"* the voice of Vaelith came through. *"We sense your distress."*

I closed my eyes, allowing the telepathic link to strengthen. *"I'm alright,"* I projected, though I knew they'd sense the lie.

"You have done more than enough," Skorn chimed in. *"Let us lend you our strength."*

I felt their concern wash over me.

"They care for you very much." Cade said softly, his lips brushing my temple.

I leaned into him. "They do. I'm a lucky girl."

"We are here, Olivia," Thyra's voice gentled through my mind. *"Always."*

Tears pricked at my eyes, and I blinked them back furiously. Now wasn't the time for weakness. *"I know,"* I whispered, the words meant for both Cade and the Dragonia. *"And it means so much to me."*

The sun was rising as we said our goodbyes to everyone. We'd agreed to meet in a couple of days in Vesparra to discuss everything that happened today. The unspoken grief of losing Grandpapa was chief among those things. But for today, we all clearly needed a day of rest. And tomorrow every kingdom needed time to bury their dead.

I felt Cade's arms tighten around me. "Let's go home, Starlight," he murmured.

I nodded. Exhaustion almost took me under as Cade's shadows wrapped around us.

In just minutes, we were standing in the quiet opulence of our chambers. Francois had thankfully kept the fireplace fire going and had the torches lit around the room. I loved the comfort and peace I immediately felt in this space.

Cade's hands on my shoulders gently led me further into the room. "Easy now, sweetheart, I've got you," he told me tenderly.

My legs felt like jelly, each step an effort, as he led me into the washroom. I caught a glimpse of myself in the ornate mirror on the wall and barely recognized the woman looking back at me.

"Cade," I whispered, "today was... it was really hard."

He turned me to face him. "Starlight, it was difficult for everyone. Please don't carry more than you should," he said his thumb brushing across my cheek. "Let me take care of you."

I leaned into his touch and closed my eyes. His gentleness was such a contrast to the warrior I'd fought beside earlier.

"It's just... I'm sorry." I said as a tear escaped my eye.

He gave me a tender kiss. "Olivia, there is nothing for you to apologize for. You could not have fought harder today. I was in awe of you."

"But," I choked out. "I couldn't keep them safe. I tried my hardest to keep everyone safe, and I couldn't. It wasn't enough. We lost people forever. Fourteen of them." Tears poured down my cheeks at the loss.

Cade pulled me against his chest. I could feel the beat of his heart. "Shh," he murmured against the top of my head. "You did all that you could, Starlight. You saved countless others."

"But I'm supposed to be the powerful Chosen One, marked by the Goddess. What good is that if I can't save everyone?"

Cade pulled back from me and cupped my face in his hands. He gave me a hard look. "You are more than enough, Olivia. No one expects you to fight alone and for us to suffer no losses. You stopped the carnage today. You closed that rift. And if you hadn't been here today, we all would have perished. And that is a fact. It's awful that we lost people today, but that is Magda's fault, not yours."

I closed my eyes and leaned into his touch. "You're right. She is where I need to direct my anger. I can be sad for the people we lost, and frustrated that I couldn't do more. But not angry at myself."

"Now, let me take care of you," he said softly, his fingers working at the clasps of my battle-worn clothing.

As the warm water of the shower cascaded over us, I felt some of the tension leave my body. Cade's hands were gentle as they worked shampoo through my hair, his fingers massaging my scalp. The familiar scent of lavender filled the air.

"You're safe here," Cade murmured, his lips close to my ear. "You don't have to be strong all the time. Not with me."

I leaned back against him, allowing myself the vulnerability I only ever showed to him. As he carefully washed away the grime and blood from my skin, I felt as though he was washing away some of the heaviness in my heart as well.

Cade's hands moved lower, his touch both reverent and purposeful. A soft gasp escaped my lips as his fingers traced down past my stomach, igniting a spark of pleasure that quickly grew into a roaring flame. I reached my hand back, gripping his neck as I stretched towards him. His strong, deft fingers moved through my folds, coaxing out moans that echoed in the steamy bathroom.

His mouth was at my ear, his voice a quiet growl. "That's it, Starlight. Take what you need from me. Your pussy is already slick for me."

He passed his fingers over my clit; the sensation caused me to moan his name.

"Always my fucking magnificent girl."

He inserted two fingers into me, pumping them in rhythm with my gyrating hips.

"Mmmm, Cade... let me come, please."

"Fuck, how can I say no when you beg so well? Let go, my love, I'll catch you."

His fingers moved out of me and straight to my clit, where he traced circles, small to large, then back to small again.

The release washed over me, my body shuddering against Cade's solid form. It was more than just physical pleasure; it was catharsis, a release of all the fear and doubt that had been plaguing me. For a moment, I forgot about the battles, the losses, the weight of responsibility. There was only this—Cade's arms around me, holding me safe as I came undone.

As the aftershocks subsided, I felt boneless, utterly spent. Cade's lips pressed against my temple, a gentle reminder of his unwavering presence.

"I love you," I murmured, my voice thick with emotion.

"And I you, my queen," he replied, reaching to turn off the water.

Cade's strong arms encircled me as he lifted me from the shower, cradling me against his chest. He stood me on the plush bathroom rug and wrapped me in a fluffy towel, then carefully dried my body. I sat on the short, padded stool in front of the mirror, where he wrung the water from my hair. I added a bit of my wind and fire magic to create a warm breeze that dried my locks while he gently brushed each strand. For me, these actions were the ultimate demonstrations of love. Every touch, every stroke of the brush screamed of how much he loved and cherished me. They were acts of devotion, a cloak of affection I wanted to wrap myself in. Our gazes met in the mirror, and the small smile he gave me all but melted my heart.

I was lost in the very essence of him when I spoke. "I adore you, Highness."

He put the brush down and gave my neck a tender kiss. "And there is nothing more valuable to me than you, Starlight, not in this realm, or any."

He scooped me into his arms, turning towards our chambers. The cool air raised goosebumps on my skin, and I shivered, burrowing closer to his warmth. He carried me to our bed, the silken sheets soft and inviting as he laid me down with infinite care.

"Let me take care of you, my love," he murmured.

I watched through heavy-lidded eyes as Cade moved above me. The flickering candlelight cast shadows across his chiseled features.

"You are so beautiful," I whispered, reaching up to trace the line of his jaw.

He turned his head, pressing a kiss to my palm. "Not nearly as beautiful as you, my queen. My Starlight."

My breath caught as he lowered himself, his lips meeting mine in a kiss that was achingly tender. I melted into him, my body recognizing its perfect counterpart. As we came together, it felt like coming home—a refuge from the chaos that swirled around us.

"I need you," I breathed against his lips, my hands sliding down his back.

"Always," he replied, his voice rough with emotion.

He entered me, his size filling me completely. "You feel so good wrapped around me."

I wrapped my legs around him, my feet digging into his perfect backside. I used this leverage to move my hips, pulling myself up and down, matching his rhythm. I couldn't get close enough.

"Gods, Starlight, what you do to me. I promised myself I'd be gentle with you."

I smiled up at him. My heavens, he was so perfect.

"I just want to feel you close to me. I need to feel you everywhere," I sighed.

He continued his delicious assault, thrusting in and out of my tight core.

"I'm so deep inside of you now, love, I feel you in my very soul. You're in my veins."

He leaned down and kissed me with a searing passion, his tongue seeming to memorize every inch of my mouth.

"Bite me."

He paused, then continued with slower thrusts.

"Are you sure, baby? You're exhausted."

"Bite me."

He pistoned harder, leaned down, and kissed me again. Then he struck. I felt his fangs enter, and my blood filled his mouth. A mind-numbing orgasm hit me all at once.

"Cade! Gods! So good…so…" Then I started drifting.

"Rest now, my love," he whispered, pressing a kiss to my forehead.

I nestled against him, my eyelids growing heavy. I still don't quite understand how the mate bond works, but I'm so grateful that the Goddess brought Cade into my life and gifted me with this bond that had given me someone who is more than a mate. He's an extension of myself.

Before sleep took me, I noticed Cade pulled the velvet roped next to his nightstand. A few moments later, I heard light footsteps outside our door.

"Your Majesty?" The valet's voice was low and respectful, barely audible from the other side of the heavy oak door.

Cade's chest rumbled as he spoke, his voice still thick with sleep. "Enter, Francois."

Cade was sure to have the bed's canopy curtains partially closed, ensuring Francois could not see me, though he would never look.

"Yes, Majesty."

Cade kept his voice low. "Can you please be sure we're not disturbed for the rest of the day?"

"Of course, sire. Would you like to have dinner in the formal dining when you receive guests the day after tomorrow?"

I felt Cade's fingers absently tracing patterns on my bare shoulder. "Yes, and you should also make sure the war room is clean as well."

I lay there for a moment, thinking about his words. Even as we rest, we always have to be considering the challenges ahead.

"Is there anything else you require, Your Majesty?" Francois asked.

Cade's arm tightened around me. "No, that will be all. Thank you, Francois."

As the valet's footsteps faded, I tilted my head to look up at Cade. He looked down at me, a question in his eyes.

"The war room?"

He nodded. "Everyone will be here, so it's the perfect opportunity for us to go over everything that happened in the last battle. And as bad as we hate it, we need to talk about Farin being taken and what that means for what comes next."

I felt a knot form in my stomach. I knew he was right. "It probably means that we're out of time. She's likely about to make her final move. Having the war room ready is probably not a bad idea. We'll probably change strategies a couple of more times before we battle her face to face. I'm just ready to have this over with."

He pulled me to his chest. "Me too, baby. Me too."

CHAPTER 22

We Won't Forget

Farin

The Underworld wreaked of despair and malice with air hot and thick. Rivers of molten lava snaked through unforgiving terrain with crimson light that cast shadows against obsidian walls. Every sound and smell was horrible. The wails of the damned rang out day and night.

When I came to, my head throbbed like it had been mistaken for a drum. Cold iron shackles bit into my wrists and ankles, each movement reminded that I was stuck here. I blinked hard into the darkness and tried to pierce the gloom and to figure out where specifically I was. I was in a cage. That was clear. The twisted metal pulsed with dark energy.

My body ached with the scars of battle. I had cuts and bruises that littered my arms and chest. But my spirit was as unyielding as ever. I pulled on my chains and felt their dark magic resist me. "Cowards," I rasped. "Too afraid to face me in the open, so you drag me her like a trophy for your queen."

The sounds of footsteps that clattered across the stone floor shattered the silence. The room lightened slightly, and a familiar figure emerged from the gloom. Nerissa. Her emerald gown shimmered with an unnatural glow and hugged her form. Her once silky dark hair hung dull, as though this hellish place had sucked the life from it. A rehearsed smile could not hide the coldness of her eyes.

She paused just outside my cage. "Farin," she purred, stopping beyond my reach. "It's been too long."

"Not long enough, Nerissa. What kind of warped game are you playing now?"

She tilted her head and looked at me as though my words injured her. "Must it be this way, darling? I came to offer you a way to escape this... unpleasantness."

"Unpleasantness? I was kidnapped from my realm, woman. I'm currently chained to a wall. I think this qualifies as more than simple unpleasantness. Of course, you've dealt in treachery for so long, I'd guess you can scarcely recognize it when it's staring you in the face." How could I have ever loved this *thing* that stands before me?

Her face hardened. Any charm she had tried for slipped away in frustration. "Think Farin. Magda is the future. If we give her what she needs, she will have us at her side. We will wield power beyond your wildest dreams." Then she tried seductive pleading. "We could be together again, rule as we were always meant to."

I couldn't hide my disgust. "You've always been a blind fool, Nerissa. You'd trade power for everything that actually matters. You'd even have sacrificed our granddaughters for your delusions of grandeur." I leaned forward, my chains straining against the wall. "I'd die a thousand deaths before I'd help you or that abomination you serve."

Her eyes narrowed in anger, stepping back into the shadows. "You'll come around to my way of thinking, Farin. One way or another." Her voice faded as she vanished.

The temperature suddenly dropped as a chill filled the air. My breath caught in my chest as a figure emerged from the darkness. She was suffocatingly beautiful. But unquestionably deadly. An evil gloom poured from her and wrapped around my throat, and made it difficult to breathe. She wore an inky gown that hugged every curve of her body and pooled around her feet, an oily puddle.

"Ah, the mighty Farin," she drawled, "Awake at last. I was beginning to think Nerissa played too rough with her toys."

I tried to keep my mouth shut. Clinching my jaw in the effort. But I knew I was a dead man, so what was the point? I looked directly into her eyes. "Spare me the theatrics, Magda. Whatever you think you'll get from me, you won't get it."

Her sultry laughter echoed around us. "Oh Farin, you underestimate me. And yourself." She flicked her wrist and the cage groaned as dark energy tore through the bars. "You possess ancient magic. It's quite powerful. I happen to need that kind of powerful magic to blend with mine. Along with your idiot wife's magic, I could make the whole of Eldoria kneel before me."

She pressed in closer to me. "Give me your power willingly, and I might be merciful. Your granddaughters might see another sunrise."

It made me furious to hear her threaten my girls. "I'll never help you rule Eldoria. I'd die first."

Magda's smile widened. "Oh, I was hoping you would say that."

She slightly raised her hand and shadows slithered into my cage. They coiled around my limbs like vise grips. Pain seared through me. I bit down, refusing to give her the satisfaction of my screams. She watched with sadistic delight.

"You're strong Farin. But everyone breaks eventually. And when you do, you'll beg to give me what I want, just so I'll stop."

My head snapped up. "You'll get nothing from me. And when I break free—I'll make sure you never harm anyone again."

Her smile faltered, her expression darkening. She waved her hand dismissively, and the shadows constricted further, forcing a grunt of pain from me. "We'll see," she hissed before melting back into the shadows, leaving me in the suffocating silence of my confinement.

I slumped against the bars, my breaths ragged. But my spirit wasn't broken. I closed my eyes and searched inward. Beneath the pain and exhaustion, I felt a spark of my power. I would not surrender. Not to Nerissa's betrayal, not to Magda's torment. If they wanted my power, they'd have to pry it from my cold, dead body.

Cade

I woke with a heavy heart. We dressed and readied ourselves to attend the funeral services for those who fell in the last battle we fought. Olivia carefully selected a dark satin gown with a delicate lace overlay. I thought it mirrored my feelings about the day perfectly. The black lace was beautiful and delicate, which aptly describes the lives of these soldiers who fought so valiantly. They lived beautiful lives doing what they loved and yet, like all lives, proved delicate, as they were here one moment and sadly gone the next.

She didn't falter as we greeted our people. They graciously received us as the priestess spoke about the soldiers that we lost. Olivia thoughtfully gave of herself to our people, sharing lovely words of encouragement in the way that only she could. While there were plenty of tears, after being in the presence of Olivia, there were plenty of smiles as well. She poured joy into their lives, and my love for her grew stronger with every hug and word she gave.

We had planned to attend the services in every kingdom, so our day was full.

We departed Vesparra in a shadow mist, her hand gripping mine with a fierce urgency as we vanished into the ethereal darkness. Our first stop was Aurelion, where Ignis and Callie awaited us.

The air in Aurelion was charged with the aftertaste of magic as we emerged onto the volcanic plateau where their fallen warriors lay in honor. Lining the jagged path, the people of Aurelion stood, heads bowed, each holding a flickering flame in their palms. The scent of sulfur was intermingled with something sweeter—the burning of resin, its smoke curling up like prayers to the sky.

Ignis stood before his people, Callie at his side. I loved the new Ignis. No longer filled with the burden of their outdated traditions, he was a man freed to rule from his heart. He addressed his people.

"Today, we honor the brave souls who gave their lives for Aurelion and our realm," he declared. "We know the Goddess received their souls and they are with her this day."

The crowd turned their eyes to Callie. They had embraced her fully—this revenant, who was once an outsider, is now their queen in all but name. She moved with grace as she and Ignis move to the traditional funeral pyres that held their dead. As she whispered, her revenant magic melded with Ignis' fire, causing the flames in their hands to burn brighter, casting a shower of light into the late morning shadows.

Beside me, Olivia observed, her expression thoughtful. She squeezed my hand, and we retreated into the mist once more.

Therionis was alive with the sounds of mourning as we arrived. The howls of shifters called through the dense forest. Here, the they honored their dead with pyres adorned with tokens of their animal forms, feathers, claws, even small wooden carvings shaped like their shifted selves.

At the center stood Amaya, their Luna. She moved among the families, her words and touch offering comfort.

"She's incredible," Olivia whispered, her voice heavy with emotion. "I always knew she had it in her."

I nodded and watched as Amaya comforted a young mother who had lost her mate. The woman's sobs filled the clearing. As Amaya allowed her own emotions to surface, she proved she shared their grief and they could trust her to be a help to them.

As the pyres were ignited, the howls intensified. Olivia's hand found mine, and we stood together, watching as the flames ascended, lifting the spirits of the fallen towards the sky. The shifters, so honest with their emotions filled all of my senses. Their grief was palpable. I thought to myself that it must be their animal instincts that gave them the freedom to so openly show how they truly felt. I almost envied them.

In Ilyndor, mourning took on a quieter, more formal tone. The fallen lay in neat rows, their bodies wrapped in silver cloth, each embroidered with the sigil of their kingdom. Miranda stood in front of the people.

"We honor those who gave everything for Ilyndor," she spoke. "Their sacrifice will not be forgotten, and their legacy will live on."

Thorne stood behind her. His face was as stoic as ever, but his eyes lingered on Miranda with pride.

Their priestess came before the congregation and gave prayers of thankfulness for each of the brave souls who died in service to Eldoria. She then asked the Goddess to receive the fallen soldiers into her care. After, a troop of guards took the bodies up the mountain pass where the priestess would conduct the ceremonial pyre alone.

Our final destination was Thalassa. Olivia had entrusted Seraphine with the task of leading the ceremonies in Farin's stead.

Seraphine took her place at the front of the congregation. The Thalassan fallen were presented similarly to those in Ilyndor. Their bodies were swathed in gold cloth, the blue emblem of Thalassa proudly displayed at the center.

Olivia and I approached to pay our respects, stepping in for Farin. His absence was felt acutely. I noticed Olivia tremble slight against my hand at her back. She placed a hand over her heart, bowing her head as she said a prayer for the dead.

My sister cleared her throat, then spoke, "Today we honor the brave men and women who faced the enemy without hesitation or regard for their own safety. The only concern they showed was for the safety of their fellow countrymen, their kingdom, their realm. They were the very best of us, and we will never forget their sacrifices."

I felt a swell of pride for my sister, stepping up during such a trying time. The people of Thalassa, already reeling from the loss of both their soldiers and their king, received Seraphine with kindness and goodwill. It was a hopeful sign for a kingdom that had endured too much.

I saw a slight look of relief on Sera's face when the priestess took over the ceremony. She walked to my side and I gave her a brief hug and whispered in her ear of how proud I was of the job she had done. Olivia squeezed her hand in thanks as well.

By the time we returned to Vesparra, we could barely keep our feet. Olivia collapsed into a chair by the hearth.

I knelt before her. "You tired, sweetheart?"

"I am. That was a tough one," she replied.

I brought her hand to my lips. "Hopefully, we won't have more days like that. Tomorrow will be a new day and we'll face it stronger than today."

"From your mouth to the Goddess's ears, honey. I do not want to experience anything like that again."

CHAPTER 23

The Spirit isn't Always Willing

Olivia

All eyes were on me as I stood at the head of the war room table. The torchlight couldn't hide the worried looks on the faces around the room. We'd gathered back at the Citadel, figuring that the central location made the most sense for a meeting. That last battle had shaken all of us to our core. But we didn't have time for worry to grab a hold of us. Magda was comin' and we had to figure out a way to take her out.

"Ok y'all. It's the same song, like, fourth verse. It seems like every time we meet our inclination is to say we're facing a threat like never before. And while I guess, that's technically true. Every threat has been basically the same, but worse by degrees."

"What exactly are we dealing with now, Olivia?" Thorne's deep voice spoke up. I glance at him and noticed his hand resting protectively on Miranda's shoulder.

"Well, first, let's address the elephant in the room." Only Callie had a clue what I meant. I almost laughed. "What I meant is, let's talk about the obvious thing we haven't talked about yet. My Grandpapa was taken in the last battle. That has to mean that Magda now has Nerissa and Farin."

I sighed and ran a hand down my long braid. "That's about as bad as it could be. With Nerissa's mastery over water and ice, and Farin's elemental abilities—I mean, more than just abilities. Heck, y'all know, they're old. I mean, y'all are all old, but they are OLD, old. Their magic is mature. Magda has tapped into a couple of sources of magic that, when combined, can likely make bad shizz happen. I think that heifer probably has the potential to breach the barrier between realms."

Murmurs erupted around the table. Cade raised his hand, silencing them. Then he spoke. "I know it sounds impossible, but we can't underestimate the raw power at her disposal."

"Right, what he said. This is as serious as it gets, y'all. I'm talkin' DEFCON 5 here." I muttered. My example of the threat level flew right over their heads.

"What we need now is a plan," I continued, forcing my voice to remain steady even as fear clawed at my insides. "Magda won't hesitate to use every weapon at her disposal, and neither can we."

As Cade outlined options, and I was running ideas through my mind. The weight of leadership felt like a mountain on my shoulders. But I looked around the table at my friends and family and I felt my faith rise a little.

We would face this threat together, and we'd figure a way to win.

Callie

I was nervous, but I needed to do this. The room fell silent as I stepped forward. Everyone turned to look at me.

"I think I can help," I said. "I can communicate with a spirit from the Underworld. It's one of my revenant powers. It's our best chance to get an edge over Magda. We can find out what her plans are and when she plans on moving."

For a minute, nobody said a word. I was starting to feel like maybe this was a bad idea.

Eldric finally spoke. "I think I could be able to help her through the ritual. It's probably a little dangerous, but it's our only way to really know what Magda is up to. And it's our only chance to get ahead of her."

Olivia spoke up. "Are you sure about this, Cal? We cannot afford to lose you."

I swallowed hard. "I'm sure I was meant to do this."

Ignis looked at me. He wasn't thrilled about this. "Callie, I don't like this. It seems like there is too much risk involved. Is it possible for Magda to take you while you do this?"

I glanced at Eldric, who then looked at Ignis.

Then Eldric spoke. "It's not one hundred percent safe. But it's very close to that."

Ignis shook his head. "If that was supposed to reassure me, it fucking failed."

I touched Ignis' arm. "I have to do this. We need whatever advantage we can get. We can't let any more people die if we can help it."

He signed, running his hand through his hair. He didn't like it, but He'd stand by me.

With a nod from Olivia, we all headed down the hall until we reached a small circular chamber at the heart of the fortress.

The scent of sage hit my nostrils as soon as we entered the room. Torches hung in iron sconces, casting shadows on the walls. In the center of the room stood a simple wooden table etched with runes that pulsed with blue energy.

Eldric made his way next to me. "This is the spot."

I took a deep breath and approached the table. Instinct drove me forward. "I feel like I know what to do." I glanced up at Eldric. "Just stay close."

He nodded down at me. Then he addressed the room. "Ok, everyone just remain still and quiet while she communicates with whatever she brings through. You may be tempted to say something, but try to fight that urge."

I looked over my shoulder at everyone then gave Ignis a reassuring smile then said, "Here we go."

I closed my eyes and reached for the well of magic that dwelled inside me. My hands lifted in the air. They began to move, tracing intricate patterns in the air the more I connected with my magic.

"Spirits of the Underworld," I murmured. "I call upon you. Hear my summons and answer my call."

The torches reacted violently. Flames stretched to unnatural heights before returning to small pinpoints of light, then correcting to their normal flames. That was odd. I tried again.

"By the power of life and death that flows through me, power that I command, I demand that you appear before us."

The air in the center of the table began to shimmer and stretch. A faint mist came together and twisted. Finally, it formed into a fairly humanoid shape.

"Holy shit," I heard someone declare behind me.

As the spirit materialized more fully, I felt a surge of power. My eyes snapped open and I knew without even looking that they held an eerie glow.

"Spirit," I commanded. "Tell us Magda's plans. What does she intend to do in Eldoria?"

The ghostly figure writhed, fighting against invisible chains. Its mouth open in an unseen scream.

"Callie," Eldric's voice came from behind me. "Be careful. Don't push too hard. Don't lose yourself."

I gritted my teeth and focused on my control.

"Tell me," I insisted. "Tell me about her plans."

The spirit shuddered, its mouth released a haunting whisper.

"The Goddess... she possesses a relic of immense power..." it rasped. "A crystal forged in the darkest pits of her realm. It will drain the very essence from its victims."

I couldn't believe such a relic existed. That's how she would take their magic.

The spirit continued. "She plans to use it on the water queen and the elemental king. Their combined strength, once absorbed will shatter the barrier between realms. She is but days away."

"How?" I demanded. "How did she create such a thing?"

The spirit's form flickered again. "The relic was not of her making alone. It required knowledge from the living realm. When the water witch was taken, a spell was used on her to reveal the relic's location. It had been hidden by a Thalassan ancestor who created it, waiting to use it."

"It doesn't matter now. It's done. When is she coming?"

The spirit was fading.

I shouted louder. "WHEN?"

Just before his form faded for good, I heard him say, "Days."

The runes on the table went dark.

Olivia looked around the room.

"Goddess, what is with those Thalassans and their rabid hunger for power?"

She was loaded for bear.

"Alright, y'all," she said, her Texas drawl in full force. "We can't let this rattle us. We gotta be ready to be hit at any moment. It's breakin' my heart to think she's hurtin' my Grandpapa, but it seems that's the facts. And she's comin' whether we're ready or not. I say we better get ready."

Cade seemed to be piecing together some kind of strategy.

"The Vale of Expanse," he announced. "That's where we make our stand."

Eldric's brow furrowed. "The Vale? It's open, exposed. We'd be vulnerable."

He nodded, a small, knowing smile on his lips. "Exactly. Magda won't expect us to choose such an exposed battleground. Plus, it gives us room to maneuver, to use our combined powers without fear of collateral damage."

As he spoke, I saw the spark of understanding ignite in everyone's eyes. Olivia stepped forward.

"We could use the runestones," she suggested. "Create a perimeter that would amplify our magic."

Ignis nodded. "And my warriors can use the open space to

their advantage with the flare arrows."

One by one, the leaders chimed in. The room buzzed with energy.

Our plans slowly came together. We at least had a better idea of a timeline for the next battle. The one that will probably be our last.

Olivia

We settled back in the war room. It seemed like a good time to go over our weapons store. The last battle had hit us hard. I just wanted to double check to be clear we all had things squared away.

"So, are we clear on weaponry?" I asked. Every kingdom had its specialty, and we needed to be sure they were in full supply.

Seraphine, now our Thalassa delegate, spoke up. "We've got water whips and ice spears ready to create barriers. If Magda tries to use her magic, we can contain it. We've also got plenty of mist orbs, water blades, aqua bows, ice arrows, and more."

"Wow, y'all got it goin' on, Sera!"

She nodded. "Eldric was instrumental in helping to make sure we were well-equipped and ready after the last battle."

Next, Ignis spoke up. "Aurelion is weapon-ready as well. Flare arrows, flame whips, and beyond, we are prepared. We'll light up the sky."

Cade smiled at me. "Vesparra has plenty of shadow shards for stealth attacks."

"Kaelen, think y'all can be positioned to flank Magda's forces?"

He gave me his typical Kaelen smile. "My sister, we can be where you need us to be."

As I spoke, I felt the energy in the room shift, coalescing into something powerful and determined.

"Miranda," I said, "your elemental wards will be the last line of defense. Make sure every warrior is equipped."

With each command, I felt a surge of pride. These weren't just allies; they were my friends, my family, ready to lay down their lives for Eldoria.

As I finished going over everything with everyone, they'd all filed out of the room. I stood alone. The slightest sliver of doubt crept in like a shadow. I thought of Grandpapa, held and twisted by Magda's evil. My heart ached, and for a moment, I allowed myself to feel the full weight of what we were about to face.

"Try to be strong, Grandpapa," I whispered, a tear tracing a path down my cheek.

The silence in the war room was deafening, broken only by the soft crackle of torches lining the walls. I ran my fingers along the rough-hewn table, tracing the map of Eldoria etched into its surface. My eyes lingered on the Vale of Expanse, where we'd soon confront Magda and her dark forces.

"Grandpapa," I whispered, my voice barely audible even to myself. "What would you say if you were here?"

I could almost hear his deep, melodic voice, imagine the warmth of his brown eyes as he'd offer some tidbit of wisdom from one of his beloved scrolls. The thought made my chest tighten.

"Dang it, Olivia," I chided myself, shaking my head. "Now's not the time to go gettin' all sentimental."

But as I turned to leave, my gaze fell on a discarded quill, its feather reminding me of the softness of Grandpapa's curls. I picked it up, twirling it between my fingers.

"I promise you," I said, my voice growing stronger. "I'll do my best to get you back on Eldoria's soil."

The weight of war bore down on me, but I straightened my shoulders, feeling the familiar pull of scar tissue on my back. Each mark was a testament to what I'd survived, what I'd overcome.

"Magda thinks she can break us," I muttered, a fire kindling in my belly. "But she doesn't know what we're made of. What

I'm made of."

I closed my eyes, picturing the faces of those I loved—Cade, Amaya, the people of Vesparra. Their trust in me was everything, my source of strength.

Cade stuck his head in the door. "Hey, my love. I thought you'd be right behind me."

"I'm sorry. Here I am, stuck in thought about what's to come, hopin' I didn't miss anything."

He wrapped me in his arms. That was my favorite place to be.

"You were magnificent today. The way you ran this meeting. I was proud to sit back and watch you command the room."

I laughed. "Oh, you stop it, you silver-tongued thing."

"I mean it. You shined like the Starlight you are. And when it comes time to face Magda on the battlefield, it's your light that's going to lead us all."

When I looked into his ice-blue eyes, I saw such love shining back.

"You're everything to me, Cadence Vesparra."

"And you, Olivia Ilyndor Vesparra, are my love and my life. And together we are going to see this through."

"Alright then," I said, squaring my shoulders. "Let's go save the world."

CHAPTER 24

It's Hard to Say Goodbye

Olivia

"Mornin'." I sat up and let the thin blanket fall away as I swung my legs over the edge of the cot. The command center was quiet, but you could feel the tension in the air. I finally stood, my bare feet hitting the cold wood floor.

Cade's hand brushed mine as I passed, a silent reminder that I wasn't alone. I gave his hand a squeeze and drew strength from his touch. We'd been through so dadgum much together, and now we faced the greatest challenge of our lives.

I walked down the dimly lit corridor, torchlight guiding my way. The facility was coming to life. I heard soft voices and the clink of silver wear drifting in from the shared kitchen. I paused in the doorway, looking around at the sight before me.

Everyone had gathered around the long table, their faces worried, movements slow. Kaelen sat at the head, his brow furrowed as he studied a map spread out before him. Miranda and Amaya sat together, their heads close as they spoke quietly to one another. Eldric wore a grim expression and leaned against the kitchen counter with his arms crossed. Sera joined him, offering him a pastry, which he refused.

As I stepped into the room; the conversation died as all eyes turned to me. "Uh, mornin', y'all."

Kaelen looked up. His intense silver eyes seemed to indicate he thought I could add to the conversation. "Olivia. We were just discussing the plan for today."

I nodded and made the move to take a seat beside him. "Ok, hit me." I reached for a mug of coffee, wrapping my hands around the warm ceramic. "What are we thinkin'?"

Kaelen sighed and pushed the map toward me. "There's been no activity. But we can't shake the feeling she's close to making her move. It's been a couple of days."

I looked at the map, knowing it wouldn't really tell us anything. She popped up wherever she dadgum well pleased whenever she flippin' wanted to.

The others started talking again, their voices low and urgent. Their words washed over me as my mind raced. I knew we were just playing a waiting game. Our only option would have been to figure out how to close the rifts permanently, and we were too late for that.

I looked up, my gaze settling on Callie. She sat apart from the others, her eyes closed, her hands clasped tightly in her lap. She thought what we all thought, but it was risky.

Kaelen's voice broke through the quiet as he stood, his chair scraped against the floor. "I have an idea, but it's dangerous."

Everyone looked at him as he took a deep breath. "We need to summon another spirit from the Underworld."

His words just hung there for a second. I glanced around the table and measured the reactions. Amaya looked away. She did not want to take part in this conversation. Meanwhile Cade, who had just entered the room, raised an eyebrow, his face saying he wasn't totally onboard with the idea. But it was Ignis who spoke first, his voice tight with worry.

"No," he said, clearly agitated at the idea. His eyes remained on Callie. "It's too dangerous. We can't ask her to do this again."

Callie met his eyes with a small smile on her face. She reached out and rested her hand gently on his arm. "I appreciate your concern, Ignis, but I can handle it. If it means giving us a better chance, I'm willing to take the risk."

Ignis shook his head, his jaw working back and forth. "You

don't know what that risk could be. The last time weakened you so much. I can't," He trailed off, "I can't stand to see you hurting."

The room fell silent. The feeling in Ignis' words sank in. I watched as Callie's expression softened, her hand slid down to intertwine with his. "You won't lose me," she promised. "I'm stronger now, and I have you by my side."

I cleared my throat. "Callie, are you sure about this? We can just wait it out if it's too much for you."

She shook her head. "No, Kaelen is right. We need every advantage we can get. I can do this."

Ignis hesitated, then squeezed her hand tighter. For a moment, I thought he might object again, but instead, he nodded. "I do trust you. Just... be careful."

Callie smiled and gave Ignis a small wink. "Aren't I always?"

We took a collective sigh. I'd like to say we relaxed a little, but we never relaxed anymore around here.

Contacting the spirit again would give us the slightest advantage, but we'd take any advantage we could get. If we could beat Magda to the battlefield even by an hour, that would help.

I stood. "Then it's settled. Callie will summon the spirit, and we'll use its power to at least see if we can figure out when Magda is making her move. It's not much, but it's somethin'." I looked up and caught Cade's tiny grin he shot my way. I gave him one right back as he moved to my side.

The others nodded, their expressions determined.

Eldric and Callie moved to the center of the living area, their footsteps echoed in the quiet space. The furniture was pushed aside, leaving a wide, open space for the summoning. We didn't have a rune table in the command center like we did at the Citadel, so we improvised. Eldric knelt, his hands steady as he traced intricate patterns on the floor with salt, forming a circle large enough for Callie to use.

I watched from the edge of the room. The others had joined

me there. The room was lit by torchlight that cast an eerie glow as the light flickered along the walls and across the floor.

Callie stepped forward, her bare feet lightly tapping across the hardwood floor.

"Are you ready?" Eldric asked his voice low.

Callie nodded, "I'm ready."

She stepped to just outside the circle, like she had done at the Citadel. She closed her eyes in concentration. The runes that Eldric had drawn on the floor glowed with a blueish light. I felt the power of Callie's magic begin to rise in the room as she raised her hands and began to move them in various shapes.

She spoke basically the same words she had the last time. "Spirits of the Underworld," she murmured, "I call upon you. Heed my summons and come forth." The candles flickered, their flames dancing wildly. I felt the energy continue to build.

Beside me, Ignis' body tensed. I felt his worry for Callie. But there was no turning back now.

A bright light shone around the room, and the spirit materialized before us. Callie seemed to be having difficulty controlling it this time.

"Spirit, I demand that you give us an update on Magda's activities."

The spirit struggled with its movements. "Magda is angry you are manipulating me."

We all froze. But Callie still spoke. "I didn't ask you what Magda thought. I asked you for an update. Is she ready to move on Eldoria yet?"

The spirit struggled. "Ehhhh…. No… she is still…draining… elemental…."

And that's all he got out before we heard a terrible scream.

Suddenly, the air beside the spirit shimmered and twisted. We held our breath as a small portal formed, its edges cracked with unstable energy. Through the twirling energy, a familiar form came into view.

Amaya gasped. "Grandpapa!" Her hand flew to her mouth in

shock.

There, on the other side of the portal, lay Grandpapa, his face etched with pain and exhaustion. He seemed to be reaching out to us.

The group surged forward. Miranda's hand was clutched at her throat with disbelief.

I dove around everyone and shouted back at Cade. "We have to get him out of there!" I'd already moved toward the portal. "We can't leave him there!"

But as I moved to act, the portal started to close.

The spirit's screeching intensified, and I was afraid I was running out of time. I had to move fast if I was going to have a chance to get him out of Magda's hands.

Without hesitation, I lunged forward, my arm outstretched as I dove toward the portal. It hissed, its edges burning against my skin as I plunged my hand through. Grandpapa's fingers brushed against mine, and I grabbed them tightly, pouring every bit of strength into my grip. The portal tugged and pulled, but I refused to let go. Cade grabbed me around the waist and pulled me back.

"Hold on, Grandpapa!" I shouted, "I've got you!"

My arm muscles screamed as I pulled with all my might. Grandpapa's face twisted in agony as he was dragged through the portal, his body twisting and stretching as if being pulled through a tiny keyhole. I gritted my teeth, my heart pounding in my chest as I summoned every last reserve of determination.

"I won't lose him again," I thought angrily. *"Not after everything we've been through."*

With a final pull, Grandpapa tumbled through the portal, his body slamming into mine as we collapsed to the floor. The portal snapped shut behind him. For a moment, the only sound was our ragged breathing.

Then a piercing scream of frustration cut through the air. The elation at getting Grandpapa out was stilled for just a moment at the dread of Magda's wrath.

"Clearly, she's not thrilled about losing him," Callie whispered, her face pale.

I clutched Grandpapa tightly. We thought Magda hated us before. Now we'd really pissed her off.

As I cradled Grandpapa in my arms, I sensed how weak he was.

Miranda and Amaya rushed to our side, their faces filled with worry. Tears filled their eyes at seeing his fragile form.

"Grandpapa," I whispered. "I thought we'd never see you again."

Slowly, his eyelids fluttered open. I looked into those brown eyes I thought I'd never see again. He managed a small smile as he raised a shaking hand to caress my cheek. "Olivia," he breathed. "My brave, beautiful girl." He tilted his head, looking at both Miranda and Amaya. "All of my granddaughters, all so strong and lovely."

Tears streamed down my face as I leaned into his touch, savoring the warmth of his skin against mine. Around us, the others gathered closer.

"What can we do for you? Let us get you some water." I was desperate to help him.

He sat up a little. "No child. I don't need any water." He rasped out. Then his gaze drifted over each face, recognition and affection shining in his eyes. "My friends," he murmured, his words filled with emotion. "I never lost faith in you, in the strength of our friendships."

He took as deep a breath as he could. His body trembled with exhaustion. "We cannot afford to linger here for long. A great danger lies ahead." His voice was urgent. He gripped my hand tightly. "Magda is coming to unleash her fury. You must be ready to face her. Protect Eldoria and all that you hold dear. Soon. She will be here sooner than you think."

His words caused a chill to run down my spine. This was our reality. We'd brought Grandpapa back from the brink of certain death, but we still had our greatest fight ahead of us. Magda would not give up.

As if he read my thoughts, Grandpapa whispered, "Together. You will face this together, as you always have."

I nodded. I understood we were stronger together. We would not let Magda destroy everything we'd worked so hard to build. Tears continued to stream down my face as I cradled him in my arms. His frail body showed the ordeal he had endured. "I don't wanna lose you," I told him tenderly. "I can't bear the thought of a world without you in it."

He reached up. Trembling fingers brushed away my tears. "Olivia, my sweet girl," he murmured. "You're always such a bright light, even in the darkest moments."

I let the memories flood my mind—how much he loved his map room, listening to his stories. Most importantly, and how he held me when I'd lost control of my magic and destroyed the ballroom, and when he calmed me and told me he loved me. The words I'd never heard before. He was the only father figure I'd ever known.

"I owe you so much," I told him.

He smiled. "And you, Olivia, taught me the true meaning of unconditional love and the power of a resilient spirit."

Around us, the others gathered closer, their faces etched with sorrow. Miranda knelt beside me, gripping his arm, tears streaming. Amaya's eyes glistened with unshed tears as she stroked his hair.

Cade stood behind me, lending me his strength.

The room was filled with a tangible sense of grief. The weight of Farin's impending loss pressed down upon us all. Yet even amid our sorrow, there was an undercurrent of love and the unbreakable bonds forged through great trials.

Farin looked at all those gathered, a glimmer of pride and affection in his eyes. "My dear friends," he said, "it has been my honor to walk this path with you all. Your courage, your dedication to your kingdoms and Eldoria, has been an inspiration to me. Goddess Speed." Those were the last words he spoke.

His words were met with tears and feelings of admiration. Each person in this room had been touched in some positive way by the life of Farin Thalassa and he will be dearly missed my all. His contribution to our effort to defeat Magda was unsurpassed. From his technology advancements to his troop allocations and movements to his final sacrifice. His calming presence will perhaps be missed the most. He was a good man. And that is something that cannot be said about many men.

A hush fell over the room, a silence so profound that even the air seemed to still in reverence. The weight of Grandpapa's passing settled upon us like a tangible presence, a shared grief that bound us together in that moment of loss.

I gently handed his body up to Cade. He took him to the nearby couch and laid him gently down. The tears that had flowed freely now dried on my cheeks.

Rising to my feet, I turned to face the others. "We cannot let his sacrifice be in vain," I said, my gaze meeting each of theirs in turn. "He warned us that Magda was on her way, and we gotta take his words seriously. We have to move, now, before it's too late."

Cade stepped forward, his hand finding mine giving it a reassuring squeeze. "Olivia is right," he said. "We have to act now, put our plans into motion. Farin bought us time, and we can't waste it."

The others nodded in agreement, their expressions a mix of sorrow and steely determination. Callie and Miranda exchanged a glance, a silent communication passing between them before they gathered their weapons and supplies.

Kaelen and Amaya moved to assist them, their movements efficient and purposeful. Ignis, his eyes still glistening with unshed tears, started packing weapons and gear, ready to face whatever lay ahead.

As we prepared to leave the command center, I looked at

Grandpapa one last time. My heart was so broken. But he would be the banner I fought behind. "We will make you proud," I whispered.

With a deep breath, I turned to join the others. My steps echoed through the halls as we set out to face whatever Magda had to throw at us.

I gave a smile graced as soon as the bright morning sun hit my face. I heard the familiar voice of Vaelith in my mind. *"Hello Little One. It looks like we are going to war today."*

"Yep, Big Guy. We're gonna have to have our ducks in a row. Cuz I intend to kick some Underworld ass today. Please pardon my language."

I could hear Dragonia rumbles of laughter all the way to where I was standing. I also heard a bit of Cade's laughter as well.

CHAPTER 25

Strategies for Survival

Cade

The command center buzzed with life. Controlled chaos unfolded before my eyes. Energy and urgency in equal parts hummed everywhere, along with sounds of steel and the scent of sweat. Soldiers from every kingdom in Eldoria made their way across the wide expanse of the Vale, eager to help wherever they could. The weight of responsibility felt heavier than I'd ever felt it.

Damn it. Farin should be here. The pang of his loss stabbed through me. His coordination would have had these troops settled in the most strategic locations with effortless efficiency. Even so, I was extremely proud of how things were coming together.

"Your Majesty," a familiar voice called out.

"Come on, Ignis," I laughed. "What's with the titles?"

"Just tying to set a good example for the underlings." He used his thumb to point over his shoulder at his general Jorvahn. Who gave him a good shove, jolting him forward.

I couldn't contain my amusement. They reminded me so much of Thorne and myself. "I can see it's working."

"Jorvahn, it's good to see you're back to your healthy self after your brush with death." A shadow crossed his handsome freckled face. That kind of thing haunted a man.

"Yes, Highness. My good king and his lady arrived just in

time. I'm forever grateful."

I didn't want them to dwell on those memories, so I hurried the conversation forward.

"So Ignis, what news from Aurelion?"

Ignis amber eyes blazed with pride. "Our troops are ready, Cade."

Jorvahn chimed in his Aurelion brogue in full force. "Aye. But it's the getting to the Vale that's the real trick innit?"

I nodded. "Troop transport is a challenge, but I believe Queen Miranda's mages have made progress on larger portals. We'll get your troops here quicker than we thought."

"This is tremendous news. We have an experimental fire portal system we thought to use." Ignis mentioned.

Jorvahn jumped in, "Aye, we do, but it works like shite at this point. I didn't want to wind up crispy after just survivin' a stabbin' with a poison blade and all."

I slapped him on his back. "Miranda has got you covered."

Ignis looked relieved. "We'll head in her direction then and get our men moving."

As they walked away, I called out, "Ignis, Jorvahn." They stopped and looked back at me. "Thank you," I told them. "I appreciate you."

Ignis nodded while Jorvahn gave me a mock salute.

I continued walking in the opposite direction and noticed Seraphine. Beside her stood the man who'd become her constant companion, Eldric.

"Brother," Sera called. I've made a decision regarding the Thalassa troops.

"And what have you decided?" I asked. Happy I had her strategic mind working with us.

She looked at Eldric. "I'm putting their oversight in Eldric's hands."

He straightened. It looked like he fully expected me to balk at her choice. "I won't let her down, Cade. I swear it."

I studied Eldric for a moment. I couldn't find a trace of the ruthless man he once had been. The man who stood before me was a man of earnest conviction who wanted to do the right thing. He'd somehow become a man of principal. And dare I say, a man who was in love with my sister?

"He is the man for the job, Cade." Sera reiterated with no apology.

Eldric looked at me. "I know my past actions don't inspire trust. But I swear to you, I will do everything in my power to be sure the Thalassan forces are prepared and positioned for battle."

I felt the weight of her decision. "Very well. You have a chance to prove yourself again, Eldric. I guess you could say, your redemption draweth nigh. And for what it's worth, I believe you."

Eldric let go of a breath I hadn't realized he'd been holding. "Thank you, Cade. I won't let you down."

As I walked away, I saw Seraphine's hand brush against Eldric's. Their fingers intertwining. The tenderness of that touch said so much. I found that I hoped that their love would be strong enough to redeem even the darkest of souls.

As I continued my walk around the perimeter of the Vale, my eyes caught on Miranda. Her dark curls fell over her shoulder and she poured over a large map on a wooden table. As expected, Thorne studied the same map right beside her.

I walked up, catching the tail end of the conversation.

"The sub-hub in Everdale is our best bet," Miranda's voice was confident. "It can handle the influx of troops from the eastern quadrant."

Thorne nodded, his armor clad frame dwarfing hers. "Agreed. We should stagger arrivals to prevent overload."

I spoke up, my curiosity getting the best of me. "Are we discussing troop movement?"

Miranda spoke eagerly, "We are. We've made significant progress with the sub-hub portal system."

Thorne added, "It's a damn sight better than marching the entire way." Then he paused. "Though I still say nothing beats a good old-fashioned forced march for building character."

Miranda rolled her eyes. "Yes, because blistered feet and exhaustion are the perfect recipe for our troops facing Magda's forces."

Those two made me smile. It was good to find humor in the places we could in the face of so much stress. "As long as our troops are here and battle ready, I don't care if they arrive on piggy back." I tossed over my shoulder as I walked away.

I noticed Zorion, Kaelen's imposing beta, had the Therionis troops running drills. His booming voice called out commands across the field.

"Archers to the eastern flank! Wolves, form up by the ridge!" His orders rang out. Each word was met by the fluid motion of his troops responding.

The shifters moved simultaneously with smooth precision. The different species of shifters grouped together and moved in harmony as though they were of one mind. It was incredible to watch.

I briefly watched my sister-in-law Amaya in her role as the pack's Luna as she moved through the ranks. Her presence seemed to calm the nerves of soldiers whose species were given to anxiety. She touched the shoulder of more than one person and almost instantly their auras changes for anxiety charged to a calm resilience.

Kaelen caught my eye, and I gave him a knowing nod. Amaya had started on shaky ground as Luna, but the Goddess knew that she was the perfect choice for him. She played a vital role with the troops preparing for this final battle.

My thoughts went to Vesparra to where my right-hand Darius had been left in charge for weeks now. While he may not fight in the field, there is not a better strategist in Eldoria. I closed my eyes and reached out with my mind, feeling the familiar presence of my oldest advisor.

Suddenly I was there, a shadowy observer in the mist-shrouded courtyard. Darius was there. He addressed my troops with a few last words and lessons.

"Remember," his rich voice echoed, "the mist is an extension of yourselves. Let it carry you, guide you, shelter you."

I watched, mesmerized, as Vesparran troops stepped into swirling shadows and vanished. The efficiency was amazing—entire battalions transported in the blink of an eye.

"Well done, old friend," I whispered. I knew he couldn't hear me, but I still felt the need to acknowledge his skill, nonetheless.

"We'll be ready, Cadence," he murmured, as though he heard me. "When the time comes, Vesparra will make the stand with you."

I released the connection and found myself back on the busy field. My confidence rising like the tide.

Just then, Miranda's voice rang out, caching my attention. "Now!" she commanded. She had gathered her mages on the western edge of the field. They moved as on, their hands weaving intricate patterns in the air. The space before them shimmered and stretched, and a portal materialized into existence. But not just any portal—this portal was easily three times the size of any I'd ever seen before.

"Holy shit," I breathed.

Miranda's eyes snapped open, a triumphant smile spread across her face. "What do you think, Cade? Big enough for you?"

I gave her a smile right back. "Duly impressed, lady. How many troops can you move through at once?"

"At least fifty," she replied, pride in her voice. "We've practiced. Turns out when you combine Ilyndor's elemental magic, and you have your cousin add her Goddess Star power... well, you get something like this." She pointed to the portal.

As if to prove her point, a contingent of Ilyndor soldiers began marching through the shimmering portal. It was an impressive sight.

"Can you repeat this portal all around Eldoria so we can get every troop here?"

She smiled. "We're doing that right now. By nightfall, every kingdom's troops will be in the Vale of Expanse."

On my way to meet Oliva I stopped by the armory. The metal masters were hard at work, their forges blazing.

"Impressive, isn't it?" Thorin, Aurelion's master smith, asked.

I nodded, watching as he twirled a newly forged rune sword. "How are preparations coming?"

His eyes shone with pride. "We're ahead of schedule. Being able to use a combination of Aurelion fire, Thalassan water magic, and Ilyndor's earth magic... we're producing weapons unlike anything I've seen before."

He handed me the rune sword. As soon as I gripped the hilt, I felt a surge of power. The runes etched along the blade flared to life as they glowed with an inner fire.

"By the gods," I whispered.

Thorin nodded. "Aye. With blades like these and the warriors to wield them... well, Magda won't know what hit her."

I nodded as I handed the sword back. My hope, which I couldn't suppress, was that what we were producing here would finally defeat Magda and the forces of darkness.

He gave me a fatherly pat on my back. "Get some rest, son. We'll be ready."

I headed towards the dragons for our planned reconnaissance flight.

"Cade!" Olivia's voice cut through the noise. I turned to see her weaving through the crowd. Gods, she was gorgeous. Even disheveled and covered in a layer of dust, she was breathtaking.

"How's it looking?" I asked as I tucked a stray strand of hair behind her ear.

She leaned into my touch. "It's coming together. The armory is set up, as I think you've seen. The healers' tents are all ready to go." She blew a stray hair out of her eyes. "Though I reckon we're gonna need a whole lot more cots if we don't kick her butt out on the first day."

"Well, we'll just need to finish the job on day one."

"You ain't kiddin' darlin'," she drawled. "But time's a'waistin', we should probably get our tails in the air for that recon flight."

I was ready to fly. "Right. Let's go."

We made our way to Vaelith and Eryndor. Their massive forms glimmered in the late afternoon sun.

I felt Eryndor's presence brush against my mind. *"Is it time, Cadence?"* His deep voice echoed in my thoughts.

"It is," I replied aloud.

Olivia quickly saddled up on Vaelith. Relaxed and confident, she was every bit a queen.

She glanced my way. "You comin' handsome, or you just gonna stand there gawkin' all day?"

"Just enjoying the view," I quipped back. Then I swung myself up onto Eryndor's back.

"Ready?" I called to Olivia.

She flashed me a brilliant smile. "Born ready, darlin.'"

With a powerful thrust, we were airborne. The ground fell away and I got the same feeling of exhilaration I always felt when we took to the skies.

As we soared, the familiar forms of the other Dragonia joined us. Nyxara's midnight blue scales shimmered, while Skorn's obsidian form seemed to absorb all light. Drathom flew in next, scarlet accents catching the light here and there.

"Took you long enough," Drathom's voice filled my mind. *"We were starting to think you chickened out."*

I laughed, shaking my head. *"Just building suspense, my friend. You know how I love a dramatic entrance."*

Olivia's laughter rang out. *"Oh please, drama queen. You just couldn't decide which outfit best showed off your broody vampire side."*

"I'll have you know this is my most practical 'saving the world' attire," I retorted.

As we banked left, the Pegasi Ariaxom and Thyra fell into formation beside us. Ariaxom's mane was a river of sparkles.

"Any sign of trouble?" I asked.

Thyra's voice chimed in the answer. *"Nothing yet, but the winds whisper of unrest. We should remain vigilant."*

I nodded, grateful for her insight. *"Agreed. Let's spread out, cover more ground. Nyxara, take the eastern flank with Skorn. Drathom, you're with Ariaxom to the west. Thyra, keep an eye on our six."*

As everyone took off to their assigned positions, I felt so grateful. Despite the looming threat, I knew how blessed we were to have these magnificent creatures in our lives.

"You know," Olivia's voice drifted over, *"if we weren't potentially flying into mortal danger, this would be pretty romantic."*

I raised an eyebrow. *"Oh? And here I thought impending doom was your idea of foreplay."*

Her laughter carried on the wind. *"Well, it does add a certain spice to things. Though I wouldn't say no to a nice, quiet evening once in a while."*

"Noted," I replied. *"When this is all over, I promise you the most boringly peaceful night of your life."*

"Careful there, Cade," Skorn's sardonic voice cut in. *"Any more sweet talk and I might lose my lunch."*

Olivia's eyes sparkled. *"Jealous, Skorn? Don't worry, there's plenty of Olivia to go around."*

Even on the eve of what could be our destruction, the bonds of our friendship were stronger than fear and duty. They go deeper.

As we continued to soar, looking for anything out of place, Vaelith tilted his head and his nostrils flared. *"Something catch your attention Vaelith?"*

He sniffed again. *"It's just something different in StarHeart's scent. A subtle change."*

I looked over at Olivia and studied her. She looked the same as always to me.

"You're right," Thyra added. *"It's like a sweetness."*

Olivia looked around at them. *"Alight y'all. What's goin' on. I've been working like crazy. I get it. I haven't been able to shower as often as usual. You don't gotta be pointing it out."*

Talk of her scent was quickly forgotten when she saw a good place for us to land for a bit.

"Hey, y'all, see that clearing up ahead? Might be a good spot to land and get our bearings."

I nodded and pushed the thoughts of Olivia's scent to the back of my mind. I'm sure it's nothing. *"Good eye, love. Let's land there for a bit."*

I shook my head, refocusing on the task at hand. "Alright, team. What did we learn from our flyover?"

Olivia's brow furrowed in concentration. "The eastern approach looks the most vulnerable. If Magda's forces come from that direction, we'll need to reinforce our defenses there."

I nodded. Her eye for tactical detail was next to none. "Agreed. We should double the patrols along that ridge."

We discussed a couple of other weak areas and how to fix them and decided we needed to head back.

With renewed purpose, we headed towards the bustling war room. It was time for final preparations for the fight of our lives.

CHAPTER 26

The Last Stand

Olivia

I awoke with a jolt, my heart pounding in my chest. The early morning sunlight filtered through the gauzy curtains of our room in the command center. Cade slept beside me, his chest moved up and down in a steady rhythm. I don't know how he slept so peacefully. Maybe it was a vampire thing. Sleeping on these portable beds didn't help either. I know, first world problems. I'm whining about the bed when in a while a literal Underworld Goddess was gonna try to kill me. Ugh.

I slipped out of bed, the wood floor was chilly on my feet. Maybe it was the electricity in the air that sent a chill up my spine. I dragged myself over to the window and looked out at the mist covered open field.

Guards from every kingdom patrolled the grounds, their hands close to their weapons. It was so still and quiet. Even the birds thought it was wise to keep their songs to themselves today. I didn't blame them. Why draw attention to yourself when that might get you whacked by a beautiful blood thirsty abomination from hell?

"Good grief," I muttered, running a hand through my tangly hair. "This is going down, for real."

The reality of what was about to happen hit me like a brick. We'd prepared as good as anyone could have. It would have to be enough. The lives of everyone I loved—heck, the fate of our entire realm—rested on this battle.

"Who you talking to?"

"HOLY SCHNEIKE! Give a girl some warning, would ya?" Cade's voice about made me jump out of my skin. He stood behind me and was also looking out the window.

He grabbed me around my waist and pulled me to his chest, resting his chin on my shoulder. "Morning, Starlight." Then he kissed my cheek.

I turned in his arms and looked into those ice-blue eyes I loved so much. I kissed him. Then I kissed him again. I kissed him like I meant it. Because I did. He wrapped his arms around me and we held each other. Gods, how I wanted to just stay here. I pulled away from him and looked at his beautiful face one more time.

"You are my everything, Cade. All of my better days. I'm so happy I chose you. I'll love forever."

He cupped my face in his hands. "I never lived until I met you, Olivia. You are my life. I love you with my whole heart."

I quickly dressed in my battle leathers. The tight leather pants were imbued with a magic layer for extra protection. A black long-sleeved turtleneck went under the long sleeve brown leather armored tunic I wore. Tall leather boots topped everything off. Not gonna lie. I looked like a badass. I felt like an imposter. But I'd seen my share of battles and kick enough hideous monster butt to qualify I guess.

I headed down the hall to join whoever else was up this early. I wasn't surprised to find everyone was up. I'd been sleeping later than everyone the past few weeks. Not oddly, their conversations died on their lips when I walked in. "Don't stop on my account. I mean, y'all weren't gossipin' about me were y'all? You know, tellin' tales outa school or anything?" Oh lord, I couldn't help myself. The looks of confusion on their faces. I died laughing. Well, Callie and I did.

I let 'em off the hook. "That was a mortal sayin," don't worry about it. "Seriously, though. what's up? Y'all ready to fight the good fight today should a deranged, power hungry goddess from hell decide that today's the day she wants to try to kill us all?"

That got a round of agreement from everyone.

"Olivia?" Eldric's voice pulled me from my thoughts. "What are your thought on deployment of the Dragonia?"

Cade walked in before I had time to answer. I looked at him and nodded.

He spoke up. "We discussed it and thought it was best if they all fought without riders. They can take on Magda's armies behind her front lines. That way, the chances of hitting any of our people will be reduced."

Everyone seemed to think that was a great tactic. We also talked about how the royals would be front and center of the battle. We had the strongest magic, so we'd lead the charge.

After we finished breakfast, everyone scattered. They all wanted to check on their troops and give last-minute encouragement. I walked out onto the large front porch and surveyed everything.

"It sure didn't take me long to fall in love with this place and her people." I told Cade who'd followed me out.

He nodded. "A testament to Eldoria is her unity. It's wonderful how all of her kingdoms carry varied magics and except for Aurelion until recently, we've all gotten along for the most part, and definitely come together in crisis."

"It's really special. Back in Texas, I never belonged anywhere. But here? I finally found a home."

Cade pulled me close. "And we will defend it with all that we have."

A wave of blonde hair caught my eye. Amaya wove through the ranks and chatted with soldiers from different battalions. I couldn't help but smile at her enthusiasm.

"Your sister really knows how to boost morale." Kaelen's voice came from behind us.

I turned to him. "Just remember Wolf King, she might be

your mate, but she's my baby sister."

His lips twitched. "Oh, believe me. I'm well aware her sister is the Chosen One. I hear it often."

We shared a small laugh but I could see as his eyes followed her there was not just a look of love but a flicker of fear for her.

"She'll be alright. You've seen her fight. She's a warrior through and through."

He nodded. "I know it. It's just… I've just found her. The thought of losing her…"

I squeezed his arm. "Hey, none of that talk. We're walking out of this fight together. All of us."

As if summoned by our conversation, Amaya bounded up the steps. "Ollie! You won't believe what I just saw! The water mages and the fire wielders have come up with this incredible combo attack. It's like a steam explosion, but controlled!"

I shared her excitement, truly. "That sounds amazing. It's that kind of innovation that will give us the edge in this fight."

That's how the morning went. We handled our business, working our weapons and strategies.

"Nervous?" Cade asked.

I looked at him. "As a whore in church."

He gave me a small grin. I think he got what I meant this time. "How 'bout you?"

Our moment was broken when the ground rumbled loudly. Then a sound shook the air.

Soldiers ran to get into formations.

"It's time," Cade said grimly.

My heart hammered against my ribs as I felt my power rising within me. It was like every hurt I'd suffered in my life. Every strike of the birch rod that left me scarred. Every bully who'd ever tormented me. Every time I was made to feel like I was less than, had culminated into this moment.

I was the Chosen One of the Goddess Vesperia and today I would prove my worth.

"Remember," I called out, my voice carrying on the wind I commanded, "we're stronger together!"

A chorus arose from the assembled forces. "TOGETHER!"

The world erupted into chaos. Magda's dark forces had appeared—not from rifts, but had seemingly shimmered into existence across the field from us. She clearly had created a large portal that they used to pour through.

Massive lines of destructive creatures surged forward, writhing masses of shadows. Her twisted magic formed every kind of unholy creature with unthinkable powers. I raised my gale blade and sent a torrent of wind that sent the first wave of attackers flailing.

"Olivia, on your left!" Cade's voice rang out.

I whipped around and faced a hulking mass of living stone. It raised its fist to strike me. I dropped and rolled quickly out of its way. But I felt the rush of air pass over my head, just missing me.

"Whew, baby! That was close!" Glad you're watchin' my back.

"Always, love." He shouted as his rune sword hacked the head off of some kind of gigantic insect man-thing.

As crazy as it sounds, having him close enough to talk to helped me.

A surge of earth magic erupted beneath me. I summoned the wind to lift me skyward on currents of air. I could see the scope of the battle from up here. Thalassan warriors used water whips that sliced through shadow creatures like a hot knife through butter. Aurelion soldiers rained flare arrows, each impact a miniature sun blooming across the battlefield.

"Ilyndor forces, shore up the eastern flank!" I shouted. "Vesparra, I need shadow cover on the western approach!"

As I touched down, I caught sight of the Dragonia making their way to take out the forces behind Magda's front lines. "Thank the Goddess. Dragonia reinforcements!"

A cheer rose up from everywhere at seeing them.

They immediately rained fire and ice on the creatures who were behind Magda. She had done a good job of keeping herself protected thus far. I needed to get to her.

I felt Cade at my back. "How are you holdin' up sugar?" I asked as I deflected a blast of dark energy.

"Never better," he replied. "Though I much prefer our workout to this."

"Focus, hot lips. Let's kill Magda. Then you can have your way with me." I told him as I wiped out two uglies by pulling vines up from the earth to strangle them.

As we fought side by side, our powers grew more and more together. When a group of Magda's minions tried to flank us, I created a vortex that lifted them into the air, then Cade's blood thorns blasted them into the ether.

But it was never ending. For every enemy we felled, two more took their place. We'd been at this too long. We had to push through to get to Magda.

"Cade," I panted, and ducked, missing a blow of pure darkness, "we've got to get to Magda. This doesn't end until we end her."

He nodded. "Lead the way, my queen. I've got your back."

I drew on every ounce of strength I had and summoned a massive gust of wind, clearing a path through the throng of enemies. As we pressed forward, I prayed to Vesperia that our allies could hold the line. This was the moment. Failure wasn't an option.

As we made our way, I saw our allies in actions. Ignis wielded fire trapping monsters here and there. "Ignis!" I called out. "Can you clear us a path to the center?"

He turned, his eyes blazing. "You got it, Olivia!" He moved with determination.

Out of the corner of my eye, I spotted Callie. Her layered blonde hair was matted with sweat and grime. She moved with deadly grace. Each move of her hands sent tendrils of darkness draining the life from Magda's minions.

"Callie's really embraced her new powers, huh?" I asked Cade.

He nodded, concerned. "I hope she doesn't lose herself in the process."

We fought on through the chaos when Eldric called out. "Olivia! Magda's forces are regrouping on the south flank. We need to cut them off."

I nodded. "Cade, can you and Eldric hold this position? I need to coordinate with the Dragonia."

Cade looked at me with worry. "Be careful, love."

"Ain't I always?" I smirked back.

As I turned to go, he grabbed my hand and pulled me in for a desperate kiss. "Come back to me."

"Always." I promised. Then I launched myself into the air on a gust of wind. I moved close enough to the Dragonia to where I could get a message to them and get them where I needed them to be.

From my aerial vantage point, I saw Magdas forces surge forward. My stomach clenched with dread. It appeared the tide had turned to her favor.

I tried to keep my panic at bay. I swooped down landing beside Miranda, her black curls matted with blood and sweat.

"We're getting our asses handed to us on a platter," she growled. Then she released a barrage of ice spears that skewered three of Magda's monstrosities.

"Not if I have anything to say about it." I replied. I closed my eyes and reached deep down for that well of power inside myself. I looked back at Miranda. "Cover me."

I felt the familiar rush of energy surge through me. My skin tingled like ants just under the surface. I opened my eyes. I could feel they glowed with purple light.

"Y'all listen up!" I shouted. "We didn't come this far to roll over and play dead. We're Eldorians, dammit, and we don't quit!"

As my aura washed over our forces, I saw the change

happen. Backs straightened and a new fire blazed in their eyes.

Thorne, in blood-spattered armor, whooped. "That's our girl! Let's show these bastards what we're made of!"

The surge of energy was intoxicating, but I knew it wouldn't be enough. We needed something more, something unexpected.

That's when I noticed Callie again. Her green eyes were blazing with an intensity that chilled me to the bone. She stood in a clearing with her hands raised to the sky.

"Callie Girl what are you—" but the words died in my throat when the ground trembled.

The earth split open and from the fissures rose... dear lord, were those hands? Skeletal fingers clawed their way out of the ground, followed by arms, torsos, and eventually full bodies. An army of the dead answered Callie's call.

"Holy crap on a cracker," I breathed.

Callie's voice split the air. "Rise fallen warriors of Eldoria. Your realm needs you once more."

The skeletal army surged forward, their hollow eye sockets aglow with unholy light. Magda's forces faltered, clearly not expecting to face the dead alongside the living.

I turned to Miranda, who looked as shocked as I was. "Well, don't just stand there mouth opened catching flies. Let's kick some demon hiney!"

We charged back into the fight, lifted by our reinforcements. Maybe we had a shot now. But not if I didn't get to Magda. I continued to claw myself in her direction. Until I was finally near.

I felt the storm rising inside me. Raw power begging to be unleashed. My eyes locked onto Magda's tall, elegant form as she strode across the battlefield.

"Hey Morticia!" I called out. "You wanna piece of me? Come at me, bro."

Her dark eyes flashed. "You really need to get a new act, you pathetic girl, trying to play at being brave."

Without a thought, I called down lightning from the sky, feeling it course through my body before directing it straight at the Goddess of the Underworld.

The bolt struck her square in the chest, sending her flying backwards. The smell of ozone and singed hair filled the air.

"That's for messing with my kingdom." I growled as I advanced on her.

Magda struggled to her feet, her perfectly coiffed hair now a smoking mess. "Why you insolent little bitch," she hissed. "You have no idea of the power you're dealing with."

I rolled my eyes. "Honey, I'm just getting started."

The sky above darkened, clouds swirling in an unnatural vortex. I raised my hands and felt the elements bend to my will. Rain began to fall, but not ordinary rain—each drop sizzled with magical energy.

"Olivia!" Cade's voice cut through my concentration. I turned to see him fighting his way towards me. "Be careful! She's—"

His warning was cut short as Magda appeared behind him, moving with inhuman speed. Before I could shout a warning, she plunged a dagger of pure shadow into his back.

Time seemed to stop. I watched in horror as Cade's eyes widened in shock, his mouth forming my name as he fell to his knees.

"No!" The scream tore from my throat, raw and primal.

In that moment, something inside me shattered that released a flood of power I did not know I possessed. My entire body began to glow. I was bathed in divine light. I heard the voice of the Goddess in my mind. *"Daughter, do what you must."*

I felt myself changing, transforming into something... more. My feet lifted off the ground as I approached Magda, who for the first time looked afraid.

I looked at my mate lying in a puddle of blood and what was left of my heart shattered even more. My rage rose. "You should not have done that. My mate was my anchor. He is what kept me human. Now? You face the Ethereal."

I advanced on Magda. I saw myself in a reflection of water. My eyes were galaxies, my hair a cascade of starlight. What *was* I?

Magda stumbled backward. "This... is impossible," she stammered.

I smiled. "Oh honey. I'm as real as it gets."

I raised my hands and felt the energy of Eldoria. My hair whipped around me.

"Time to go home, Magda. For good." My voice echoed with power that made the ground tremble.

Magda's eyed widened in terror. "No, please! You don't know what you're doing."

I wanted to laugh. After all she'd done, after striking down my mate, she thought she could beg? "Oh, I reckon I understand just fine. It's called the BANISHING SMITE, sugar. And if anyone has earned it, it's YOU."

With a thought, I summoned all the elemental forces at my command. They swirled around me, raw power.

I locked eyes with Magda one last time. "Give my regards to the Underworld."

Then I unleashed hell.

The BANISHING SMITE erupted from me in a blinding flash of white-hot energy. It struck Magda full force. She screamed. It was the sound of pure anguish.

As the light faded, I saw Magda's form disintegrate, breaking apart into tiny dots of darkness that were sucked down into a wide portal. Her minions were right behind her, all of them sucked back into the Underworld.

The last thing I saw was Magda's face. There was no beauty there, evil or otherwise. Just a face twisted in hatred and fear before she vanished completely.

Silence fell over the Vale of Expanse. I floated there for a moment, still glowing with ethereal energy. Then, as suddenly as it had come, the power left me. I felt myself falling. My transformation was over as quickly as it had begun. The last thing I remember before darkness claimed me was the feeling of powerful arms catching me and that voice, "I've got you, Starlight."

Then, blissful silence.

CHAPTER 27

A Lesson in Life and A Dragonia's Promise

Olivia

I clawed my way back to consciousness, but my head throbbed like a mofo. Other than that, I felt fine. Wait. "Cade!"

"Starlight, I'm right here." Stars. I didn't think I was gonna hear his voice again.

"But, you fell. I saw her stab you." He stood next to our bed, so I reached up and pull on him to sit next to me. "What time is it? What *day* is it? How long was I out?"

"Slow down, love. It's late. But not a day has passed since the battle. Yes, Magda *did* stab me with some kind of shadow blade. It hurt enough to knock me out for a bit, but the dumb bitch either didn't know or forgot. I'm the king of shadow magic. I healed before she was good and back in the Underworld. By the time you were finished with her and your extra special magic let you go, I was able to catch you."

I laid back with a sigh. "What a weird day."

"It was an extra-Olivia day, that's for sure. I would have crawled in bed with you, but I wanted to wait until you woke back up to be sure you were alright first."

I looked down at myself. I looked perfectly clean and dressed for bed.

"How come I look no worse for wear?"

He gave me a signature Cade Vesparra smile. "I knew you'd hate getting into a clean bed if you were not, so I gave you a thorough bath, complete with washing your hair. Then I dressed you in a fresh gown and popped you under the covers."

I leaned up and gave him a kiss, and yawned into his mouth. "Ahh 'scuse me." I laughed, covering my mouth.

He stood from my side and walked around to his side of the bed. He was already in a pair of silk sleep pants, so he crawled under the covers with me. "I can sleep now that I know you're fine."

I tucked into his side and instantly drifted back to sleep.

***

The morning sun filtered through the curtains of our bedchamber. I stretched, regretting the movement as a wave of nausea rolled through me.

"Ah geez," I muttered, clamping a hand over my mouth as I bolted to the washroom. I barely made it in time, as I heaved into the toilet. "Eww, lovely."

I knelt there for a minute to make sure that was everything, when a memory made its way into my brain. The Dragonias' words from the other day, what did they say? *"Your scent... it's different"*

I hauled myself up and caught the sight of reflection in the mirror. I looked tired, dark circles under my eyes. But seriously. I've been worried about Magda for weeks now. Yuck. I needed to get the taste out of my mouth. As I reached for my toothbrush, I noticed a tremble in my hand.

"Get it together, Olivia," I mutter to myself. But as I mechanically went through the motions of brushing, my mind raced.

Could I be? Nah. Surely not. But, maybe?

The bathroom door creaked open, and Cade's reflection appeared behind me in the mirror. He wasn't in bed when I'd gotten up. He must have been ordering brunch.

"Good morning, Starlight," he murmured as he wrapped his

arms around my waist.

I leaned over and spit used toothpaste in the sink, then rinsed. "Morning, sugar."

He turned me in his arms. "Remember when we were fighting those creatures?"

I smiled, "Mmm hmmm."

"Well, you promised me I could ravage you when we won. And we won, so...."

"I don't think I used those exact words... but..." I slowly walked into our bedchamber. I wanted this man.

I sat at the foot of the bed and opened my robe. "Show me what the vampire king can do."

He growled as he stalked up to me and dropped his silk sleep pants. If there was ever a prettier erection on a man in any realm, I wouldn't believe it. I moaned at the sight.

"Highness, I *do* love that." I pointed down at his cock.

"Do you Starlight? If you're a really, really, good fucking girl, maybe later, I'll let you take it down your throat. How does that sound?"

I looked from his cock to his icy blue eyes. "That sounds delicious."

He was stroking himself. "You are such a naughty, fucking girl. And you're mine."

He stood over me and grasped my face in his hands and plunged his tongue into my mouth in a claiming kiss. It wasn't gentle. Not sweet. He owned my mouth. His tongue, lips, teeth were everywhere. He kissed me like he'd never have another chance.

I laid back, my knees were still hanging over the foot of the bed.

He raised himself over me, his hands on either side of my head, his arms extended.

"Gods, I've never seen a woman more beautiful that you. Or magnificent. When you fought yesterday, I thought I'd come in my leathers. You wouldn't even have to touch me. There is no one in this realm or any other who compares to you Starlight."

Then he proceeded to lick and kiss his way down my body. Starting at my neck, he kissed and nibbled one side and then the next all while his hands played my body like an instrument, plucking at one nipple, then the next. He grabbed handfuls of my breasts, kneading and pulling eliciting sounds from me I'd never made before.

"Oh Gods, mmm, 'sgood, so good."

Next, he circled my navel with his tongue, then peppered small kisses all around. It tickled and I cried out laughter, and tried to pull my knees up.

"Nah ah, those knees stay where they are my darling. I haven't gotten to my prize yet."

He continued on to my pelvic bone, tracing just under my tummy with his tongue. How'd he get so good with that thing?

"Mmm, Cade, please. Get to where you're going. I need it."

"Oh, now listen to my badass queen beg. Is it wrong for me to love to hear you beg? Because if it is, I do not fucking want to be right."

He dipped down to his knees and spread my knees wide. I leaned up on my elbows so I could watch every bit of what he did. Gods, he was so freakin' sexy. So beautiful.

He rubbed his nose across me.

"This is the most beautiful pus—"

"Starlight?"

I was looking right into his eyes over my pubic bone.

"Cade?"

"Your scent, it's…"

"It's what, Cade?"

"How are you feeling, Olivia?"

"I've been feeling tired. This morning I threw up."

He slowly stood. He was still hard as a rock.

"Do you know what your scent tells me?"

I still held his eyes. "That… I'm pregnant?"

"Yes Starlight! Yes! You're pregnant!"

He was on the bed now and had me in his arms, hugging and kissing me.

"Cade."

"Yes, love?"

"I'm also, really, really horny. Can you please make love to me?"

His laughter filled the room.. "Yes my love. There is nothing I'd rather do."

He laid my head on the pillow, and very gently he was over me. When he entered me, it felt so right. Like we had come full circle. It was right in every way. From meeting him in my dreams to knowing him as my True Fated Mate. And now he is the father of my child.

I wrapped my legs around him as he moved in and out of me with determined thrusts.

"Please, Highness. Don't start treating me like I'm fragile."

His thrusts became increasingly harder and faster.

"I can feel you everywhere Starlight. You are a part of me."

He reached between us and rubbed my clit as I moved my hips, meeting his rhythm stroke for stroke.

"I'm so close Cade."

When my release hit, he tumbled over at the same time. I felt him fill me up, and I felt so complete.

"I love you, Highness."

"I love you, Starlight."

We laid there, catching our breaths, him still inside me. I still felt myself throbbing against him.

"We're going to be parents," he whispered.

I nodded. "I reckon we are."

Cade pulled me into his arms, and I melted against him. It felt like home. His hand moved to rest on my still-flat stomach, and a shiver ran through me.

"I never thought..." Cade's voice trailed off. "After

everything we've been through, all the battles and the pain... this feels like a miracle."

I pulled back slightly, looking up at him. "You not scared are you?"

A low chuckle rumbled in his chest. "Terrified," he admitted. "But also... unbelievably happy." "We've faced demons and dark magic, my love. I think we can handle a little one."

I laughed. "I don't know, sugar. Babies can be pretty dang terrifying."

"We should probably head down for brunch," I said reluctantly. "The others will be waiting."

He groaned and led me to the washroom for a quick shower before we headed downstairs.

As we stepped into the dining room, all eyes turned to us. A sea of voices sounded so happy that I was alright. The last time they'd seen me, I was passed out on the battlefield.

"Y'all know me. I always go for the dramatic." I said, as laughter filled the room. But I could tell they'd all been worried. It melted my heart just knowing that I finally had a family who loved me. I was no longer that little girl that nobody wanted.

I took a deep breath, the scent of cinnamon and coffee filling my lungs. "Actually," I began, "we've got some news to share."

Cade slipped his arm around my waist and pulled me close. "Olivia and I," he announced, his voice full of pride, "are expecting a child."

The room erupted in a flurry of cheers and exclamations.

Amaya jumped up and pulled me into a hug. "I'm gonna be an aunt! I'm so excited to get her her first little stuffed wolf!"

I gave her a funny look. "How do you know it's gonna be a girl?"

She just smiled. "I don't know, I just have a feeling."

"So," I drawled, "any of y'all got ideas for names?" 'Cause, I gotta tell y'all, comin' up with a name fit for vampire royalty is a tad bit intimidating."

Cade intertwined his fingers with mine under the table. "Well, I know we just found out, but I was thinking of Cadence Farin for a boy."

And then I added, "For a girl how 'bout Faralynn Mayana?"

Everyone had tears in their eyes at the mention of Farin. We really hadn't had time to grieve for his passing. But naming our baby after him would be such a nice way to keep his legacy alive. Adding my mother's name would also be a nice to remember her as well.

"Those are beautiful choices," someone murmured, and I felt a tear fall down my cheek.

As the conversations flowed about nursery decor and baby showers, then turning to the battle and next steps, I found myself a little overwhelmed.

I told Cade I'd like to take a few minutes for myself alone. He kissed my hand and told me he'd see me in a little while. I slipped away from the brunch, my heart full but my mind whirling.

The garden seemed like the perfect spot to rest my mind. The fountain bubbled away and I thought about the day Cade and I came here and he trained me on how to control my magic.

"This is just as beautiful as I remember." I murmured, running my hand through the fountain, the smell of jasmin in the air.

As I rounded a corner, I saw a figure hunched over a bed of tulips. He seemed familiar, but I couldn't place him.

"Hi there," I called out.

The gardener stood, turning to face me. I knew immediately who he was even though I'd never seen him. His eyes were ancient and filled with wisdom.

"All-Father?" I whispered.

He smiled, the corners of his eyes crinkling. "Hello, Olivia. I thought I might see you today."

My mind reeled. The creator of Eldoria and all the realms,

and the source of all magic, was standing before me wearing dirty overalls. I couldn't help shake my head at how absurd this seemed.

"I'm sorry." It's just… I didn't expect to find the most powerful being in existence, pullin' weeds."

He gave his shoulders a little shrug. "Even gods need hobbies, and there's something satisfying about growing things with your own hands."

I nodded. "I suppose I get that. Though, while you're here, I *do* have some questions that have been botherin' me.

All-Father looked at me with understanding. "I imagine you do. The path you've walked has not been an easy one."

"That's puttin' it mildly," I said. "I mean, and I don't mean to sound ungrateful, cuz, I know I have so much to be thankful for today. But it's just gettin' here. Why did I have to endure so much pain when other people seem to seem to get to live on easy street? Why did I have to live through so many horrible things?"

He sat next to me on a nearby bench.

All-Father's eyes met mine. "Olivia, fate is a difficult thing to understand. The hardships you went through were never punishment but preparation."

I felt a lump form in my throat. "Preparation for what? My life has been a tragedy. I was beaten unmercifully for years, my parents murdered, my grandmother betrayed me. Were you preparing me for disappointment and pain?"

He reached out, his hands gently covering mine.

"It was preparation for the strength you now possess," he said softly. "For the compassion that you are so willing to show others. For the love you have with Cade, and the baby you now carry."

"But couldn't I have learned all of those things another way? A way without pain?"

"If you hadn't experienced things as they happened, little Amaya would never have met Kaelen because you'd have never have met Cade. And even if you had found Cade, he would have forever lost you because there would have been no Callie to save you from Magda's grasp. Then Ignis would have been lost without Callie, and his people would still be bound in their tradition of isolation."

I sat still as he spoke, putting things together.

He went on. "And even poor Eldric. He'd have continued on his path of destruction, never seeking or finding redemption and love. Had it not been for you, even sweet Miranda would not have found Thorne."

All-Father sighed. "So you see, pain and joy are closely related, Olivia. You cannot truly appreciate the light without having known the darkness. Your struggles have made you into the remarkable woman you are today—a leader, a warrior, Cade's pride and joy."

"I think I finally understand," I admitted. "But what about Grandpapa? His death… it crushed me. I tried to save him."

He gave me a smile. "Ah, Farin. His death was noble, as was he. And I can assure you, he is at peace. He lived well and is much deserving of a wonderful afterlife. Yes, child, I promise you, your grandfather is quite happy."

My eyebrows shot up. "Happy? How can you be so sure?"

"Because he's with me."

I wasn't surprised to hear that of any place my beautiful Grandpapa would spend eternity, it would be in Elysium. That eased my mind.

"All-Father, when you see him, please let him know we won. and that everyone is ok."

He stood and gave me a smile that was as bright as the cosmos and said, "He knows, child, he knows." And with that, he followed the path in the direction I had come from. The further he walked the more he faded from my sight until he simply was no longer there.

I sat on the bench and enjoyed the flowers, wondering if I'd lost my ever-lovin' mind.

A while later, I heard footsteps coming up the path. I'd know those footsteps anywhere. He sat next to me. "Did the fountain bring back memories?"

I smiled. "They did. You helped me wrangle two types of magic at once. Boy, if you only had known at the time, I'd call down lightning from the sky!"

He pulled me to his side. "Well, you certainly had had me seeing stars."

I laughed. "He's got jokes."

He kissed my forehead.

We sat quietly for a few more minutes. Then I was hit with the saddest thought.

"What happens now, Cade? Are the Dragonia gonna leave me? The legend said they only awaken in times that they are needed. I mean, *I* need 'em. But the realm technically doesn't need them." I couldn't stop the tears. "I don't want to lose anybody else."

I felt a familiar presence brush up against my mind. *"StarHeart. Don't cry. We'd like to talk to you. Please come for a visit."*

Cade and I made our way towards the caves. The Dragonia met us halfway.

"Vaelith, remember when y'all said my scent seemed different? We'll you were right. We're gonna have a baby." My tears started to fall all over again.

The valley rumbled with Dragonia hums. Our minds were filled with their good wishes.

Drathom lowered his gray wyvern head. and leaned on the tips of his great wings. *"Little One, is that why you are crying?"*

My hand trembled as I reached for his neck. My heart ached with the weight of my emotions. "It's not because I'm pregnant. It's just that the war is over and the threat has passed. And according to the legend, Dragonia are only awakened by a Wyldcaster when a threat to the realm is present and they are needed. Tears continued to stream down my face as I struggled to continue. But I need you, and the thought of you leaving me is almost more than I can stand."

"But as much as I want you to stay, I'd *never* ask y'all to if your hearts are in Wyldhaven. I know that's your home. It just breaks my heart to think that our baby won't have the chance to grow up surrounded by our loving Dragonia family and won't get the chance to know y'all. We'll just have share stories with her of the other part of our family and how they made such a difference in our lives."

Thyra nudged my shoulder. *"Child, you're not giving us a chance to speak."*

Cade reached into his pocket and pulled out a handkerchief and handed it to me. "Here, Starlight. You need this. You have a little, uh. Snot."

I snatched it from him and wiped my nose.

"I'm sorry Thyra. Please tell me what happens next."

She gently spoke. *"I think Vaelith should be the one to talk to you."*

Vaelith's silver scales shimmered like molten starlight as he lowered his massive head, his turquoise eyes reflecting fragments of the late afternoon sky. The ground trembled faintly beneath his claws as he shifted, sending ripples through the wildflowers blooming at his feet.

"StarHeart," he began, *"you have said things as though you think we are bound by ancient laws etched in stone. But you forget —we are Dragonia. We bend with time; we do not break beneath its weight."* His tail swept gently across the meadow. *"Wyldhaven is where we were born and where we have slept... but Eldoria?"* A rumble rose in his chest. *"Eldoria is alive. It breathes with **your** laughter now. Your child will be born into its song... and we would hear that song deepen."*

Thyra's wings unfurled behind her. Her voice chimed in. *"Did you think we would leave before counting all ten fingers? All ten toes?"* Her muzzle brushed my belly lightly, strands of her mane tickling my skin. *"Every child needs guardians who can teach them to taste storms and outrace moonlight."*

Eryndor snorted, a shower of ember-sparks erupting from his serpentine nostrils. *"And who else will ensure this hatchling learns proper mischief?"* He cocked his wedge-shaped head, amber eyes slitting with mock seriousness. *"You humans barely know how to scorch a forest without apologizing."*

The other Dragonia began to gather closer. Their collective hum swelled into a harmony that made the air itself shiver.

Vaelith's muzzle hovered inches from my face, his breath warm, carrying the scent of smoke. *"We do not stay because Eldoria needs us,"* he murmured. *"We stay because **you** do."* His gaze slid to Cade, then down to my stomach, where our daughter's tiny magic already buzzed against my ribs. *"And because she will need stories told by more than echoes."*

Vaelith lingered longest, his tail curling protectively around our little trio as twilight deepened into violet. *"Rest now,"* he said—words vibrating through soil and soul alike. *"We will be here when morning comes... And when **she** does."*

EPILOGUE

5 YEARS LATER

Cade

Sweat beaded on Olivia's brow. She'd labored for about six hours now and our newest little bundle of joy hadn't yet decided to leave the comfort of his or her mother's womb. She twisted in discomfort as I tried to prop another pillow under her back to give her some relief.

"OHH!" She rubbed her round belly. "Now, look her you stubborn little peanut. Time's up! I know you're nice and warm in there, but you gotta go on, git!"

I place a cool cloth on her forehead. Even in pain, she was the most gorgeous thing I'd ever seen. Knowing she worked so hard to bring our child into this world only made me love her more. If I could take this pain from her and put it on myself, Goddess knows I would do it.

"You're doing great, Starlight. I'm so proud of you."

"Oh yeah? You're proud of me? Well, that and a quarter will buy me a CUP O' JACK SQUAT!" Her grip on my hand had become painful as I tried to decipher what in all hell she just said. Another contraction hit her hard. Her face contorted as she squeezed her eyes shut tight. I held on to her for dear life. My own heart beat raced in my chest. We had to be getting close.

"Cade? Do you still love me?" She asked me weakly.

"Of course I do, baby. How could you even ask me that?"

Tears streamed down her face, "cuz I'm bein' so mean to you."

"You're not, sweetheart, you're just in pain."

"You're right, and it's all your fault."

I couldn't help but laugh.

I think I loved her most when she was unreasonable and said things the way that only she could. It never got old. The bond that connected us was the strongest weapon in my arsenal, the thing that I held onto the tightest.

The intense quiet spell of the moment was broken when the chaos that was our five-year-old daughter, Faralynn crashed through the door. She was her mother in miniature form with the same dark hair and penchant for saying whatever was on her mind. The only difference was in her ice-blue eyes.

She stood at Olivia's bedside. "Momma! Momma!" She exclaimed, oblivious to her mother's situation. "Kieran hid Garrik's toy wolf and won't tell him where!"

I couldn't hide my amusement despite the stress as I touched her shoulders and maneuvered her towards the door. She looked up at me. "But Papa—he's being mean!" She wore a pout like her mother did when she thought I wasn't listening.

"I heard you angel. But Momma is having the baby right now. We shouldn't disturb her for just a little longer."

She caught her little breath and looked around me at her mother with wide eyes. "Mercy!" She cried. "I forgot. I just wanted you to teach Kieran a lesson like you to Uncle Eldric sometimes when your shadows sneak up on him and scare him." She giggled.

Olivia moaned again. "Honey, I think it's time."

Amaya pushed the door the rest of the way open apologetically. "I'm so sorry, she got away from me!" My poor sister-in-law looked mortified.

I laughed, "She does that. Don't worry about it."

"Kieran's just actin' like an old cowpie, being mean to his cousin."

I just shook my head and looked at Maya. "She *is* her mother's daughter."

Olivia yelled out at Amaya. "Ahh, Amaya, get the midwife. The baby is finally ready to exit!"

"Oh, my Goddess! I'll go grab her. Come on Faralynn, time to go!" She pulled her out the door.

The midwife worked with amazing efficiency. She whispered incantations that wove spells that sparkled through the air. Thankfully, Olivia's pain ceased. She gripped my hand once more in anticipation as she pushed as directed by the midwife.

"You're almost there, love," I told her. I was filled with anticipation, excited to meet my child.

With a final grunt and a big push, my child burst forth into the midwife's hands. A wail pierced the room. A girl—Tahlia had arrived. I looked at the squirming bundle and my heart sang. The midwife placed her on Olivia's breast. The tiny thing wanted to feel her mother's skin against hers. She quieted immediately.

"Just look at her, Cade," Olivia's voice was filled with wonder and exhaustion. The miracle of life always took our breaths away.

I couldn't look away. Tahlia's hair was as black as the midnight realms of Vesparra. When she finally blinked her eyes opened, they glowed as amethyst as her mothers.

"She's beautiful," I breathed, my voice filled with pride. My daughter. Our daughter.

All at once, I caught a distant sound. It happened with the birth of each of our children. It was a chant, harmonious and beautiful. The song of the Dragonia welcoming a new life. There were no words for us to understand, be we knew they were saying, "welcome Tahlia, our new baby, we cannot wait to meet you."

When I looked at Olivia, I saw my own joy reflected back at me. The Dragonias' connection to us, to our children, and the boundless love that would guide our daughter to her destiny was infinite.

The midwife took Tahlia and gently cleaned her and wrapped her in a soft blanket. I helped Olivia into the washroom and helped her wash as well. She changed into a clean gown, knowing we'd have visitors soon.

Once back in bed and propped up and pillows, I gently laid Tahlia back in her arms. She was noisily sucking on her fist. I left the room to give Olivia some time to nurse while I went downstairs to tell Faralynn and Kieran that their sister had been born.

"Can we see her now? Please?" Faralynn was excited to meet her new sister. In her wake, Kieran wasn't sure what to expect. But he knew it was important to meet this new member of the family.

"Come," I called, unable to hide my joy. They approached Olivia's side their steps hesitant. Kieran held tight to Faralynn's hand.

Olivia extended her arm, allowing them to come close. Faralynn's eyes widened in wonder.

"She's so tiny."

"Tiny but fierce, just like you were," I assured her.

"Will she play with me?" Kieran asked.

"Of course," I replied. "But not just yet, little man. She needs to grow a bit first."

"We'll protect her," Faralynn declared. It was a vow, simple and profound.

"Good," I said. "She's going to need her big brother and sister to look out for her."

I looked up as the door slowly opened. My sister and Eldric quietly entered the room along with Amaya, Kaelen, and their son Garrick.

"Everyone," I greeted. "Come and meet your niece."

"Look at her, Cade," Seraphine cooed as she walked up to the bedside. Their daughter Elaris clung to her mother's skirt, peeking around.

"Isn't she pretty, Uncle Eldric?" Faralynn asked, pulling on Eldric's trousers.

"Indeed, she is little miss, just beautiful." He replied to her satisfaction.

"May I" Sera asked, gesturing to the baby. Olivia nodded and Sera carefully cradled the babe in her arms. She glanced at Eldric. "Honey, this gives me ideas." She sing songed to him.

A smile and a hint of pink cheeks were his answer to her.

"Welcome to the family, little Tahlia," Eldric spoke, looking over Sera's shoulder. "You are so loved."

Amaya was beside herself as she peeked over Sera's shoulder as well. "Ollie, she's gorgeous!" Then she looked over at Kaelen. "Do you not see your son and nephew wreaking havoc in the corner?" as Garrick and Kieren were up to mischief making a fort out of the baby blankets.

***

After a few days, we'd settled into our new three-child routine. We hired a nanny to help, so Olivia didn't have to work so hard. We'd gotten back into our normal breakfast routine, although it was usually just the two of us and the children now that everyone was married and had families of their own.

One morning Olivia brought up the subject of the children's education. It was something I'd not given much thought to.

"How exactly does school work for our children?"

I set my coffee cup down. "It's pretty straightforward. Faralynn will start in a few months, given her age. Our children will have private tutors who will come in. There is a room here that has always been used for education. It's in a wing near the gardens. We've just never ventured there."

I told her some things they'd learn at home. "They'll be taught all the important skills you learned in the mortal realm. Reading and mathematics. Of course, they'll be taught to read a few different languages. But then, they'll also be taught to speak those languages as well. They'll learn the history of all the kingdoms in Eldoria, along with their customs. And they'll study larger kingdoms in the most important realms."

Olivia just stared at me.

"Good grief. That seems like so much!"

I laughed. "Well, there's much more, but remember, Starlight, this is over years and years. They'll be in school until they are twenty years old. Then they'll head off to the Fae realm of Elunara to learn court diplomacy, art of negotiation, realm laws, elemental combat training, shadow magic, things like that."

Her face was priceless.. "Oh, things like that." She mocked.

I tried to ease her mind. "My family has attended there for generations. It will be fine. Plus, everyone's kids will go there. And speaking of, don't we have a birthday party to go to?"

I can't believe I'm being saved by a kid's party.

She jumped up. "Stars! Yes, we need to get to Callie's for Embry's party."

***

The scent of roasted grapes and honey cakes wrapped around me like an old friend as I stepped through the arched gateway, Tahlia's sleepy weight perfect in my arms. Callie's laughter cut through the chatter before I spotted her—that raspy, too-loud sound she'd never quite managed to smooth into royalty.

"Well, look what the hellhound dragged in!" She materialized from a swirl of silk-clad courtiers, her blonde curls catching flecks of amber light from the floating lanterns. The faded scar along her jawline puckered as she grinned, already reaching for the baby. "C'mere, sugar plum. Let Auntie Callie corrupt you before your eyes even focus proper."

Ignis appeared behind her shoulder like smoke resolving

into form, his crown of braided copper threads glinting. "A pleasure as always, Olivia," he said, the lilt of his voice turning formality into something warmer, fingers brushing my elbow in greeting. His gaze lingered on Callie's hands, cradling Tahlia's head.

I laid my Texas on thick, just to watch his royal composure twitch. "Y'all throw a shindig, or did the whole realm just spontaneously decide to get rowdy in your rose bushes?" The look he gave me made me giggle.

The garden pulsed around us—children's shrieks bouncing off canyon stone terraces, the sticky-sweet tang of pomegranate wine mingling with charred lamb fat dripping into firepits. Nobles from the frost-bitten north rubbed shoulders with desert traders in their indigo veils, all sipping Aurelion's famed crimson vintages from glass chalices that threw rubies across the sandstone paths.

"Tag! You're cursed!" Faralynn's voice arrowed through the din, all five-year-old superiority. My daughter stood atop a low limestone wall, sunflower-yellow skirts whipping around her legs as she pointed at Kieran. The boy froze mid-sneak-attack, his shadow stretching long and jagged across the herb beds.

Embry crouched behind a topiary shaped like a phoenix, her pearl-sewn party dress blending with the white blossoms. "No fair using magic!" she hissed, though the spark in her citrine eyes betrayed her.

Kieran's answering grin flashed wolf-sharp. "Says who?" He vaulted over a marble bench, scattering a flock of jewel-toned songbirds. They erupted skyward in a clatter of trills, wings beating time with Embry's startled yelp as he lunged.

"Hey, that's my sister!" three-year-old Nyx stated as he heard her cry out.

Tahlia stirred against Callie's shoulder, a tiny fist brushing the hollow of the queen's collarbone.

"They've been... enthusiastic," Ignis said, gaze tracking the children's spiraling chase past a grove of twisted olive trees.

Callie snorted. "Those are your blood talking, firebug." Her thumb traced idle circles on the baby's back, the gesture older than kingdoms. She glanced at me. "Remember when we could get away by hiding in the wine cellar during state dinners?"

The memory rose sudden and bright—smuggled cinnamon buns crumbling on our laps, Callie's laughter muffled against my shoulder as guards' boots echoed overhead. So many lifetimes ago, when crowns felt heavier than war hammers and we just wanted a moment of peace away from courtiers.

Now Faralynn's bare feet sent up puffs of terracotta dust as she streaked past, Kieran's whoop chasing her toward the dessert tables. Embry and Nyx followed at a careful sprint, all vulnerability shed like last year's snakeskin. My chest tightened watching them—these fierce, unbroken things we'd made after those hard-fought battles.

"Mama! Look!" Faralynn skidded to a halt below us, brandishing a stolen honeycomb dripping gold onto the flagstones. Her braids had come half-undone, lavender ribbons tangled with willow leaves. "Tastes like summer!"

Kieran materialized at her elbow, breathing hard. "Stole it right from under the pastry master's nose," he announced, pride puffing his narrow chest. Behind him, Embry carefully wiped sticky fingers on her sash, trying too hard to look innocent.

I raised an eyebrow. "Y'all know the rules about thievin' before supper."

Four pairs of eyes blinked up at me—Faralynn's ice-blue stare all practiced guilelessness, Kieran's gleaming with mischief, Embry's wide and luminous enough to melt glaciers and Nyx's sweet face so precious. Callie muffled a laugh into Tahlia's blanket.

"Run along now," Ignis said, mouth twitching beneath his beard. "Before I'm forced to imprison you in the lemon grove." He looked to Cade. "Don't you think a brief stay there would be time for them to think about their crimes?"

Cade put on his best official voice, "Why yes, King Ignis. That sounds appropriate for children who don't get out from under their parents' feet."

They scattered like dandelion seeds, laughter trailing behind them. The late afternoon light caught in the metallic threads of Faralynn's skirt as she vanished around a hedge, Kieran's shadow stretching long and lean ahead of her. Embry paused just long enough for her little brother to catch up before following.

Tahlia made a soft chirping noise against Callie's neck, all unknowing trust. I pressed a hand to my lower back where the scars lay buried beneath silk, the ghosts of old wounds humming beneath this new, impossible tenderness.

The crunch of gravel beneath paws snapped my attention sideways. A blur of white fur streaked past my ankles, sending peacock feathers scattering from a nearby planter. Little Garrick skidded to a halt beside me, his wolf pup's tail thumping against the cobblestones as Kieran offered him a stolen honey cake.

"Shouldn't let him eat sweets before sunset," Amaya called, her laughter weaving through the citrus trees like wind chimes. She emerged arm-in-arm with Kaelen, her cerulean skirts swirling around ankles still bare despite her royal status. "He'll be up howling at the moon till dawn."

Kaelen's chuckle rumbled deep enough to vibrate through the goblet in my hand. "Our son takes after his mother in matters of stubbornness." He caught Amaya's wrist as she mock-swatted his chest, pressing a kiss to her knuckles that softened her pretended scowl into something private and warm.

Miranda's and Seraphine's laughter cut through the garden's buzz like a cool spring brook. "If it's chaos you crave..." Miranda said as they swept into the clearing, "this one," she pointed to her daughter Ryn in Thorne's arms, "chewed through three nursemaids' sleeves before breakfast." He deposited the wriggling girl gently beside Elaris who Eldric had just released from his arms.

Garrick had veered in next to them both nipping at their heels. Thorne inclined his head toward Kaelen, the ghost of a smile playing at his lips. "Your boy's got a fine hunting stance."

"For a three-year-old?" Amaya snorted, plucking a sprig of mint from Kaelen's hair. "He mistook Lord Brysden's ceremonial robes for a deer pelt yesterday." With that, she hauled her squirming pup into a nearby cabana so he could shift and put on clothing for the rest of the party.

The crash of cymbals shattered our laughter. Across the lawn, servants wheeled out a towering confection shimmering with edible gold leaf. Embry stood tip-toe on a marble bench, her tiny face illuminated by five flickering flames. Callie's hands hovered protectively near her daughter's waist while Ignis murmured something that made the girl's nose scrunch in concentration.

"Make the wish count, firefly," Ignis said, fingers brushing Callie's hipbone. I thought it was amazing that we had incorporated the mortal custom of birthday parties into our family's traditions.

The candles died in a single breath. Embry whirled, scattering wax droplets that hardened into opalescent beads before hitting the grass. "Papa! Did you—"

"Swear on the Eternal Flame." Ignis' solemn tone belied the mischief in his eyes as he hoisted her onto his shoulders. Callie leaned into his side, her smile softer than I'd ever seen it in our warrior days.

I drifted toward the refreshment tables where a Vesparran envoy was demonstrating how to layer smoked eel onto rye crackers. "Try it with the cloudberry preserves," urged a Thalassan herbalist, her fingertips still stained blue from mixing healing tonics. Behind us, two Therionis blacksmiths debated the merits of moon steel versus solar-forged blades, their argument punctuated by the clink of ale horns.

The squeal hit my ears before the commotion did—that particular pitch only achieved by overexcited three-year-olds and possibly banshees. I turned just in time to see Kieran skid behind the lemon trees, his father's jet hair flying wildly around a grin full of mischief. His arms cradled something fuzzy and gray that definitely wasn't supposed to leave Garrick's side.

"Ki-bird, you put Mr. Snuffles down this instant!" The command would've carried more weight if Amaya hadn't been biting her lip to keep from laughing. Her son stood trembling at the edge of the rose bushes, golden eyes gone wide and watery. Not even the soft wolf's ears peeking through his chestnut curls made him look fierce right now.

Crouching behind a marble planter, I caught the flash of Kieran's crimson tunic. "Y'all might wanna duck," I stage-whispered to Sera and Eldric who had drifted beside me.

Garrick's howl shook petals from the hibiscus. The air shimmered around him as he shifted—not fully, thank the Goddess, but enough that his sprint after Kieran left claw marks in the grass. Embry's delighted shriek joined the fray as she leapt from her perch on Ignis's shoulders, birthday ribbons streaming behind her like war banners.

"Twenty silver marks on the wolf cub." Eldric flicked a coin between his knuckles.

"You're on." I nodded toward where Ryn had materialized atop the pergola, the Ilyndor's girl's braids swinging as she calculated trajectories with unnerving precision. "That one's got her mama's tactical genius."

The crash came from the dessert table. Flour clouds erupted around a toppled tiered cake stand, two giggling blurs racing through the powdered sugar haze. Callie's gasp cut through the chaos.

"Oh, no she didn't!" My best friend's hands went to her hips, green eyes blazing even as Ignis muffled his laughter against her hair. "Embry Olivia Aurelion, you get back here and—"

The rest dissolved into sputtered indignation as a cream puff sailed past her ear. I pressed my sleeve to my mouth, shoulders shaking. Across the wreckage of petit fours, Cade caught my eye. Our daughter slept peacefully against his chest, oblivious to the sugary carnage as her kingly father used shadow magic to float a surviving macaron into his palm. The corner of his mouth quirked—our silent joke about battlefield clean-up being easier than parenting.

When the first lyre notes drifted from the musicians' pavilion, I took the baby from Cade's arms and slipped away. The scent of crushed mint followed me down the garden path, clinging to the hem of my sage-green dress. Past the bubbling fountain where water nymphs danced liquid patterns for giggling guests, beyond the arbor dripping with star jasmine…

Laughter echoed faintly through the trees. Through the green veil, I watched kingdoms that almost had fallen. A Therionis shifter adjusted the drape of a Vesparran noble's cloak, sunlight glinting off the moon steel embroidery. Two Ilyndorian earth mages demonstrated vine-weaving techniques to an enraptured group of Aurelian fire starters.

Tahlia's sleepy murmur against my collarbone startled me. I nuzzled her dark curls, inhaling the milky sweetness only newborns carry. "Don't grow up too fast, darlin'. Let Mama enjoy—"

"Contemplating escape routes?" Warm hands slid around my waist, familiar lips brushing the shell of my ear. The minstrels started a rather provocative version of 'The Maiden and the Moonstag.'

I leaned back into Cade's chest, his chuckle vibrating through me. "Just storing up the quiet moments. Never know when…"

His arms tightened. No need to finish. We both still saw shadows in sunlit places, heard war drums beneath celebration songs. But when his mouth found the sensitive spot below my ear, the shiver it drew was all present, no past.

The clearing erupted with fireflies as we returned. Or perhaps they were actually Aurelian sparks—hard to tell when half the guests had elemental magic crackling at their fingertips. Platters of seared citrus-glazed pheasant circulated alongside Thalassa's famous oyster towers, the briny scent mingling with wood smoke from roasting chestnuts. Someone had enchanted the lanterns to drift in hypnotic patterns, their golden light glinting off jeweled goblets and children's sticky cheeks alike.

"Took your time." Callie bumped her shoulder against mine, passing a honeycomb pastry. "Ignis owes Marin three barrels of aged whiskey."

I followed her gaze to where the massive Thalassan commander was arm-wrestling a grinning Ignis, their linked hands hovering over a growing puddle of mead. "Your husband's gonna regret teaching that man about drinking games."

"Mm, but the view's worth it." Her sigh was pure cat-that-got-the-cream as Ignis' tunic rode up, revealing sun-kissed skin. "You saw—oh sweet Vesperia, Kaelen! Not the hydrangeas!"

We moved as one, our time of battlefield synergy intact even in this domestic skirmish. I quickly handed her the baby as I shot a gust of wind in their direction, but the damage was done. Amaya's mate stood knee-deep in trampled blossoms, Garrick's toy wolf clutched triumphantly overhead. The boy's answering whoop stirred nesting starlings from the rafters.

Later, when the youngest revelers had been corralled onto makeshift pallets and the wine flowed thicker, I found my husband beneath the wisteria arch. Tahlia's tiny hand gripped his thumb, her eyes reflecting the bioluminescent blooms twining through his hair—my doing, though I'd never admit it.

Cade didn't speak as I tucked myself against him. He didn't need to. His kiss tasted of promises kept and tomorrows waiting, of quiet victories woven through ordinary moments.

Somewhere beyond the garden walls, the world breathed easy.

The scent of smoked venison and honeysuckle mead still clung to my hair when I found myself leaning against an oak older than most kingdoms. Tahlia's weight had been lessened, wrapped around me with a wide silk scarf, her breaths soft as moth wings against my neck. Across the lawn, Kieran's laughter had died down with the lute strings as he laid on soft blankets. Faralynn was telling stories to the children who were still awake.

Cade's shadow fell across us before his hand did, calloused palms brushing the scars beneath the sild of my dress. "They're gonna find that toy wolf in the soup tureen," he murmured, breath warm where my neck met shoulder. "Bet you three foaling seasons."

I snorted, tipping my head back against the bark that hummed with ancient earth magic. "You're on, darlin'. That hellion's got your sneaky streak." The words vibrated with the deep contentment of a barn cat in sunshine.

Beyond the firepit where Ignis was demonstrating Aurelion fire-dances—badly—Callie caught my eye. Her smile flashed, all mischief and molten gold, as she lobbed a honey cake at her mate's head. The treat dissolved midair in a shower of ember sparks, drawing cheers from Therionis warriors clinking runestone tankards.

Amaya's chuckle carried over the din as she emerged from the hydrangeas, Garrick slung over one shoulder like a sack of grain. "Found the culprit!" She shook the giggling boy gently, moonlight catching the ice crystals forming in her braids. "Tried burying evidence near the rosebushes."

"Standard shifter protocol," Kaelen called from where he arm-wrestled a Thalassan admiral, the table groaning under their linked grip. "Dig, deny, demand treats."

Laughter bubbled up raw and bright in my chest—the kind that used to surprise me in its simplicity. Tahlia stirred, a tiny fist curling around the amulet at my throat. Cade's thumb brushed her knuckles, shadows pooling lovingly around his fingertips.

"Remember..." His voice roughened, gaze fixed on Ryn attempting to climb Miranda's leg like a tree. "That day when I first took you into the Vesparra village?"

I turned my face into his palm, tasting salt and smoke. "When you told me to only tell you I love you when I was sure?"

His kiss was a vow against my temple. "I was so afraid that you might not."

The music swelled then, fiddles and elemental harmonies weaving through fireflies rising from the lavender beds. Around us, the tapestry of our making unfolded—shifters and elementals trading dance steps, a Vesparran general teaching Thalassan children to balance daggers on their noses, Embry's delighted shriek as Garrick pounced from behind a topiary wolf.

I looked into his beautiful ice-blue eyes. "How could I not? You were the better days I'd always searched for. I loved you then. I love you more now."

MY SINCERE THANKS

Thank you—wholeheartedly—for embarking on this journey through the Kingdoms of Eldoria. Writing this trilogy as my debut series has been a labor of love (and occasional tears!), and I'm endlessly grateful you chose to spend your time in this world amid the choice of countless romantasy tales. Like any first adventure, this one may have its imperfections, but I hope Olivia, Cade, and their found family swept you into their triumphs and heartaches as deeply as they did me. Saying goodbye while writing those final pages? Let's just say tissues were mandatory.

Your Voice Matters
If Eldoria's tale lingered with you, I'd be so grateful if you'd share a few words in an honest review—it doesn't need to be lengthy! (Though if *"OMG THIS BOOK"* wants to escape your soul in all-caps? Well... I'll never complain about five stars.) Reader support means everything to new authors like me, and your thoughts help this story reach others who might adore it too.

Let's Stay Connected!
I'd love to meet you beyond these pages! As someone still building my circle, I'm thrilled to chat about future stories, behind-the-scenes secrets, or even your favorite fictional crushes (Cade fans: I see you). Join me on Facebook, subscribe

for updates via my newsletter- subscribe on my website, or catch me on TikTok or over on Instagram —let's turn this epilogue into the start of our friendship!

With gratitude and love,
Dex

P.S. Keep an eye out for bonus content, original songs, videos, character Q&As, giveaways, and more coming soon to subscribers—you won't want to miss it!

There's a new series on the horizon. Stay in touch to learn more.

ABOUT THE AUTHOR

Dex Haven

Writing has been a part of my life for years, though it wasn't always the kind of writing I'm doing now. I started blogging after we lost our son-in-law in 2013 — a little outlet for my heart. Over time, I wrote about crafts, home decor, and random bursts of inspiration. Later, I dipped into copywriting, penning articles that were basically ads in disguise (but hey, it paid the bills). Then, in 2023, I met an author who became a good friend. Watching him bring stories to life sparked something in me — a hunger I couldn't shake. I realized I had my own stories swirling around in my head, and it was about time I got them down on paper.

And that's how the Starlight Trilogy was born.

I'm lucky to have a husband who's as steady as he is supportive. Decades together and he still cheers me on like I'm chasing down gold medals. This whole writing journey has been wild, wonderful, and humbling. Knowing that so many of you are falling in love with these characters and this world I've built? It blows me away every single day.

Olivia, my main character, has a special place in my heart. Not because I grew up in foster care or ride dragons (though how cool would that be?!), but because she's a fighter. A lot of us know what it's like to have a rough start, to face challenges head-on and claw our way forward. Olivia's story is for all of us who've found our own magic and fought off the monsters — the ones outside us and the ones within.

And yes, let's talk about the heat. I write the kind of spice that's for you. For every woman who's spent her day juggling kids, work, house chores, and a never-ending to-do list. For the women who feel like their spark has been buried under "all the things" — this is for you. My books are your escape. Your reminder that you're still that sexy, powerful, wild creature with so much to offer. And, trust me, your man definitely notices.

Thanks for being here. I'm so glad you've found your way to my little corner of the world. I hope my stories remind you to fight for your magic and, just maybe, give you a reason to stay up way too late reading "just one more chapter."

Made in the USA
Coppell, TX
16 February 2025